Momentary lapses in concentration

Phil Thomson

Momentary lapses in concentration

Cover photographs courtesy of the author

ISBN 978-1-911319-89-1

APS Publications,
4 Oakleigh Road,
Stourbridge,
West Midlands,
DY8 2JX

www.andrewsparke.com

for Sebastian

we hear and see only the edges of things…
for the rest, we travel

Wk.1413
52° 8' N   111° 40' W

'It's a one-way mirror.' she said, leaning into view in front of the glass. 'I'm sure we are being watched.'

'Everyone's being watched. Well, actually, no; if you believe in God, you're being watched.' Stonie was surprised by his response. He did not know what to say next. The remark was meant to tease, fill a space, not start a sermon. Perhaps his nerves were showing. Bhavani was leaving and he had no address or telephone number. She tried again, shifting her weight from foot to foot and circling playfully around him with her hands clasped behind her back.

'Don't you think so? I mean, I'm staring into this smoky mirror and all I see is myself, right? Who knows who's really looking back? Maybe that isn't me after all. In any case, it is someone I do not recognise,' she said, turning in the direction of the darkened ticket office window. 'See, there she is. Can you see her now from where you are? It's weird how darkness changes us.'

'Actually, it's impossible to recognise you,' Stonie said. 'You're a stranger.'

'I always have been.' Stonie made the connection for the first time. Why bother with the exotic. The idea was preposterous. They were oceans apart. Not oceans, worlds; anyway, it was far too late for soul-searching. He knew that now, but he felt he had to play along, just one more time. In the reflection, the two figures were intertwined.

'Ok, but I don't recognise myself; it's a darker version of me. I'm a ghost, really,' he said. 'No, that's not right. I'm an alien. It's more like a black hole, infinity. And I'm seeing through a glass darkly.'

'I don't know what you mean by that,' Bhavani said. Stonie was ready to tell her it was a metaphor, from the Holy Bible, but small talk was his undoing. There was always a bigger picture and he could never quite grasp the significance at the time, caught up in endless, inconsequential detail. Perhaps, after all, this lady was from another dimension. Most of his love interests were.

'Oh, nothing to worry about, I don't know what I mean,' he said, 'it's just - ' Stonie was interrupted.

'If that's the real me in there, beyond the glass, she won't be able to connect with you… all she can do is imagine you are looking back at her. All she can do is hope you are looking back at her. Right?' He was sure Bhavani winked at him. Was this some kind of teasing, last minute come on? Her cool restrained voice trailed off into the hiss of the streets below the station. She was playing stupid games, surely, filling time. Killing time.

To Stonie, the two figures were playing out an Edward Hopper painting. He warmed to the idea, caught between a past which yet again was leading nowhere and a future, which was sure to confirm his worst fears. As he paused to savour the moment, the clock hand jerked between the roman numerals, cutting into the silence.

'Is that the right time?' There was no answer. Again, the awkward pause. These silences had been a feature of their unfinished lives. They were at the mercy of the impenetrable distance between them. When the station lamp stuttered, it was as if some dry storm had cracked open a hair-line scratch of blue-white onto the black horizon, the back of his eyes. That flicker put an end to the game. What was really on offer was practiced restraint, resignation. If he was honest, he knew the protocol, how inappropriate it would be if Bhavani made a personal response, say, hold his hand, stroke his hair. Being close, intimate, was all anyone ever wanted. But it had never happened. No chance now.

'You are sad, aren't you? I can tell.' she said, surprising him with the coolness of her voice.' Stonie nodded in agreement but said nothing. 'Well, I shall take that as a compliment,' she went on. He moved a few paces away from her.

'There are twenty-four wooden slats on that wall,' he said, with a limp wave in the direction of the kiosk, 'all overlapping each other. Like the hours we've spent trying to link our lives together, to make them connect, dovetail, that sort of thing.' His tone had hardened into mock sincerity. He turned to face her, one arm across his body as if in contrition, his palm, for some reason, flat against his chest. He could feel his heart, count the still-beats in these final awkward moments. He had no idea why he found himself in these situations.

'They will never dovetail,' Bhavani said with a polite smile. 'You know that.' The 'never' came over slowly. A cooling breeze wafted across the platform, a welcome edge. Now every word had to be a search, every nuance to be fully exploited. He would like to think she was unprepared for the way she felt, ill at ease with this awakening. Yet she remained poised. There were no clues.

'Here, I want you to have this,' she said quietly, moving over to her luggage and turning to him holding a loosely wrapped parcel. 'I bought it for you in the market at home…on impulse. You said you needed one. It's for you. Go on, take it. You must.' It was a leather satchel. An act she would never have undertaken before, something she would never have been allowed to do back home. He took it from her hesitantly, conscious that refusal would be an insult. Nothing this dangerous had ever happened in Bhavani's world, he was sure of that. This was her moment of closure.

'How will I find out where you are, what you are doing, who you are with?' Stonie asked aware that his question had revealed too much. 'I mean, a voice on the telephone, it's already history, so detached from…' He paused, hoping for some playful interruption, but the silence made Bhavani hold back, told her instinctively to build the mystery rather than to destroy it. Mystery was all she owned. 'And letters, well they are fiction by the time we set eyes on them,' Stonie went on. 'There has to be more.' He wanted to continue but nothing came. He was left with the muted panic of knowing there was something definitive to be added. It was out there in Hollywood or Mills and Boon or some 'B' list soap opera dream about how it was all supposed to end. But it was certainly not in his head. Wanting more is why we breathe, he thought. The hunger for more is everything. Lust for life; lust. Stonie chanced a steadier look over her wistful face, roving, prodding, intent on finding her eyes. In any case, there would be too many obstacles, too high a price for the goodbye. He must always have known that. He would have to be content with her darting, intense restlessness. To know that in these few remaining moments there was an imprint and it would be deep, lasting. It would out-live memory; it would journey far beyond both of them. After the formalities - thank you, you shouldn't have, not a problem, it was the least I could do – both of them had fallen silent.

'I hate turquoise,' she said, finally, stretching the 'ay' and turning her eyes upwards towards the flaking, encrusted palings of the ceiling. The accent now seemed much more pronounced. 'I can't stand its incipience, its lack of character, you know; the kind of colour that just sits there, being limp and pastel and non-committal.

Affecting your mood. You just know it would never fight for you, stick by you, give you something to rely on.' She pursed her lips inward - a resigned, well-rehearsed gesture. This was exactly the kind of oblique, riveting conversation they'd had from the start. Pure mischief. Anything alternative that came to mind, they would say. Those were the rules. Stonie gave a wry smile.

'Turquoise, eh?'

'Tell me you prefer blue,' she said. 'Or royal purple.' It was a question rather than a command, yet it had all the hallmarks of interrogation. And it was avoidance. Without waiting for an answer, she danced away from him and trailed her hand across the slats under the window, deliberately touching each one in turn. The touch of a single finger. 'There are twenty-five, not twenty four,' she announced, pirouetting around to face him full on. Her arms were open, bent at the elbow in a welcoming dance-like gesture, her gold bracelets sliding up onto her slender wrists as the long sparkling silks twisted through the air and folded against her. Stonie had narrowed his eyes to a fine mist. He was no longer listening, no longer present. The feeling was weightlessness. The sequins were stars, pulsating, fading. Bhavani stared intently at him for a few seconds. She had seen this look before. This was consistent. Stonie moves into a space then forgets why he is there.

'Hey, over here,' she said, waving one arm high in the air. The move accentuated her breasts, her petite, perfect frame. One embrace would have been enough.

Stonie forced a smile. Behind her, the train was in sight. 'I lied, yeh, twenty five,' he said slowly, staring past her beyond the factory roofs and chimneys and the neat station canopy, staring at the darkening autumn sky, looking for that first real jewel. He was losing count of these small beginnings that lead to nothing. They were becoming interruptions. That was it, interruptions. 'Alright, I admit it. I needed to connect with you, something to say in a hurry, I just wanted to fill the space. Most of the time people talk rubbish.' He paused, enough to recognise his familiar desperation. As the train approached, the carriage blocked out the thin strip of sky. Stonie turned, preparing for some kind of contact, but her suitcase was already between them. He took a deep breath. His stranger was tipping her luggage away from him, mouthing something over the low, tightening squeal of the brakes. So this was it. He made no move forward this time. As she slowly distanced herself in the glow of the station lamps, the young woman twisted around and looked back, raising the flat of her hand in a gentle wave, for the first time locking her eyes against his. There was no point in goodbye. He made a faltering gesture, as if blessing the space between them, the carriage, the train, the past gathering speed in front of him.

Stonie walked away from the station, head bowed. He felt hollow, felt the familiar drift. It was never going to work. One minute casual, the next, a finely tuned cultural minefield. He stopped beside some coloured marks that had been hurriedly daubed onto the pavement. The stare brought on a déjà vu. Someone, some artist had cut out an actual piece of pavement once. At least that was what was intended. He remembered seeing it, framed, in a gallery, hanging on a wall. Double yellow lines. Kerb. Maybe a cast iron drain. In minute detail. He had decided it wasn't real. It was resin, oils, plaster; made to look real. In other words, fake. Fake, but perpendicular and called Art. You were meant to look at it in a different way. That's what the artist forced on you. And the chance of love; you were meant to look at it in a different way. But surely you had to be in the mood for either. He looked up and took in his surroundings. The desolate pavements. Marks on the ground, marks on the sky - it was perfunctory, the obligation to interpret whatever was in front of your eyes, to insist that you knew, that you understood. This was what everyone expected.

There was a time when he dared to believe it was all meant for him, whatever the message. Not any more. It had all gone wrong. His encounter with art, with women, with God. He felt sweat in the small of his back, the kind of sweat that said he ought to know, ought to be in control. He walked on, more and more conscious of the night between buildings. Soon the back-to-backs gave way to several redbrick industrial units then open space, unfenced, even dirtier and full of other people's crap. God, his mind was full of other people's crap. This would be the short cut. Looking across the open space, he noticed up to twenty crows spread out along the dipping telephone wires at the far end. Most were stationary, squawking, arguing their particular position. That it was an odd time of day for active crows did not occur to him. In his head he was arguing his own position. Anyhow, the pattern had fused, had become the notation that drove the song within, the rhythm of his breathing. He tried to read the notes, make up his own tune to them and laughed at the idea. The painted arrows and numbers on the pavement had to be some kind of hieroglyphic branding, flagging up a change in ownership of his life. It was a sign, a reminder. And now these city birds with their meaningless existence and endless routine, living by instinct, dipping in and out of the detritus in his head with their song.

He stood by the belisha crossing, blinking in time with the yellow black phrasing of the moment. The kerb was yet another contract with the world, trying to guide his steps. He crossed the road, still with his head down, scanning the concrete for meaning. More marks. Blue for water, green for gas, red for electricity. More odd numbers. Perhaps they were silent warnings of mortality, the civil engineers unknowingly forcing their portent of degradation on his path; a pavement graffiti instruction on how to lay waste to a memory, a skyline, the pipelines and wires beneath his feet. Planning its destruction. Here was the angel of death daubing the lintel, blood trickling down in absolution. This one lives, this one dies. That's the way it felt. They had no right. Six months from now, the wrecker's ball would strike and all his landmarks would be history. No wonder he looked to the sky.

Stonie didn't belong in these surroundings. He didn't need to be there. In any case, it was all being wrested from his grasp. The old ways. Better to become a stranger right now, while the route provided him with barriers, pointers, this way and that according to whim. The rubble would soon slope and crumble under his feet. He would have to make decisions for himself. Yellow stroke with red. Two over four with arrow. Pretzel in green with blue colon. The brush-stroke messages, the fractions, seemed precise, immediate; for him. Yet there was no way he could penetrate the mystery, the contrivance. The speculators would have their way. He walked on, the scuff of his feet the only rhythm. Within a few minutes he could see the canal, its oil slick rubbish pock-marking the black shine. He was back in his old patch, but it brought him no comfort.

He was being spoken to, from his past, from his future. About how he listened for clouds, about how he chose his stars. And it was dark enough now to choose. As he walked, he felt a dust spec in his eye, manufacturing a tear. It made him press a finger against the duct, swearing silently at the gust. An irritation. An interruption.

Wk.1414
52° 8' N 111° 40' W

The friends of Stonie were all deep inside his head, worlds within worlds. They would never touch each other's lives. Not directly. He saw them as stars in their own little firmament. They would shine for him alone. That way, he could know them without being known, without having to be talked about. He could travel with them and not have to face the scrutiny. Stonie hated prolonged negotiations, contracts, those awkward little questions, people tip-toeing around each other, trying to make it to the next level. Inside his head, he could fit into Gemima's sophisticated town set, hold court with aplomb. He could smell her fragrance whenever he wanted. He knew he could. Or have an argument with wild-eyed Kate. Everyone argued with Kate; you could see it coming, have a good laugh afterwards. There was always the potential for whatever people wanted from him. Always on his terms. Except for Zach, full name Zacharias P. Graffenheimer III.

Stonie was working on himself. He had hit one of those rare moments. Mulling; that was the term: after a long Sunday of doing nothing much. After the Bhavani goodbye. He was in the pub and in first person. Let's see, one morning in the Spring of '69, would-be artist Stonie Reuladair decides he is not a photographer. He leaves behind the seeds of what might have been. There is a restlessness in his gaze, fuelled by the fleeting flower power of London and the siren call of the Big Apple. Yet some remnant is left to mark what he chooses not to be, the moment he walks away from one future and into another. Stonie took a sip of his beer. Walking away had been the easy bit.

He looked up from his drink. They're all one type or another, he thought. They all look like someone I've seen before, talked to, been a passing stranger to, that's the way with race and genes and cosmic stuff. Look at them. A Latin babe here, a house-husband over there, a war veteran in the alcove. Got to be a war veteran, the way he holds himself. I talk to anyone who looks me in the eye. Why can't I just nod? That's the trouble. Don't want to talk, just can't help myself. God, I can't help myself. This was the noise he lived with. But it never led anywhere, the conversations. You learn nothing just hearing yourself all over again. That guy keeps pigeons. This one's mid-European, has the look of a Romany. It was all rattling around in his head. This was how he prepared himself for another useless week, at a loose end, waiting for some big life-moment, some Damascus Road. Well, it could have been Bhavani, he mused. He cut a sad figure, cramped against the pillar with his collar up.

Stonie became aware of a presence near to him, in his peripheral vision, too close, really. It was in the shape of the shoulders and hair, the angularity of the frame. There seemed no particular reason to single anyone out, yet a vague unease crept over him. He could never tell where they came from, those tricks of memory, how they were selected inside his head, primed for recall. He was always plagued by the nano-seconds. His brain was always taking the law into its own hands, spewing out random music, stories, memories, inventing other people's lives. There he was, singing the same song over and over again inside his skull. It was always like this. No respite. He looked across the room, over the bobbing heads, out through the far window to check the sky. Cloud. Thin, but no good.

This guy, maybe there is some kind of force field around him and I'm one of the sensitive ones, maybe I'm on the edge of his aura. He took a swig from his beer and immediately thought swig was a funny word. He thought aura was a funny word. His mind worked in that way. Pretending not to notice, that was another ploy, trying to blend in. But he would keep on watching, even although he promised himself he would avoid talking to any random person who happened to be in view. There had to be genuine eye contact or it did not count. It is what he craved and loathed, the encounter.

Here was the paradox. He liked the idea of being a private person, but he never knew how. This was the price of being a part of a fallen race. Being constantly let down. Always watching the sky, staring at the ceiling each night thinking, it isn't the ceiling that keeps him flat on his back. Beyond the ceiling is the roof, then above that, this crazy force which prevents him from escaping. He could not go up. Down was not an option; down was finite. Like pot-holers or miners. A few fissures, seams. Once you've found the core you would have to return to where the search started.

And what about sideways? Keep going around and there's a good chance you would come right back up, but somewhere else. You just can't walk off the planet, he would say when pressed. Complete the circle, he would say, only it wouldn't quite be a circle. You would be out by a few feet or a hundred miles, maybe a millimetre. Stonie could see the back of the man's collar. It had a weird animal pattern on it, a kind of hell-for-leather, charging bison. He began to think of Calderpark Zoo as he took another drink, then he was flitting to some tacky circus he was taken to by his father when he was eight. All Cowboys and Indians and scary and like nothing he had ever seen before. No. It was scary till the Indian Chief's feather head-dress caught alight and the whole thing came off and they were stamping all over it. Now that was a real war dance. Or was it Kelvin Hall; the auditorium? Some kind of slow moving stampede of Billy Graham converts and this little boy being dragged along under the very nose of the great man, all tears and runny nose and "Just as I am without one plea" rolling off the choir stalls. He could always remember first lines. It seemed there were people crowding in on him at all times of the day, at all angles. Still were. He needed space. Part of him was trying to practice not talking.

Stonie edged closer, tilted his head to the side of the pillar. If the stranger was about to speak, he wanted to hear what he had to say. The man would be one of those characters with accusing, hooded blue eyes which could stare straight through him, spikey high cheek bones, long eyebrows, a lived-in face. There would be an accent, or course. And the guy would lean close, so close to him that he would have to threaten the stranger with some expletive, or hint broadly about foreigners taking over the city. Stonie could rehearse these things, the aggression, the clever word. He could clench his fists and get ready for something to happen. That would add the frisson. Fat chance. The man had already found his victim and was launching forth. Stonie twisted round as much as he could and watched. There was enough space for him to lean back against the pillar to listen in.

'Sound and fury,' the character finally muttered through the froth on his glass. 'Is that what they say?' Stonie had another of those pictures – a fleeting glimpse of a previous existence. A cove of shingle, huge, screaming sky, an accusing moon picking off the odd star and the ebb and draw of a million pebbles roaring to the howl of the sea and there he was, running naked towards the foam, finally splashing face up, into the shallows; a cold, clear starry night for a dare. Stonie was horrified. Here I am as far from the sea as I can get. Why the hell is this in my head. Why the hell is anything in my head. I have to get out of the place, he thought. He felt he had to get out of everywhere. The Old Crown seemed to be crawling with misfits all trying to out-do each other. He was one of them.

Instead, he waited, wondering what this man in a suit might say next. That was the game. The Suit started it – that vaguely self-conscious, over-dressed pose, silvering hair tightly drawn to a taper, with the faintest of pleated rat's tails falling off his neck and over his collar. Stonie noticed the ponytail had a green bead in it, hard against the nape, saying I'm still hip, three years after the sixties disappeared. Still hip.

Suits in a pub - they're always on their way to somewhere or just coming back but they don't want to admit it. Never the pub for the sake of it. Stonie began to wonder if the man was talking to himself after all, nodding from time to time, robotic and stiff; no use of the hands or arms. Perhaps he was just innocently drinking; yet something in the man's pose annoyed him. He would have to stick with it, stick with this world in the corner of his eye. He would pass the time. It's either him or me. I wonder how I can will him out of the place? One of the rules. People-watchers take on such roles. I should will him out of the place. The pace of Stonie's drinking was measured. This is as far as his boredom had taken him.

The other attraction was Kate, several tables away, intensely engaged in heated handwriting with the same two men as before. There was some laughter. They must be friends. They were touching each other on the arm, the shoulder. Stonie acknowledged her glance, yet instinctively decided not to break in. Perhaps later. Perhaps tonight would be conversation number nine and this time all to himself. The most he had managed was a phone number, but so far, no call.

Stonie watched the stranger draw his finger around the rim of his glass, as if the siren sound would add a sentiment or two to the conversation. The man was becoming more animated, which made him strain even harder to listen. 'It was all hell-fire and damnation, is that what they say? The preacher was pointing at us all the time.' The man was speaking to his companion with slow, deliberate movement of the lips across the little round table. The Listener had a polite, why-ask-me look on his face; why talk to me? Stonie caught his eye, tried a smile. He was no good with rhetorical questions himself. He watched the stranger down half a pint in one gulp in a precursor to a rapid exit – or perhaps some eyebrow-raising diatribe. Stonie was fond of searching out such details, trying to figure out the back story. The Listener wiped a foam moustache from under his nose and burped though pursed lips.

'I am sorry,' he said.

Stonie was homing in on the conversation amongst the chatter, warming to it. Why not. He sat forward a little, relaxed, took a few sips of beer and took stock. Better not look at The Listener for too long. The other option was to crash the party, thoroughly break it up. Don't mind if I join you loners, do you. Don't mind if I liven up your boring little tête à tête? Here was another calculation. How many split seconds before a look becomes a stare? That was something to work on.

'Yeh, I know exactly what you mean,' The Listener said, nodding, feigning sympathy. 'I grew up with churchfuls of bubbling, emotional dwarfs screaming repentance at me from the pulpit, very blinkered.' Even with these fragments to piece together, Stonie decided the man was talking rubbish. 'It's alright as a kid, when you can't answer back, but eventually you walk away, find the real world.' Find the real world. Honestly, this is the real world? Stonie pulled back and looked around the pub. All these people shifting pints and mindless banter...the real world? He had heard enough.

'It is not what I expected from a funeral service,' the Pony Tail added. Stonie waited for the man to drain the dregs, making the most of that final jerk of the neck to catch the last drop. That was the point to leave, with the stranger's head at full tilt. It would not have mattered. That's what he should have done.

'Oh, I see,' was all The Listener could muster. Stonie was growing more curious. Maybe he did like this game after all and should try even harder to filter out the chatter around him.

'This is what you wear in honour of the dead, this suit, is it not?' The Pony Tail said. Stonie watched the fake, quizzical expression of The Listener, watched till the people around the two men were out of focus, concentrating now on gleaning something worthwhile, something noteworthy from the encounter. He was tempted to jot down the phrases, turn the whole thing into Godot. There was a quality in the tone of voice, the exchange which fascinated him. But he was hemmed in and not quite close enough. He tried to position himself for a clearer view, with his head lowered and his hand spread out against his cheek. The Suit now felt creepy and that was what he was reading on the Listener's face. Both men had fallen silent. Stonie knew that, left to himself, he would have had to fill the space. It was what he always did. Silences were threatening. Better to say anything than nothing. The rest of the bar was teeming, boisterous, but Stonie had centred down; there was something here to experience after all. 'Sorry, I didn't catch that it was a funeral. My condolences.' The Listener said, picking up his empty glass and placing it formally in front of him with both hands and some deliberation.

'Tell me, who are your people?' The Suit enquired. A turn of phrase. The dialogue between the two men was becoming surreal. It was crazy, dangerous to listen in and none of his business; or harmless. Just a way of being entertained. Surely.

'You mean, my ancestors,' The Listener answered. His tone had become unconvincingly playful. 'You're first time over here?' he asked.

Stonie was still missing bits of the conversation and didn't catch the response. But he decided it was all rehearsed. These guys know each other, and they want to be heard. This is for me, this charade. He could feel his own mood darkening. He didn't want to be in any kind of mood. The one guy knows nothing. The other guy is mental. Why listen.

'And the man making the signs in the air, who was he?' the Pony Tail enquired, much louder this time. That was it. The kind of moment when you seriously take stock of who you're talking to, or who you are listening to. It isn't small talk any more, it is strategic. Something is going on. Messing with your brain. The priest, stupid, the bloody priest, Stonie shouted inside his head. What planet are you on? Don't you know anything? Where's the phrase book? Leave the guy alone, you fucking weirdo. He doesn't even want to listen. With the conversation becoming barely audible over the growing pub noise, it was time to wrap things up. Time to get out. But Stonie had too much in his glass to rush things; was damned if he was going to abandon his pint. He watched as The Listener spoke again.

‘Always a difficult time. Was it, eh, someone you knew well?’ There was a pause.

‘Suspicious circumstances,’ came the slow, cryptic reply. Stonie studied The Listener’s face for clues, but he was looking bored. He could hear the words from The Suit coming out in tiny little bites, almost like a game; it simply did not feel like a conversation; the man opposite him was definitely being told stuff. His expressions were on cue. Stonie decided The Suit, The Pony Tail, had been beamed in. The alien was looking out across the room, as if checking, as if searching for someone. He seemed agitated as he twisted in his seat. From his position on the other side of the pillar, Stonie could not lean any further back and still look natural. The Suit tipped himself forward, forearms on his knees, looking as if he was about to reveal some intimate secret to his companion across the table.

Perhaps there was, after all, unfinished business. One minute the guy wanted to talk. Then he was distant and disengaged. His companion had begun looking up nervously at the garish baubles and beaten-up tinsel leftovers, fiddling with the Bumper Santa Menu, clearly intent on making an escape. Stonie hadn’t noticed it before. Christmas food in the middle of January and here he was sitting opposite some fake mourner who was dumping all kinds of inconsequential crap on other lone drinkers. They are all lone drinkers. This guy’s been let out.

Stonie put down his drink, looked out across the faces and checked the sky again, as much of it as he could see. Light pollution, no stars. He could easily walk away without even a nod. He thought for a second. It’s always the same, closure. When something is over but you don’t know it, don’t know what to do with it. Well, he crossed into my space, into my world, distracted me. One more drink and that’s it.

He found a wall spot to stare at, curls of yellowing sticky tape, several rusting drawing pins and threads from endless years of festive decoration. They usually marked out The Plough or Big Bear on the smoke hardened frieze or made you swear they were bugs; maybe harvesters, endlessly pulsating up and down on their invisible legs. You can always find crawlies and peeling paint and coagulating tar drops in the ceiling crannies if you look closely enough. You just couldn’t tell anyone it was a pastime. Stonie always insisted on a back-to-the-wall pub seat in clear view of a window; not just any window, but a canal-side window. In that position he had the assurance that someone was going somewhere, as the multi-coloured flower pots on the roof of the narrow boat eased through at sill height – then the bicycle, followed by the green Wellington boots and the sleeping mongrel – all at four and a half miles per hour - then the peeling red and white life-belt, more withering geraniums and lastly the retired, faintly smiling pipe-smoker with the lived-in face, tipping his beat-up leather cap, fingers lightly wrapped around the tiller. Funny how, in the narrowest of cuts, you still need a rudder.

With strangers, you can usually find a polite way to avert the gaze if you want to; that split second before you make a choice to look away. It is a practiced art with some people. Locking eyes inevitably leads to endless weather forecasts or some drunk spitting on his palm and trying to shake your hand. Stonie was still tempted to get up from his seat, move round the pillar and take a good, full-on look at The Suit, just for the sake of it; more like serious probing than people-watching. Usually, he preferred observing; there were options, endless strands of conversations, introductions to other worlds. But The Suit drew him in. The man was drifting, swaying slightly, panning the room, twisting away from the table without moving his bum, then arching back and filling his lungs with these long deep breaths. Stonie could see his shoulders were locked up, his whole frame frozen. That's what held him. The body language. He was, at times, a Madame Tussauds dummy; stiff as a poker. It was not normal behaviour. A guest on ATV, a varsity stunt, a new refugee, some absent-minded PhD who has lost his way back to Edgbaston? For most of those he surveyed, he had an explanation, a category.

Stonie picked up his glass and knocked back the rest of his drink. Time to let this stranger get on with his life. It was enough sport. He could see The Suit in his peripheral vision. Nothing was actually happening. It would hardly be a wrench. He squeezed between the chairs and the standers folding in around him and edged out towards the door. The moment had gone. He needed to be elsewhere. But it didn't work out like that.

Something in him was stirring. The city always delivered, always guaranteed to prod you out of your comfort zone. It was love and hate in equal measure. He decided, just for the hell of it, to linger, give it a few more minutes. He turned and pushed back to his table before anyone had occupied the space. The world around him was animated, fictional, distant. This alien presence, still with his back to him behind the pillar, still with one hand fixed firmly to his glass of beer, was becoming some kind of mysterious, intimate stranger, a social experiment, a personal encounter of sorts. There were choices. He could spirit himself away into the crowd, continue with the stalking game, or create a drum roll and leap onto the table waving an accusing finger. If he he'd consumed enough drink. If he'd had enough of the holy huddle. Stonie closed his eyes, ready for one final decision. The Drinker was still there, a few robotic degrees in front of him, but there was at least, some movement. As his shoulders went slack, he looked as if he was about to stand up. Stonie couldn't leave now. He strained forward. Maybe, after all, he would find a way for them to nod at each other, trade pleasantries. A ridiculous fixation. Unfortunately, he could not position himself, though, crazy as it seemed, he was beginning to feel he needed to button-hole the man, just to spice things up, learn something about *himself*. It was that kind of evening. He was always contradicting everything he planned to do, setting himself useless goals. Might as well engage a complete stranger in a packed pub for no reason, fill in the missing pieces, go home and write a poem about it. Target practice.

'Oh well, all the goodbyes are over,' he was sure he heard the Pony Tail say through a long slow sigh. Then nothing. The man stood up abruptly, shouldered forward into the standing crowd and was gone, straight ahead, still with his back to Stonie, all in the time it had taken Stonie to look through the bottom of his glass. He made to follow but changed his mind, his gaze fixed on the disappearing silver pony tail, that green bead. But he resisted the impulse to follow. He turned round to check his seat and make sure nothing was left, hesitating long enough for The Listener to make a gesture, waving towards the empty chair. 'Saw you taking an interest,' he said. 'Couldn't help it.'

'Good idea,' Stonie said. 'but hold the seat, I'll be back. Can I get you a drink?'

'I'm alright for now,' the man replied. 'Thanks.'

Stonie sat down and stared ahead for a moment, forgetting the offer he had just made. There was nothing in his brain any more. This was simply another inconsequential episode in his life; where he had just been. He sat on the edge of his seat, steeling himself to fill the hour before closing time.

'Tell you what, I'll get them,' The Listener said. Stonie barely nodded.

When the man returned, Stonie was ready for him. 'Interesting character, the guy in the pony tail.'

'Hell, that was tricky.' The Listener said. 'Don't like sharing a table with someone who sets your teeth on edge, yeh, not easy.'

'I couldn't help overhearing some of it, I have to say,' Stonie admitted, drawing his drink up to his lips in defence, giving him time. The stranger filled the space.

'Yeh, I noticed. Found myself talking bloody drivel, I did. Definitely foreign. Don't think I was rude but he was hard work. Was I rude?'

'I wouldn't have thought it mattered now,' Stonie answered, with a muted laugh, placing his glass on a beer mat, half on, half off. He slid his finger slowly down the side of the glass to correct the move, tipping it back towards the centre. Perhaps it was time to go after all. There was a scribbled, hand-written scrawl on the damp beer mat, in brown ink, still wet. The trickle of condensation on the outside of the cold glass had created a small arc through the writing, beginning to fur the lines. Curious, Stonie slid the mat out from under the glass and took a closer look. It was blurred, written in a faltering hand. Stonie raised the mat towards a better light and slowly whispered the words to himself. "Mica Cambareri is dead."

The blood rushed to Stonie's head in the time it takes the sound to hit the brain and tell the heart - and the blood was thumping. His ears were about to burst. He had to remember to breathe. It was those sharp little intakes as the brain panics. He swallowed hard, desperate to create a normal response.

He tried to take a sip of beer with no more than a fumble at his glass, his eyes unnaturally wide, fixed on where The Suit had disappeared. Nothing was in focus, he was hardly conscious of anyone's presence. 'Unusual name,' was the best he could do, pointing at the scribbled mat. 'Who…I mean - ' Nothing would come.

'You alright?' He could hear someone's voice filtering through the pub noise. 'Better lean your head back mate. I'll get you some water.'

Stonie was thankful for the dim light. He could feel the colour draining out of his face. The Listener was saying something. He heard, but did not listen. That is wrong, I read it wrong. He was standing, he was sitting, it did not matter. He couldn't tell. Perhaps The Listener was smirking at Stonie. Would he care? He could feel heat around his eyes, pressure on the drums. He had no saliva. He was aware he had farted, was half-standing, trembling, that his chest was tight, that he couldn't move, the voice in his head screaming with shock. He was gripping the glass. Any second it would break. 'Mica' was my name for her. Only *I* knew it. It was ours.

'She - ' he began, then faltered. 'I'll be okay…I'll be - ' There was an awkward pause. Stonie wanted to say, I knew someone once called Jay Cambareri. To me, she was Mica; not the Biblical Micah, but *Mica*, my own name for her, feminine, see? Least I thought so. It says something, you know, when you have a special name, does it not? I didn't use it in public, oh no, just our private moments, you understand? Something warm, to laugh about between us. Can't remember how it started. She was in my poems as Mica, my whispers, my dreams. He wanted to say, but nothing came. All he could hear was the scream.

The pub was busy, smokier, noisier than usual, but with the wrong kind of drinker. He had the proof. Stonie drew his tongue over his dry lips and began again. 'The guy in the pony tail, has he gone then?' he asked. He was staring but saw nothing, not even as a glass flew over his head. It hit the flashing star on the plastic Christmas tree, sent the whole lot flying, before the offender was set upon on.

'Shit! Did you see that! Just missed your ear,' someone shouted. Stonie barely moved. A mouthful of sick had forced itself up into his throat. All he could muster was a slow nod.

'Third week in January, for God's sake, and they haven't even taken away the Christmas tree, honestly. So much for Christmas cheer, eh?' The Listener was animated. 'Are you alright mate?' The star light, the pub's crowning glory, had exploded into a million tiny shards of thin white glass, purple dust spraying across the tables before anyone had time to move a muscle. Yeh, Stonie was about to say, there's a thing, my name for her. He was about to tell him, tell The Listener, tell his new companion. Not the Biblical spelling, you understand? Special. Maybe like the mineral. Without the 'h'. A gem as far as I'm concerned. Now there's a coincidence. My name for mine. Dead?

Stonie focused enough to see Kate leaving by a side door at the far end of the pub. Another opportunity gone. The scuffle behind him had been dealt with in seconds in a mixture of screams and laughter and fucking stardust jokes as one or two of the heavier drinkers pounced. He sat still, unwilling to join in any conversation. The drinks were lightly dusted, but eventually he took a sip of his beer and stared intently at the fellow trying to talk to him. The shoulders and collar of his companion's dark shirt were flecked. Stonie decided this was the point to stand up. He took hold of his own collar and shook off the star dust. The stranger seemed not to care. In the sweat of his thinning pate there lay several sparkles of glass and tiny shreds of coloured ribbon. Makes him look a bit camp, Stonie thought, ready for a party. The slight giggle inside was enough. He swept the dust and pine needles from the table and turned away to dry spit some irritating grit from his lips. He was trying hard to create a memory in his brain, to capture something. Mica, dead?

'Happened last week too. A black woman and a white guy. Local stuff. Nothing to worry about. You having another drink?' Stonie said nothing. The Listener pushed up from his chair, dropping more dust onto the table. 'Another one, right? There's just time. You look as if you need one.'

Stonie managed a pathetic squeak of thanks. Some bar staff were fussing around, clearing up the rest of the mess, apologising. Yeh, buy me a drink, he whispered. Let's toast the news. There was no celebratory ting of the tills, jangle of money or fired-off guffaws, no rasping, sing-songy gossip to pick up on, no duke-box angst, only this dull, eerie drone crimping its way like a deep fever through his body. He was rooted. All he could hear was his war drum heart. He was under siege. Every single drinker had turned on him. He squeezed his eyes tight shut, gurning his whole face, staring deeply into the skin of his eyes. Hieronymus Bosch would have loved it. Dark shadows coming to life, entrails and flames belching at him, thousands of hollow, darting shards, the deadly kilter of teeth gnashing at his heels, great big, bloody fish-mouths grinning at him, their spears at the ready, beaks sharpened. Riven bodies falling upwards into every orifice, their faces screaming at him. He could read their lips in the whirl. Now do you believe us? What did we tell you? It's over. You had it coming to you. Want to hear more? The truth for a change? Leave if you dare.

Twenty minutes passed before Stonie found a sound enough breath to bring some composure. The drinks had failed to return. But Stonie had no plan, no course of action. He was numb. Mica's face was fading every time he tried to see her in his head. It was not possible that she was dead. Not his Mica. His heart was still thumping. He drew in as much of the smoky air as his lungs could take and tucked himself back into his seat. I'm meant to go searching, chase after this guy, The Listener; or the green bead, whatever. One of them will be across the street from me, in a doorway, watching. I'll be stalked, bundled into a car. They'll want to know how long I knew her, how we met. Never heard of the lady. Who is Zach? Yeh, The Listener was a part of it; some elaborate game. And The Pony Tail. He's the key. Come to think of it…the accent was foreign, maybe American. So, what if Kate is Afro. No she doesn't know a Gemima. Yeh, she can get feisty. Don't know what she does for a living. None of your damn business. None of your damn business and how on earth can I possibly say where Zach goes and do I care. No I do not. Stonie's mind went back to the phone calls. Two short, disturbing phone calls over two days, waking him at four-thirty in the morning each time. Never talked about Jay, did I? Never said anything to Zach, nor anyone else before for that matter. He would ring Zach. He would know who The Suit was. Zach, somewhere over the Atlantic. Hi. I'm not available at the moment, please leave a message.

Drinking alone is always tricky. Perhaps in some bolt-hole with endless jugs of coffee and a notebook and a window onto the street, inventing people's stories as they drift through their day. Maybe on the raffia-strewn deck of some palm café, leaning against the bar in the warm waft of an empty midnight dance floor, watching the only dancing couple left alive pacing it out to the blind piano player, dark waves crashing onto the white sands below. Even that late-night broken promise fourth single malt, staring out over the rooftops of your untidy bed-sit with mountains of next-day paperwork thrashing about at your feet. But this was Sunday evening in a Fellini saloon with barely the taxi fare home and the whole bloody world thumping in your veins. Stonie was desperate. He was trying to even out his breathing. Trying to think, sitting exactly on the edge of his seat, bolt upright. His buttocks were rigid. He could feel his feet. They were lead, weren't moving when he told them to. The pub seemed shuffling and tawdry, the people cowed into submission by the sheer weight of eternity. All in slow motion. He made no gesture as the seat opposite became occupied. They sat in silence, Stonie and the next stranger. In every mirror, tile and picture glass, in the coffee spoons and baubles and the darkening canal windows, the late drinkers were mouthing and blowing smoke and making silent, empty gestures of fellowship.

Stonie made an excuse and headed for the street to soak up some night air, steady himself. That would be enough for now. On the way he caught sight of Kate again, nodded but kept on going. He was out of chat-up lines. The door swung back against his heels as he stood in the entrance, trying to take charge. With the move came the doubts. You must have read that all wrong, some mistake, a weird trick of the mind. There will be more than one Mica. He dug deep but there was no beer mat in his pocket. For a moment, he thought he would fight his way back to the table, find the mat, but he wasn't going back. There was no going back. He moved out into the street. He could feel himself swaying on the kerbside as he held onto the rail, the traffic piling up in front of him, snarling, growing ever more menacing. This was sick-making. He started walking. Every step flung it around inside his knotted middle. The filth on the brickwork was coming off on his fingers as he trailed his hand, brick by bloody brick, like some blind man prodding his way along the wall, tilting his head at the world. He stopped at the end of the building and began peeling and scraping at the layers of a torn 'Strike now!' poster plastered on the boarded up windows. That was a good feeling, just ripping; the simple act of destroying. It was something physical to do. What next. Cross the road. Why? No reason. Leap over the railings into the path of a bus. Good idea. What would the final moment feel like? A quicker way to get somewhere. Anywhere.

We were ships that passed in the night, he murmured. The guy's got to have meant someone else, his own Mica. I'll find him. But there were rules. Never talk about Mica to anyone. No one knew the story. It was separate lives. It was Jay, a distant friend. It was over; in a way, she *was* dead. He would have to sweat this one out. Somebody was playing a weird trick. I knew there was something about The Pony Tail. Just knew it. I need a plan. Log the tears, plot the distance between breakdowns. Search warrant? Unlikely, but any photograph to be torn, burnt, trashed. Books given to charity, sent back in jiffy bags with no return address. Pages torn out of the diary, scratched off the calendar. Joke coffee mugs binned. The attic, there were things in the attic. Stuff we thought our kids would laugh at. Must have been The Suit who left the beer mat. It was on his table. Need to read it again. What about the key-ring, the fob? The cheap locket with the badly cut-out photo. And the Charlie Brown pencil case, what was in the pencil case? Doesn't matter; that had to go. And the lock of hair, what kind of stupid, last century thing was that, in its little glass box? Stonie panicked. There were so many traces, too many hooks.

He leaned on the pub door just enough for a thin shaft of light to pierce through. Inside, everything seemed to be in slow motion. He knew he had to pull himself together. Maybe he would find The Suit, buy him a drink, delay him. Or maybe tomorrow night. The street was empty. He stood in the foyer, swaying, trying to make up his mind what to do next. He could see that The Listener was back in the same place, as if he had never risen from the table at all. Stonie rubbed his puffy eyes, trying to focus through the yellow half-light. He's only going to small-talk me in any case. Most likely a darkness will set in. Mention funerals and it does that to people. But whose funeral? Stonie was thinking faster now. He stepped inside the room, forced his way to the bar and bought two beers, all the time watching his adversary in the mock period mirrors. As he approached, The Listener looked up and straight at him, as if expecting his return, as if he himself had timed everything to perfection.

There was not a word about the previous conversation. No comment about flying beers or smashing stars or the weather. Or a death. Nothing. He wondered what The Listener knew. Stonie was about to angle a question. But before he could find the right opening, the right question, The Listener spoke.

'Sorry. Met someone, had a chat. I was thinking it was like they wheeled someone on to discuss post self-realisation depression. Needed to see a shrink, that guy' he chuckled. 'I mean, that character in the ponytail. You feeling a bit better?'

Stonie took a deep breath and cast his eye round the room, trying to work out if he should leave without another word. Maybe The Listener was just as crazy. 'Yeh, I'll be okay. Just remembered something. It upset me. I'll be fine,' he said.

'Perhaps it's some kind of foreign sense of humour,' The Listener continued. 'Know what...it looked like a plant, some sort of student prank kind of thing, one of those out-of-work actors working a home-made script.' He nodded at Stonie. 'Yeh, that's it.'

Stonie was becoming agitated. 'Well, I wouldn't be impressed by what people do to get their fifteen minutes of fame. You know…art in a public space, that sort of thing. It's all old hat,' he replied, meaning where the hell is this leading to, you freaky bastard, just get on with it, say it, come out with it. You know what happened to Mica, don't you. It's a set up. Well, I'm damned if I'm going to leap back across the burning bridges. Now, cut the cryptic, you asshole, get to the point. Why are you here?

'Sounds a bit alternative, a bit too weird for me,' Stonie said. 'Just a loner, that's all. If I were you, I would pay no attention to it. It's just a pub conversation. You forget most of what you say right away in any case. Just evaporates.' He was trying to stay calm, his head thumping, his brain in overdrive. There was still this awful heat. He was sure he had used the back of his grubby hand to wipe his face, get rid of the tears. The tips of his fingers, the poster black nails, the filled-in palm prints with bits of printed lead type from yesterday's news, skin to skin. He could still hear the scraping-across-the-boards sound, see the text ripping through the layers. Trade Unions bashing the government, calls for the brotherhood to strike, Scargill's face all scarred. That appealed. He had stopped talking. Someone's bound to notice when you're red eyed and grubby. Maybe he didn't remember, didn't even care what had actually happened. He was exhausted. There were dirty streaks all across his cheeks and forehead. War paint.

'Had a weird way of talking, then?' Stonie asked. 'The guy in the pony tail?'

'The foreigner. Yeh, I reckon they listen to the television in their rooms,' The Listener replied. 'I've heard tell. Can't afford the language classes, the books, you know.'

'Right. The television.' Stonie said. He waited, but no explanation came. He did nothing, said nothing. The Listener would surely elaborate.

'The guy in the pony tail, the one you were staring at - '

'Wasn't staring, really,' Stonie said.

'Staring...'. The listener paused, shifting position. He took a sip of his beer and nodded at Stonie. 'You were staring over at him. Anyway, said he saw the TV as a new friend. Said it talked to him about the Christ and something they called heavy metal music and it showed him an angry old man called Steptoe and his wise son. I had to turn away to stifle a snigger or two, I did. Well you would, wouldn't you? Not polite. Definitely new to England.'

Stonie listened impatiently. More drivel, more confusion.

'I have never heard anything so weird, really,' The Listener said. 'Christ, we all know about…and the sitcom thing but…the way it all came out - '

This was no good. Stonie needed to find out what had really been talked about. He was convinced it was all about him, in some kind of code. The beer mat had been a plant. It seemed so disjointed. All he wanted was to find out who The Pony Tail was, what was the connection with Mica. There had to be a clue to where he might find him. He watched as the Listener put down his pint and leaned forward.

'Could see you were kinda interested, half-leaning round the pillar, though. Maybe not exactly staring. Don't blame you. Maybe you didn't catch it all, but he said things like "Everything is strange when you first set out on a journey". Like some guru.' The Listener closed his eyes and continued. 'Oh, yeh, then he went on...said something like "The journey itself becomes comforting; the search is the treasure." I remember that much. Heavy, eh?'

'Strange. Definitely very odd,' Stonie replied, hardly piecing together anything which made sense. It was all oblique nonsense, existential, whatever, and he was in no mood to take it in. He tried to breathe deeply, worried he might retch again, all the time grinding his teeth and moaning gently to himself. The noise in his jawbone was deafening. He could barely register what the The

Listener was saying and didn't care any more. He was in no condition for whimsy. Or maybe he did care; if this was his Mica, their three years pulsating in his brain. How could the minutia be suddenly compacted into a barely suppressed scream? Her face was laughing beneath the skin of his eyes, her black dress teasing its way out into the world, that half-smiling strip-me-now sparkle in her eyes. He shook his head violently, drew deep, deliberately widened his eyes and opened his mouth as wide as a yawn.

The Listener was looking at him in silence. Staring at him, saying we've got you where we want you, paralysed, nothing to say for yourself. *Your* Mica, eh? What you waiting for, go on, your turn. Your take on Canaletto…Kate in Ann Arbor. Think Zach's for real, Mr. Reuladair? Do you, do you? We know more than you think. Speak up, can't hear you. Thought you could hide it from the world? Stonie wiped his palm down across his nose and mouth. He was scared. The last time he saw Mica, in the morning, in the room, the fine silk sheet drawn up over her head, her motionless figure; there was a starling on the window ledge. And a day moon, a crescent on the horizon; and one star.

'That's an interesting concept, don't you think?' Stonie said finally. 'I could make it part of my creed, all that search is the treasure stuff.'

The Listener nodded vaguely, closing his eyes yet again as he drew his pint glass up to his face. There was a script in here, Stonie thought, an unfolding. He could hear himself speaking and it was out-of-body. The real Stonie was crawling his way into some metaphysical hole to sweat this one out. He was not going to get what he wanted. The best he could do was muster one-sided generalisations, big denominational themes. He heard himself talking about the state the world was in, the three day week, sorry about poor old Spanish Prime Minister what's-his-name-Blanco did-you-hear-about-that yes, Luis Carrero gunned down in cold blood. Politics, religion, all the same after all. He heard himself wittering on about a bad church life, steeling himself for the bad sex life joke at any minute. It was tabloid conversation. He was in two places at once. Not a pleasant hour.

The Listener was beginning to look uncomfortable, waiting for Stonie's recovery, an explanation. Stonie tried to anticipate the pauses, to keep things going with deeper breathing and more deliberate sips of beer, still hoping for a significant revelation as he tried to compose himself. Loners get seriously confessional, especially in pubs. Somehow, through all the pressure, he sensed this one was unlikely to come close. Stonie's anger was now wariness. I can't unpack the last three years to some retard alien who ought to be sectioned or, better still, piled on to the next plane with a one-way ticket. Come to think of it, this guy looks foreign too. I just won't go that far, won't make myself that vulnerable, Stonie argued. No, not on this earth. He tried his trick of going into first person, to look differently at the guy, listen differently, the way artists do. But he couldn't make it work, couldn't get far enough back. Do you have a bison on the back of your collar too? He would save that one up. Good for an awkward silence. Reminds me of when I was a kid, you know. This Wild West thing we went to, my dad and I. Fucking fright I got when the Red Indian leaned over and screamed right in front of my face and I was so scared I was peeing myself and I imagine I got a bloody hiding when I got home. People in tenements got hidings. Imagine, getting your arse kicked in for peeing yourself when you thought the world was coming to an end and did The Pony Tail wear it for a reason, your late friend, The Bison, that is, that little mark on the back of your neck, his neck, fuck, your collar. Is it a secret society, then, the hair, that pathetic little green bead, have you got a little green bead hidden away back there too - and why do you talk in tiny bursts of crap - you're not from these parts are you, you're just like the guy who upped and left and by the way who was she, this Mica character, this...other Mica, you frigging weirdo, what the hell happened? Did he tell you what the hell happened? He wrote it down on a beer mat. Bet you knew her. How did you know her? I'll fucking let go your throat when you tell me the truth, right? Choking? I don't give a tinker's curse. What is she to you? Who's pulling your strings, eh? I'll take my boot off your face when you admit you're in on this. What happened…I mean these so-called suspicious circumstances. Yeh? You heard that much, didn't you, you fucking little creep.

Stonie hadn't moved a muscle, but he was shaking, nauseous, The Suit's scribbled announcement was still burning into his skull, burning so forcefully into his brain that it was impossible to concentrate. It took a supreme effort not to scream, not to kick over a table or two. You have no idea what it has taken to move on. No idea. Do you realise what you've done, you bastards, you…you. I had it under control. I was over her. I-was-over-her. I chose to be reborn, here, at this moment, on this precious little arc of earth. And I can do elliptical too. I can do cryptic. It was all under control. I can do obtuse you fucking little bastard. I had a new life. Stonie felt he was choking. He closed his eyes and swallowed hard. His fists were clenched. Who sent you? Somebody bloody sent you. She was already dead, he could hear himself shouting, already dead.

'Must go. Been a pleasure to meet you,' The Listener announced, interrupting Stonie's head in mid-flow. Stonie looked at him intently. The face gave nothing away. It was as if the man was talking to himself again, as if he had received instructions in an earpiece. This has been a waste of time - coming back into the pub. A waste. I need some air. He could find no way to hold the man's attention. Alright, so up until now she was really only gone. Now this. Now this…finality. Moves everything onto a different plain, does it not? Don't you think? Different kind of memory. Different kind of loss. How do you, personally I mean, how do you deal with loss? We should carry on, discuss what we know right here. Compare notes. Talk about what I'm going to do now, you know. What am I going to do? Over a pint or two, as two congenial strangers. I mean, with no agenda. Clichés, That would surely be enough.

'Must go,' Stonie heard him say again. With that, the stranger turned and pushed his way through the crowd; his last action, to grab a beer mat from the table as he turned. No sign of a high five or a stay cool, dude, or 'may the stars guide your way'. Stonie was offering him his hand – no name, just his hand; then he held back, bit his lip. No name was about right.

He was being followed. That's how it felt. Maybe the alcohol was doing the arguing. Suddenly it didn't seem such a good idea to drop off the pavement onto the towpath. That secret garden of a door in Gas Street had sucked him in again, only this time it didn't feel right, not at 1.30 in the morning. One-thirty? What have I been doing since…since..? Stonie tried to picture the evening he'd just been through, quickening his steps, with every few yards clawing back the remnants. A good Saturday night's jazz simply wasting away in a fuddle. There's always someone ready to spoil the party.

His brain was ranting at him, on playback, piling on the confusion. The jazz. I went to the Old Crown for the jazz, never got upstairs. Heard it all from downstairs. Yeh, and the kiosk in the entrance, that was it.

The phone calls. Hello Gem, it's me. Need to talk. Ok it's damn near midnight I know, but I need to talk. Saw you earlier. There's no one else…I haven't ever told anyone…I need to let someone in on…no, not phone call stuff, you're right. Can I come round? Yes, now. Won't wait till the morning, just have to…will wait till the morning. Bye. Gemima. Svelte, cool, a sophisticate, the still waters. Had her own rather mysterious consultancy and plenty of money, the bitch. She'd be the one to sit down last when anyone gathered. Maybe it was a power thing. Maybe she wasn't to be trusted. Bet she's rarely in her own bed.

Hi, Kate. Sorry, bad line. I've no one else to…sorry, I just thought that after our tiny little frisson I thought you'd be the one to turn to…it *is* damned important, more important than you realise. Did I wake you up? Course. Sorry. Yeh, middle of the night. Kate would burst into a room with her long tousled black hair crazily back-combed by the wind, beaming dark freckles on her dark skin. She'd be the one to give you a kiss on the back of the head if she's over you, thrust her cold fingers into your eyeballs and say 'guess who' and you'd always say 'now let me think…' Hey Kate, night person… Yeh, well it is a bit late. It's always a bit late…never an appropriate time, you're right. See you. Stonie's head was pounding.

For goodness sake. That was it, Stonie whispered in sung speech. I was running out of coins and there was shouting, noise, this muffled Take Five in the background. Should have started with Zach. We all know it's short for something Biblical, poor guy. Just Zach. Yeh, Zacharias. Find me another Zach, I say. One syllable. Guess it'll have to do. Takes off home to good old Yankee doodle land. Where's the bloody number? Which one's Gem's, no Zach's. What do I really know about these people? Come to think about it, they know nothing about each other; never met. So what does it matter? Must keep it that way. Why start now? Come on Zach, answer the bloody phone. Never does. Must try phoning Zach again, yeh, right on. Mustn't phone Zach, trans-atlantic calls cost a fortune. No, mustn't phone anyone. Nothing they can do. No one knows Mica and me…the split. No one was in on it. What the hell. Why would I tell them anything? Stonie was breathing so hard into the black mouthpiece, it stank back. Stale smoke, spirits, curry, lipstick. He could hear his heart pounding in his ears. God, everyone else's bugs and my own breath pumping up my nose, he mouthed. Fuck all of you, you wouldn't have an answer if someone tortured you for it. There was never any answer. To the phone. To the questions; to anything. He burped, swayed and replaced the receiver slowly. God, I'll bet if he'd been there he would have been there.

Canal junctions. Do I take the beautiful, rusting old cast-iron bridge or scramble up over the fence and across some rat-infested back yard, bouncing on damp mattresses and rotting piles of undelivered election manifestos, all in the hope of escaping out onto the road? Stonie simply could not remember where the next set of steps would take him. He was out of breath, but more from muted panic than any physical effort. He was being followed, after all. And there was this voice gnawing away at his insides. 'Just a few more questions if you don't mind. Perhaps you would care to call in at the station'. Next thing, they'll be drinking pints and blending in. You never know who you're talking to in pubs.

He stopped for breath. Canal paths are much longer in the dark. There will be one of those we-have-had-our-eye-on-you inspectors, probably called Morrell or Shaw or Delaney, who's sole purpose in life is to fuck you up and just happens to be an expert at reading faces. Bet he gets hunches. They all get hunches. We believe...what do you mean, you believe…you bloody saw me...we believe you were engaged in conversation with a man in a suit in a pub. The Old Crown, we believe. A thin man with tight silver hair and a short pony tail. Sallow complexion. Don't forget the bloody green bead at the nape, you scumbags. I never got to talk to him once, you idiots, I was sitting behind him. We have reason to believe you know who he is. Yeh, well I don't. Get off my case. I missed the jazz because of it. Mica is dead. You lot aren't likely to shed a tear. Charge me or let me get on with my life. Come to think of it, get your own life. Some weird-looking robotic stranger's got one over me here, acting all mesmeric. And his frigging empty-headed foreign mate. I meant to go upstairs, listen to the jazz band. That was all I was there to do. Stonie was getting tired of putting one foot in front of the other. He stopped under a road bridge.

The crowds had thinned. Overhead, the top deck of a bus slid past. Instinctively, in the sudden glow, he tucked himself further into the shadow of the arch. There was hardly a sound to be heard down on this watery road, just the hollow gravel as he shuffled, his rasping breath, the drips from the oozing, crumbling brickwork dropping in slow motion onto the canal with sweet, soporific clarity, each plinking note suspended in the hush. He watched overlapping circles melt ever outwards into the black glassy reflection from the light of the yellow streetlamps on the water. A drip from the low curved brickwork caught the inside of his collar, ran cold between his shoulder blades, making him shiver. He didn't like the nagging, this feeling that someone might be looking for clues, that Morrell and his cronies, with so little to go on, had put a tail on him. That would be his name. Morrell. Fanciful, perhaps. Stonie set off again, slowly. Every gantry and looming warehouse was leaning into his path. He kept his head down, watching for dog-shit and those big metal rings that could roll you head first into the oily water if you dragged your foot. It's what canals can do if you dream too much, or you show them you're scared.

A few drinks in a pub then for no reason, capow! - you're some comic-strip fugitive being outrun by dark forces from twenty pages further on. If Mica was dead he needed proof. If he tried to get proof, he'd be talking about her. The word 'dead' made his heart jump. Every few yards, he glanced over his shoulder. No one. Yet the feeling persisted. Canals have few alleys, no side roads. It would be easy to follow him from the front, be there for his next choice. The benign, idle waterways with their slinky, multi-coloured oil-trails and sun-burst wakes in the wash of scatty ducks, they turned menacing at this hour. He was a rat in a rat run. Forward or back? He could easily be anticipated from above. His accusers, dark bramble patches, mini sub-station boxes, abandoned sofas, they were all closing in. Those tethered narrow boats, there were eyes at the port holes, for certain. Someone in that phone box up there on the road was calling ahead to the next lock. Any minute now some homburg would step out onto his path in those last few feet of freedom. I have no idea what happened to her. Honestly. It's a case of mistaken identity, the Bison Tie said so himself. Stonie's walking had reached a dragging crawl.

As he reached the sign for his bridge, the cobbled ramp, with those familiar rooftops caught in the street lights, he paused, leaned forward and put his hands on his trembling knees to steady himself. Nearly home. Drawing a long deep breath and holding it in, that was a mistake. The cold air was too much. The vomit spurted out, a long arc of pasta straight into the water. He swayed and steadied himself, crouching to his hunches to lock the violent retching. For a moment, he thought he would tip into the canal himself, his head so light he could see stars. He tucked himself down, rocked back and forth, arms around his knees. He was thinking, these aren't the stars I had planned for myself, this isn't the new world I was trying to invent. It made him laugh, one of those tearful laughs. He looked up, bent his head fully back till his chin was pointing at the clouds then fell backwards onto the dirt with a stupid little laugh. There were nettles burning onto his ears and neck, but he didn't care. The sky was moving and that was pure entertainment. Little flecks, thin, scratchy lines, tiny pearls of neatly spaced yellow. He let his whole body relax for a moment or two then tried to take control again, slaking the bitter tang of the sick with as much saliva as he could massage out of his burning throat. Cool young professional, check, puffing away on his meerschaum with a pint and some jazz, check, everything under control, un-phased, making things happen eh? I don't think so. We sleep to wake, we fall to rise, we are baffled to fight better. I don't think so. Anyway, it isn't working. It doesn't matter if I stay here all night. Nobody gives a shit.

He tested himself with a long slow intake of breath. It felt good not to be running. It was in situations like these that he would talk to God. That is what he thought he was doing; observations, rhetorical questions, big stuff. After that, he would talk to himself. Get up, he said out loud. What are you doing here, he said. Tell me, Stonie, what are your plans for tomorrow? Tomorrow, you'll be in the studio producing your little scamps for the creatives and the whiz-kid account executives and getting a measly crumb for coming up with brilliant ideas. Brilliant ideas and no fucking credit. Yeh, and you'll have written at least one phenomenal slogan that goes national and nobody will give a monkey's and if she's really gone, the last vestige of hope will have finally gone too. He shivered. No, I didn't want to find her. I should have looked back once more, I should have checked.

He stood up and pulled at his jeans, damp and cold from the grass. There seemed to be no beautiful memory to reclaim. He fancied that Morrell would have had a way of listening to every last little word, and the thought spurred him on. Right now, Mr Reuladair, within half a minute, you will be turning the key in the lock of your own front door, just think of that. He could feel the sick sitting there, just below the sternum. He liked to think that a few deep breaths, a few short steps later, he was clicking the door of his flat behind him with his bum. He knew he banged the light switch on with his forehead. He had the scar.

Stonie woke to a half moon at the window. It took a little time to focus. On the third pane, a spider marked time between stars. He could hear the clock. He could hear his neck creaking. From his position on the carpet, he could hear a police siren streets away. Layers of sound folding in on each other. He finally made it onto the armchair. It felt comfortable, the kind of comfort that said no point in moving, no point in thinking. His whole body was at the mercy of those last few hours. But he pushed himself up off the armchair and went over to the window. One more look. The spider was still there, but at a guess, the stars had moved a few million light years. He was never any good with distances, never could put any discernible distance between those blissful years and the present he deserved. At least, that's the way he saw it. He swore he could still smell Mica in his nostrils, taste her. The bite on his lip, the electric silk of her perfect thighs. He'd been reading too much poetry. All it took was discovering a hair-grip caught in the skirting board, a shrivelled-up rose bud behind the bookshelves.

He stared out into the dark. This was the time to disappear into the night. Your friends would turn up late one afternoon, knock and knock and knock then go away. Then they would phone you all through that same evening and get no answer till someone plucked up the courage to call the police and they'd all come together and break down the door at one in the morning to find the place empty, stripped bare. No recognisable stick of furniture anywhere. Maybe there would be a crumpled envelope, ripped open, with a sender address on the back and that would be the clue everybody would be taking apart; that would be the lead the uniforms would follow. Before long, you'd make it into the local rags, appear on milk cartons and bollards at traffic lights, that kind of thing. Someone would donate a photograph of you at fourteen years old bearing no resemblance whatsoever to who you see in the mirror. And out there, holed up in some damp, poorly-lit bedsit over-looking a goods yard, you'd be peering through moth-eaten curtains at this alien, sad old world, desperate to be found.

The speech nailed it. A sea of adoring East Coast elite. As the applause died away, Zach stepped down from the podium and eased himself slowly through the crowd, nodding, sipping at his wine, smiling, shaking hands. One of those evenings when it was impossible to look anyone in the eye. You would be looking over the shoulder, catching the room, the drift of important people. Tonight, it was his turn. He would allow himself a few hours of importance. It was a rare condition, but the Private View was going well, press interviews, local TV, dignitaries. He was elated. Broke, but elated. The punters would start buying soon, he was certain of that. All it would take was one red dot. The gallery would take care of it. Okay, so this was New York. Hard as nails, over-indulged. He needed Europe.

'Mr. Graffenheimer, excuse me sir, there is a call for you'. Zach felt a touch on his shoulder. 'This way, please.' He squeezed through the guests and was directed to a wall phone at the end of the bar counter. A server was waiting, elbow on the bar, the receiver dangling unprofessionally from her limp hand. Zach shook his head and took the phone from her impatiently.

'Hello, Zach here.'

'Hi, we don't know each other but I wonder if we could meet, Mr. Graffenheimer. I have a proposal which might interest you.' Stonie did not recognise the voice.

'Who am I speaking to? I'm sorry...there is a lot of background noise. Definitely not the best time to - 'Zach cupped his free hand to his ear, straining to keep up with the fragmented conversation. This was it. The commission, the break. 'Yeh, yes, I understand. Sounds intriguing. Yeh, so, right now? Got that. Well I'm very busy. Does seem a little unusual. Give me a few minutes. Guess I could do with some air.' He pressed the receiver harder against his ear, but the rest was lost. He was high, pumped up, open to anything. A waitress pushed a flute of bubbly across the desk on a pink doily. Zach waived it away as he replaced the hand- set. His watch read ten minutes after midnight.

He could not figure out the urgency, but sure enough, when he stepped outside, across the courtyard he could see the white Buick, parked up alongside one of those clear, plastic phone booths which always reminded him of his early days, space helmets, rockets, being captain of his own spaceship. He stood for a moment on the top step, tasting the wine on the back of his throat, weighing up the situation. It was a warm night, with the subtle smell of fallen eucalyptus leaves, the soft yellow of the tree lights and the hum of the city a welcome break from the raucous, densely perfumed claustrophobia of the gallery. He felt safe, curious, in control. This was *his* evening. As he approached the car, the smoked glass of the passenger's window dropped six or eight inches and a hand thrust out, a gloved hand, holding a silver business card.

'I appreciate it's an inappropriate time, but you should call in at my office within a couple of days. No more. We'll expect you.' It was the same voice. Slightly husky, mid-paced, a refined up-state accent. Zach bent closer to get a better look. His visitor was alone in the back of the car, staring straight ahead. He was wearing a thin striped charcoal suit, dark glasses, a black fedora completing the range of shadows. Zach recognised it as a Borsalino. The man's profile was deep-lined, tanned, sculpted. Zach shifted his position and narrowed his eyes, trying to read the cuff-links.

'My boss, he is looking for an artist who takes pictures, who's going places. Potential. Thinks you are promising. He'll make it worth your while.'

Zach straightened up. 'Might I ask which agency...I mean, well, won't you join us, take a look right now, the gallery. Let me get you my card. It's a perfect time.' He was trembling, excited. 'You'll be able to view the – '

'That's okay. We know your work. It's okay.' This time the tone was one of irritation.

Know your work. Know your work? This was his first time out of the mid-west. How? Zach couldn't get any questions ready in time.

'Right, thank you, Mr....' He held up the card to the light, searching for a name as the engine burst into life, the window began to close and the car slowly rolled forward.

'Save it, Mr. Graffenheimer. Just say Battjes sent for you.' The Buick gathered speed, leaving Zach breathing exhaust fumes, staring after the car, too late to catch the number plate.

Wk.1178
32º 39.3 N   114º 36.2 W

Luca 'Canaletto' Cambareri cursed whatever gods he could think of, crossing himself in contrition at the very thought of blasphemy. His breathing was short, shallow, rapid, even in the act of standing up. He was angry. His pass had been revoked, the guard could not find his clearance number, any details – and now, after all the waiting, They wanted to carry out a body search. There were mutterings, phone calls, print-outs. He could see himself in staccato slow motion on the security monitor, the bald patch on his crown, greasy and shining in the stark light, filling the frame. Distortion, it was all distortion. He could watch himself from above, as if it was some monochromed out-of-body dream, and he didn't like looking down on the person he saw. He hurriedly replaced his cap, forcing the peak down hard onto the bridge of his nose. Why insist on the uniform. He had so little occasion for it these days.

Endless waiting. He was in shock. He had no idea it would take him so long to get into his own compound, his own laboratory. And the search; who ordered that? Three years in and out of the same building, and now this. Two years of insurance claims flying around, and now this - everyone passing the buck; one year of disability allowance, but no explanation for the symptoms and all the time, he had faithfully filed his reports. One thing he could never understand – none of the research had ever been published. Not to his knowledge, at any rate. No abstracts, not a word. It was 'out of Their hands' he was told. Not what They promised when he took the post. Even the prognosis kept changing.

The bulb finally flicked alive, a voice rasped through the speak-here grill and the door lock clicked. He stood motionless for a moment, unsure how to respond, then realised he had to pull open the door; it was not automatic, not sliding, just buzzing. He curled his fingers round the door handle, arm at full stretch, but made no move to bend his arm, no attempt to pull the door towards him, as if frozen; or, somewhere deep within him, as if checking against the possibility this was a one-way journey. Once inside, he let his arm fall by his side and gently wiped the sweat of his palm against the trim of his trousers. The door made to slam behind him, frightening Luca into a sudden, defensive twist of the shoulders, then it cushioned itself for the last few inches, settling gently into place with that final suck of air. Another room. One table, plastic topped, one chair, one high shelf, a security camera and several coat hooks. The whole area was bathed in a pale blue light from some hidden ceiling recess. He wanted to find the light, to know where it was coming from. There were no signs on the shiny white walls. What was remarkable was that Luca could not hear his feet. No steel-capped scratching across the floor, no click. He could always hear his feet, always knew they were there. It was his connection, his certainty; the steady clack as he walked, marched, took the stairs, shuffled against the sides of the elevator; it was his metronome, his rhythm. But this time, not even a scratch. He turned, but his minder had already gone.

Let's see...it's 1969, check; I'm forty-six years, eight months and eleven days old, check; it's morning; eight twenty nine and eleven seconds, check. He looked at the back of his hand, stared at it for a long time. The veins stood out, like someone twice his age. He could see the shake, feel it more by the day. He stretched out both arms in front of him, palms downwards and spread his fingers as wide as he could. None of his knuckles would straighten. His cuticles were dry, his nails streaked with cream lines. Very slowly, he drew his fingers together and turned his hands flat against each other in a horizontal prayer, fingers absolutely matched. The pose took him back. He was diving. This was the start of the dive. This was the moment of balance, of being in control, his body, taut, every nerve and sinew primed and in agreement with his brain, the knees slightly bent, the toes curled over the board above the pool, his breathing in perfect harmony with his intentions. He would not look down. He would see with his eyes closed. But he did look down. After emptying himself of all thought but the point of entry, he did look down. And there she was, Bethany. On the edge, deep below him. He could see just enough of her to recognise the flash of golden hair, the perfect symmetry of her breasts rising and falling in expectation of the dive. The water danced. To him, the deep ceramic blue lines, twisting and coiling upwards from the sparkling depths were binding the two of them together. The distance between them had narrowed. He would marry in England, honeymoon in Italy, first home in Boston. A Mount Kisco kid living in Boston. A good plan. But Arizona beckoned. A good plan till he took the commission. He studied his hands. They were lean and straight. Steady fingers which knew the salute, knew the commands. Once.

'Canaletto!' The voice startled him. 'Ca-na-lett-o.' How he hated people calling him Canaletto. This was the gifted amateur, cleared of fakery in a blaze of gallery madness and forever made to pay for the joke. A painting genius and anti-hero at eighteen, throwing it all in for God and country. There was no forgiveness; the name was part of the territory. It stuck long after the novelty wore off. Long after he'd seen action. Long after the serious transformation to man of science and the too-old-for-war trick. Turning to forensic, turning to research was the natural progression; the minutiae, the careful building up of quite a different kind of picture; it appealed to his sense of what was masked, what was revealed.

'Hey, Luca, I had no idea it was you – just had a number. There's been a mistake. How are you, old buddy?' Luca turned to find himself inches from a familiar face. Battjes was gushing. No other word for it; always had been. But this was more phony than ever. Luca was already feeling sick. He was in no mood for pleasantries.

'What d'you mean a mistake?' he said, pulling away from the hand on his shoulder. He was unsteady on his feet but summoned up enough indignation to mount a challenge. 'What kind of mistake?'

'The search,' Battjes replied, tapping Luca playfully on the shoulder.

'Don't touch me,' Luca said, recoiling far enough to crash against the table and drop down onto the seat.

'They got that bit wrong, that's all,' Battjes said. He beckoned Luca to follow him out into the corridor. 'Three for an eight; someone needs glasses in this department; read a three when it should have been an eight, that's all. You're a clerical error,' he chuckled. He was walking slightly ahead of Luca, very much aware of the distance between him and his charge. 'There's no search.'

Luca was ushered into an office. There were framed photographs of white coats, medalled uniform types, smug looking uniform types, he thought – dripping off the walls around the room; no one he recognised. Battjes with the President took centre stage. A Stars and Stripes was draped behind the only desk, some kind of walnut desk with a leather inlay top, gold marquetry patterns around the edges – and a white phone; the all-important phone. The drawer of a grey filing cabinet lay open, with several papers strewn across the tops of the drop files.

'Please, take a seat.'

Luca made no move to obey. He stood in the middle of the room, wondering if he was standing to attention. Battjes swung into his chair and leaned both elbows on the desk. 'So, what's it been, then? Three years? Has to be at least two and one half. I had no idea you'd joined the programme. It's a big operation, lots of people coming and going all the time.' He was talking in that quick-fire, artificially friendly manner, quite definitely leaving little space for Luca.

'Right, I'll - '

Luca caught sight of himself in the smoked glass window. There were figures moving behind his reflection, sure there were; it was a one-way mirror; had to be. Figures moving inside his head. Sure they were. There was certainly no one else in the room.

'Right,' Battjes began again, 'You may like to know I have assigned an intern to your section; to organise the technicians, lab reports, that sort of thing. Been here...oh...a couple of months. Name's Graffenheimer. Zacharias P. The third. Good man. Just while you are on the road to recovery, that's all, Luca; while you are being assessed, you understand? Rehab. Your work...eh was going well. That is until you fell ill of course. Unfortunate business.'

'What do you want from me?' Luca asked. 'What do They want from me? Cut the sweet talk. I've nothing to lose here; that's for sure. Why am I being hounded, no help, no explanation. I've been stepped down, can't get to my desk, can't get clearance - ' His voice was trembling.

'Well now, Canaletto,' Battjes dropped a tone 'There are a number of …ah…security issues and of course, your condition. We - ' He stopped mid-sentence. Luca was staring straight ahead, disengaged. His arms were stiff by his side in a stand-to-attention lock, his fingers frenetically piano playing, his shoulders rigid.

'Who's fucking me up here, what's the charge, what have I done? Somebody fucking tell me what's going on. And less of the Canaletto shit. You should know better than that.'

'Would you please sit down, Luca. Take a seat. Here, have something to drink.' Jay was mechanical. Luca could hear the ice cubes rattling in the glass as he was led to a chair. He knew he was cracking, hated showing emotion.

'You're kid's gone to her mother, then? New start.' Luca tried to rehearse a response. Never told you anything, never will. She flies next week, tomorrow; maybe tomorrow, weeks ago - what's it to you. What's it got to do with the Centre, ass-hole? Somebody tell me what's wrong with me. Battjes took another line. 'Walsall. Got it down as Warsaw first time round; Warsaw UK, dumb clerk. Dangerous mistake. Local intern, see? Found it in time and no harm done. You can understand why it caused a flutter for an hour or two. You can see that, can't you. They tell me Birmingham's the black country. Hell, there's a coincidence for you – I mean Birmingham, Alabama and all them niggers. Black country, right?' There was nothing for the scientist to do but listen. 'Kinda lonely for you, what with you being sick and all.'

Luca put the glass to his mouth but hesitated. 'Lime juice, nothing else,' he heard the man say. Jay was talking through him. 'We'll put you back together, don't worry. You can take some leave. Go visit. Get your strength back. Been looking at your case, your work load. Everybody has a review. Hell, I get a review myself; nothing special in that.'

Luca knew Battjes would ignore anything he tried to say. This wasn't conversation. It was softening up, Luca knew that; knew there was more to come. He let his shoulders relax, took a sip from the glass and looked across at The Director of Operations.

'No business of yours, my life. Who put a tail on me? Who's listening to my calls? Leave my family out of it...you - ' His voice trailed off. He knew he was stringing bits of sentences together, struggling to get any flow. He sat awkwardly against the back of the chair. He was exhausted; he could hardly think straight, hardly get his mind around the latest developments. The hunter becoming the hunted: what if the divorce was just one more *arrangement*? Of course, he'd seen it coming. Weeks of late nights at the centre; Beth at home, or maybe not at home. Regular notes by the phone 'Call Kurt. Kurt rang 3.45pm. Message for mom, ring Kurt right away'. It was 3.45pm regular. The rage came in stutters. Over the years, she'd taken the beatings, the outbursts, the other women; taken him back, lived with his clawing remorse. Taken the money. There was nothing left to fight over. Let the law take its course. There were only recent memories. Short trips home; longer stays in hospital. No sympathy, no calls apart from Beth's attorney. That part was all flooding back but it didn't add up to much. There was no trace of the man they called Kurt.

'Heard from Jay, I guess? Making friends. Taking to her new school? Polytechnic, that's what they call it over there? Beth's got folks in the neighbourhood, she'll make out just fine, she'll be just fine.' This man Battjes was bad at sincerity. His voice droned on. Luca closed his eyes. Who the hell is Jay? Oh yeh, Jay. My kid. Where was she? That's what he wanted to know. But Luca Cambareri didn't know how to ask. He usually took. He could not remember things any more. He had a wife, still had a wife; oh yes, for a few more days; Bethany, if that was her name, she never…was that her name? She never settled. Jay, *his* beautiful Jay, daughter, star in his firmament - now she… This was the point of tears; the flashes; more embarrassing as he had no idea why he was in tears. He just never knew how to connect, how to make them understand his needs. There was an echo in his head - 'Heard from Jay, then? Taken to her new school?'

'You already know, what's the point in asking me?' Luca whispered loudly.

If he heard at all, Battjes made no response. He was bowed over his desk, writing. For Luca, the effort of selecting his words was making him catch his breath in several short gulps of air. He closed his eyes. He was back several weeks; the night of the phone calls, two in one night. He always remembered conversations on the telephone; the distant, disembodied voice. He could listen more intently. There was something comforting in not seeing the person speaking to you. Two calls from England. Straight to his hospital bed. He was sure this was the first time his daughter had ever spent time with him as a grown up.

'How's Beth? I mean, your mother?'

'Well, home but like, might as well be on foreign soil, being back here. Can't say, might take a while.' Jay didn't add Walsall sucks; I'm coming back to the U.S. Jay didn't want to give him anything. 'You alright? They gave me this number. Mom says you are in a *clinic*. I thought you were recovering at home' Jay's voice was steady, unemotional. She allowed the silences. Luca didn't say, how's your mom, how are you. Miss you.

'So-so...look, I was thinking, you need to know something about the family. Something Beth...you're mom might never get round to telling you. You still there?' He was never sure if Jay had ever listened to anything he said. He'd been ready to tell her, then. Something he needed to confess. It was time. But she had cut across him; always did. Not with venom, but she did sound cold; that's what he heard, cold.

'Been a one-night-stand for twenty years, you and mom,' she'd said. 'All hell breaking loose, then you gone for months on end, working in that damned government laboratory. Me having to polish your buttons but not allowed to sit on your knee. That's what I remember. Mom will get by. You must have known it would come to this.' Must have known. Must have known.' Each time, the voice hardened.

Luca swirled the ice in his glass. Clockwise, then the other way. It was harder anti-clockwise. These were the things he noticed. 'Hell, no, there were plenty of good times, he had whispered to Jay, with his hand clasped over the mouthpiece. Plenty. You were just too young, too young to - ' That's when the line had gone dead. He didn't know how to return the call, didn't know if he wanted to. He had held the receiver to his ear for a long time, until a nurse prised it free and replaced it. It rang again, almost immediately. 'What do you want with me this time?' had blurted out of his mouth even before he'd taken stock. 'Oh, the letter, yes, I got the letter; thank you. I'll reply, I promise. Yeh, I'll write. Looking after myself, right. Always do.'

Luca fumbled in his inside pocket. No envelope, but several crumpled pages were teased out. He had been going to write.

'I was going to write.' he said, looking across at Battjes. Luca was sitting to attention. Battjes got up from his seat and walked around his desk. He gently prised the paper from Luca's fist, smoothed out the sheets and scanned through the pages.

"...fourteen crumbling high-rises – they call them tenements here – two boarded up public houses (that's a bar to us) and a chained playground, swings as twisted as the aftermath of an WW2 air raid. That's the view from my window. Every afternoon, the kids from the

block hang out on a muddy little grass mound by a row of stores, kinda broken down and covered in graffiti – they fight and smoke and they're all round shoulders and unhealthy looking and they all smoke the same cigarette while they're waiting for their working mothers, I guess. It's pretty bleak.
I can tell you the one who's gonna take a leak in the bus shelter, then there's one ginger kid, can't be more than twelve and he's the tough guy. I've seen him sticking his grubby little hands down a girl's pants in full view. Oh, and I've been on a double decker bus, it's the only way to get anywhere out here. Got a timetable.
Mom's depressed. Taking pills for it, think she's self-harming but what do you care.
Just thought you oughta be told. Don't know what I'm doing here, I swear. Has anyone told you my condo in Ann Arbour was burgled and I was attacked as I arrived home. You couldn't have done much anyway in your state. That was another reason for quitting school. God, this place is boring, no wonder mom escaped when you showed up. Married you to get out of this hell-hole, I swear. Bet nothing's changed here in twenty years. Let me tell you that on the few clear days when you can see it, there's some kinda power station thing like a sand timer and it belches out all this smoke and steam then you can't see the allotments. That's the word for a yard when you don't own one. Anyway, it rains a lot and there's all these rows of grey slab roofs with no detail and there's no sense of time passing and no escape. Just buses spewing out their kids and pensioners and I swear I AM GOING INSANE. There's no hope here but I got nothing to come home for. This is supposed to be home now. No hope – maybe except for the yellow line on the horizon at night. That's the city and all I do is sit and write messages to the angels in my breath on the window, but you wouldn't understand. Guess am just feeling sorry for myself but I don't know anyone and I'm lonely and mom doesn't give a shit. Says she does. Just like you said. Mom wants to come back for Thanksgiving, might do her good and I might as well come back with her. You know what she's like, all mixed up. I mean she couldn't wait to get over here and now, well...only for a couple of weeks, though, to see folks. She says she might visit with you. Don't rightly know why. Guess I might tag along. But it could get better here. I made a few calls to the polytechnic (that's school) Thought

you oughta be proud I'm gonna try for a batchelors degree. Yeh, well you know me, say what I have to. I don't mean stuff but well, anyhow, I met a guy on a train and he was"

There was no more to read. In any case, Battjes had read it before. He liked the shitty attitude of the girl. No love lost. He folded the notepaper slowly and pushed the sheets into the top pocket of Luca's jacket. Luca showed no desire for dialogue. He sat, motionless, both hands in his lap, hardly daring to speak.

He could sense he was slurring words, taking longer to formulate a response, trying more and more desperately to hold onto his dignity. The rules are changing by the minute, he thought to himself. He knew damn well They were playing with him. It was one thing knowing the game, quite a different matter playing it.

'It's no game.' Battjes said. The retort jolted Luca from his reverie. 'It's no game, Cambareri – no one's playing here.' The tone was severe. There was singular emphasis on each word. Luca shivered. He hadn't spoken out. He could swear he had not uttered a sound. Had he? It was all part of it; yes, that's the way it is with these things. They want me to lose my grip on reality. Hell, he thought - clicks on the line, disinformation, FBI files, clearance problems, strip don't strip, people I hardly know being all buddy-buddy and telling me what they've no right to know. He was breathing noisily to cover any movement of his lips. He had found a moment so lucid, the adrenalin was at his beck and call. So it has come to this. Set up. Turned into some kind of sadistic case study. The illness? He was in a cold sweat. He could hear this guy Battjes talking to him, the hollow, tinny monologue reverberating around his skull. His head was pounding, his heart thudding. He was becoming paralysed by the truth. Unable to blink. The illness was, is the experiment. The mysterious condition, the experiment; the data, the samples, the reports – all the experiment. Between spells in hospital, he had, in effect, been researching himself.

For the first time, Luca knew he would never get well again, never breathe deep, run upstairs, play ball. He struggled to find words which would take away the feeling it was all drifting away, that it was all over. There was nothing left to fight with, no fire in his belly, no anger. A warmth, a faintly burning warmth crept through him from the inside. His eyelids felt rough, his mouth dry and tight and it was time, yes it was time simply to be led, to do nothing of his own free will. He tried to speak, but all that squeaked out were numbers, groups of numbers. Could he reconcile the numbers, make connections. No matter how hard he tried, none of it made sense.

'Best if we get a move on, Luca, get you back to base.' This time, it wasn't the Battjes character holding onto his elbow. He looked up. The identity card was swaying around. He narrowed his eyes and swayed with it, just enough focus to register the "Zac..." before the tag was trapped in the man's uniform. 'Best if you get in here,' the driver beckoned. 'This way.'

Luca became aware he was by the security huts, being ushered across flagstones towards a jeep and two uniformed men. It was the first time in an eternity he could hear his footsteps. He was sure he had been away somewhere and was coming home. That was the feeling. Everything would be back to normal. He opened his mouth to speak but could not hear any noise. He knew it was late afternoon. He knew it was early autumn. Most of all he knew he had completed three hundred and ninety-two six forty-ones, innumerable D3 checking procedures – probably just over four thousand five hundred – submitted three formal data sheets code Eagle 51, ran fifty-nine cobalts, rotated eighteen hundred and twenty three samples a month, filed one hundred and seventy-two reports in three and a half years. He knew. The one set of numbers that mattered drew a smile. Scratched with a pin into the back of a photograph, a small black and white mug shot; someone he once knew. The jeep gathered speed, leaving a trail of desert dust in its wake, the pale canopy ahead of them fusing to peach then turquoise then darker blue. Luca was rolling limply with the acceleration, his neck at an angle against the quilted plastic of the headrest, staring emptily out through the glass at a falling sky. 'The rag star,' he mouthed.

Wk. 1213 (8482)

52°23.2' N 1°47.7' W

'Umpteenth.' He could still hear the sex in her voice. Even after all these years. 'Well, ah…I'm afraid it is a word the origins of which are beyond me.' The origins of which. Stonie never spoke in that manner; he was just caught out, searching for a way to respond. He couldn't quite make out the accent at first, the 'excuse-me-sir' of it, the unnerving way she had said it without ever looking up, not even a glance. That's what took him by surprise. The 'who, me?' reaction when there was no other soul in the railway carriage. He had always reckoned train journeys were a metaphor. He could always romanticise their searching, unresolved banality. Staring out of the window but seeing only the reflected fellow-travellers ghosting their way through the countryside, living out their body language in some kind of ritual game, some kind of pastiche. Who they are escaping from, what dramas they will return to, how much they know about each other. The wonder was always whose conversation to break into, the temptation, to scream "let me deal with the bastards, I'll sort them out, marry him and be done with it. You should have bought the hush-puppies instead, face it, the fucking shares are worthless". The lady had sat there, implacable, moving only at the whim of the train. Not once had she looked across at him. Women seemed to be able to look at a man without using their eyes. Just sat there. It had a B-movie feel to it, especially the newspaper. Some prop.

Stonie slumped even further into his armchair, unsure what to do with the memory. The flat was cooling down. After the canal, the paranoia, the vomit, there was something pleasingly perverse in sitting in the dark watching the luminous green hands of the kitchen clock moving imperceptibly towards dawn. How many times had he found himself turning over that first encounter with Jay on the train, reliving it, inventing subtle new beginnings, compensations for the irretrievable loss to the senses. He shifted position. From his angle, he could watch for stars that had not been earmarked for satellites, half closing his eyes to make shapes with the planets. His neck and shoulders were hard in spite of his pose, his mind relishing that first rolling, train-ride stare with regret. Umpteenth indeed.

She had finally looked up, looked straight at him as she lowered her newspaper. That was it. A slow, deliberate action – meant to say, I know you've been staring at me for ages, picking at the hunger, getting those juices going, trying to fit me into your sad little world, searching for a label, a history. Trying not to be the one to start a conversation. It was all there in that first split second of eye contact.

'That's what you do when you've known someone forever.' he had said. 'That's what happens; the kind of knowing, disarming familiarity, years of practice at being elsewhere in your heart, but still intimate enough to read each other without looking up, without confirming that you're connecting.' He had dug a hole for himself. Philosophical, may be, but bottomless. The train was rolling – and with it, the story of his next few years.

'What exactly do you mean?' Recalling those first few exchanges with Jay made his skin creep. She was beautiful, she was confident, she was in control.

'Well, we've been sitting here for, say, twenty minutes, no one else in this section of the train. Then out of nowhere, you ask the world where the word 'umpteenth' comes from – and since I'm the only ears around, I assume it's for me. But you don't look up, there's the merest flicker of a smile as you say it.' He had intoned in a slightly scolding way. The attitude in his voice had crept under her porcelain skin.

'You were staring that intensely?' It had been rhetorical. But it was true. You can feel someone looking at you, a sense of something projected. That's the way it started. A hint of playfulness. She was definitely sparring. On the day, it was worth the gamble. As the train rumbled on, there had been nothing better to do than hope.

'You were undressing me,' she had said. 'They all do, can't help themselves.' He remembered his unconvincing indignation, the 'now wait a minute' he'd fired back.

'We're not all pervs, I - '

She'd had the cheek to say, if the glove fits - and the argument really took off. A real teaser. Stonie shifted his position on the rug, aroused by the picture he was trying to hold on to. Half-past four in the morning and not an ounce of sleep in him. The room felt even colder but he refused to do anything about it. He was not going to bed. He was moving to the sound of the train. 'Cap. It's cap. If the cap fits.' he recalled. 'The expression - ' In his mind, the reason for the umpteenth was her crossword puzzle, that newspaper. No matter, she had persevered by insisting that the word to be used was 'glove'. Stonie smiled at the way she had handled it. She had closed and folded her newspaper in a most methodical and haughty manner and leaned further back against the high, padded seat, her head tilted slightly against the window, her elbow firmly on the armrest. She began by tapping the window with the backs of her fingernails, drumming out some random beat while staring through the glass at the passing countryside, staring through the passing countryside at him. This was a game. How he had wanted to move things on. Perhaps this would be a pyrrhic victory; the way it can be with passing strangers. He remembered the distinctive lurch and roll of the train, the tiny silences which seemed like hours, the definite feeling that the stakes were indeed rising the closer they were to their destination.

'As I said, not looking…not looking up at me…that was so - ' Somewhere in his mind there had been a word for it. 'So clever.' She had repeated the word, fixing him with some bemusement, both of them knowing how deliberate every minor adjustment had become. He was hooked.

Stonie felt the need to dig deeper into the past, to fit the sounds, the fleeting images, her fragrance into his nether world. There was no point in going to bed. He had his head at full tilt over the back of the armchair, staring at the ceiling, his legs and arms outstretched in a long, controlled yawn. Somewhere between the roar of the clock and the silence of the stars, he had lost the art of rage. It had been one of those inconsequential business journeys through nondescript countryside in the middle of the day. Broken clouds, endless fields, nowhere in particular to rest the eyes, massage the ears. He had been bored with reading and had no inspiration to write. There had been only the soporific drifting in and out of reality enclaves, like prayer, or day-dreaming or making up lists of things to do, or wondering what next to look forward to, as if we all search for those infrequent little rewards which help to make travail and striving worth steeling ourselves against. This one beautiful encounter should stay in his imagination. It would have been better there. After all, he had spent his life so far living on the cusp. Why take risks. Why another interruption.

But in truth, he lived for interruption. Interruption relieved the boredom, even if it was of his own making. It was bound to expand into something out of control, whether it lasted three hours, three weeks or three years. Stonie could not breathe deeply enough to uncoil the tension. The Train was making sure of that. It was a memory of a dream or a dream of a memory, an invention, certainties which had long ago vanished. The sky was upside down. Stonie wondered how he knew that, wondered if it was possible to have an upside down sky. He changed angle and the roofs came into view. He recognised St. Margaret's. The bell never seemed to peal until he was desperately trying to relax. He stared at the window, trying to frame Mica's face, but the picture still would not come. The affair was over, it was all still to be invented, it would never leave his head. All these years and the encounter still made
him smile.

'That man-woman thing, talking without looking at each other,' he had said, finally breaking the silence as the train rumbled closer to the city. 'Surely that's what you do to each other when you've had enough of each other, become too familiar, you're trying…when you've switched off to them, like…to deny them something. I mean when you are politely trying to ignore them, get rid of them.' He rolled himself off the chair and lay down, flat on his back again, positioned to take in the pure sky, to wait for the thin skein of cloud to give way to stars. He remembered feeling the desperation, looking straight at Jay, straight into her eyes for the first time as the train rumbled on through the countryside. She had held her nerve, waited her moment. 'Or the opposite,' she had replied. 'The opposite.'

Wk.1415

52° 8' N 111° 40' W.

Stonie slammed the door shut behind him, breathed in the cool morning air and stood for a few minutes on the step, wondering if Jesus would come back. That would solve everything. Today, he was not going to be Whitman. He was not going to be Lawrence Ferlinghetti. It would be another day at the ad agency, at everyone else's bidding. The canal was chugging, the morning sun was piercing through each kitchen window, right through the best rooms and out onto the cobbled stones; back-lit kids were cheeking up the milkman. So he would walk to the phone box and make the call. The coins clanked into an empty box.

'Been the same all weekend.' he said in his best tonsillitis voice. 'No point in spreading it around. Will you manage without me?' Will you manage without me? It was dumb and arrogant, he decided. But necessary. A couple more of those and another bridge would have been burned. But humming Take Five and kicking stones till they pinged off the wrought iron railings into the canal seemed an infinitely better option. He decided to retrace his steps along the towpath. Last night, somewhere between Blue Rondo a la Turk and the pasta arcing its way into the dark water, his plans had unravelled. Of course he wasn't being followed. There was no Morrell, was there? How would anyone know if Mica was no longer…if Jay was -. His slow walk ground to a halt. He was back with the faint hiss of early light through the propped open window, that fingernail moon tacked onto the morning sky, the first motes of sunlight, the starlings, the curled figure motionless under the silk sheet. Perhaps he dreamt it all. The room, the stillness, But the two strangers, they were real. The Pony Tail, The Listener. They had to be real.

There were dark shadows in the cut. This was what the canal was good for. He could choose his spaces. He stopped for a moment, turned slowly and moved till he felt the sun on his face then closed his eyes. Not for the first time, he had no idea what he was going to do next. In the pause, he saw Gem rise from her comfortable sofa chair, felt the soft cheek of the air kisses she dispensed so gracefully as she leaned over him. He was drinking in the waft of familiar perfume. Then she was gone, the hotel's revolving door spinning her into an angel rising above the traffic.

The pub was awash with sixties throwbacks. On tiptoe, Stonie could see Zach, drink in hand and uncharacteristically animated. He was in full flow, close to the small stage. Stonie, holding back in the shadow of an alcove, took stock. What disturbed him was Zach. Back in the UK and no call to say so. An excuse to regard everyone as stanger. He instinctively drew the flattened knuckles of his hand up over his nose and sniffed for perfume hard and long, pressing the skin against one of his nostrils. It had been a few hours, but there must surely be some small trace of Gem; the beginnings of something new.

The walls were typical Old Crown, plastered in past triumphs: the mix of murky Mingus shots, Blakey in full grin, posters of unknowns with autograph. There were autographs everywhere. Stonie spotted a poster of a young Roger McGough with the sanguine Edwin Brock. One day, he promised himself. There was a full-size black and white picture of Long John Baldry. Now, that was impressive. Stonie felt comfortable. Everything was in black and white. Gives a better feel, I always think; colour's too soppy, too…too obvious. That's what he always told people. He also told people the same thing time after time, found himself in full flight, kept promising never again. I mean, aren't we just substituting one uniform for another? Why people have to define themselves by what they *do*, after all, my occupation says nothing about what occupies me. I mean, I work for a living. Nobody learns how to *be*. Well, it's a kind of mask, isn't it? There was always silence from the other side while he dug his hole. From maxim to maxim; he could hear himself. We're human beings, not human doings. No one ever seemed to jump in to save him. Stonie had developed a disgust for polite, dishonest listeners. During pub time, he would swing from cool to Holden Caulfield, as certain as ever he was not the only phoney in the building. If it's going to be an evening of stupid conversations, that's okay by me. Just as long as I do the listening. Everyone needs stupid conversations. Everyone else. As far as I'm concerned, that's what pubs are for. Small talk. Banter. The hunter and the hunted, looking for something to feast the eyes on. And the stomach, hardly the mind. Just don't ask what I did last night, or last year. Let's not get real about this. He shivered. What he did last night. There was a chance The Suit would be back. Or perhaps The Listener. The feeling brought a tight knot to his stomach.

The room was dim and humid and filling up fast at the front with die-hards, milling with post-broadcast crews and jazz sensibilities, all wondering when retro would set in. The Opposite Locke, Marian Montgomery and Newcastle Brown were for later. The unions, the strikes, Scargill versus anyone. It was all raw. It needed to be tucked away for the day. Stonie scanned the room. This night, he was tuned to being distant. Tonight, every sinew was honed to the one moment he would set eyes on The Suit. But it was the same old faces. Nothing unusual, everything familiar. There it was again. How come, in every crowd, there's someone you think you know. There are always types, shapes, bone structures, hairstyles; memories, people who remind you of people. Short, sharp facts, no nuances, no allusions. And, if they could possibly allow themselves the luxury, no agendas. He was angry. He had already buried Mica. Now, it seems, so had someone else. He shivered. He was on the edge.

'Your turn,' someone called out. 'Tell us the truth or a lie about yourself and make it convincing. We'll decide. Lose and it's your round.' Stonie winced but played along.

'Okay, I'm good at that – truth, fiction, whatever? With no rules?' Stonie asked. He hated games, ice-breakers; why couldn't people just deal with life normally. Why do they insist on stuff like this? Honestly. He looked around. People who thought they belonged. He made a mental note to buttonhole Zach as soon as he could make it across the room.

'Okay, well...what I did the other night - ' He was talking quietly against the background chatter. Maybe they would move on. Anyhow, it would annoy the hell out of them. 'Nothing funny or particularly exciting but...well - ' One of the gang leaned forward. She was backlit, dark, pretty. Another possibility. Her accent was impeccable.

'Go on, then, my dear, get on with it, we're waiting. What's it to be? What was your big idea? Let's get it over with.'

'Well, I lay on my back on the park bench near to my flat and stared at the stars.' He paused. 'I have this seat, outside where I live, right? It's got my name on it on a little brass plate. Anyhow, it was a very clear night, okay? I do this every Friday at exactly the same time. Seven forty-five. Even if it's raining. Well, from my bedroom window, if there's cloud, I just imagine them, if I'm honest. I close my eyes and imagine them. I mean, if it's raining, I can still see them in my head.'

'That's it? Get on with it,' someone interrupted. Stonie was thinking fast.

'Wait for it,' he answered, trying not to look at anyone in particular. 'Allowing for light pollution, I pick out my very favourite star, planet, that kind of thing. Always the strongest ones, of course. Then just stare and stare until they have become a picture, until all the other stars have become a blur, until there's a connection. Takes a lot of concentration, you know.' Stonie knew he was in for a ribbing; it was juvenile at best but it seemed lateral enough for the way the drink was flowing. As an after thought, he bowed in a grand manner, touching his forehead and swinging his arms behind him, his voice rising in conclusion. 'And then, and then I write a poem about it for my next anthology and draw the picture the stars make and it accompanies the poem. I've been writing poems about the stars since I was nine years old. That's it this time.' He glanced around, trying not to catch anyone's eye.

'False', came a shout from the back of the group, and everyone began talking over each other. Stonie didn't want to prove anything. It was a risk – a favourite star indeed. Twinkle, twinkle, that was the level. Yet somewhere deep inside himself there was a point to it. He liked the idea, taking time out to ponder, to gaze at the stars. He looked around and was surprised at the general approval. Fortunately, the band were beginning to assemble. He had no desire to say any more about it. He wanted the band to play, loud, crank up the volume. He really did not wish to elaborate.

'And after that?' the same girl shouted at him, with a cool, dismissive look, sipping at her glass of wine with a barely disguised I-told-you-so narrowing of the eyes. There was a ragged chorus of 'I know, I've got it, okay then, then you see a... a teddy bear and a bunny rabbit…and, and, and...a teensy weensy li'l mouse.'

'After that,' Stonie shouted very deliberately, cutting the air with his hand to silence his detractors. So different from last night; one minute a loner, next the life and soul. He took a long draw on his glass of beer 'After that - '

'You haven't a clue, admit it, you haven't got the foggiest idea,' someone piped up.

'Okay, so you take this plan - ' It was Zach. 'Don't tell us. We need to guess. Tell you what, let someone else play around with it from here.' Stonie felt a sense of relief. He was not good at fitting in. Everything was too raw. It was time to withdraw, time to ease himself out as the music kicked in. All he could see was the beer mat. The scribbled line. All he could think of was how to retrace his steps, keep an eye open for The Pony Tail. As for the firmament, he knew exactly where that was going. But the drums rolled, high hats and a screeching sax cut loose and the rescue package was complete.

He need take it no further. For now, it was an irrelevance. There were other, more serious games to play. Amidst laughter, whey-heys and chinking glasses he shook his head and took another long, grateful gulp.

'Too much noise,' he shouted. 'Tell you all later.' It was back to drinking, foot-tapping, lip-reading, sizing each other up. Just where they had all come in.

'So what are you going to do with these blessed stars, then?' Zach enquired. 'What's the plan?' The two men were about to walk in different directions some way from the pub. The jazz was all talked out.

'Oh, nothing, really,' Stonie said with a bit of a chuckle 'Just rambling, letting it flow, improvising to see what would happen. Didn't go well, though. Not my thing.'

'Living dangerously, eh?'

'Could say that,' Stonie admitted. There was an awkward pause. 'Oh yeh, the new show. You said something crazy about getting invited to a Biennale. Italy or somewhere, you said. And you were having a gig in New York.'

'Ah, well, no, I met someone who loved my work, said she'd like to recommend me. She's a powerful figure, an agent. Told me she could get me written up, build up the exposure, that kind of thing. It's all pie in the sky, I guess. Man, there is so much money to be made if your name fits.' Stonie nodded slowly, trying to appear interested.

'Yeh, well it all has to start somewhere. Connections, golf club, casting couch, free masonry.' It was the wrong thing to say, but it was worth an embarrassed chuckle.

'Hey, steady on.'

'Yeh, well, why not?' Stonie said, tipping his head cheekily to one side. Zach looked quizzically at him.

'Not my style. You can't be serious.'

'No, of course not. Bad taste. Must go, got an early start...oh... and let me know next time.' he said, squaring up to Zach. 'I was expecting a call. You said it would be the first thing you'd do when you got here. It would be good to have some quality time - '

'Ah, yes...sorry' Zach cut across him. 'I will definitely call, tomorrow.' For a moment, Stonie was tempted to double back, check out who was left in the pub. Maybe the backlit girl. Lets see, she says she flies kites, drives a mini, has a kitten. She is resting between relationships. That's the important bit. She walks into the agency reception, sees Stonie in the studio through the glass. Lunch? She nods approval. He mouths something about her waiting a moment, rushes out to her. He gives her a good-to-see-you gentle pat on the arm. Do you want a look round the agency? She lifts her hand to cover his and holds it in place. Longer than would be expected. It is the start of something new.

'You look tired, or you've had too much to drink,' Stonie said. Zach started to back off but hung in for the courtesy handshake, the slap on the back.

'Yeh, well...time zones and stuff' he said. 'I meant to call. Never quite know my next move but I will call, next time.' With that, he was gone. Zach knew how to disappear quickly.

Walking briskly against the damp night air, Stonie was finally thankful for his own space. There had been no green-beaded Pony Tail. Too much to hope for. Perversely, he enjoyed mystery, simply hated unfinished business. Not when it was as personal as this, not while it was so raw, so unresolved. It was hard to know how to react, but for now he was calm. He stopped under a broken street lamp to look at the clear sky, aware of his visible breath drifting across him. He tried making smoke rings with the pumping silence, chin up against the light and the clear sky. Stupid, really, it never works with moisture, he thought, clicking his jaw furiously. It was another of those strange, disconnected reflexes. A trial moment. Something else he would never share with anybody.

Stonie tensed his shoulders, thrust his hands deep into his pockets and leaned against the lamp. He was thinking of his plan for the stars. He had always had a plan. Take a large acetate print of whatever configuration is above your head at a significant time and lay it on a map of Great Britain – something to scale, something to cover your tracks. Pitting the astronomical against the intimate. Plot the points your chosen stars make on this little patch of earth. Plot them exactly; the longitude and latitude. Start with the nearest. That's the place to go to, these are the stories to find. He could set out on his quest, arriving at each tiny pin-hole of earth, meet the people, paint the picture, talk about inter-connectedness and significant interruptions. It could be the middle of a seagull-wheeling rock stack. Right in the dank, paint-peeling bowels of a high-rise stairwell, the foul-mouthed kitchen of a greasy transport café. Something ordinary, like a gridlocked motorway slip road. He'd want it to be a freshly-mown village cricket square, full of ancient tales of heroic struggles against absentee landlords and questionable practices by Morris dancers; headless ghosts still haunting the churchyard, all the clichés. He'd want it to be some gently tidal dockland, salt-o'-the-earth, sunshine beaming workshop full of near-retirement worthies, topping each other with ocean-liner bravado and picking baccy bits from their teeth. More likely, though, it would be some methane silted cut full of supermarket trolleys and rat-eaten sofas with half abandoned ten year olds threatening to do unspeakable things to his mother if they could find her. Well, after all, it's their patch. More likely, it would be smack in the middle of some very nasty domestic punch-up in the west wing of a decrepit country pile. A good plan. He just had to work out everything he didn't know about constellations.

Wk.1408
52º 29' N 1º 56.6' W

Home. And the wind-down seemed particularly difficult. It was always the most awkward part of the day, deciding deliberately to stop reliving whatever it was that was worth savouring and making some stab at organising all his tomorrows. But Stonie was not sure he had any. In the flat, the presence of Mica was everywhere. He tried again to relive the last contact. That night. Drifting on some elemental time line. Forward, back. Months back. Everything about the place felt uncomfortable. He fixed himself a coffee and snacked a little, tried a line or two of a new poem. He could feel his shoulders becoming more tense. He wanted to write, needed to write. There were scraps of paper everywhere. But it was one of those times when the need outstrips the inspiration. One of those times when you *know* you're no bloody good at anything. And what are you going to do about it, then? Anything that matters, that is.

He opened the window, maybe an inch. It was a cooling draught. Someone in the opposite roof skylight was playing a guitar, strumming, picking out an old Pentangle number. It might be 'The Circle Game', good old Joni Mitchell. Something, something in the carousel of time. He lay down, turned off the bedside light and began to drift. He was nearly over, slipping into that saliva-on-the-pillow moment. Probably throwing stones at first floor windows with their lights on, in Main Street, Durango, trying to raise a Navaho buck or two from all-night painters making love to their easels. He had to keep on going. Every time the dream ran out, there would be another sky he was lying under, staring, shivering, longing for an alien abduction. Something to get his name in the papers, a cheap motel.

The phone rang. It's one-something in the morning and the phone's ringing. Who the hell's on to me, he thought. His heart leapt just for a moment with sudden shock, in that bad news kind of way. Then the trek to the phone; it seemed fraught with toe-stubbing obstacles.

'Yeh, hello.' There was a tiny moment of silence, then her voice, *that* voice; it just…he hardly knew how to describe those deep layers of muted pain being inflicted on every fibre. You don't know you are reacting, don't know you're being damaged – like a heart monitor recording the race, even when you're being told to breathe slowly, deeply. You swear blind you are rested, that you are perfectly calm, lying flat on your back, all wired up for a read-out, certain of a clean bill of health.

'It's the photograph. I need my father's photograph. I left it in *The Little Prince*. I just have to have it back.' Mica's voice seemed very ordinary. It could have been a daytime conversation about the weather or the evening meal. 'I need to get it. Send it.' Click. Purr. That's the noise you get.

One hundred and twenty-fifth of a second at f8, that's a long time in the life of a photograph, but not long enough to die. You need time for the chemicals to do their worst. Or was it radiation? Nobody knew, nobody was saying. It could well have been a yearbook shot, the look so assured, so clean, the bromide sheen glinting through his memory. Stonie had no idea, of course, he possessed the only photograph of Luca that existed on this side of the Atlantic, or possibly anywhere. For one fleeting moment, he was tempted to tear it up. There was deep anger, a get-even wave of petty helplessness.

One lousy snapshot, what was so special? He found the book, well thumbed, underlined, dog-eared. Those hats and elephants and snakes and stars, the flower to take care of and that endless desert. *Like laughing stars, your joy brightens my planet.* He found the book, found the story easing through his subconscious. He had always liked the sound of a high night plane droning under the open sky, nothing but stars above and those vast tracks of earth beneath. All those options on where to point the craft, that going somewhere feeling, tucked up in the cockpit, staring out at the horizon.

There was always a glow-line somewhere. You were always moving away from one dark fusion of earth-sky to another, certain there was some skinny line of dawn to aim for, some hope of arrival. He'd fall asleep much easier if even one plane scratched its way across his square of sky. He would stop breathing to hear its distant trail fade into the whispering canopy, imagining he was finally free. Perhaps it was a way of easing himself into the future. This time, only silence.

Wk. 1199

42º 16.6' N 83º 44' W

The deli was almost empty. Hours had passed, it seemed, and still Jay could not make up her mind. Staying in the U.S. had always been the best option. Moving to some god-forsaken corner of the United Kingdom held no fascination at all. She had ordered a root beer and a coffee at the same time, and was picking over the crumbs of pie on her plate, dipping her wet finger in the grains of sugar. Something to do. The rain drummed on the window panes.

'Penny for them,' a voice whispered over her head. 'You're miles away.'

'Oh, Miss Kate.' Jay turned to the figure stooping over the table.

'Hi, well I hate to interrupt your flight of fancy. Not in school?'

Jay hesitated, then snapped back into life, flicking her auburn hair away from her eyes and half standing to give Kate an air kiss on both cheeks. 'Hey, sit down, want some coffee? I'll order another coffee – or would you rather have some pop. Have some pie, I'll get some pie.'

'Whoa, wait…what's the panic…in a minute or two,' Kate replied, trying to find the space. 'Let me catch my breath. I was running to dodge the rain out there.'

‘No, didn’t take any classes today,’ Jay said. Kate was waiting for more, but it didn’t come. Her student, not much younger than herself, seemed preoccupied.

‘Here, let me get rid of these,’ Jay said, gathering her note-pad, pen and a scarf from the table and stuffing them into an open cloth bag which was hooked over the empty chair. Kate noted several maps jutting out.

‘Planning a holiday? Now that’s a really neat idea. Wish I could,’ she said. ‘Anywhere’s better than this campus in the rain; more dead than usual.’ She could tell it was going to be hard work. It was like bouncing a ball against a pillow.

Before Jay had time to respond, Kate was off on one of those cheeky tangents that had soon earned her the sobriquet of Mrs Einstein among her colleagues. It was her way of breaking in. One-sided conversations. ‘So if I run faster to get out of the rain, do I end up being more wet because I’ve met up with all the little drops of rain faster than if I’d walked at a normal speed. I mean, does it make any difference? I’ve always wondered that? Haven’t you always wondered that, Jay?’

Jay, her chin cupped in her hands, her elbows straddling her plate, made direct eye contact with Kate, and measured her response. ‘Miss Katherine, am I allowed to say you are faintly ridiculous, you do know that?’ It was a risk, but she was smiling.

‘Mind if I ask you a question?’ Kate was desperately trying to measure Jay’s real mood. The talk was, Jay was losing the plot, missing class, staying out of everyone’s way. She wanted to ask Jay about the parcel. There it was again, on the floor this time. Her foot was kicking against it. She was really curious about the package. Both women sat back slightly as the waitress brought fresh drinks, brushed the table, laid out new napkins.

‘Go on, then,’ Jay said. ‘What’s on your mind?’

‘I should ask you what’s on yours,’ Kate replied. Perhaps this was the opportunity. She might as well go for it. She’d be the first to know. Everyone was talking about it. ‘Well, I hope you don’t mind me asking, but for months now…well, it seems like months you’ve been carrying that package around with you, it’s never out of your sight. You take it into the rest room, you have it in lectures, it’s always on the back seat of your car…like, it’s here now. You - ’

Jay abruptly dropped down and retrieved the tightly wrapped brown parcel from between her feet, sat back, placed it neatly on her lap and squared up to Kate. She took a long, slow, deep breath, opened her mouth to speak – and froze. Kate shuffled awkwardly in her seat as the silence lengthened.

'I didn't mean to pry, I - '

Jay raised one finger slowly in front of her face, reached over and almost touched Kate's lips. Kate leaned back and tucked her falling curls behind her hair. 'It's okay,' she whispered, 'really it is. I should talk to someone, I guess.' She liked Einstein. Better her than some of the others. Full of conundrums she might be, but she also knew when to stay silent, knew when it mattered to day nothing. This was a different kind of black woman than the ones she was used to.

Jay's face was ashen, her look strained. She was biting her lower lip again. She sat back in her seat, cradled the package against her chest and stared at Kate. Nothing was said, probably for five minutes. Kate knew this was not the time to be lateral. No quips, no interruptions. She could hear the gusts of wind, the rain spattering against the glass, the gurgle of the ice machine, the hissing coffee maker, everything in tension in the deserted diner. A truck splashed by outside the window. She watched condensation trickle down the inside of the pane for a few seconds – anything to avert her gaze. She was desperate to break the silence, coax Jay back into the world. This had better be good. It's a test, she thought. I'm doing very well. She risked a glance across the table. Tears were welling up. Kate felt she needed to say something, made to say it's okay, leave it, it will wait, you don't need to explain - but Jay beat her to it.

'It's my father's ashes.'

Kate sat still, absolutely nothing to offer. She slowly straightened her back, quietly drawing breath as she clasped her hands onto her lap and stared across at her student. She could hear a faint whimper.

'It's Luca's ashes,' Jay whispered, then as if finding the right volume, a certain amount of composure, she added 'I'm supposed to send them to England. They released them months ago.' She cleared her throat. 'I'm supposed to send them to England.' Kate could feel her own tears. She knew she was meant to be grown up, strong and matter-of-fact, but there was no rule book. She stretched over and placed her hand on Jay's arm. Jay hugged the parcel even tighter.

'I'm supposed to *take* them to England. I don't know what to do. I don't know…it's what my mother - '

Kate leaned over, both arms outstretched and clasped behind Jay's shoulders, drawing her in across the table, embracing her gently. Jay began sobbing quietly, rocking back and forth, the package buried beneath folds of her long hair.

'I owe you an explanation,' Jay said, laying the parcel once more under the table. 'Mother and father…well, for years they just didn't get along, it was all disintegrating.' She drew her finger across her face to catch a tear.

'Look, I don't need to know the details, it's alright…another time, if you wish, it really doesn't matter. I mean, if I can do anything.'

'No, I want to, I need to talk about it,' Jay insisted, dabbing at her eyes with a table napkin. 'I look a mess, your coffee's going cold, I'm sorry.' She pushed her chair backwards. 'Excuse me, I need to go to the rest room.'

'Were you born in Italy?' Kate asked as soon as Jay sat down again. 'Look, I ordered fresh drinks. Cream?'

'Goodness no,' Jay said. 'Mother's English.'

Kate interrupted her. 'Hence the *mother* thing rather than 'mom' – I always wondered.'

'I guess so. I believe they met in England. My father was posted there briefly, stationed or something. My grandparents emigrated from Milan when Luca was eight. I don't know the details. But I am good old U. S. of A. through and through, whatever that may mean. How they ended up in Mount Kisco is a mystery. In fact, an awful lot of my childhood is shrouded in mystery. Anyhow, there are loads of us Cambareris in Mount Kisco. My folks, they didn't go in for photographs. Nobody seemed to write to each other either. Not much that I knew about. Different generation.'

Jay's voice was becoming more assured. She was glad of the company. She found herself wanting to explain things, as if they would become clearer in her own mind, as if there might just be some clues for her on what do next.

'I've never told anyone this but...what the heck, mother even hinted once she wasn't all that sure Luca was my father. Imagine. Sent a chill down my spine. Can you imagine? I can still feel it. She was drunk at the time and I went berserk, hitting out at her, punching and scratching, I was so shocked. She was grabbing me, I was scratching at her face. She got really, really angry, said she'd beat the hell out of me if I ever brought it up again, disown me, that kind of thing. It ruined freshers for me. I couldn't handle it.' Slowly, Jay shook her head. 'Never asked her about it after that, never brought it up.'

'And you couldn't have asked your father.'

Jay gave a wry smile and tilted her head. 'No, I do not think that would have been a very good idea.' Both paused and took a sip of coffee in unison. 'You know, I really don't remember if me and my father ever did get along. I know I wanted to – and I was always dressed up for him coming home. God, I can remember this awful dress that mother made me wear. All puffed shoulders, lilac ribbons and bows. I hated it.' There was a pause, one which Kate decided not to fill. 'Can you honestly imagine anyone being able to casually drop that kind of thing into a conversation?' Jay continued. 'I still get a shiver when I think about it. I can get angry. It was cruel. I tried to find some papers in a bureau but it was all too much of a mess. Guess I blocked it out – too awful to think about. Not my parents, no way, Miss Kate. I couldn't bring it up again. They were dysfunctional most of the time in any case. Father away a lot doing military stuff, mother hitting the bottle. She always said she'd go back if anything happened…back to the UK, I mean.'

Kate resisted the urge to dig deeper on what had happened to Luca Cambareri. She felt uncomfortable enough with what she had heard and the conversation was faltering. It was time to leave. Jay, sensing the change, became animated, began to stack the crockery, organise the table and turned towards the counter as if to summon the waitress.

'So, what...eh...what brought you to America, Miss Kate?'

'You really want to know right now? It can wait,' Kate said.

'No, I've decided...ah...especially if I'm supposed to live there, I need to know why you left, right? Maybe pick up some ideas.' Jay felt emboldened by the presence of her tutor, distracted. It was a good idea to talk.

'Well now, this looks like an excuse for another drink. Can you stand another one?'

'Sure,' Jay nodded and sat back.

'I applied for an internship at SUNY Buffalo, sounded romantic, really. Just the way to…further my studies. Got caught up in wondering where I came from, you know, the Afro-Caribbean thing. It's a long story. It was either there, or Louisiana. Deep South, But it was too scary down there, from what I read, even for me, and I mean, I'm pretty confident, outspoken, can handle myself. Complete apartheid, it seemed.'

'It's everywhere, who are they kidding,' Jay said. 'Detroit black, Dearborn white. That's it. Everyone knows their place.'

'Any road, Buffalo didn't want me in their faculty, but they suggested Michigan was recruiting. Now that was pretty decent of them. American Studies was all new stuff to us in the UK, well, at least to me but they liked my writing. They had the programme. Where else better to study than in the land of the free? Of course, I was making it up as I went along.'

'So you were that crazy? And desperate to get away?' For the first time, Jay was smiling.

'Yeh, kinda crazy, liberal stuff; pretty good at it too, I was. I wanted to be a journalist, liked current affairs, history, that kind of stuff. Started off writing about what was going on right on my doorstep, quite literally. A guy called Enoch Powell, an MP. He'd been stirring it up. It was the topic of the moment.'

'MP? That's Military Policeman. What's that got to do with - '

'No, no – Member of Parliament. Her Majesty's Government. He was trying to be some kind of prophet. He just ended up stirring things up. Prophet of Doom, really. It was about immigration. The country was being ruined according to his way of thinking. Mixed races as evil. Great Britain being overrun by people like me. He was famous for a speech warning about rivers of blood because of the influx. It was plain racist and very messy. I swear they would have opened a chapter of the Ku Klux Klan if they could have got away with it.' Jay started doodling on her napkin.

'Powell should have been wearing a pointed white hood and burning crosses, couldn't have done more damage. It was all around where I lived, my home town. The edge of the Black Country. It caused riots.' Jay gave Kate a quizzical look.

'Not that kind of black. I know, I know. It got the name from the industrial revolution. All the iron and steel, smelting...coal mining, factories, plain old smoke and dirt. Anyhow, I was still at university, just finishing. Not in the Black Country; I was in the city. Birmingham, well, Edgbaston. It was what they called old school, cricket, big houses, well-off. Almost entirely white people, so we felt a bit like token blacks, me and my friends. I made myself speak differently from what was expected, where my crowd came from; my accent changed – I'm a bit ashamed of it now, to be honest. I kept out of the way of my own kind while I was studying, well, that was until I wanted a story. I never gave up on my roots, though. I would go back home to the Black Country some weekends.' Kate hesitated for a moment. 'You look bored. Had enough?' Jay shook her head, waved her permission to continue.

'Oh, sorry, just tired,' she replied. 'You still haven't said how you came to be here, how you came to be teaching class.' Kate drained her cup and sat back in her chair. The story felt strange, someone else's life, as she recalled the events. In her work it had become fiction.

'Ah, well, in my final year I used to hang out at a pub called The Old Crown, just because it was full of hacks, TV people, theatre people. Hacks are journalists in case you didn't know. Don't know where the term came from. Anyhow, I was trying to make connections and they were all pretty interesting people, a little bit crazy. That's where one of the TV producers, well, he became a friend and...never mind. I got the notion to get away. I liked the idea. There were all kinds of great people around, but not too much opportunity for racial minorities, especially in the media. I didn't feel I fitted in at first and that made me a bit angry, so studying was a way of escape. Anyhow, I think I got scared when I went home; scared I'd get trapped. And I was plain restless by the end of my studies. I mean, it was a white pub, The Crown. They were a nice enough bunch. It wasn't as if there were no-go areas or anything like that. Though a guy did set on me once, a disgusting individual, white guy, he came on to me, really unexpected it was. It was just after Christmas and he was wearing a Santa hat and he dragged me onto his knee. I tried to fend him off and he smacked me on the face and started throwing things around. That was freaky, but I still went back. I liked the jazz, the poetry. Yeh, it was all very cool. And I wasn't ready for work.' Jay laughed at the idea.

'Better not tell me things like that, I'll just keep on taking classes,' she said.

'You know, Jay, I just wanted to study so much I made a nuisance of myself, worked harder and harder than ever and won a scholarship and now I'm working my way through a PhD. All this research…I guess I'm a bit of a detective, finding things out. I needed to do it. Maybe it's a different kind of healing.'

'What do you mean?'

'Oh, nothing, really. Another time. Couldn't have done it back in Brum in any case. I think I've got the best of both worlds here.' Kate felt she had said enough.

'Brum?'

'Our local word for Birmingham. There's a few others but they sound rude.'

'So you ended up here in Ann Arbor with...well, Detroit and Motown..and people like me! Best of both worlds, right?' Kate paused for a second.

'And that's the good part, right?' she said, looking straight at Jay. Jay had begun fiddling with her wrist watch.

'Yes,' she said, 'definitely. Apart from Flat Rock.' She looked across at Kate. 'Oh, never mind. Just don't ask me to take you there. Good Lord, I've been in here for four and a half hours,' she announced. 'Time to go.'

Kate took a steadied look across the table, trying to read Jay's face.

'Oh, look at the time. Yes, I have some things to be getting on with too. Will we see you in school?' The exchange had become more formal.

'Don't know how tomorrow will shape up,' Jay replied, 'but thanks for your company. It's been real nice to have someone to talk to.' She was hesitating slightly. Kate turned to face her as they both began to walk towards the door.

'Oh, and I would sure be glad if you didn't tell anyone about - '

'My goodness, no, you have my word,' Kate cut in. Jay straightened her jacket and began gathering up her belongings methodically, almost too slowly to be natural, as if leaving hadn't really been a part of the plan.

'Well, if I'm honest, I've nothing to go home to, nothing much to go home for,' she said as she picked up the package.

'So, come home with me, right?' Kate replied. 'We'll cook up, watch some TV. I have student lodgers. We can invite them to visit. They're a real nice group.'

Jay sat down again, drew a deep breath and sighed.

'That's a neat idea, thanks, don't get me wrong, I mean, I really do appreciate your being with me and all, but I'd ah…thinking about it, I'd rather have some time to myself in spite of…I'm not very good company. I'm just not very good company right now.'

Kate instinctively knew not to press the point. She felt uncomfortable about the package but checked herself. She had found out more than she had ever expected to. It was time to distance herself. That's the trouble, she thought; you just never know the stories people carry. Jay was looking straight at Kate, now in a business-like manner. Kate did not know whether to offer a hand or a sympathetic hug.

'I have to sort this out once and for all - my past, my future, you know - once and for all, if you don't mind. You do understand? Call me if you want in a day or two.'

The path to Jay's front door was strewn with leaves. She kicked her way through them, her mind racing with the 'what if's' – all those arguments and possibilities. Living at home with mother and little sister held no attraction, but keeping up payments on the lease by herself was proving difficult. She faced a foreign country, no friends, a strange system; beginning her studies again. Yet what was left to cling to here? As the key turned in the lock, the door eased open with no effort. She drew back for an instant, one of those tiny dislocations, something not within the pattern of things, something which focuses the attention. She moved into the hallway with some deliberation. The kitchen light was burning. Jay was fastidious when it came to switches. This was not normal. Of course, all the worry, the roller-coaster emotions, there was bound to be fall-out, not being herself, not on top of things. You can have all those little conversations with yourself when you live alone, you talk things through. She was good at connecting all the tiny bits of her day, careful on the rituals for survival. This time, something simply did not feel right.

She bent her knees a little to lay her bag on the floor, still with her back straight and staring intently at the open kitchen door. She knew she had clicked the door shut before leaving. She always registered that click sound. It was her marker, her way of moving on to the next stage in her day. As the bag strap went limp, she was struck just above the waist, sent flying through the hall in a football tackle, sliding on the carpet into the kitchen as her head thudded onto the floor. She could smell alcohol, see a streak of light bulb, watch her keys flying in slow motion against the window. She was on her side, cheek squashed against the cold linoleum by the attacker's chest, tiny slivers of straw matting piercing her skin, one arm trapped beneath her.

There was no scream, just the weight of a heart beat thumping against her head, the whistle of constricted airways. She was winded, numb, barely able to draw breath but with enough presence of mind to register there were muttering expletives, a rasping voice growling at her as she briefly attempted to struggle free. She tried to pick up on the accent any kind of recognisable clue. She could feel heat pouring down the bridge of her nose. Staying awake, staying absolutely still became her immediate priority, realising instantly that to struggle was futile. She was cold, with a creeping warmth around her nose and lips. She knew the taste of blood, but could never have imagined bathing in her own.

'Where is it? Where's the pig-shitting tag? Where's the package?' her attacker growled. As the weight lifted, Jay felt as if she was rising, floating, but resisted the temptation to move; not one muscle, not even an eyelash. When a boot crunched into her stomach, vomit spurted up into her mouth. She fixed her lips tight shut. The second kick brought the burning acid taste up through her nostrils. Still, she refused to let her body respond. She was concentrating on dying. There had to be an accent to grasp, something to hold onto, a reason. That was her focus. Stillness might just save her from worse. Her attacker had the toe of his boot pressed against her chin.

'I…I…don't know what you mean. I don't have…you're hurting me. I'm bleeding, God. What are you after?' She knew she was saying something in her head, there were words, but there was no point in moving her lips. She knew she was drooling. It was the merest whisper, a breath away, nothing the assailant could hear. Jay steeled herself against the next blow; so still, so frozen her eyeballs ached. In the pumping white noise in her ears, in an eternity of knotted, piercing gut, there would be no give-away muscle trembling, no reflex; she would stay in control. She had already departed. Someone was ranting, ransacking, blaspheming their way through her last breath. She could hear the musical clock, the ting-aling pink ballerina grinding to a halt; the blood-of-Jesus choirs wafting up into the cowering balcony; there was the hollow tumbling ten-pin bowling alley laughter; oh yes, and the grotesque, bare-teethed faces leering through the waves of bubbling, cascading water falling onto her open-eyed baptism; down down through the bubbles till she couldn't breathe, thrust into eternity at all costs amid the amens, the screaming hallelujahs; oh for that sudden, gasping spray of tears. There was no way of knowing where she had been, how much time had passed, who she was with in this nether world.

Jay opened the eye closest to the floor and could see the window and a reflection of the ceiling reflected in the shiny dark surface spread before her. In this mirror, there was a half moon creeping round the curtain, a wave of branches, the odd star pricking the sky. She knew; this was a pool of blood, her blood: creeping round the skin of her temple; the world around her reduced to a reflection in her own blood. She tried to swallow, but her throat was burning with the flux. Time to listen. Time to wait. It was almost dark before she decided to move. Crawling, then easing herself upright took several painful minutes. She sat in the stickiness, too shocked for tears, trying to swallow, trying to create saliva, drawing her tongue across the caked scabs of blood on her lip. She had seen a knife. Her attacker had swept around her with some kind of blade flashing as they fell together. She looked down at herself, gathering her torn shirt into her fist at the waist. Half her bra was ripped away and her left breast was cut. She cupped her hand up over the wound, drawing the gash and the nipple together with the tips of her fingers. "Through my coat…stabbed, no, cut but not cut open. ". It seemed reassuring to make a noise, to hear the sound of her own voice.

Jay eased herself onto her knees and struggled to pull herself up to a standing position; one shoe was missing. She breathed in deeply, holding her breath for as long as she could, then slowly relaxed her shoulders, steadying herself against the kitchen bench as she turned to switch on the light. That noise, that soft click was the trigger. Her brain emptied, she could feel her eyes going back uncontrollably, rolling the room into a golden spin and with it, her ability to hold on any longer. Her knees buckled; she knew she was going, could hear the dull thud as she crumpled against the chairs, sending them clattering against the wall.

A faint draught of wind played strands of hair across the limp body, the only visible signs of movement till a breeze caught the front door, slapping it gently against the open shutters. Both creaked on their hinges with the rocking of the slow fading light – finally, in a gust, snapping shut and dropping the catch, as if the quiet Michigan suburb was turning a blind October eye to all it had witnessed. Somewhere in Ann Arbor, Kate sat flicking channels, fretting the 'should have' kind of fret. She was at a loose end. That made it easy to think through her day. Jay needed time, she mused. Her own space.

Wk.1202
42° 16.6' N 83° 44' W

It was a bleak Christmas, punctuated by fruitless investigations, endless interviews which lead nowhere. Bethany, back in the US, nursed and fussed her way through the family visits, the gifts, the healing, barely containing her resentment at having to look after her daughter. Jay would fix up better without her. This, after all, was foreign soil. She wanted, needed to be back in Walsall. She made it abundantly clear that life stateside had been over for many years. She was finally rid of her twenty year one-night-stand. She had made the break. Canaletto indeed. Perhaps his life had always been a forgery. And now, the final irony, even the package was gone. His ashes. Every trace. The family were told little at first, then they were informed it was the wrong Cambareri; records showed. No one seemed able to provide them with an explanation. Jay was certain that if they did, they would fake it, although at least it would be closure of sorts. At every turn, Luca's status within the military was cited; security reasons, a difficult case falling somewhere between the state and civil authorities, classified information. Details were scarce. Bethany, however, had no interest in proof. The dog-tag scientist was history. She had binned all she possessed that reminded her of their life together, burned every image. Why would she now want a photograph in uniform, the very thing she had grown to detest. Luca Cambareri had been expunged. It was the only thing that made her smile. She refused to have anything to do with the official investigation, insisting that she just did not have the stomach for it, slipping further into depression, ever more reliant on tablets, ever more paranoid over her daughter's unsupervised life. All that mattered was getting back home to the UK.

Each day, Jay would position herself close to the front room window and stare out at the dreary Midlands housing estate she had been forced to adopt. She had to be doing something else as well as eating; usually, breakfast of French toast and milky coffee while watching a tired and disparate group of commuters gather at the bus shelter. She was getting to know who caught the 8.15am, the 8.40, the 9.05. It was not what she had planned for herself: the fading memory of a father she had hardly known, a neurotic mother she was now supposed to look after and an enforced break from studies. She had no passion, no goal. Just guilt and responsibility in equal measure. It was hard sharing house with her 'mom' again. She felt as if she had been thrown without mercy into an alien culture. There was nothing in the newspapers about 'rivers of blood'. What was Dr Kate talking about, Dr. Kate Huggins? She was still someone to look up to. Jay missed her more than anyone, missed the Ann Arbour years. Perhaps the lady was somewhere in England. Somewhere in the Midlands.

Jay knew she had to do something about her boredom, channel her anger. There would be no harking back. Sometime during the early spring of '70, she decided that feeling sorry for herself was no longer an option. This was where the train journeys began. She was keeping a list. Pretty Stratford, with its well-rehearsed Shakespearean rhetoric and dreadful service. Bridgnorth with its weird little funicular railway. Oxford's not-so-dreamy spires in the pounding rain, Coventry's shapeless centre, cathedral spires and stupid nude. It was all building up, playing to her fierce independence. She would move out of the family home with barely a conscience for her increasingly erratic single parent. As far as she was concerned, mother could languish in her crumbling Shelfield semi with nothing but the goldfish to feed and the milkman to avoid. No more beck and call.

Wk.1179
32º 31.4’ N   113º 31.1’ W

Walking back to Gila Bend seemed the best option. Stonie could barely work out how far; it had been endless desert with the stifling, soporific rasp of the truck whipping clouds of dust up around his eyes. The sides of his mouth were caked with it; his eyes, gritty and barely focusing. He stood for a moment, collecting his thoughts. At least there would be life, a few friendly faces, some food and a telephone. He was just south of Atlantic City, he reckoned, but there was nothing to see on any horizon. The ghost town must have taken thirty to forty seconds to pass through, the ‘City for Sale’ sign the most memorable moment. On the edge, he recalled seeing a rusting old Winnebago, way beyond the electric fence, its little stamp of land marked out in end-to-end motorcycles, bikes, trikes and various assorted wheels – there was even a pram – like some Salvador Dali stockade. No sign of life; just the pallor of shimmering decay. The pick-up had been throwing him around so much he could hardly take much notice of what was going by. Could there be someone in the Winnebago, maybe a telephone line, maybe a lift back to Gila Bend. He squinted his eyes against the shimmer. Which road to take. He was no longer sure of what road to take. He could hear the grit crunching under his feet. It set his teeth on edge. Time to regret accepting the ride; more time to wonder if his supply of water would hold out. His flask was all he had left. He was exhausted. His first ‘ride’ in many hours had turned out to be half-mental, the driver an almost incomprehensible and very dangerous old hillbilly.

Stonie was still trying to work out if there was anything he could have done, some foolhardy gesture that would have paid off just once. But not at gunpoint. Forced to jump down onto the roadside, with the old timer still in his cab, poking both barrels through the broken back window of the cab; there was no upper hand to be gained. Stonie had to watch him hurtling off towards the foothills, taking with him his backpack; had to watch helplessly as the fading ball of dust tailed out behind him. He must have stood motionless for at least half an hour, unable to think, unable to do anything but stare. This was not something he had allowed for – not in the Age of Aquarius.

The nights would be cold. This was a hard-won rites of passage gone wrong. He finally dropped to his hunches and picked at the dirt, as if trying to find inspiration, looking out beyond this single wire fence. What was being protected, he wondered: as far as he could see, on either side of the road, a well-maintained electric fence was strung out, fifty feet or so from the edge of the road. The sun was dropping fast. There was 180 degrees of sky wherever he turned. Just stones, sand, hardy, drought-resistant greens. Saguaro shadows were fingering the tiny outcrops. This could be the moon. On the cracked tar, with its yellow arrow marking the turn-off, a tarantula was catching the last rays of the sun. No vehicle had come through in two hours. Was it two hours? His watch had gone, in one of the pockets. He had no ideas. This was a place where nothing moved.

Stonie looked up at the sky, picking out the stronger stars in the deepening blue. 'There's a man up there,' he said out loud. 'Hey, can you hear me? I'm on the moon too, or are you on the earth?' he shouted. Someone was actually walking about on that shiny little crescent, he thought to himself. 'Can you fucking hear me?' he yelled in frustration. Not even an echo. He slumped into the dirt. The short stubby hairs on his bare knees pricked into his fore arms. God, I'm in shorts…sandals. Scorpion country, rattlesnakes. Now and again he could hear a soft, crack as a rock cooled. There was nothing else it could be, but it was an uncomfortable sound, as if someone was creeping up behind him. Wonder how you're getting along up there? The moon held her peace. 'I saw the new moon late yestreen, wi' the old moon in her arms, and if we gang to sea, maister, I fear we'll come to harms' he began to sing. How does it go, Stonie? He was half whispering, standing up, taking quarter turns to face each crossroad in some meaningless ritual. He would have to start walking; there was nothing else for it. 'We hadnae gone a league, a league, a league but barely three,' he recited 'when the night fell dark…when the sky went dark…the wind grew loud and gurly grew the sea. Right. Gurly, now there's a word'. Stonie began to wheel around faster, stopping at each of the four roads. He was panting. He was talking out loud, could hear his heart thumping. 'Nothing everywhere,' he announced to the world. 'I'm going to die out here. Cold or poison or the sheer boredom of having to listen to myself. Stupid boy. Accepting a ride.' He took a long deep breath, filling his lungs, threw his head back as far as he could and stared straight up at the stars. The sweat patches on his shirt were clinging, cold and uncomfortable. With his head still pushed back to catch the stars directly above him, he started walking. Soon he was in stride, relaxing; one minute, staring at the stars, the next, squinting at the road ahead. It felt good to have made a decision, even if the choice made no difference. First the road, then the stars, then the road again.

At least, it created a rhythm, a way of marking out the minutes. I wonder how far I can walk with my eyes closed? This seemed like a useful diversion. How many paces? You can't always sense when you are going off track, when you are departing from the true way. He imagined he was thinking more slowly, drawing his breaths through the words, as if there is a speed to how thoughts are formed. All he could hear were the sounds of his body. All he could feel was the emptiness, that familiar, aching emptiness. Should have stayed home, held on to the job, waited just a few months longer. Should have. Something would have come along. For a fleeting moment he was sure he could smell Gem. He stuck his palm against his nose. What I'd give for a pint among strangers, he thought. A stupid ice-breaker.

When he opened his eyes, the sky had finally wrapped itself around him, blue black; only the far horizon was blood red. What a useless moon. He spoke out, louder this time, so that he could hear himself. He could hardly see his feet. 'Some job up there, you guys…turn on the light.' he shouted. He had never been lost before; at least, not in this way. 'I will not fear though I walk through the shadow of the valley of…the valley of the shadow of....' the words petered out. He simply could not utter the final word. His money, clothes, passport and his *year of finding out* had vanished in a cloud of dust. He began to cry. It didn't matter anyway – there was no one to kiss the tears. It was as if it had always been like this. He just could not recognise his own fear. In Jerome, he'd heard the Harley Davidson stories, and they had scared the shit out of him. He felt vulnerable, homesick with precious little to be homesick about. You can roll off the road at a hundred and twenty and no car passing for ten, maybe fourteen hours. Word is there's a fatality a week out there. Pretty mean country, yes sir. Best tell people where you think you're going. Very unwise not to; unforgiving, no respecter, see?

He had to admit the Big Idea had taken a twist. But there was no wry smile this time, no feeling he could fake it. No pub jokes here. Every few hundred yards of road, he would turn and head back for the crossroads. He was trying to work out what he should do. He had always used each interruption to create another one. And what about the ultimate plan. The acetate in his head, it was still the sky above his bed, the precise constellation – selected, pin-pointed: 12 December 1973, 1.31am, the last time he'd heard her voice. The first time he knew he had to travel.

Stonie stopped abruptly and closed his eyes again. His feet were stinging. What precise spot was this, what longitude and latitude; it has a number, maybe even a name. Never think about that, do we? He could see his first floor drawing board view of the High Street, his *position*; at least the figures on the street below seemed to be going somewhere. There he was, grinding out other people's ideas, some dire clip-art world blessed by the union stamp. Slade Art Union; stupid people with small minds. God, Unions. Yeh, visualising, copy-writing. Why did he always feel he was telling lies? He despised the sanctions, the black-lists, toeing the party line. There had to be more than the petty racist skirmishes, the power workers whinging, the god-awful miners with their placards and foul-mouthed sloganeering. What was wrong with them all? The country was a mess. Yet, just for once, he'd like to be part of the mess. He began to cry again, began walking again, the fourth road this time, somewhere different; or was it the one he'd just returned from. He had the same kind of knotted feeling as in the last days of Mica. It said, something big is happening, something beyond you; there's nothing you can do.

Wk.1179

32º 31.4' N   113º 31.3' W

As he paused to wipe the grit from the sweat and the salt, something sparkled. Stonie blinked hard, stared, drew the edge of his shirt across his eyebrows. This was no fire-fly country. It had to be a car or truck, and the light was getting stronger. Stonie began to rip his shirt up over his head; he needed a flag. He had to be seen.

'Stop, for Christ sake stop. Bloody see me,' he screamed and jumped around, completely oblivious to his position on the road. 'Get me outa here.' He could hear the 'outa' and gave an almost laughable cry, sniffing and grunting and throwing himself around. He had to be noticed. Being mown down simply did not enter his head. 'One car in fucking hours,' he bawled. 'Bloody stop.' The lights were still some way off, but Stonie was taking no measure of distance. This was pure panic; all that mattered was survival. The vehicle drew to a halt a few feet from this dancing figure, still yelling at the top of his voice, barely aware of his rescuers. The headlights of the Jeep were caked with bugs. Steam and dust belched out around the grill. 'Thank God,' Stonie screamed. 'Thank God.' He gasped, swallowing hard and dropping to his knees. 'I eh, I...going my way?' he managed to quip 'Like...anywhere?' There was a long pause.

'What you doin' out here, buddy? Where's the party? Got a shindig going on?' The back-lit voice in the headlights was slow, a nasal drawl. Stonie shuffled towards the open door, then thought the better of it.

'Easy now,' the voice warned. 'Coulda got yourself killed, hollerin' and leaping around like that.' Stonie shielded his eyes from the glare, trying to make out who was blocking his path. The figure seemed to tower over him.

'Good thing I ain't drivin' hard, might have missed you. Hell, coulda made mincemeat out of you, more likely.'

'I just need to get out of this God-forsaken...' He stopped, suddenly aware that the silhouette in front of him sported a gun holster. The military policeman, a tall, lean ranger, held himself stiff, ready for anything. His finger was tapping close to the trigger.

'You look like you could use a drink. Where you come from...time of night...hell, there's nowhere to go and nowhere to come from out here in any case. You got some wheels? Got some company back there?'

Stonie was heaving, but gained enough composure to button up his shirt and look up. The driver was still back-lit, standing legs apart. He glanced at the number plate, barely visible through the clouds of beetles bombing the headlights, but it did not make sense to him. A rasping conversation broke his breathing pattern, the airwaves crackling with local radio banter. He was trying to contain his emotion.

'I was robbed,' he began. 'I was hitching a ride from Cottonwood…no, Jerome, it was Jerome. But the guy, some old farmer, he pulled a gun on me, took out this beat-up rifle, took my things. All my stuff, then just drove off." He could feel the tears welling up. 'I'm exhausted, lost, penniless – can't even prove who I am.' He backed away from the man and sat at the edge of the road, dropping to his haunches and tipping back onto the dirt, his arms behind him to support himself. "I'm exhausted. I would very much appreciate being taken back to civilisation.' He wanted to lie flat out on his back, but checked himself; he was vulnerable enough. The driver idled over to the passenger side of the jeep, signalling to his companion to kill the engine. Stonie could hear the muffled conversation. He tried to pick out anything that was not in the vernacular, but his heartbeat was pounding in his ears. He felt sure he was about to be left there, abandoned to the wilderness; what was there to discuss? Surely he could not be left to this emptiness, left in this state.

'Please, you've got to help me. You're locals, must know the area, right? Just get me to a motel.' Stonie felt as if he was pleading for his life.'

'Wouldn't know an Arizona from a Texan accent, son. Now just you hold on there' one of the rangers said, moving towards him. The radio crackled but there was nothing Stonie could pick up on. The other driver came back over to where Stonie was sitting, stood for a moment over him, then spat into the dirt inches from his shoulder.

'Not so straight forward,' Stonie said under his breath. 'Might have known.' He was shivering. 'What the hell, maybe I don't care anyway.' He sat still, muttering to himself, his lips trembling with cold, and slowly drew his arms round his knees. 'I'll waken up soon.'

As they sped away from the roadside, Stonie leaned back, sank back as far as he could against the plastic headrest and sighed deeply. One of his fingernails had broken the skin on his palm. That was the price of the tension, the sheer rage. It was bleeding and stinging with the sweat. All that mattered was that he was going somewhere. The stupid moon was still pricking a corner of the sky. Otherwise, there was nothing between him and the universe but the glass. He tapped his forehead against the window several times, as if to assure himself he was actually staring through a window and not at the sky itself. No details; nothing visual to register movement – just the whine of rubber, the rocking of the springs, the sparse, cryptic conversation from up front. The lull was enough to send him to sleep. When he came to, there was a thin, yellow-white glow on the horizon, the tips of a thousand cacti catching the light. He tried to focus, get a clear picture of what was in front of his eyes, what the feeling of movement was, at first, simply aware that the crescent moon was gone – and if it was a dream, he had no idea who these people were or where he was headed. His neck was stiff, his shirt stretched tight against his waist, his shorts cutting into his groin. He tried to swallow but his mouth felt sticky. He pulled his shoulder blades back, trying to stretch his arms out in the cramped space, anticipating the build up of a yawn. 'Dust. Nothing but dust' he whispered. Perhaps it was wiser to wait until he could look these guys in the eye before pronouncing on the terrain, before asking awkward questions. You get the truth in the eye contact; not like talking to the back of someone's neck; not like looking away while you're talking to somebody. Anyway, he had nothing they could rob; they had believed his story; at least, he was going somewhere.

Stonie stretched his arms upwards and over his head, pressing his fingers against the roof of the jeep. The metal was warm already, even from the low sun pushing across the plain. As he yawned, he kicked his legs forward and one of them jarred, causing him some pain. Looking down, he saw that he had been shackled. His left leg was chained to a metal loop on the floor. The shock made him yell out. 'Hell, what the hell, what are you doing, what the fuck! I'm shackled!' Stonie stiffened, immediately fully awake, wide-eyed, pin sharp. He sat fully upright. The chain rattled around the pinions as he strained on it, cutting into his ankle. The driver and his mate both reacted with a half turn, but said nothing.

'Come on, guys. This some kind of joke? Who the hell do you think you are?' Stonie's voice was trembling, his mind racing. These were two rangers, right? Military policemen, highway patrol officers; maybe not. It was hard to tell them apart. In the darkness, it didn't matter. He needed to know what he was dealing with. Yet they never seemed to use each other's names. Nor nicknames. There had to be numbers on their shirts, a county, a state. But it was still too dark for details. All he could see was that one was bleached, the other, light brown. He would call them 'Blond' and 'Tan', if anything at all. Blond seemed to be slightly taller in his seat. He was doing the driving.

'Woken up, have we?' one of them said.

'What on earth are you playing at, I'm no felon.' The word fell into place, a good word, one they would understand. He was surprised at himself. 'I'm no criminal, done nothing...you can't do this to a complete stranger, it's…'

'Strictly regulation. This is a military vehicle and we're taking a chance…well, taking no chances.' The interruption had a chilling ring to it. 'Not supposed to carry non-service personnel, see? This is restricted territory, see? How we supposed to tell who you are, shit we're doing you a favour in any case. Just ain't hospitable being out here all night; now just you calm down.' The driver spat out of the open window.

Stonie caught the spray on his cheek before he had a chance to draw his arm up across his face. This was becoming more fearful than any night desert. There was no other vehicle in sight, no houses, no minor tracks. No road signs. And the jeep was rocking and swaying dangerously, causing Stonie to hold on even tighter to the back door rail. He felt nauseous, tight chested. He was sure they had speeded up after the driver had realised he was awake. Gone was the steady fifty-five miles an hour. The metal was scraping his leg. His heart was thumping. Everything around him was darkness. 'Just find me a motel, I'll call someone,' he yelled over the engine noise. 'I can sort this out…there's no point in…'

He was shouted down. 'Any more lip we'll throw you back out there, big cats'n all, coyotes, nasty spiders, the like…yeh most likely the vultures would get you.' There was a chuckle from both of the men. In his head, Stonie was trying to work out if he was driving through vultures or big cat country – or if this was also part of some elaborate prank; by now he could not remember a single telephone number. His mind was racing, desperately trying to figure out their next move.

'So where are you taking me?' he yelled again in frustration. Before there was any answer, the jeep dropped off the half-tarred road and bumped alongside some low, unmarked shacks. Stonie was sitting so bolt upright, his back so rigid that he jarred his head on the roof. The vehicle slewed to a halt, kicking up a cloud of dust. Dust, with yellow shards of sunlight streaming through it.

All was silent for a moment, the two men making no move to get out of the jeep. Stonie had been locked into the seat at the back of the vehicle. In front of him, the bench seat immediately behind the driver suddenly squeaked and moved, then a hand grasped the back of the upright strapping. Another person had been travelling with them. The figure laboriously pulled himself up, his dishevelled sleeve and crumpled collar clearly visible over the top of the quilted headrest. Stonie fell back against the door, startled that there had been someone else riding with them. The man had close-cropped, greying hair and skin like leather. He looked round-shouldered, skinny and from what Stonie could make out, he was shaking. He seemed to be ill. He might have been wearing a military shirt, but Stonie had fewer and fewer reference points to hold onto. The man made no attempt to turn round; he just sat in his seat at an awkward angle, half-propped up on one elbow, making tiny nodding movements of his head.

'You alright there, two three?' Blond asked, twisting round in his seat. Stonie watched, waiting for something he could say that would make a difference.

'Wish you'd stop doing that, you know, that number thing,' Tan said, hitting his companion playfully on the arm with the back of his hand.

'Hey, that hurt. Doing what, dude?' he replied.

'Don't you dude me, you know what ah'm saying – the critter's got a name,' came the response. The driver jumped down onto the gravel. 'Hell, they're all numbers,' he snapped, slamming the door. 'That right, two three?'

Stonie had the presence of mind to keep quiet. He really did not want an explanation, just an English voice on the other end of the line, a familiar face in his head. There was absolutely nothing to tell him where the jeep had stopped, no clues to what might happen next. One of the rangers sidled round to the back of the truck and threw open the back doors. Stonie swung his free leg round into the gap. 'Would you mind telling me what's going on? All I wanted was a lift, and I'm very grateful...now, if you don't mind...' Stonie couldn't help himself. He knew he was saying the wrong thing, that silence was a stronger card.

'You'll what?' came the chorus from both sides. The wizened fellow traveller, sandwiched between Stonie and his saviours for so long, slowly lowered himself back into a horizontal position, disappearing from view. One leg was bent underneath the seat. Stonie could see that he, too, was cuffed and shackled. He hadn't uttered a word. 'You will what? We didn't hear you.' Blond came back at him. 'Hey, gimme that name again.' Stonie took a deep breath.

'Stonie," he said. 'Stonie.'

'Stow-nee,' the co-driver wheezed. 'Now, what kinda name is that?' Stonie's sense of relief had long given way to unease, then outright fear. What was he supposed to say. A night under the stars would have been preferable to this unfolding nightmare. The man stroked his chin and shook his head.

'Well now, Stow-nee - ' Blond's drawl seemed more pronounced, the tone more official, the uniform more formal. Tan pulled open the side door. Stonie, sitting with his body twisting away from his seat, took the opportunity to stretch his leg down over the sill. The guard took a key to the manacle and Stonie swung fully towards the back. 'Easy now.' Blond's voice was warning enough. Stonie resisted the temptation to leap out. Instead, he leaned forward slowly and massaged his ankle, smoothing his skin with his palm and pulling his toes up towards his shin. 'About time,' he thought.

'Could turn you loose right now,' his captor said, stepping back several paces, 'but, see here…all those towers out there, in the distance, that fence or two, or maybe hundred miles of it, well now, that's gonna be a problem for you. This area is gonna be a problem for you, right? Times a stray had a bullet in the back just for going too close. Wouldn't want that, would we?'

Blond dropped his arm towards his trouser pocket. Stonie was watching every move. There was simply no cover, nowhere to run to. There would be no meeting of eyes through those dark glasses; gestures were everything. For a split second, he thought he might be shot at point blank range, right there by the side of the road. Both men were standing a few paces away from the vehicle by this time, legs astride, arms folded. That was the stance. Admiring their find…that's what it looks like, Stonie muttered as he finally jumped down from the back seat. His legs buckled under him when he hit the ground and he toppled unceremoniously onto his side. He lay still for a few seconds, breathing heavily. Military boots at eye level, grinding grey dust, a sky of perfect blue. The jeep was leaking fuel from a pipe, just a drip. He focused on this, on watching tiny bugs jumping amongst the stones, on the grooves of sand his slow breathing was carving out of the sand, on waiting for the boots to move. In the few moments of stillness, he tried to compose himself, find another level of entreaty. There was nothing to do but pick himself up. Painfully, he made it to an upright position, leaned back against the open door and hauled himself to his feet. There was sand and grit sticking into every inch of exposed sweaty skin. He stood before the two men, panting, pitiful, angry, then took a couple of steps towards them. Both men stiffened. There he was, reflected four times in their sunglasses. 'Look,' he said, 'I can prove who I am. I can remember a number,' he lied. 'Just get me to a telephone. Can you just get through on your radio to someone? Run a check. Where are we anyway?'

'I'll wager we need a tad longer to get you outa here safely,' Blond said, ignoring Stonie. 'Just have to inform my superiors. Routine. There's a rest room in that there building,' he said, nodding with a spit in the direction of the shacks.

'Now don't go getting any fancy ideas, hell no, we're your best hope, son.'

Blond shuffled forward with a sideways motion, till he was no more than a few inches from his captive's face, but staring straight ahead over Stonie's shoulder. Stonie stood his ground this time, realising that Blond was more intent on what was behind him in the jeep. His colleague broke the awkward silence.

'Shit, two three's fine,' Tan said in a whining voice, 'just fine. It'll be hours before he's any trouble.'

'Yeh, yeh, I know. Just making sure,' Blond replied. He was irate. 'Gonna be a hot one today, no doubt on that,' he added, wiping his brow with his fore arm. 'You gonna use the jon or what?'

Without saying anything, Stonie broke away towards the shacks, moving with the discomfort of a full bladder and hours cramped in one position. The path dipped till he was temporarily out of site of the road. No point in making a run for it. The simpering heat, the stultifying silence, the watery mirage on the far the horizon, it was all turning from black nightmare to white nightmare for the backpacker. This was the land of the free. He had only ever had a spliff once and it didn't do this. Some form of rapture wouldn't have been a bad idea, an acid trip, transfiguration. There weren't even any pieces to fit together.

It was insane. He pushed open the door of the first shack to be confronted by another door. Some joker had scratched a warning onto the peeling paintwork - "Abandon hope all ye who enter here". There was a seat-less pan, long dried up, but it seemed the proper thing to do, even a little absurd in this vast wasteland. Stonie listened to his pee rattling the inside of the dry pan and closed his eyes. He could feel himself swaying. He tried to let his shoulders drop, to find some cooler air in the shadows. As he shook off, there was a rasping sound just beyond the skin of the hut and the door slammed shut behind him, metal on metal. The kind of screech that dries out your gums. He wheeled round and lunged towards the front of the hut at the unmistakable crunch of footsteps on gravel. Running, escaping, giving up on him. He reached forward and tried the latch. It was stuck fast.

As he thumped against the door with his fists, dust, large flakes of rust and old cobwebs rained down on him. But it would not budge. The shack, mostly tin and wood, shuddered as he tried again, kicking and yelling. He was breathing in old spider skin, powdered insect wing and paint flakes and years of desert. He choked, cleared his throat and spat with a curse. Splinters of sunlight cut through the murky air. He was sure he had heard a motor engine on the road, even through all the creaking and crashing around him. He stopped for a moment to listen. Nothing but his own heaving chest. Warily, he pushed his face against a tiny hole in the corrugated wall to the side of the door. From what little he could see of the road, there was no jeep in sight, no one: his erstwhile saviours had vanished. He tried another slit several inches away. Nothing. Now he would suffocate. He had been abandoned.

Perhaps Tan and Blond were lying in wait some distance away, ready to have a pop, a bit of sport; taking bets on how long it would take him to fry. It was probably 8.30am, he surmised, and already the air was boiling. The only window had been boarded up. Everything was tinder dry. They could set it alight. They could wait till he was pleading for mercy, they could...he tried to steady himself against the thought he might pass out, simply shrivel up in the heat. These are sick, twisted psychos. They're just waiting to cart me off to some other playpen if I hack my way out. This is…unreal, the end of everything. Nothing left. Stonie was breathing as deeply as he could, stuttering out a whisper with his eyes closed and a picture of good old Zach flitting though his mind. Now what would Zach do if he'd already surrendered his watch, ring, chain, pen, penknife, maps - all he owned, to a toothless half-mad farmer, if he'd been chained up and driven nowhere for hours only to find his freedom was in the hands of a couple of dodgy uniforms hell-bent on frying him alive, or using him as target practice. What would he do?

There was little point in doing nothing. Stepping back along the hallway, crunching over flattened beer cans, and sweeping aside matted newspapers, he kicked and scuffed a path through the rubbish, then launched forward, hurling himself at the door with a scream, both arms across his chest, his shoulders fixed for the shock. Everything gave way as the door flew off its lintel, hinges twisting dangerously close to his eyes as he burst free. Clouds of dirt, splinters and debris rained down on him. But he was flying, that slow-motion sensation of having no physical contact with this world, a split-second singing wind in his ears before he crashed down, bruised and cut at the shoulder, with the outside of his right arm scraped raw. He lay sprawled, winded, eyes tight shut, the corrugated metal branding his skin. There was no breath in or out – just the sound of grit against his temple. Rolling over to one side, he stiffened up, expecting something to happen to him. A thud, a piercing blow, some gut-wrenching rip. Nothing. He opened his eyes to a blast of light and squinted painfully till he could make out the ridge above him. The same arc, the same meeting of earth and sky and the shimmering ache between them. Not even a bug in the air. For a moment, Stonie watched his breath carve a tiny crater in the glass-sparkling sand, certain there was a presence near him. With some difficulty, he propped himself onto his left fore arm and began to check for blood. Most of his skin was stinging, raw-white when touched. He eased his head onto a rock, stared straight upwards into the blue and consciously tried to slow his breathing. There was the taste of sick in his mouth. He closed his eyes and all he could see were tiny stars. All this, Stonie had known before.

If he could have seen beyond the hollow, he would have proof he was no more than the turn of a single grain of sand in the vast hollow world, the scrape of the valley stretching silently into a shimmering distance. He would have known there was no one to hear his whimper, no one to believe the one-sided conversations in his head. Stonie wriggled out a cooler layer of sand for his bum, sat up slowly and began picking at the stones embedded in his arm, wiping sand and grit out of his eyes. Blood had eased out along the etched skin on his arms and thigh. He dabbed at it with a corner of his shirt, wincing at the touch, slaking his throat as he tried to find some saliva for his tongue, something to draw across his lips. What now? There was no shade apart from the stinking shack and nothing to say which direction he should take. He waited, drawing in the hot air, listening beyond every measured breath. When he found the right moment, he stood up gingerly, stumbled up the path onto the road and sat down on a protruding clump of grass, leaning onto the road surface with this hand to ease himself down. Tiny dots of tar stuck to his palm, making him recoil at once. The road was cooking. He flattened his palm into a deep patch of sand to cool it off. As he did so, something else caught his eye, a glint of silver, just where the jeep had been parked a few feet away from where he was sitting. He had time, it seemed, in this timeless emptiness, to examine every detail around him.

Perhaps, not taking stock, not taking care of the small things, had drawn him into this mess in the first place. He was too trusting, too much of a romantic, he decided. He would examine everything. This particular detail proved to be a dog chain. On his travels, he had met a number of Viet Nam vets. This was definitely a dog chain. Further over, in the grass, he spotted the tag. He picked it up but dropped it immediately, letting out a gasp as it burned into his fingers. The noise of his voice caught him off guard. He spat on the metal, blew on it, then juggled with it from hand to hand until it felt comfortable enough to hold.

'Luca Cambareri 2323046,' he read. He paused for a moment, examining both sides of the thin plate, then, with mock pomposity, announced 'Luca Cambareri, I return your chain to your tag, but apologise that I cannot in this god-awful furnace, find you a dog'. For the moment, everything would be voiced. He polished the plate against his shorts and dropped the chain through the hole, connecting it up and dangling it on his index finger. 'Now that's a hell of a new dog tag,' he decided, raising it to eye level. 'Hardly a scratch on it; must have only just got there.' He thought for a moment. It hadn't been lying in the dirt for long; it wasn't a bashed up, trampled, worn at the edges, bullet-taking piece of metal. He dropped it into his palm. 'No,' he said, 'it can't have been in the dirt for long. Hardly a mark on it…lying there, didn't have to dig it out of the sand.' Perhaps he was making something out of nothing, losing all proportion. He eased himself to his feet and walked over to where he had just been sitting, wondering what else he might find. As he did so, a wave of nausea flooded over him, dizziness, his legs weak and trembling. He tried to focus, but the swaying was enough to make him fall to one knee. The shock of the burning sand to his skin brought him abruptly upright again, tightened every muscle. This time he would concentrate. He knew he had to keep a clear head, make a plan. So far there had been no shots.

The jeep's wheels had dug deep with the fast acceleration. Close to the deeper tracks where the vehicle had been parked, Stonie could make out some letters hesitantly scratched into the dirt. "C A N E" he began "C A N A L…letters, a word, whatever, they're new, darker than the surface grit, definitely new, definitely a message" he muttered. "Now what on earth can that be about" he continued, interrogating himself. Everything was a commentary, an attempt to distract himself from the overpowering heat. He needed to keep his mind active; he needed to make a decision. Later, he would wonder about a dog tag and a canal. It was probably a good idea to move back down to the huts. It seemed as if the sun had been overhead ever since he had fallen out of the jeep, but there was shade to one side. He would hunker down, take stock, conserve his energy; the thirst was affecting his breathing. He rubbed the shiny dog tag between thumb and forefinger inside his pocket, perhaps to reassure himself it was still there, wondering what story lay behind it. Yet there were other, more pressing things to worry about. How long he would last, what horizon he should make for, the possibility he was still being watched, that the jeep would return, that he would pass out. The noise of his breathing was interfering with his ability to listen. At any moment, there could be a bullet in the back.

Stonie could taste the heat. The last time he had been this parched he was being filled with the Holy Spirit. All it took was the preacher's thumb, one middle finger to the temple and he was gone, legs akimbo. He had crumpled like jelly. The power, from somewhere above him, simply waved over him and down he went. Not even his catcher knew where he would end up. That was his most significant fall. Perhaps that was his most significant interruption. There were bodies everywhere, laughing hysterically, crying, foetal, rocking, carpet thumping. Others just stood there swaying, wafting in the divine wind. For him, it had been the stillness, the silence. He could sense there was the faintest of curls at the edges of his mouth. Could this be the beginnings of a smile? The taste had lasted for days. Here, out of the searing eternal desert, the same crushing torpor was descending. At first, there was nothing to slake his thirst, till finally there was no thirst, only the electric pall of an arid wasteland and that same euphoric isolation. He could see little white sparks before his eyes, which moved with every change of view, with every roll. What if this, at last, was permanent, lasting, *real*? He stood up, leaning back against the side of the shack, trying to blink more rapidly, circling his eyeballs back and up into their sockets. Then the grimace, drawing his eyes tight shut till his long eyebrows tickled his cheeks. He hated the taut skin, the cracked lips, every last drop of sweat being wrung out of his weary frame. He could see further with eyes half closed, with the palm of his hand capped against his forehead, staring intently out into the brightness of the desert. The world through the mesh of the hairs of his eyelashes.

'Okay, Mr. Wanderlust, ' he shouted at the sky, finally pushing with the back of his head against the side of the shack. The effect tipped him fully upright. 'Decision made. Leave a sign for help, an arrow or something by the roadside, move only at night, that is, if there's a moon.' He was trying to be methodical, apply some kind of logic. Talking out loud helped him remember what he had decided to do. 'Walk south, there's nothing the way we came, nothing.' He took a long sigh. 'Nothing to the north. We came from the south east. No, came east. The sun rose over...we drove in from the north west. Anyway, at last I have a plan.'

He was sure he had a plan. Start right away. Surely somewhere, there would be relief from the merciless, screaming canopy of blue. He took his first deliberate step, kicking up powder puffs of dust as he scuffed out of the shadows, summoning up every ounce of energy for the sloping track up onto the road. Each lurch forward was a struggle. His head was pounding.

He was sure he could hear the glory coming down, the tongues, the whooping, baying congregation swirling around him. He could feel the music, only this time he was hardly in touch with the dance. He steadied himself, trying to breathe freely. This was the ultimate fire tunnel, the test. The effort hurt. Somewhere in his rib cage there was pain. He was slamming into the door again, the thin, prolonged tuning fork of a sound echoing in his head. He could hear the evangelist yelling comfort at him. In the name of Jesus, he could swear there were all those outstretched arms swaying like a breeze-blown fringe against his face. This time he was by-passing his brain. This time he would say yes. This time. He could feel his feet melting tackily onto the tar with every step. But he was there. He'd received it, the blessing. He was crying, relieved, stumbling erratically towards a promised new life.

Wk.1180

32° 41.9' N 114° 37.5' W

'Don't make no sense any which way. He's dumb, that's all there is to it – else he plain won't utter a sound. Nothing. For some kinda stubborn reason…maybe that bleeding head wound…it done for his brain.'

'Been over this,' came the reply. After a pause, the man and the woman spat, one after the other into the scrub.

'Still just grunts. A fella can grunt in any language, hell, don't get no accent with a holler. Like he's had his tongue'n all burnt out.' The sky had cooled over the open yard, both figures adopting their late afternoon pose, another of the rituals, staring at the sky, examining the sky, as if planning the weather. They seemed to move at the pace of the clouds.

'What's it been, six months, darn near?' The two nurses sauntered idly towards the doorway, staring through the mesh at their charge, a gaunt, slightly stooping figure dressed in blue and white check shirt, khaki shorts and open toe sandals. The shutters were creaking, nudging against the flaking, encrusted walls. Flies flicked and bombed the single lamp, which had been placed dead centre on a faded, embroidered napkin spread out on the trestle table on the veranda. Night was closing in fast, dropping onto the ramshackle clutch of picket-fenced houses. It was the only human life, this backwater, last ditch of the elderly and infirm south east of Yuma. Faceless bureaucracy had chosen well. The nearest homestead was some sixty miles. A good place to bang up the unwanted, a perfect place to rot. The home, more a compound of several misshapen houses, seemed to have grown out of swells of scrubland by default, some way off the smallest of country tracks and almost completely ignored by the late sixties. This was hardly the proudest the county could offer. But it made no difference to the mystery man scraped off the desert floor only hours from death.

'Should have been vulture fodder and no mistake. Got lucky.' The woman spat again, picking tobacco strands from her teeth, all the time, talking to the sky. Both figures were side by side, leaning over the veranda rail and staring out into the yard.

'We gonna keep him?' Her companion shouldered her gently.

'I swear you taken a shine, yeh that's it. Didn't get in touch with the authorities, did ya? That was what you s'posed to do.' There was no one to answer to, nothing to explain. The stranger had no papers, no tell-tale birthmarks, no tattoos, no voice. Something has seriously shut him up. It was the gash to the temple; it was exposure to the searing Arizona furnace. There were two jokes: he really had a biblical brush with The Almighty, or he never could speak in the first place. The thought that the man might be naturally dumb was a triumph of the obvious. Warder Two was pleased with herself over that little piece of wisdom.

Few enquiries were ever made in these cracks in the landscape. The morning sun took longer to hit the gully floor, the shadows built up suddenly, late afternoon. From the highway, it simply did not exist. The residents did not exist. The stranger had folded into featureless surroundings and routines like all the others with unquestioning faith. This latest resident had no discernible health problems, ate modestly, slept fitfully, occasionally strayed beyond the reception building. No one could be bothered to get him registered with the authorities. That was a hundred and twenty mile round trip. There was no picking up on 'Blu's' story. Blu was easy to spell, they reckoned and in any case that was the colour of his eyes. God knows they had looked into them often enough to find out if there was anything going on in his brain. So little response, so acquiescent. That was the gentle bit, which sure as hell made them feel guilty when they'd had enough running after him and left him on his own for a day or two. He was work. Several of the residents never ventured outside their rooms, but this one, there was the odd moment when they had lost him.

This was a place where everyone thought that someone else was taking care of business. Then there was the invisible military. You got used to not asking questions, keeping your counsel. Shooting the breeze could mean real bullets. So the MD would come and go - usually one side or the other of death's door - local supplies were plied with hardly a murmur and visitors were discouraged by the simple expedient of an absence of signposts, anywhere.

This was nether world and proud of it.

'Hell, a lot of things just don't exist around here,' One was fond of exclaiming. He was at it again, the loop, the comfortable observation. It was his phrase. It had come to mean any number of things. In this instance, he was in full flow on what was likely to be going on inside Blu's brain. 'Don't recall him getting that far before, ever. Coulda got clean away this time. Clean away.' One was leaning on the rail of the porch, squashing ants with his middle finger as they rounded on his bare arm.

'Best if we don't go chasing after him next time,' Two replied.

A tinny bell rang out, announcing food for the mobile residents. Blu appeared in the doorway of the common room. Shuffling between the two nurses, he lurched down the two or three steps and scuffed his way towards the bell with not a flicker on his vacant face. Nothing registered. At food time, in particular, nothing registered. Within half an hour, he was back in the room, choosing his chair. No one could move his chair; it had to face forward, towards the window, back of the chair against the wall. Facing out. That was one of the few times he would become agitated, when the chair was not facing towards the window, pointing towards the sky, back to the wall.

These were short days. All too soon, the light was gone. In the rooms, stooped figures passed between windows, shuffled across open doorways. On the board walk, One stumped a fresh cigarette three or four times each end on the side of the pack, scratched a match on his teeth and drew the flame through the light. 'Never seen you do that before,' Two said.

'What d'you mean next time?' One cleared his throat and swallowed before he remembered to spit, formed a word on his lips then thought the better of it.

'Blu's never been anywhere, much. No trouble. Don't recall he's ever wandered off that far before,' Two continued.

'Yep, no trouble. Still, like as not…we could take him for a ride one night, you and I,' came One's more measured reply. 'Lose him. I mean, he wandered off, didn't he? Just took off into the night. Ten, maybe fifteen miles wouldn't be too far. Other side of the world to him.' He paused, half expecting Two to cut in. 'Kinda…fell over, smashed his head in on the rocks again. This time for good. What's the point in him living like this? Could be arranged. I've a mind to…'

He was interrupted by a set of headlights sweeping through the compound, straight towards where they were standing. In twenty minutes and three smokes, the sun had fully set, the temperature had dropped sharply and Blu had made several trips across his room to kick the television. The pick-up drew slowly alongside the front of the window and crunched to a halt. The reflected lounge light on the cab window meant that neither of the two carers could make out exactly who had pulled up. The engine died, but nothing else stirred. The driver, with a rather tentative push, stretched the cab door till it was half open, held the angle, and dropped one leg onto the running board. It was as if he was ready to change his mind. Finally, he pulled himself free of his seat, stooped out and stood to height, making direct eye contact with One. He drew his right hand up to his left shoulder, fist against collarbone in a time-honoured greeting, then stepped forward towards the deck. He had the poise and timing of his breed, the dim cast of the house lights serving only to heighten his sculpted frame.

'Well I'll be damned,' Two said, drawing the last little glow from her cigarette butt and stubbing it out almost theatrically on the handrail. 'I'll be damned.' She moved half a step, glanced round at the window to check that Blu was still slumped in the armchair, and stepped down from the deck. 'You're the guy who brought him in…you the scout who found him,' she said, tipping her head backwards in the direction of Blu without looking. Tonight, Blu would move to an eternal soundtrack of canned laughter, making no distinction between Lucille Ball, Ed, the talking horse and Dan

Rather. His shoulders would roll a little, then he would more or less disappear below the back of the armchair. This was an empty space, offering nothing but the grey flicker of a hollow world.

'You ki-woo-she-an,' One said, easing himself into a wicker chair. He leaned forward, rocking slightly, elbows fixed on the narrow arms. 'Never forget a name. Yeh, you the one alright. Sorry state he was in. Some guardian angel... hell, he was a goner, then you - ' The Indian looked at both nurses in quick succession as he cut across the conversation.

'My name is Wendy Soon.' He began moving tentatively away from the truck, his arm connecting with the open cab door behind him as he spoke. 'My name is Wendy Soon. I am Quechen.'. The door remained as it was, an escape route.

The two uniforms burst into a muted cackle. 'Wendy?' One asked, his hand cupped to his mouth, stroking his upper lip and making mock coughing sounds. 'Wendy, as I recall you took off pretty damn quick. Didn't rightly get the chance to talk, I mean, you and I, the night you brought him in.'

'Hell, I swear you ought to have some recall on that moniker,' Two said with a sneer.

'I never forget a name...never.' One slapped his hands on the arms of the chair and leaned back. 'Aint your real name now, that's for sure.'

'So what you doing out here this time?' his companion asked. 'No matter, wrong time of day to be visiting with folks.' Two's tone had become edgy; it had the practiced delivery of a disturbed mind. She stood right in front of Wendy Soon and without taking her eyes off him for a second, added 'He sure got you on that one, my friend. So, what's your business, what you doing here? That's what I asked already.'

Behind Two's confrontational pose, One could see the Indian steadying himself, preparing to back up into his truck. 'Hell, sit down, take no account of the bitch, she just mouthing off. Take a seat,' he said, waving Two to one side. 'Yeh, pull up that chair. Need a drink...been a long drive, what's your business, where you heading?' Without waiting for answers, he continued 'See, Wendy...well, Wendy, that's for woman folks, right? White women,' he sniggered. 'S'what we're used to, see?' He slowed, quietened his voice. 'Don't sound right on a man, could get him into trouble' he said through the beginnings of a smile.

The Indian sat down on the rim of the seat, carefully, with his back straight, his arms outstretched, his hands placed firmly on his knees. There would be no friendly banter, no breaking of the ice. One moment there was irritation, the next, peace. There were always mixed signals from white people.

'I understand this,' he replied. His voice betrayed no fear, yet he knew there were risks in relaxing with the occupiers. He saw nothing in their values to warm his heart. It was a time for caution. He knew that some white men were easily turned black - with rage or cowardice or the sickness of power. They could use their position to bad effect. As far as he knew, they believed Hollywood, bought the whole damned package. He had heard of the unrest at Gila Bend. This was many generations of bad blood.

'A drink then?'

'Yes, I would like a drink. I have been out at Sundad and Papago,' he said, offering some information. It was no reason to relax. Two finally drew a third seat side-on against the table and sat down. In the light breeze, the candle flame seemed to be twisting to the rise and fall of the TV in some inevitable dance of accommodation. This visit was not cosy, but necessary. Perhaps, after all, the Indian would simply say his piece and make his excuses. One pulled himself free of his chair and disappeared into the darkness with no further announcement.

'Papago? Christ, there's nothing out there but kit fox,' Two replied. 'Anyways, that's half way cross Maracupa. What you doing way east?'

Wendy Soon had been expecting the interrogation. This would be the first of the many sacrifices he would make. 'I have a relative, a cousin, in Buckeye,' he lied. 'He is ill and it is two summers since I saw him.' He knew how to play the white man game. He did not wish them to know he had made a special journey.

'You Quechen, then, right? Yeh, yeh that's what you said already,' Two continued. 'Well your kind, you border tribes, all kinda look the same to me. Suppose you could have been Cocopa. No matter, never could tell. So, what you…eh - ' She paused, sat back, folded her arms and stared intently at the visitor. 'Sure you ain't up to something, are you? You all kinda shifty far as I'm concerned.' Wendy Soon chose not to respond. There was an awkward silence, each of them waiting for the other.

'Feeling generous tonight, ge-ne-rous,' One shouted as he shuffled back across the yard a few minutes later. 'Sure don't know why, but you better make the most of it.' He was clutching several bottles of beer, a bag of ice and three stacked glasses, all haphazardly embraced tightly against his chest. 'Don't rightly know why, but I do.' He bent his knees to ease the bottles onto the table. 'Look at me, bowing to the warrior,' he quipped, dropping chunks of ice as he steadied the glasses. Both guards scrambled to catch the ice. One began sweeping the lumps off the table into the glasses, along with whatever grit and frazzled mosquito happened to be in the way. Then he held each bottle by the neck, its top against the edge of the table and thumped it open. 'There, get that down you,' Two said, sliding a bottle in the direction of the Indian. 'You Cocopa, me human being.' she went on 'Am sorry, interruptin' your pow wow an' all.'

"Cool it, woman," One cut across her, sounding annoyed. 'Show a tad more respect, will you. The Indian's gotta have a reason for being here. That right, my friend?'

'That is right,' Wendy Soon replied, confused that the atmosphere between them had suddenly mellowed. He ignored the glass and its dirty ice, picked up the bottle and took a long slow drink. In the chirp and rasp of the dusty night air, he could hear a dog howling and the faint, muffled exhortations of the compere from the little TV set in the lounge. Blu hadn't moved. For all his wanderings, Blu was one of the easy ones to look after, easy to forget. Through the open door, Wendy soon could just make out the figure pressed into the back of an armchair. He instinctively knew this was the one he had rescued. He remembered the fear in his eyes in the moment he had lifted him from the roadside. He could feel the stiffening, wide-eyed delirium of the man's racked body as he carried him to the truck, wiped the caked blood from his face and poured life-giving water onto his parched lips. He would not forget.

'Well then, get on with it,' One said. 'What can I...what can we do for you at this god-forsaken hour of the day?'

Wendy Soon took another drink from the lukewarm bottle. He knew that to correct their ignorance would be folly. He wanted to tell them that Kw'st'An were the sacred sites of his people. He wanted to protest that Indian Pass was still under threat of being taken over. But his hosts were the ignorant descendants of arrogant cowboy settlers; that was obvious from their body language. What would they know about roots, about a man's place under the stars? All Indians were savages, of course. He could hear himself setting them right about the 1872 Mining Law, reciting it passage by thieving passage. He had rehearsed it often enough out on the road. It was all compressed, bottled up; the plans for the mile-wide open pit mine that would destroy forever their ancient spiritual landscape. Giving up their souls for an ounce of gold was not an option. But these were dark forces. Correcting their pronunciation would not be helpful. They knew best. He was here on other business.

'So you from Kofa way? A guide or something?' Two asked. Wendy Soon made to answer, but was distracted just enough to pause. Blu was standing now, some way back from the window, rocking gently on his heels in the ghostly flicker of the TV: a normal figure, a *presence*, in the half-light; just another beating heart. Wendy Soon had questions of his own, but in the instant, he renewed eye contact with Two as she followed up. She was unpredictable.

'No. I am not out of Kofa'

'Heading west? I mean, can't stay here. Don't let no Indians stay. That's the rules.'. She shifted in her chair as she made the pronouncement.

'I will leave in a moment.'

Wendy Soon felt more in charge. For now, he felt equal to them. He settled back in his chair and waited, the invitation of silence.

'D'you say you found Blu…called him Blu on account of his eyes, did I say that? Anyhow, we don't rightly have any other information. You got some information?' One asked, trying to speed things up.

'South of Vicksburg, that right, close to I-10,' Two said. 'Say between 45 and 53 – hell, reckon further east, below 69 and 81. Don't matter.' Two was almost talking to herself, filling the spaces. Then it was One's turn. Wendy Soon waited for an opportunity to speak. To the white men, he waited too long. Neither of the nurses was comfortable with silence. Neither of the nurses was comfortable being civil. It would have been easy for them to see him off. Yet for some reason, he was being entertained. Somewhere in the heart lurked the common gesture, that grudging whisper of mortality; there was some good to salvage.

'Hell, don't matter anyhow. Never did fill in a form at the time,' One admitted. 'Now don't you go blabbin' – don't make no border issue, see?' One suddenly had a hint of agitation in his voice. He was never one for confessionals. He didn't like the way this visit was shaping up after all. Wendy Soon raised the bottle of beer to his lips and took in a slow draft. Drinking was a useful way of taking stock. This was his first alcohol; his first sacrifice. He placed the bottle on the table, pushing it slowly away from the edge. He could sense the guards were cooling off. As he thrust his hand deep into the pocket of his cape, both wardens reacted instinctively, unsure of the move. Wendy Soon pulled out a dog tag and threw it under-arm onto the table. 'It is the only clue,' he said. 'You should have it.'

Both One and Two sat upright and reached for the tag simultaneously, leaning forward and thumping their glasses onto the table. Two won, and bent over the flame to examine the markings. 'I found it in my wagon some weeks after I got back from here,' Wendy Soon explained. 'I meant to send it but I did not have an address. I am sorry. I thought it might help. This was my first opportunity.'

'Mil-i-ta-ry, now there's a thing,' Two said. 'Luca Cambareri? Some kinda foreign name. Hell, don't rightly help much.' She stood up without warning, throwing the tag at One. 'Gotta go, things to do,' she announced abruptly. A scraggy grey dog, lying curled up at the bottom of the steps jumped at her, growled and ran off, snapping at her heels as she disappeared into the darkness of the yard.

'Might just about solve the mystery,' One said, pushing his chair back and rising over the Indian. 'Sure is a mystery. Now…is that your business here?' Wendy Soon stood to face him.

'I will go now. Thank you for the drink. I have one other thing to say.' One shuffled impatiently. In the flickering light, he was sure he caught sight of a smirk or the beginnings of a smile on the Indian's face. As far as he was concerned, he had never seen an Indian smile. They knew nothing of humour. This would be a first. Wendy Soon drew his fist up across his chest to signal goodbye and looked straight into One's eyes. 'I have never been offered a drink by a white man,' he began. 'I have paid for everything or made a companion of thirst". One picked up his glass and drained the last few drops simply to fill the space.

'My people live in fear of uniforms,'Wendy Soon continued 'yet for the white man I come here. You have allowed me to sit with you. Thank you. I leave with no fear. I have done my duty.' One made a move to offer his hand, but before he knew what to do with the urge, Wendy Soon had turned around and stooped into the cab. There was no looking back. The engine burst into life as the cab door slammed shut.

The headlights immediately picked out the hollow-glazed pellet eyes of a staring guard dog skulking on the far side of the yard. It was restrained by a long chain. Wendy Soon swung the truck round. Something else caught the headlights. As the beam swept the yard, he could see the tailgates of two heavy jeeps tucked between the low buildings. There were drivers in the cabs. Their red eyes had also caught the beam. The jeeps had no state plates. He felt a chill down his back as he pulled hard on the steering wheel and pointed for the dirt track and open road. 'Something going on,' he muttered to himself. 'This is not an ordinary rest home.' He thrust his foot to the floor, the tyres whipping dust and stones out behind him till he felt them grip the solid road. There were twenty miles between him and the cut before he realised how tightly he was holding the wheel. He breathed in deeply and slowly, drawing his shoulder blades together. He could relax, loosen his knuckle-white grip. Somehow, doing his duty brought with it bad omens. How long could he feel sorry for a white man? Blu was none of his business. 'Blu,' he announced to the night. 'Blu is a stupid name. No imagination.' He checked his mirror for headlights.

Blu's dreams had him raging though the Mica years in minute detail, every last second scrutinised for clues. Somewhere inside his head he had missed something, failed to empathise. Failed to persuade. Love wasn't enough. The truth was there, in the teasing, minute pulses, the tiny split-second spurts of clarity. He knew it was all going on, the replay. He could even anticipate the moment, but the *sense* was lost to him, the years compressed between TV and armchair, armchair and TV. The uniform in the photograph…he is dying, was dead, had never been alive, just a figment, an impression. His face...that was it, the last time he had talked to her, the man had robbed him, denied him Mica. The man in the cap. Some father...there were stars on the cap. Blu talked to him, loudly inside his head. 'And we'll all go round and round in the circle game…' It was your fault I lived through the silences, the distance. Silk sheets and silences. What you did to her, not me. Your imprint. He ranted. But no one could tell. In the grey flicker, in the cool orange glow of an Arizona dawn, in the suffocating glare of noon. Even close up. No one could tell.

Wendy Soon drew himself upright with a start, shook himself back to the driving. It had been several miles since he had looked in his rear mirror. Still no headlights. From the rocks on his left to the scrub on his right, nothing but stars. The pearls on the posts danced towards him. He picked out a star on the horizon. He had the imagination. There was little to do but ease his craft free of terra firma, gently smoothing his way up into the velvet. The night bugs were asteroids racing past his visor; the nearer outcrops, planets. He twisted the knob on the radio through tortured music till it crackled instructions. "This is W-FTBO with a word from our sponsors…just gone midnight here at…" The signal split to a rasping storm of sound, dipping back into a fervent southern evangelist raging hell-fire into the ether. That was too much. He leaned forward and switched off the tremulant soul-searcher, at once re-connecting with the power of flight and the distant hum of eternity. Suddenly, space, freedom seemed too complicated. Perhaps, after all, the firmament would wait. Perhaps he simply needed to go back, to set course for where it all began. There were high hill tracks and river trails to trace, lakes to dance on, the moon's reflection to chase. Keep it simple. Keep it young. He would sail the dunes, brush the tips of the trees, roll through the deep canyons with the rocks and raging white water barely inches away, the windows open, the cool spray against his cheeks. Yes, this was more like it; staying close and going far. Yet the road, the sky, those pearls of pink wrapped around him, they were cold comfort in the uncertain still-beat of his heart.

The car seemed to be driving itself. He could see his ghost-like face in the windscreen. Blue, green, red off the dashboard. The face was speaking to him, mouthing something. It was his father. He was his father. The face spoke in a low whisper. 'Time to begin your journey, Wendy Soon. Start with what you know. Build on where you are. In time the heart will know. You have to find her.' Wendy

Soon shook his head, closed his eyes briefly, listened hard. Nothing but the whine of the engine, the rattle of the vent, pumping warm air at him. 'You have to find her,' He stared long and hard at his reflection, at his father, at the generations of stars beyond the glass. 'Far beyond this arc of earth.' The voice and the road-whispers wrapped themselves around him in the cabin.

With every mile, Wendy Soon's conscience sharpened. He could see his dying mother, her beautiful, etched skin, nothing but protruding bones, gasping for air, calm and certain of her destiny. This was the legacy of a hundred thousand journeys. No one had told the people on the reservation that every open-mined step would draw them downwards into the very dust they carried. His own family was sick; the generations before them, already gone – agonising, stoic, premature. There were sad stories, back-breaking gangs of miners, the alcohol, the gambling, the patronage and pittance. No one voiced their fears. No protests, nothing to strike out against. The white men, they knew better. He had never spoken of it, only reserved contempt for his race, for the arrogant dignity of resignation. He would learn to live *outside*. He had nothing. He could taste his young bride, smell her hair, the touch of her silk skin gently on his cheek. He could feel the tears of the pyre. She had lasted one year. Bride for one year. It was the year in which he found the manual, learned the chemistry yet never once admitted that he could read. He knew now. It would happen all over again. The tribal chiefs had been paid for their silence. He was certain of this. Their children and their children's children were paying with their lives. The thought made him straighten the arch of his back, lean forward, as if searching for the fleeting father image. There had been no land light since he sped away from the home. Only dark traces between earth and sky. There was only the tapering beam of his headlights confounding the emptiness ahead.

Wendy Soon chose his third star. The road had found its own way south. He loosened his grip again on the steering wheel and talked to his body, in time becoming aware of a faint yellow glow in the sky ahead. Yuma.

Wk.1417
52° 29' N 1° 56.6' W

'Open the bloody door, will you. Just get me out of - '

Stonie thought he knew the voice. 'It's ten minutes after midnight. Quit the screaming…what's the problem?' He shouted in a whisper, trying to get to the door before any neighbours pounced. The first thing he saw was a hand through the letter box.

'I'm stuck; my hand...it's stuck.'

'What the hell are you doing with your hand inside my letterbox?' The tone was calm, slow. He had to decide how to act. He knew the voice.

'Ayeea, easy, bloody plastic rim, cutting my wrist. I've cut my wrist.'

'Doesn't sound like a bad idea,' Stonie said, as he began to push back the bolt.

'Shit…my arm, let me get it out first.'

'Who do you think you are?' Stonie asked. He was becoming more agitated as he took in the situation, unsure if he should even open the door at all.

'Just open the bloody door, it's me, Zach. It *is* you in there, isn't it? My mate Stonie?'

Stonie twisted the handle and peered round the edge of the door, keeping one hand firmly on the half drawn bolt.

'I was in bed; well, not in bed, about to get ready,' Stonie said, unhooking the safety chain but holding on to it, with the door barely open. He had one foot lodged firmly against the wood, warily weighing up the situation. 'Who did you say you are?' Zach was in pain, twisting his wrist to free it. He was taken aback by the response. He found himself searching for the next line, working out how to explain what he was doing.

'Just thought I'd drop round. Never been to your place before. Time to catch up. No particular reason really. Time to catch up…was wondering if you might like to join us for a late beer…you sure you're okay? Yeh well shit, that was hours ago, come to think of it. Well, honestly now, remembered I was close by your pad. Look at the bloody time; missed the bus, see, I couldn't go back to my place. No money for..a...taxi. Spending too much time in the pub, eh? Gets to be a habit. Knew you wouldn't mind a friendly intruder. Well thought you'd gone away, to be honest. Was going to crash out. Devil of a place to find. Good place to hole up for the night, though.'

'Who said anything about friendly?' Stonie said. He was picturing thc pub. Thc word games, the bonhomie, being nice to each other. The company. He could never make up his mind if he enjoyed any kind of company. There was Gem. On the edge of everything. First time he had seen her in his head for a long time. Every face was usually Mica.

'Thought you were away, quite honestly. Sure you said once you kept a key hanging up where you could reach…ayeeha… hold the frame…am still stuck.'

'Oh, so you know me, do you? Well tell me who I am then, you drunk? Think yourself lucky I don't leave you there and call the police.'

Stonie pretended to push the door shut, then without warning let go. The door flew open with Zach still attached by the letterbox and running out of expletives. 'Got an idea.' Within a few moments, Stonie was back clutching a shoe horn and a bar of soap.

'Fat lot of good a shoe horn...bloody don't pull...and don't push either.' Zach slowed the manoeuvre down. 'Ah, fucking...careful, will you.' Zach pushed Stonie away. Finally, he managed to straighten his fingers and prise his wrist free. It was bruised red and slightly bleeding where he had been twisting against the plastic rim. 'Bloody bad design,' he said, nursing his arm.

'Good design, I'd say,' Stonie said muttering something under his breath. He shuffled awkwardly aside to allow Zach to enter the hallway, almost immediately turning his back and walking off towards the darkness of the living room. Zach began to trail after him nursing his scratched wrist. 'Better get on your knees and clip the frame back, d'you hear?' Stonie said. He leaned round the edge of the door and switched on the kitchen light, leaving the main room in semi-darkness. 'Serves you bloody right.'

Zach felt uncomfortable, embarrassed; this was a joke, this vague response. He had been expecting an empty flat. Or he had not been expecting to be greeted as a stranger. One or the other. It was time to make up the truth. 'Well you weren't answering your phone, nobody had seen you around. Word was you'd upped and left without any goodbyes. I thought maybe you'd packed in the agency. Thought there was something up.' Zach was staring intently at his friend. Enough to prompt Stonie to a response.

'Oh, I was thinking of going out, just didn't get round to it. Who did you say you are?' he joked. He knew full well. Zach leant awkwardly against the wall, trying to measure the timing, the gestures, the whole unexpected weirdness. He's drunk, drugged or something. We've spent endless nights together. He was about to recall some moments.

'Yeh, good times, eh? The Old Crown.' Stonie said. Zach waited for more.

'Mind if I sit down. I'm tired.' Stonie swung his arm in an after-you gesture

'No, go ahead…find something else to wreck.'

'Sorry. Stupid really. Had a few drinks.'

Zach burped and leaned back in his chair. Stonie looked odd; the mustard cord shirt, a green handkerchief hanging from the breast pocket, faded dark blue denim; round his neck, a mother of pearl bolo which he kept fingering. His hair was unkempt and he was bare-footed. Not going out. Zach took stock of the room: a pile of newspapers and unopened mail on the low table between them; dates from several weeks ago: the smell of sleep, unaired, old food. There were dead flies on the window sill, dangling cobwebs. There was dust everywhere, tea-stained mugs, yellowing half-poem notes, a shrivelled-up orange in an ashtray on the mantelpiece, acting as a paperweight for several lists. Always lists, Zach thought. But he could not see anything out of the ordinary; the guy's *been away*, that's all. Stonie reached back and fumbled for the light switch on an old, tilting standard lamp. As it rocked, he steadied it and sat down on the cushioned arm of a chair.

'That's better. Yes, I was away for a while,' he said, anticipating the response. 'Not been too well, but you know how it is. Didn't mean to be rude. Bit of a shock, thinking I had an intruder. Well in a way, I have. Been weeks since we were in touch. Takes two. Well, anyhow, how's your work going these days? Any new shows?' He stood up again and positioned himself behind the sofa, as if suddenly conscious of his appearance.

'Fine. Slow progress, but I'm following up some good leads.' There was an awkward silence, then both made to speak at the same time.

'You can stay,' Stonie said, what the hell, I can easily make up a bed on the sofa.' 'Want a drink? What's your poison?' Making no attempt to follow up on his offer, Stonie sat down opposite Zach and leaned forward, his elbows on his knees, head in his hands, talking through his fingers. 'Yeh, the Old Crown. Some crowd. Took me a minute or two.'

'You alright?' Zach asked. Zach was feeling the alcohol and it set him on edge. He didn't like waiting for an answer. 'Are you going to tell me what's been going on? Something's changed. I know that much.'

Stonie was slow to respond. Yet again he was having to re-invent himself. Where he had been, who he had been, the shape of the wounds, the Arizona *spaces*, how long it had taken to get back. There were moments when everything had to be renamed, remembered. For months shown what to do, where to go; the slurred words, the scribbles, vaguely familiar sounds and aromas. He would grasp at them then it would all go blank. That would signal the panic attacks, people rushing everywhere, talking him round; the injections, holding him down. He did not want to be held. There were locked rooms, food lines, the smell of pills; the strange, deep set eyes when he gazed into the mirror. Surely they knew *he wanted to be somewhere else.* He remembered. He had become the star of the conference circuit; wheeled out, examined, questioned. He knew how to perform for those West Coast medics, all those patronising bastards who wired him up, talked in loud whispers behind his back. All his life, people had talked behind his back. And the hacks; thankfully, he was no longer a story.

Zach brushed past him into the kitchen, sure that Stonie was about to break into tears. He watched him check in his pockets, pull off his jacket and hang it over the arm of the chair; checking and re-checking.

'You're really on edge, I must say; giving me the feeling half the city's trying to track you down. Coffee?' Stonie spoke but didn't move. Finally he nodded. 'Yeh. Coffee. Good idea.' He took a long time over the last four words.

'White, two sugars, right?' Zach asked.

'Black, 'Stonie answered, finally looking over to where Zach was leaning against the lintel, holding two mugs and weighing up the best place to sit.

'I know, I know, it was a bit cheeky. Sorry to be a nuisance. Well, not sorry really. Seemed like a good idea at the time. Just remembered your place, thought it was a bit of a ruse, though...well, didn't think, I suppose.'

'No, nothing like that, nobody's after me. Least I don't think so,' Stonie said. 'Just trying to pick up the pieces; know how it is when you've been out of town for a few weeks. Haven't seen many people lately.' Stonie fell silent, unsure what to say next. Zach's presence was adding another thread, knitting new memories into his waking hours. He would make little appraisals, lists. Kate flew kites. Her 'hello' was always full on the lips, and those lips always tasted of strawberries. Gem drove a Porsche. Guaranteed to organise everyone. The latest discovery, Kate and her PhD: Dr. Kate. That was a new one. And the idea about the stars. Zach, sitting here. Had the breeding, the background; loved details, was full of wonder, travelled. Artist extraordinaire. Stonie steeled himself. There was more to add to the list. The world he inhabited was expanding. Any minute there would be some new revelation about his own life, something would wave over him, something he ought to know about; a stupid, inconsequential detail. And he would fake it. With enough time, he could fake it, absorb it into the facts. Yet there were always doubts. Perhaps this was no social call.

Zach's task was simple. Find out the contents of the package. Not the ashes; the tag, the information, any photographs, anything unusual. There must be a connection. Battjes wanted results. 'Black,' he shouted through. 'Yeh, I remember.' Stonie stood up, walked over to the window and drew the curtain gently to one side, positioning himself against the wall. He tilted his head to peer out through the slit. It was the distinctive move of the best cloak and dagger movies. It had the foreign film about it. Soon he'd be speaking in sub-titles, leaning his forearm against the mantelpiece, caressing a packet of Gauloises and staring at a cracked black and white photograph of some swimsuit couple with their smiling arms around each other's necks. He'd probably tap a cigarette two or three times each end in close up and touch it delicately to his lips before the soundtrack exploded as the match rasped across the box and burst into life; then silence, while the camera felt its way through the smoke to find the mascara stained eyes of his about-to-be-jilted lover.

There was nothing beyond the window but rooftops and a glimpse of the end of the cul-de-sac. Lock No.13 was empty. One street lamp was broken. There was a light behind the yellow curtain on the third window of the second narrow boat in the cut. There was never a light on in the narrow boat at this time in the morning. There had to be a reason. Stonie had always lacked one thing in life – the ability to *not care*. 'Life is a comedy to those who think and a tragedy to those who feel' – rang loud in his sub-conscious and he lived permanently in the tragedic. So, there was someone out there, in the cut, slinking around, awaiting their moment of triumph. Waiting to say, 'He's the one', he did it', though he never had the faintest idea what he was guilty of; he smoothed out the curtain and turned to the perplexed figure of his companion.

'You can have the sofa', I'll find a duvet or something'

Zach slumped down on the cushions with a sigh, hooked one foot behind the other and flicked off his shoes. There was no point in sleeping. The hours amounted to fending off some scratchy foreign news station that was seeping through from next door while puffing up the threadbare sofa cushions. He threw off the travel blanket and rolled out onto the carpet. Stonie's jacket was on the floor where he had dropped it; his trousers were hanging on the door knob. He could see through the open door to where Stonie was snoring at the world, loud enough to mask his movements. Zach decided to take the risk and began rifling through Stonie's pockets. He could make it look as if he was picking things up, folding, tidying after him. There was a photograph: it was a cowboy re-enactment; Stonie, complete with badly fitting headgear and awful make-up. You can be a proud Indian without all that ridiculous fakery, Zach thought: Hollywood has a lot to answer for. There were scraps of paper – bus tickets, a receipt for dry cleaning, a list of classical music albums. He gathered up the loose pieces of paper and stuffed them back in as random a way as they had fallen out – surely no one would have noted the order to such a degree. He had his back to the open door and glanced round; more snoring – he was safe, so far. He decided to risk the wallet: notes, bank guarantee card, a compliment slip for Candice Judson Dance Company – Private Lessons – local, with scribbled prices - surely not line-dancing; a couple of insurance broker cards – all very boring, Zach thought. He was pushing his luck and it felt slightly unnecessary. Then there was a faint shine from the top, inside pocket; a clear plastic sleeve. He eased it out to find that it contained a map. That seemed worth a look.

In the half-light of the bedroom, Stonie rolled and grunted, enough to frighten Zach into dropping the jacket onto the handle before he had taken a proper look. Zach froze for a moment, then slid the sleeve out and turned it towards the table lamp. It looked like a detailed ordnance survey map, but it was definitely not British. He steadied himself and peered closer. There were Interstate symbols, Mexican sounding names, some lines drawn in biro. On the uppermost folded section, the numbers which were ringed were 45 and 69 and there were arrows pointing away from a couple of names towards the fold: one from Maricopa and the other from Cocopah. What was Stonie doing with a detailed foreign map in his pocket? Zach could feel himself breathing more heavily, wondered how noisy he had become; he was taking too much time, paying too much attention. A loud cough signalled the end of the rummage, causing Zach to thrust the map deep into the jacket pocket and move back a few feet across the carpet. Stonie slept on. The first real opportunity and pretty much no clues, Zach thought, but the adrenalin had kicked in. He would need to take another look, if possible, try to make something out of it. This was an unexpected opportunity.

He decided to try one more pocket. He knew the way to stay ahead; information. He fiddled with an appointment card; it was the Neurology Department of the local hospital, full of fastidious small writing. He squinted. There were entries every two weeks for the past two months, with the latest two days hence. He stuck the card back with a real twinge: a brain tumour, long-term drug damage, Parkinson's? Who was this *mate* of his in any case. The muscles between his shoulders had locked tight; he could feel a brittle, edgy tension creeping over him. This was not right. He needed the money but this was not right. Zach sat back on the edge of the sofa, surveying the tiny bedsit, trying to gather together what he thought he knew. Perhaps it was one pocket too far. The yield, however, was beyond what he had expected. Strange, unconnected details. He addressed Stonie in his head. The stuff we don't know about each other, eh? Wrapped up in our own survival… all these dramas being played out around us; what do we know about anyone's history, it's all so…I mean, dressing up as a Red Indian; who would have thought? There was no time to write it down. He would have to make notes from memory, have other conversations, listen out for connections. They would have to do something, together. Perhaps a short trip, sustained proximity, ease of revelation. But he was due back in thc statcs. Battjes wanted something, anything. They were running out of patience.

Wk.1418
53° 23.2' N   1° 47.7' W

'So let me get this right. The San Diego people told you where you came from?' Zach was trying to read Stonie's expression, but Stonie was standing up, against the sky, back lit. Zach was looking for a clue, certain it was some kind of wind up, some kind of spoiler. Sometimes, he felt sure Stonie was in complete control of his past. Anyhow, he was finding him more and more difficult to process, more difficult to be in mode. He was irritated. This time, he could hear himself. The voice measured, the practiced art of faking it, biding time, nothing out of the ordinary. But he was growing increasingly disillusioned with what he was doing, wishing he'd never taken on the assignment.

'Well...yeh...the guys in Yuma didn't have any of my things. I didn't have anything anyway. Everything was taken. It was the medics who began to piece it together from interviews as far as I know. Fragments of conversation. The right kind of questions, I guess. Over a number of weeks, maybe a number of months. I'm sure I was in LA for a time...didn't ask. Funny thing, that, I've never asked. Maybe I don't want to know how long I was lost.'

Stonie was engaging with the world by degrees. He liked it that way. Always had. Now he had an excuse. Perverse, or just mildly affecting, the notion of eccentricity had never occurred to him, but maybe this was what it amounted to. Life was made up of momentary lapses in concentration. For Zach, it was a brain tumour. A rogue gene. A flaw. A deliberate ploy. For Stonie, it was at once a game, then a very real one-sided conversation regarding his survival. He had a choice. In his more forgiving moments, it did not matter which. Private words were a nuisance.

For now, working their narrow boat through Knowle, Zach had more immediate preoccupations. The plan was vague, but nothing to worry about; they would know when to stop. In the past few days, he'd made no mention of what else he knew of Stonie. There had been conversations; he'd come close; but he knew when to hold back.

'Surely there has to be someone, some agency who has records here?'

'Haven't got that far. Never was on the electoral register, never voted.' Stonie said. 'No police record. Can you imagine it, I mean...I go into the local police station, smile politely and say, hey can you tell me who I am, do I exist or what? Sure.'

'But what about your family? What about missing persons stuff?' The engine stuttered as Zach throttled back and began to tuck in towards the bank. There was just enough clearance for an on-coming narrow boat to edge past with the customary greeting and clipped news of water traffic. Stonie registered nothing at the mention of family.

'I don't know how to ask people who I am. Don't feel that strong, Zach.' He paused. He knew he was opening up. Sometimes he would steel himself against a revelation, some tiny fragment so huge it would overwhelm him. There was only so much self-realisation you could take. Zach had laughed at that idea. He had made a joke of it. Stonie dropped his arm and tipped across the side of the rail to let his fingers trail in the water.

'Hey, careful; don't lean over too far, you'll get your fingers squashed. It's my insurance. I don't want a casualty on my hands.' Zach was master. He had his hands on the tiller.

'Okay, okay,' Stonie said. 'Well I was driven up here by personnel from Brize Norton, of all people. I didn't understand the military connection at the time, still don't, really. Bit of a VIP I was. I had a B&B for a week or two till someone found me the flat in the mews. I must say, that bit seemed the worst. Being left on my own. Now there's the thing, they must have known it was my own place. All part of the rehab, I suppose.' He stretched out his legs and leaned back to feel the full tremble of the narrow boat. Four and a half miles an hour. It was the right pace to get in touch with the world, reassuring; he could cope with that, taking stock. He could deal with the action. Stonie was more used to other people being in control. Yet he was beginning to sense a hunger, some kind of prompting to take the initiative.

'So what don't you remember?' Zach enquired in all seriousness.

'Yeh, yeh. You being funny? How would I know?' Stonie answered, letting out a long, contented sigh. This was a day to savour. He was out and about, feeling confident. He was being trusted with himself. Zach's idea, and so far, a good one. On canal matters, he didn't mind being told what to do. He didn't know how he would deal with Hatton Locks, but that was an hour away and anyway, Zach had the knowledge. Stonie closed his eyes. There were things to confess; that's the way he felt, but closing his eyes wouldn't help. He took a deep breath and picked out an overhanging branch to focus on.

'I lived close to the cut. I think I had given up my job, but I don't remember what I'm good at; I do know where I earned a living but I hardly dare go back to the agency to ask what I did there. Not yet. Funny that; you'd think it would all piece together. There's stuff about in the flat that would tell me, but I haven't looked all that closely. Don't have the urge.' Stonie looked sheepishly across at Zach. He knew it seemed implausible, but he really didn't care. This time he didn't care.

'Clever guys, those psychiatrists or whatever they are. I mean, letting you loose back in your own space, even if you didn't recognise it at first,' Zach said. 'Must have known you were capable of making your own way.' Stonie nodded.

'Nobody seems to recognise me much when I'm out and about, you know. See, they all keep to themselves, even in these so-called inner city communities. Admittedly, I haven't really been out much. Just to collect some money.'

'Yep, recognising our own space; interesting idea.' Zach said. 'So what's in yours now, then? I mean, what kind of things are in it?' He was ready to try anything. Stonie looked uncomfortable with the question and ignored it.

'I can't get back to where I was; maybe I don't want to. Don't know who to ask in any case. My counsellor suggested I keep a record of what I find out. Said it would all come back, eventually. I mean, how do I know who to ask? Anyhow, how much do I need to know about who I am? It's too much trouble keeping notes.'

'Medics?' Zach needed to pace himself. He already had information; both of them were trying to piece together the same story. 'So it's a blank? Bits of it not there? I don't get it.' Zach said, with a theatrical nod of the head. He didn't know if he was pushing too hard.

'Strange thing the brain.'

Stonie made his way tentatively, hand on roof rail, towards the bow of the boat.

'Well, I found you where you used to live.' Zach shouted. 'Same house.'

'Yeh, but I didn't know that at first; you are telling me what you know. I'm having a hard time trying to piece together the last few months. It was all a blank. I pick up books and they're not mine; I roll back the duvet, it's not mine; I find a blender in the kitchen, it's not mine. The window onto the street, it is unfamiliar territory. The phone rings and for a moment I find myself saying wrong number. Nothing feels owned. Only tiny little moments have a history. It's like everyone is telling me who I am and I'm having to believe them. Makes me a lot of different people. It's...it's all very weird.'

The conversation became more fragmented, each of the boaters willingly distracted by the rich grassy swells and willow-strewn edges of the journey: a heron rising in slow motion to tangle with the yellowing tufts of broom; a couple of excited children leaning dangerously over the crumbling stone parapet waving them on through bridge No. 5; ducks and coots sidling out of reach as they cut through the tension of the faintly oiled surface ahead of them. Zach stooped to avoid a dipping bough as he lined up the narrow boat for the wider section of the canal up ahead. To Stonie, Zach's tone was slightly mocking. Stonie needed to be taken seriously. Zach was logical, wanted explanations. There was no forgiveness in logic – and Stonie felt he needed to be understood, to be waited on: courted, not questioned. It was significant enough what you reveal to yourself.

On the nearby country lane, an ageing Triumph Herald was lurching forward at approximately four and a half miles an hour, the low stutter of its engine muffled by the high hedgerow and the purr of the boat. The car eased itself onto the gravel edge and crept to a halt, tucked in against the hawthorn. Waiting. The driver had sight of the narrow boat again – through a long, wide stretch this time –

tapering ahead through a gap in the hedge, across a small, mole-ridden field. The lady silenced the engine and took out a notebook from the glove compartment. It was easier staking out by car. It was a private world. Unaccountable. At the Old Crown, she was conspicuous. At church, she would be judged for not listening.

Zach was sensing a distance in the way Stonie reeled off the facts, his mind as much on Stonie's expression as on the far bank. How much was invention he could hardly tell. The day was warming up, the countryside easy on the eye. But he was becoming increasingly uncomfortable in his role. After a few moments of silence, he spoke.

'I just can't get my head round this. I have to go over it again, just for my own sanity. You disappear. Probably everyone thinks you're busy or your company has sent you abroad or you got fed up with your mates and took up with another crowd. That's what you said at first, right? And now, this…this crazy story about a missing chunk of your life. Intriguing.'

Stonie nodded but said nothing. 'I take it you're still seeing a doctor or shrink or something, just to make sure it's all going in the right direction?' Zach checked himself. Too personal.

'Not really,' Stonie replied, rather cagily. 'It's all going in the right direction now.'

'Yeh, well who knows what's normal in any case, eh?' It was rhetorical and went unacknowledged. 'My, I just love these Midland canals,' Zach continued. He was not waiting for an answer this time. The mention of Midlands prompted an immediate reaction in Stonie. Gemima. Another flash back. Another fragrance. He was at the Midland Hotel. He was telling her about his future, about getting away. He was not telling her why.

'Yes, it definitely is all getting back to the way it used to be' Stonie went on. 'And I have to say, you have been a great help – well, that is, when you've been here.' Stonie watched for a reaction and steadied himself as the boat gently nudged the bank. The engine noise was soporific, comforting; the relaxing massage of the boards, up through his palms, his thighs, the soles of his feet. He positioned himself against the cabin wall, lay back, rested his head on the edge of the bench and began to close his eyes. He could feel the crinkled peeling paint against the side of his face, smell the diesel and the damp rope and the squeak of the rusting hinges. He was looking up, out; his world reduced to the tips of slow moving trees and passing clouds, the occasional crow and sparrow. Somehow he knew there would be no drama now, just the warm, unhurried acceptance of the faintly familiar. He was having pictures. It was coming back to him.

'Next thing you'll be swearing on an alien abduction.' Zach hammed up the alien abduction. At once he could feel it was entirely the wrong pitch. Stonie laughed this time but Zach could feel he was losing it. Stonie looked over and gave a wry smile.

'Confused. Been more than confused, I'd have to say.' But he was no longer confused. He could remember Mica, and for the moment, that was all that mattered.

Not for the first time, Zach felt self-conscious, guilty. He said nothing after that. Guiding the craft had to come first. He revved the engine for no reason.

'I've been frightened, to be honest with you.' Stonie spoke slowly. 'It's all there, in hiding... bits of my life. It's like...episodes. But connecting them together... something happened - ' Stonie's voice tailed off again. Zach could not make up his mind if this was building to something traumatic or was merely for effect. The unfinished sentences were the worst. The temptation was to fill in, to tell Stonie what he knew. 'It just didn't register when I wanted it to, Zach. But I'm beginning to believe it's all there. I get glimpses of what I think is missing. Anyhow, I guess I drift with the good bits.'

'Ah, selective memory. Great game,' Zach said. The comment made Stonie angry, nervous. He began clambering back to the tiller.

'No game, my friend. But admittedly, other people's stories remind me of my own, and I go looking inside my head.' Stonie countered, then hesitated, distracted by almost losing his balance. 'Actually, I don't know what I mean by that. But I do know that it wasn't alien stuff. That's taking it too far.' He felt more confident; acknowledging the existence of Mica, the end of Mica, why he had cut loose in the first place, the good intentions for the trip - that he had enough reason.

The last threads of mist were rolling out of the shadows of the overhangs on the canal, curling round the reeds, wisping their way through the late morning sun. From his low angle, Stonie could see the banks were more manicured, the weeds cropped to reveal an ancient edge of weathered stone, the occasional rusted tie-up ring. A few feet from the bank, the hedge had become fence, painted and looked after. The towpath was being found, reclaimed.

'Sorry,' Zach said. 'Sorry. Didn't mean to make light of it. Better get yourself right up to the front and grab that rope now. You'll need to leap off onto the bank in a minute - at the right moment, when we ease into the side.' Zach throttled back as the boat rounded a slow curve to reveal The Navigator. Time to glide into lunch...

'Lord, I'm hungry. It's these bloody locks. It's all the exertion' Zach was speaking with his mouth full. 'Pass the pepper, would you?' Stonie saw the break as a chance to take charge, put a few things straight. The emotional metronome was tick-tocking it's way through his subconscious. But at least, now there was a rhythm. He knew he was having a hard time keeping up with Zach's questions, the persistent teasing out and Zach's quiet insistence. Time to go for it. The public space didn't matter. Another pub, another towpath, as familiar and strange as they had ever been.

'Right. Within two weeks we were lovers.' There was a determination in Stonie's voice. 'Jay and I were convinced we knew all there was to know about each other. There were no wild claims of devotion. It was all animal without the destiny.' Stonie dried up as he glanced over at Zach, looking for clues to how he was being received. He leaned across the table and fixed Zach with a stare, saying don't interrupt, let me get started, it's my turn to lead. He could sense he was walking into the spotlight. He had rehearsed his lines. He could hear the applause. Zach waited. When nothing happened, he spoke up.

'You mean you fell in love with an American accent? The lady was living dangerously and you were being opportunist.' Stonie looked surprised.

'How did you know she is American, *was* American? I didn't say...haven't talked about - '

'Yeh, well you said it, sure you did.' Zach stiffened; a moment of muted panic. Part of the job. A reminder to be careful what he revealed.

'Well anyway, she had those liquid eyes, bloody teasing mouth; one of those hair-flicking smiles – and she smelled of…yeh, well you know.' Stonie was waxing eloquent on the rush. This was new, dangerous. Every frame brought her closer. 'I tore up the pictures of her, of course, her photographs. Did I tell you that? I tore them up. Couldn't stand living with them.' In his head it was no longer a face of pure, innocent beauty but a mask; sallow cheeks, a calculating smile, a knowing look caught behind those flowing locks, the mystery he was powerless to ignore. She always knew what she was doing to him. Right from that first moment on the train.

'And you couldn't help yourself, I know. What else was a guy to do, right?' Stonie looked up to find what he thought was the faintest of leering smiles.

'Could say that,' Stonie answered. 'But she was hardly an innocent abroad. There was always a sense of danger. Guess it had all the hallmarks of an ill-planned recce. Somehow you'll make it back, somehow all the points can be plotted to reveal the bigger picture. It's just the destination that's missing.' Stonie took a breath. 'Anyhow, you're jealous.'

'Yeh, well, don't want too much detail, do I? Not good for me.'

Stonie seemed comfortable in his confessional free-fall, hurtling into a fanciful world of what might have been. Embellishing, leaving stuff out. Back and forth. It might be difficult to sort out truth from fiction after all. Nothing new there. All he knew was that the memories were bringing him alive, making his fingers tips tingle. There seemed to be a physical connection with his past. Zach had noted the change of pace.

'Yeh, well, there were all those barely disguised mysteries, real teasers, like her troubled school years in Boston, the 'incident' at Ann Arbour, the Italian connections. There seemed to be so many lopped off branches of the family tree. And her father, Jay used to dismiss father with a one-liner so cut and dried there was no possible way to continue. Died in the military. The tone warned me not even to attempt sympathy. I just couldn't get my head around the silences, and those were the deepest of all.'

'Pretty intense, then?' Zach said. He recalled some of this from his briefing. But there were new leads, embellishments. He had to remind himself, they didn't know what item they were looking for, how the information had been rendered. The two friends were interrupted by the food and drinks, both of them leaning back in their chairs as the waitress systematically emptied her tray. This was a good moment for Stonie to choose his next revelation.

'Yeh, well she was nuts about e.e. cummings and Antoine de Saint-Exupéry.' Stonie began again, this time between mouthfuls. 'That did it for me.'

'Do me a favour,' Zach said, 'You wouldn't have noticed if she'd spoken logorithms at you in Mandarin.' He paused to pick a fish bone from his teeth, rather pleased with the compound image. Stonie ignored the observation. He was in a serious frame of mind and hardly reacted to the provocation. He was in discovery mode.

'Pastrami, she ate buckets of it. Sucked ice cubes, knew loads of Sinatra's lyrics, lines from Uncle Vanya, the Beatitudes, in that order.' Zach made no attempt to break in. It didn't really matter how the past emerged, only if it was truth or fiction. The trouble was, once it was gone, it was all fiction. Minutes passed before he interrupted.

'Love at first sight, then?' he asked.

'Love at all costs.' Stonie said. The pictures were increasingly uncomfortable. 'The moral low ground, body and soul with body in the ascendancy.'

'That's because you're an artist, Stonie. I mean. Look at Rodin. Takes the highest form of worship to transcend mere sex. Or is it the highest form of sex to transcend mere worship? Any road, you were religious about it, right?' Stonie looked bemused. 'Screwed all his models, didn't he?' Zach said.

'Oh really? I wouldn't know. Anyhow, why am I telling you this? What's that got to do with it? Nothing to do with being an artist, writer, whatever.'

'Everything to do with it. The pursuit of art is a form of surrogate spirituality and so is sex. Everyone knows that. As fundamental to our search for meaning, for fulfilment. Deny ourselves and we are incomplete.'

Stonie stared at Zach open-mouthed. 'What are you talking about? Do you want to - ' He stopped in mid sentence, chewing for a moment to let the agitation subside. Zach said nothing, waiting for Stonie to compose himself. After a moment or two, Stonie began again.

'Well, anyhow, know the first thing I ever heard her say, the first word?'

Zach fidgeted. The balance, as ever, was how to be a professional as well as a friend.

'Umpteenth. Now is that surreal or what? Umpteenth. One single word in a pool of silence. Out of the blue and definitely directed towards me.' Stonie was attacking his meal with renewed vigour, head down, mechanical, each portion a deliberate act of survival. With his head gently rocking from side to side, he carried on talking. 'The way I was feeling on that train when she - ' The fork of food was almost on his lips as the sound drained away. He lowered it slowly to his plate, his mouth still open, a look of wide-eyed incredulity spreading over his face. 'That was it. That was the moment, the first time I laid eyes on her,' he said quietly. 'The train back from London. The train - '

'Yeh, I got that bit' Zach said quietly, trying not to disturb the flow.

Stonie took his knife and slowly scraped the food off the fork back onto the plate, as if to begin again creating the picture in his mind. He leaned against the back of his chair, took a deep breath and looked straight at Zach. 'God she was a teaser. I mean, not sexually. Playful, I'd say - and you knew you were up for the game. Well, there were rewards. Nobody in their right mind would walk away, would they? Not…no… you just - ' Once again, there was silence. Stonie had run out of memory, overdosed on the emotion of the moment, enough to register. He went quite still, his face closing down, his breathing slower.

'You okay?' Zach said, reaching forward to touch Stonie's arm. Zach didn't do much touching, not these days, but this was different. He needed to connect, to make sure this was not some precursor to isolation, to a complete shut out. He could not feel the guilt; that was what worried him most. He had the picture of an eagle targeting his prey from a great height, soaring, distant on the thermals, wings poised against the gale. Still, but still moving. He wanted to be closer. There was, after all, the beginnings of a tear.

Stonie sat with his hands spread out on either side of his plate, palms down, as if waiting for some signal, for permission to continue with his meal. After a few moments, Zach broke the silence. 'Getting cold, mate. Eat up. I'll get another couple of pints in. Better still, how about a bottle of wine? No, two.'

Stonie could hear the patter and shuffle of birds on the roof. He squinted at his watch; five minutes to two. He eased his ear off the pillow and pressed his head hard against the inner skin of the narrow boat. Whispers, the muted rasping of wood on wood, his own blood coursing into his brain, the wake from some industrious water rodent; it was all set to amplify through the space he imagined was his, the emerging echoes of an unfamiliar world. He was looking for markers, touchstones: the stars through the glass, the black, black sky, the edge of something. He was always looking for the edge of something. He pressed his forehead against the moist window; cool against the wine glow. The shock made him swallow, it was the slime of old merlot, the slake of a palate in desperate thirst, the sudden realisation that there was saliva drooling down the right side of his chin. But his mouth felt dry, grainy. Last time he'd woken like that was on some droning, dust-blown highway, staring out of a jeep at a huge spattered sky. The last time, he was also in chains. The same sense of fear caught him for an instant, shook him wide awake. He sat up and swung his legs out over the side of the bunk, wrapping his hands around both ankles. No manacle. His feet brushed against a small sheet of notepaper. He gripped it between both big toes, bent his knees and eased it up until he could reach it. So he had been writing.

'We lost count of all those morning suns on naked breast, skin taut and silky, those motes caught in the first beams as we looked out on the world; sparrows scratching crumbs on the window sill, the first buzz of a house fly; that suspended moment of decision – face the day, or drift beyond the tree line, the hollow blue fingernail of moon hanging in the rush hour air, the barking, muffled edge; out into that elusive nothingness. We lost track of all those stars rising past the slit in the window at dusk. Cold coffee cups, full, untouched; the odd rich digestive crunched into the carpet, the phone off the hook, legs between legs, the ceiling cracks widening. No sensation; no guilt. Months went by'

'Mmm.' Stonie's audible murmur tickled his lips. He lay back with his head at an awkward angle, forcing his chin against his chest, then wriggled himself flat, his feet pushing down into his cocoon. Somewhere between midnight and Lapworth he was back in the only safe place, if he was honest, the only safe place he knew:

Mica was making a breakfast announcement, one of her infrequent assessments of what point they had reached in their relationship. 'Post flower power licence.' She was dressed and ready for college, ready for a fight. She would stand in the same place, with her coat on, her back to the sink, the small of her back hard against the edge of the kitchen-top, moving her body gently, cradling her cup of coffee in both hands, her head down, shoulders rounded enough to tumble her hair across her face. Her pose.

'That's where we are.' He said nothing. It was always best to hold back.

'You like Sonny Terry and Brownie McGee and I like Neil Diamond.' He had considered a pre-emptive strike before war was declared, searching for something meaningful to say, something to ensure fair play. Guns of peace. Nothing came. Both of them were desperately trying to avoid the first mistake of the day. He did not need reminding. That was the pattern. He was in love with a stranger. That gnawing fact rankled. Was it the Boston chic, the New Jersey frisson she somehow managed between them? Here was a new distraction - the morning conversations which would peter out. Guaranteed. Conversations where the butter knife would come to a halt halfway across the toast, glued to the bread, as some deeper truth dawned. Then there would be a sigh.

'We lived on a military base. All rules and regulations, mostly adult company. Nothing for us kids.' She would look as if she'd forgotten how to spread the butter, staring emptily out of the window. 'He'd be in the house, my father that is, but the only time you knew it was when he'd shout at me or when he pointed at things that were out of place. He remembered everything that was out of place. You just don't know what that was like.'

'Go on,' Stonie would urge.

'I…I…well –'

The mention of father. That would be the signal. She would rise from the breakfast table and move slowly to the kitchen sink to wash her hands, thoroughly wash her hands – as if in some ritual cleansing, as if ridding herself of some stain. Then she would whirl around and say something like 'look, I can't talk about this, can't talk about…him. Upsets me. Should have known better.' Then silence. More than once, she would finish it off, walking away muttering to herself. 'Good old Canaletto,' she would say in a tone which warned, don't go there. Stonie could recall this detail. Canaletto. Somewhere inside his head, he was beginning to make connections.

The berth was a safe place for now, the duvet up over his chin, his hands behind his head, staring up at the low ceiling of the narrow boat. He had worked out the way things were. How the end came. Say she was off in the morning with a lightness in her step: she would come back home to the flat and the minute he heard the key in the door, he knew he was cut out.
Something in the timing, the deliberation. The day was over for him. 'Canaletto' would have set off three days of random shut-out between them. They would drift from room to room without eye contact. Stonie would leave notes. Mica never left notes. There were rules. He learned to say nothing; no body language; no pent up frustration spilling out as he opened stubborn biscuit tin lids or wrestled with the length of his tie in the morning. They would eat separately. At night, on those nights, they made love in silence. It was perfunctory, a mime show; imperfectly choreographed. He would punish her by being with another woman in his head – only for one fleeting second - till the fatuous, unhealthy truth of it dawned on him. She would be brittle, but never break, her angry body on the offensive. Then, in slow motion, the dancing would begin; the dance of accommodation. There would be intense, intimate glances; the occasional shuffle, the lingering touch; a hot mug of coffee waiting for him when he came through to the kitchen in the morning, a comment about a voice on the radio, a reluctant smile. A softening. It had to be neutral; the lifting of something heavy or the discovery of lost keys - that would suffice: the wry, replaced by the unguarded: a flower on the pillow, two places set at table. But it was no green light to pry. It was the other Mica; more like Jay, the one on the train; the voice in his head saying, this is all you will ever know; don't ask, for the umpteenth time, just do not ask.

Stonie stretched out, clasped his hands behind his head and arched his back. He was tense, and the thin mattress of the bunk bed hardly absorbed the tension. He breathed in, as slowly and deeply as his tired body would allow. The tiny lamp had dimmed. He should have known better than keep this going, now that his memory seemed to be in free-fall. Yet he hadn't known how to go back, how to find the story.

Letters from America began arriving, post-marked Yuma, Arizona; letters Mica never opened. They would be propped up on the toaster, moved behind the vase for the day, then stashed on the top shelf, above the coat hooks, well back, jammed between the electric meter and the cupboard wall in the hallway. It would take the letters three days to reach this point. He had grown tired of asking what was going on; it was simply another opportunity for Mica to be evasive. There seemed to be no common future and no shared past; just one continuous, numbing present, stripped of that rich sense of journey. Mica was tiring of him. He knew that much.

Stonie could see himself trailing behind her through the flat, shouting 'What kind of game are we playing here?' and blurting out 'enough is enough'. It was a mistake to think he could force Mica to confront her ghosts. Every time he tried… The thought drew him back to the present, staring at the wood grain ceiling of the narrow boat, his face covered up to his nose in duvet. It was time to make some coffee. He eased himself down through the boat to the galley and lit the gas under the kettle. The next lucid moment came as the steam sang from the open nozzle. There were moments like this – tracks of time when there was nothing in his mind, nothing he could go back over. Then Mica was there. Something about her was always there, lingering. Even after all this time. He finished stirring the drink and made his way out under the awning.

The night clouds were breaking up in places to reveal a lighter sky. The bench was cold and damp, but the air was sharp and fresh; he drew in deeply. It was good finally to be taking charge of things, making decisions. He could have his memories, survive the present, live with his waking dream. Was some of it made up? In the wrong order? That did not seem to matter anymore. He had crossed his bridge into the past. He was deep in thought when Zach stumbled out onto the open deck, squinting at the early morning light.

'You look worse than I feel,' Stonie said, greeting him with a tepid mug of coffee. 'Here, I'm on my third; couldn't sleep. I made this for you just in case.'

'Yeh, well, wine and me - '

'Wine and I,' Stonie said. The cool of the canal had sharpened him. There was a roll of mist creeping off the surface, swirling up through the roots of the trees to meet the first rays of sunlight. He felt good about talking, he decided. He would talk more.

'Must you be so pedantic?' Zach asked, only half expecting an answer.

'I have to be,' Stonie answered. 'I have to be. I have to pick over everything… and…. I've made a decision.'

'Like going back to bed. It's only 6.30am,' Zach cut in. '…far too early to begin the rest of my life, or is it the rest of your life. I don't care. Can't this wait?' Stonie ignored him. He felt no fatigue, no hangover.

'I was completely baffled at the time.' Stonie began. 'About how it all came to an end. I blame Canaletto.' The voice was matter-of-fact. Zach let out a long, deliberate sigh and sat down on the edge of the boat.

'Canaletto? For God's sake, what's the painter got to do with anything?' There was this photograph, Stonie was about to say. A photograph with strange scratchy writing on the back of it. Still got it. But the sentence petered out in his head. 'Sure this can't wait? Hardly awake, you know. Need the tail of the dog, that sort of thing.'

Stonie looked over at him, fixed him with a determined stare but said nothing for a moment or two. His heart was racing. Time to go back to Mica. Back to the reason for walking away from everything.

'So, what's the riddle this time, Stonie? I'm ready as I'll ever be,' Zach responded, with mock resignation.

'No, I'm serious; take me seriously; I want to get this out of my system. I'm trying to draw a line under it, closed chapter, whatever. I need to lay down a marker. You're the one who's been badgering me. Anyhow, you're the only one within earshot.' Zach ran his fingers though his hair. It was going to be a long morning. 'Can't you see I'm trying to get back to normal life?'

'Before breakfast?' Zach yawned. He already knew the answer.

'Three years of my life came to an end just before we met. I was angry. You have no idea how much of a rage - ' Stonie stopped for a moment and took a deep breath of air. A slow breath of air.

'So who or what was Canaletto?' Zach asked. The tone was resigned, detached.

'Look, you've got memories, right? Try stringing them together, I mean all the small, seemingly insignificant stuff. One thing that took place before or after something else, who knew whom, was it someone else's story or pure invention? Who you were with at a particular time, place, event. You find yourself having to go back and check what went on in your own life, when or if somebody was in your life at all. It gets tricky.' Zach remained silent. Jay and I were living together, right? It was kind of falling apart. Just tiny things, but enough to unsettle. Then these letters started coming through the post for her, but she never opened them. Just never opened them. Can you imagine; just piled them up, for God's sake. Seemed like hundreds of them and she wouldn't explain anything to me.' Stonie looked up. 'Right, okay, yeh, yeh, I've already told you that.'

'Yup.' Zach said. He was distracted. He wanted to find a phone box. He was trying to picture the last mile or so of water, the lane where it touched the canal, the conversation; had he said anything. He was thousands of miles away, explaining his failure to Battjes, how he had drawn a blank so far. How he had made a mistake. Battjes could have his money back. There would be other deals. Canals, oh yeh, at the Stedelijk, arguing with Kees Vuyk over a gallery show, trying to remember his Dutch. Where did that come from? This is when he did not like his brain, what it did to him. Tell me something, Stonie – when is Jay Mica and when is Mica Jay. Or was it San Diego, before the offer? I can put things right.

A duck squawked up from the reeds and echoed round the canopy of willow, startling both men. Stonie rose from the bench.

'I need a top up.'

'I'm listening, honest,' Zach said. 'The letters.' It was his job to be grateful for any information, always hopeful that there would be enough to piece Stonie together, get what he wanted; what *they* wanted. He leaned back and tipped the dregs of his coffee over the side.

'Well, I would follow her through the kitchen door as she ceremoniously propped up the first letter of the week. There might have been two or three in one week, sometimes none. But it became a ritual. I'd be ready to grab the envelope and tear it open. I mean, it was weird, bizarre. But I didn't; there was a line to cross so I didn't and she wouldn't explain what she was up to. I tell you, I was losing it. So bloody annoyed. I just couldn't leave it alone; well, could *you*?' Zach looked across and nodded vaguely.

‘So, was she beautiful? I mean, really drop dead gorgeous?’

‘What on earth has that got to do with it?’ Stonie said. He was irritated. ‘Don’t even ask. I tore up every image of her, remember?’ He was trying to concentrate on the events, the sequence. He needed to make sure he’d got it right. It was a serious issue, understanding the distinction between the truth and his imagination.

‘I was so beside myself one morning over breakfast, I swept the lot off the table, every damn thing, every piece of crockery. Smashed. Didn’t feel any better. She just came back into the kitchen laughing and put her umbrella up. Completely random, then she said something like “Oh yeh, it’s bad luck to get it up in the kitchen.” and we’d both laugh awkwardly and she was gone for the day; I was left in my own mess.’

Zach didn’t feel like pushing the joke any further. It was the kind of memory to memorise, keep ready. He looked along the canal, as if searching for inspiration, for the next question, watching the faint wisps rolling off the surface of the water. Every so often the low sun would fire yellow darts through the drifting mist. Lines of light. Zach sensed he had to hold back, wait for more from Stonie rather than push too hard. He offered the odd murmur, a sympathetic nod of the head. It felt right to be vocal.

‘I’d say, “Look we have to talk” right?’ Stonie went on, ‘and she’d say “Ah, the letters; one-a-week is a bad week and three is a good week, dear” or something like that and she’d be off with a sing-songy “Byee” and I’d be shouting after her “For God’s sake, Mica”…well, Jay to you, “For God’s sake, we have to sort this out” and all that would come back was “Not now, not a good time” and I’d be left there in the hall somewhere between expletives and tears, saying to myself yeh well maybe there’s never a good time, ever. It was just becoming impossible. I knew we’d lost it.’ With that, Stonie stood up and stretched. ‘I swear I was being punished for something.’

‘So, was she beautiful?’ Stonie shook his head and said nothing.

Stonie would like to have been Kerouac, he decided. Or Ginsberg. Heading out who knows where with his back to everything, holding court by streams of consciousness, a clutch of unfinished poems and acolytes scattered around him, the angst of self-esteem in his wake. Instead, he could see himself trapped in his kitchen, threatening to steam open some mysterious letter over a boiling kettle in a Moseley bed-sit under slab grey skies, knowing in the end he wouldn't crack, that he would not risk it, not even for peace of mind. He must have walked a mile on the towpath, kicking the odd stone out into the water, running at a squawking duck, picking a berry or two to plop onto the surface. It was a tiny sound. That, and the tinkle of gravel as he scraped it sideways with his foot over the edge and into the canal. The water seemed receptive. Things floated away, or simply disappeared. Nothing else. Nothing stayed. Either way, the surface soon became itself again.

Those letters. Mica had never seemed curious at all about the contents. She must have known who they were from, what they were about and didn't care - or feared them. But none of them were ever torn up, just ceremoniously stashed. Stonie was deep in thought, his pace along the towpath even slower, his gaze more fixed than ever on those soulful weeks. The nights were the worst, lying awake trying to convince himself to let go. It didn't matter; it was none of his business. The argument: how much of each other do we own? That was the prevailing theme. Yet it had seemed not worth trading in for a lonely bed. All those unopened letters. He was almost at a standstill, trailing his feet.

There was Mica, hiding those thin white ankles under silk and talking of angels, dreaming, always in someone else's city, where the sparrows argued between buildings and at dusk, starlings urged the traffic skyward. He'd made a poem of it. They would stay in their room all day, the two of them, and follow the sun as it crossed the floor. Then, as evening folded in on them, they'd watch for stars. That was it. Watching the sky together. He liked telling her to do that. It was their square of sky, wherever they were. Stonie could feel his face change, soften for a moment at the thought. He could smile at the mornings, in the warm light of day, at her walking fingers over his thigh, puppet-toes with biro faces peeping up over the blanket, the art of talking with a nipple in his mouth.

A wave of heat rolled behind his eyes, as if that last morning was being projected through his skull. Stonie felt dizzy. He slumped down, facing the canal, leaned against a concrete fence post, head back, stretched out his arms on either side, and wrapped his fingers around the middle wires to steady himself. The memory had hardened. The barbed wire was cutting into his hands, and he knew it. But it was of no concern. He was entwined with Mica. Somewhere in their muffled laughter, in the gentle rasp of hair on skin, in the silly digressions between thrusts, something snapped. “The scar”. He could still hear his cold, measured voice. “The scar through your breast – how on earth did it get there? I have to know; I really do have to know. You have never told me and I have to know. We have to know everything about each other. No secrets, remember?” He was ear against ear, clutching her shoulders, breathing hard, his nails digging deeper and deeper. Mica twisted out from under him, back arched, knees closing up to her chin. He could see her. She was on her side, rocking, foetal. Then her faint whimpering gave way to silence.

On the towpath, Stonie heaved and looked heavenward. He tried to stop the picture, tried to blank everything out. He was in that silence again, motionless, The silence which haunted him, watching the figure in the room drawing the bed sheet up across Mica’s naked body till her head was covered, standing over the shroud, tracing with his finger down her spine the last folds to fall. The sun was stabbing through the barely open curtains, those familiar sounds, everyone rushing to start their day. Queue, make calls, type memos, fill shopping trolleys, cluster sleepily around bus stops, pick up letters from the mat. How long had he stood in the room, listening to the rustling world beyond, trying to find a still-beat, plotting the path the sun might take across the floor; searching for a language of disintegration.

On the towpath, Zach had walked more than a mile when he spotted Stonie. Now he ran, stumbled towards him, hardly stopping for breath. He was angry. He had already taken the canal track the wrong way. He was hungry. ‘Why you…for God’s sake…there you are. What are you playing at Stonie, taking off? Breakfast, we were about to do breakfast, remember?’ He was still several feet away and shouting when it dawned on him that Stonie wasn’t moving. The figure was crucified against the field, half-hidden by rye grass and rowan, head forward, outstretched arms against the joint, the knees hunched up towards the chest. ‘What the hell? What’s happened? Who did this to you?’ Stonie slowly raised his head. ‘Lord, look at you. How did you get…’ Zach wasn’t expecting an answer. He prised first one hand off the wire, then the other, and, with his forearms through Stonie's armpits, eased him upright, trying to avoid the blood dripping off Stonie's fingertips.

'I'm…I'll be…hey it's my mate Zach'

'You stupid idiot, look at the state you're in. Hey, tears eh? Good for you, just as good as a laugh. Hey, come on.' Stonie was limp, his head tilted to one side. At first, his legs offered no support. Zach waited for a few moments, his hands clasped behind the figure to hold his weight till he sensed Stonie was ready to take control. Gradually Stonie pushed himself straight enough for Zach to release him. He was shivering, biting his lip, muttering something about blood and altars and unintentional sacrifice.

'All cried out, then? Yeh, well Zach's here, yeh maybe we can put things right.' Stonie swayed back against the fence post, drawing in air with shallow, intermittent gasps. His face was gaunt, his puffy eyes barely registering.

'Sorry, mate. Did you bring any plasters?' He made a grimace of a smile as Zach tried to straighten his fingers.

'Good Lord, what kind of masochist - ' Zach stopped there. He knew there was no point in a rant. Something had broken.

Wk. 1440

32º 39' N   89º 57' W

'2323946 did you say?' One more call; yet another lengthy wait. 'One moment please. I have to connect you to another department.' The voice was expressionless. Wendy Soon was running short of dimes but was accustomed to the clipped, monotone responses, the silences. He was always being put on hold, the phone going dead. This time, at least, a second voice cut in. 'Mr. Soon?'

'Yes, Mr. Soon; I am trying to find a friend of mine. I think he came back from Viet Nam in '70 and was pensioned off in Mid West. I lost touch with him. He gave my son his tag as a memento, that is how I have his number. Luca Cambareri, I will spell it for you.' He waited. There were no long shots here. There was nothing. Every voice tailed off, every authority in denial. The lies, the generalisations yielded not one single lead. All those counties, state departments, veterans' associations, GI charities. It was the same at every turn. 'We have no one of that name, I'm afraid.'

The tar strips between the concrete slabs were bubbling, the metal booth was untouchable, the sweat beginning to bead across Wendy Soon's forehead, matting his hair. He had been shifting his stance for almost two hours, determined to beat the arc of the sun. He was sure that with every dog tag there was a soldier, a story, a mother's son. This would be his quest, his destiny, giving back what had been taken away. The utter helplessness of having no voice - the lot of the Indian – this time it would not stand in his way. He had to speak for Blu. He had to follow what was in his spirit. This was the wish of his father. He would know, when the time came, why. Somehow he would know. In the choking heat he was close to tears.

More than once, Wendy Soon was sure he had had enough. What was the point? One chain, a tag and a docile mute. Perhaps the yellowing, dog-ridden Arizona rest home would simply fade into history, with the forlorn, vacant drifter he had picked up and laid down, pacing out the rest of his life between armchairs, in sweet surrender to oblivion. In a way, he *was* Blu, random, helpless, at the mercy of forces beyond his control. He should let well alone. Yet he was drawn to the danger, to the mystery, felt strangely connected. Wendy Soon was beginning to believe he was more than chance. Every day, in his dusty, rolling brushwood alley he would see some ghost tramping between gantries, tinkering with the hydrants, staring through the windows of the bar, waiting for nothing in particular to happen. The sun, at its height, brought silence, inertia – everyone slinking in the deep shadows, disowning the town, hungry for the evening beer and consumed by stultifying boredom.

He was already escaping in his mind. He would no longer be another soul under the stars with no voice, no journey, abandoned. All those phone calls, every cent dropping into the box, it was about dignity, presence, honouring the beating heart. Surely now, to be Quechen was to search. This was something he had forgotten.

The Reservation boasted this one public call box. Wendy Soon knew every stain and flaking scratch of its rusting ribs. He could see continents in the paint, great flood plains and feathered, rain-soaked mountain screes in the distressed metal. In the early mornings, ahead of the heat, he would lean against the thin, panelled frame, long relieved of its glass, and stare at the fading poster, plotting every coloured dot as he held the line. But he had never considered the invitation: the old advert picture exhorting him to try the fast food joint, the only diner for miles. He could see the building through the broken glass, no more than spitting distance from the highway. He'd often looked at the poster of the woman, stared intently into her wide eyes, wondered about her pearl white teeth, that flicking bounce of hair curling onto her shoulder, that steaming food tray, never growing cold. Food, comfort, relief, it was always there, beckoning to him through those hours of drifting in and out of the phone calls, hanging on to a promise, losing himself in the waitress' story. She would have a strong pubis, pale, porcelain breasts. Under that apron, her spikey fur would bristle, her nipples would harden as she moved towards him, her lips would grow moist. The nipples were important; the first oral stimulation for the infant, the first food, the first connection after the severed cord. Forbidden fruit, the white woman – but no one could travel inside his head. He would lie with her inside his head.

And what if he did try this pizza, those fries - the Leaning Tower food? He had no appetite for such dishes. Perhaps it was time. All his phone numbers were used up. For hours each day he had followed any lead, and now, though numbed to the constant rejection, he was indeed ready to give up. He had run out of patience and money and ideas. This was the afternoon he would step free of the booth for the last time and admit defeat. He could see Blu pacing between the armchairs in that grey glow, hear the barbed comments of the nurses in their sinister world. He knew they would make sport of him. And in another year, the mute would still be slumped in his chair, oblivious to the garbled, spit-filled rants of his protectors. He would still be locked in a lonely, silent world he did not deserve. For a split second, Wendy Soon could see the face in the windscreen, hear the quick-breathing, scary, yelling whoop of a promise he'd made to his father. Surely he could not give up. He returned the receiver to its hook and slowly pushed against the door with his shoulder. There was one last gesture for the day, one final sacrifice. He turned towards the diner. Never in his life had he crossed the threshold. His kind stayed away.

Once inside, he chose a seat as far away from the counter as possible. The faintly smoky atmosphere caught his throat, causing him to swallow hard. He sat for a while, anxiously looking out through the dulled, film grease of the window at the lengthening finger shadows clawing their way across the rail yard. He hardly dare look around. This was a world in which he did not feel welcome. He wedged his elbows firmly against the trim, and with his head in his hands, sighed deeply, his breath momentarily frosting a patch of glass. He was waiting. He would be asked to leave. It was clear he had no plan, nor any real intention of buying food or drink. The formica shelf which edged the window was barely wide enough to balance a coffee mug, but as he pressed his nose against the glass and took stock, he became aware of the waitress sliding a drink towards his arm.

'Here, that's on the house. Like as not you need something inside you after the hours you spending propped up over there,' she said, with a nod in the direction of the telephone booth. 'What you doing anyway, making all those calls? Must know a power of folks to be talking like that. And have plenty of dimes. Never seen one of your kind doin' so much - ' She stopped, realising that she was getting no response. Wendy Soon was looking at her, barely acknowledging her presence, trying to work out how to behave. 'Anyhow,' she continued, unperturbed 'Anyhow, fries are off. Can do parmesan and side salad, some dressing. Yeh and tomato pizza. You like some tomato pizza?' She continued talking as she made her way back to the hatch, her voice tailing off in a dispassionate manner. Wendy Soon twisted around to watch her. The waitress was a disappointment. She was chewing gum, slouching, rolling her shoulders. The veins in her legs were blue. That's the trouble with white women, he mused; no grace.

'Thank you,' he shouted after her, watching as she carried her childbearing bulk through the 'in' door. 'I am very grateful for your kindness.'

Perhaps this was the pert waitress of the phone booth advertisement many years on, the plate of pasta gone cold, her hair dyed, her dreams gone. And her children many miles and arguments away. This was not someone to walk with into old age. Her skin was limp, her eyes ringed. He opened his pouch and took out his notebook. It was well thumbed and dog-eared, full of doodles, idle moments among the hundreds of numbers. He hated numbers. There was a tyranny in the myriad combinations more thunderous than all the stars. They railed against him in their blinding persistence. Somewhere, behind one of those phone calls, was a lie. For the first time, he realised what Holden Caulfield meant; it was all phoney.

Nobody gave a damn, no matter how innocent and trusting you were prepared to be. Perhaps there was no Catcher in this story; he was destined to amount to nothing after all. He sat motionless, elbows locked, his mug of coffee cradled against his chin. All his learning probably amounted to nothing after all. Indians are never literate. They know their place. He had never found a way of using what he knew.

It had never before occurred to him to lie about anything. There was no need. His forefathers spoke in pictures, talked of invention, taught him to regard the story as the mask for the ultimate good. For this purpose, he had a son who had been given a dog tag. For this reason, he had a nephew in Buckeye. How else would he be believed. He, a Quechan, speaking into a non-Quechan world thousands of miles away and only yards from the edge of the reservation? Those were distances of the heart.

The waitress bumped and clattered behind the counter, singing in a language Wendy Soon did not recognise. He could see his face in the glass. He watched the waitress behind him. Behind this ghost in the window, rolling stock shunted into view, the turquoise and peach and pink sky dropping to purple. The pinpricks of stars grew more intense. Wendy Soon sipped the bitter dregs of his coffee; it was time to leave. As the door of the diner slapped behind him and he breathed in the cooling air, something charged his brain. He stood, immovable for a moment, then turned round, pulled the door open in an uncharacteristically brisk manner and walked back into the diner, straight up to the counter. The waitress was still singing quietly to herself, head down, arms, hands and elbows swirling around in the soapy sink. She pretended to ignore him, then when she knew she had made some kind of point, without looking up, said 'Nothing left but coffee. Food's off. Bagels, I can do a couple of bagels.'

'No thank you, I do not want to eat,' Wendy Soon replied. There was a silence between them. He paused until the lady was forced to look up, look straight at him. 'Can you tell me your name? I want to know your name,'

The waitress lowered her eyes, leaned deliberately forward and continued to wash the dishes. 'Well, there's a thing, really something.' She chuckled. 'Didn't rightly know you Indians, you Kwu-tsan,' she said pointedly, 'Didn't know you got a line. Don't you know you not supposed to sweet-talk white ladies?' She was talking without looking. Wendy Soon had learned not to trust people who talked without looking.

'But you are not really white,' he answered. He stood stiffly before her, watching her every move. The only two other people in the diner had slipped away, leaving the stage empty for the interrogation.

'Lippy for an Indian, sure are,' she countered. 'You're a might too lippy. Swear I never heard one of your kind string a sentence together in months'. This time she was looking straight into the eyes of the Indian. 'Not white, eh?'

'No.' Wendy Soon stood his ground. He found the conversation exhilarating. He liked the danger; he knew exactly what he was after. 'Your skin,' he went on, 'It is not the skin of a white woman. You must tell me, who are your people?' The waitress looked as if she was losing patience. She drew herself up to her full height, as if relishing the new-found challenge.

'Well, I am kinda sallow,' she replied. 'You bold one and no mistake. I'm a kinda yellow, maybe ochre; know what ochre look like? Yellow brown, call it tan. Hell, I can never rightly find the words. What it matter to you? This is crazy.' Her mood seemed to change with the explanation; she was uncomfortable with the scrutiny, unsure of the intrusion. 'So, am definitely no pink, eh? That satisfy you?' She stopped washing the glasses in the sink and shook the suds from her hands. 'Getting personal, ain't you? Maybe you better think about leaving.' Wendy Soon said nothing. He was standing close against the counter, his shoulders straight, his hands gripping the shiny edge. Perhaps he had gone too far, but he would hold his nerve. 'Yeh, well I'm no pink,' she repeated. The realisation seemed to soften her stance. Wendy Soon felt he had won a battle with himself, with the lady; sensed she might break into a smile. 'Well, since you so forward, my name is Silviena. 'I own this place. Now - '

'You have other names?' he persisted.

'Belicci.' That my family name. Now, you better go.' Wendy Soon processed the information, nodded his head and continued.

'And what is your country?' he asked. 'Where are your ancestors?' The waitress dried her hands on her apron, turned her back on him and began stacking plates. She could follow his movements in the mirror wall.

'Five children, all girls, all growed up and my country is Arizona, just like you,' she said. He caught her eye as he gazed past her into the mirror. 'Just like you,' she repeated.

'But *we* are not white. I am definitely not American, I am Quechan,' he said. He had never had such a strange conversation. Not with an alien. He stood watching the waitress. She was deliberately finding things to do which would keep her with her back to him. Any minute, she might order him out, chase him away. Perhaps she couldn't make up her mind. The Indian was surprising himself. Wendy Soon had almost forgotten what he wanted, almost didn't care where it was leading. He had come back into the diner to follow his head; now his heart was taking over. The romantic heart still belonged to his wife. This was the elation of being treated as an equal.

'And I am Italian, least my parents were. Settled in Mount Kisco way out east. I don't remember. I was very young when we moved.' She slowed down, paused for a moment, then changed her tone. 'Hey now, what am I doin' telling this to you, a complete stranger, telling all this stuff. Better say your piece and get on your way.'

'Italian names,' Wendy Soon began. 'Do they all end in the 'i' letter?' The waitress laughed at the question, the kind of gentle laugh you would offer an inquisitive child. 'Quite a few,' she said, turning to face him. 'What's this all about? You're asking far too many questions. You have to go now, I'm locking up the diner.' She moved towards the gap in the bar and waved him away, closing the hinged lid and sliding the bolt.

'I - ' Wendy Soon looked as if he would block her path. 'I need to find someone,' he said, unsure of his ground. 'I have been searching for him.'

'Well, I don't rightly see how I can help you. I'm sorry. Now would you kindly leave?' Silviena's voice had hardened. 'You have to go.' This was the first time in months an Indian had entered the premises. There was no one around to come to her assistance. Mostly, she was used to the rough and tumble of the rail yard gangs, the hobos, the ex-pats. This was different. This was altogether more calculated. Indians stayed away. Now this emboldened primitive was taxing her patience. She had lost the thread, couldn't make sense of where it was all leading.

Wendy Soon knew the signals. He had no intention of being run in by some uniform. He moved slowly towards the door, following through with a half-hearted salute. 'His name is Luca, Luca Cambareri.' he offered as a parting shot. 'He was…he is a soldier. I will leave now.' As he pulled open the bug shutter, he could hear crockery being firmly dropped onto the back shelf. Out of the corner of his eye, he noticed that Silviena had turned around and was raising her arm, as if asking him to wait.

'Well now, that's Italian,' she said. 'Sure you got that bit right? How d'you spell it? No worry, I've seen that name plenty.' Wendy Soon stood with his back to the door, looking at the floor. 'Why you want to find him?' Silviena asked. Wendy Soon kept his distance. The waitress, without taking her eyes off him, sat back in a slow and deliberate manner onto a high stool behind the counter and leaned her elbow on the shelf. She dipped into her apron pocket and took out a packet of cigarettes which she shook open enough to feed one between her lips. This was another slow act. She was finding time to think, putting herself in charge. She pushed open a box of matches, lit up and took a long draw till all the smoke disappeared into her throat. Then she made a swirling motion with her arm. 'There's a story here,' she said, the smoke streaming from her mouth and nostrils as she spoke. 'You gonna tell me?'

'The man has been found, but he doesn't know it,' Wendy Soon began.

'So you no actually looking for him?' Silviena asked. 'You can do better than that. What's the game?'

'Can I sit down?' Wendy Soon moved back to his window seat. The waitress had her head resting on the mirror, her arms folded against each other, with a lengthening stalk of ash angled at the tip of her cigarette. She watched the Indian take out his battered notebook and pencil and several pieces of ripped newspaper, which he fastidiously laid out on the table. Wendy Soon was excited. This was the first time he had told anyone. Somehow he felt safe with this Miss Silviena Belicci. Her name had the rhythm of Cambareri. There would be a connection. He knew, in that empty diner on his first ever visit alone with a woman, with a complete stranger, that there would be a connection. He would share his mission, tell his tale.

Wendy Soon's unlikely liaison with his waitress proved to be fertile territory for the gossips. This was breaking new ground. He had never heard the word gigolo before, never had to fend off accusations of being 'kept'. Every few days he could be seen in deep discussion at *his* window seat, an innocent abroad, learning to deal with a knowing world. His mentor was more than a match for the asides, the tight-lipped stares. Silviena was engrossed, driven, unconcerned. She had her drifters, she had her rail yard workers – and now, the bewildering sight of more and more Quechens joining the mix. Good for business. What had taken them so long to break the spell, the unwritten apartheid which until then, few had dared to challenge? The pair would lay out their maps, notebooks, newspaper cuttings across the worn plastic table cover and methodically pour over every detail: an improbable war cabinet, intent on beating the odds.

The Indian was convinced that no one else would want to know about his find. He trusted the waitress. She, in turn, had found a cause, something to relieve the boredom. She would write letters until she received an answer. One address in particular. There was a sister, a mother, a daughter to be reached. Wendy Soon knew it. The waitress would break from serving, cleaning, dealing with customers at every opportunity to sit opposite the Indian, making notes, holding up another military rejection, ripping spiral bound pages from her notebook and taping them to the window. They had rules. They were never to be seen together after hours, in the phone booth, eating meals together. They would rarely spend more than half an hour across the table in any one morning or afternoon. They would never be seen touching one another. They agreed. They would always hold conversations by looking each other in the eye.

Wk.1423

52° 8' N   111° 40' W

Stoney clipped the door fast behind him, took a deep breath and made for the end of the cul-de-sac at a brisk pace. He hated watching a bus go by. There would never be a bus just about to pull into view as he rounded the corner, not for him. He knew that. Yet if he ambled, one would flash past at the end of the road. One of those laws. Soon he was slumped down in a top deck window seat, drifting through the sunbursts between buildings, the warm darts of morning light crystallizing on his faintly closed eyelids. He liked tightening the muscles around his eyes. Squinting at the world. First day back at Brunnings. Don't think about it. Pretend. That's what they all do in any case. It will all come back. Every day he was reclaiming something. At times it was a smell, maybe a snatch of a song on the radio or a vaguely familiar face in the crowd. More than once he was sure The Bison Tie was out there, just a profile, a fleeting, distant look. The back of a head. Inevitably, in one of those rare, ridiculous moments when he felt good for no reason.

Here, on the top deck of the bus, he could control the light, summon the dark, see what no one else could see. He turned his head in the direction of the sun and closed his eyes. He enjoyed seeing what no one else could see. Light through the skein of soft skin, blood lines, pulsating, multi-coloured shapes. In front of his eyes, tiny white sparks, the pale geometry of a million bursting diamonds gorged with pink lightening powering their way through his subconscious drift. It was a signal. Dark, light, light dark. There was the scrape of the hot corrugated sheeting, the screech of sand against skin. This was the dance, this was the heat, this, the dry sand caked against his cheek. He could feel his eyes rolling back under his eyebrows. He could see the swirling wisps of cloud, of dust, of sand, the everlasting blue dizzying down into his brain. He could see the Indian. The face was a ghost talking. He was looking up into lovat eyes, deep, glacé pools of dark. The breath came closer, the mouth closing over his lips. It was aniseed, it was mint, it was tobacco oil seeping out of his nostrils, pressing his drums, filling every corner of his gaping throat, the warm, choking stench of life pumping through his veins. He had stopped breathing. Stonie sat bolt upright with a start, screeching an intake of breath as curdling as a night vixen.

'The Suit,' he gulped, 'the Bison Tie'. He swallowed hard. 'The Old Crown.' The moment was audible. He was heaving, his heart pounding in his ears as he began to take control. There was scant response from other passengers. They stared, they turned away. Stonie tried to breathe out more slowly.

'You alright, mate?' someone asked. He nodded jerkily, slaking on as much saliva as he could find and swallowing hard. He leaned back, arms outstretched, his sweaty palms painfully wrapped around the chrome bar in front of his seat.

Within seconds, he was hurtling downstairs, ramming his thumb against the bell and swaying recklessly from the platform. As the bus leaned against a slow corner, he edged to the door, leapt for the pavement through the open gap and propelled himself forward, arms flailing to retain his balance, yelling at the shop fronts. His legs jarred as he made contact with the tarmac, but he was running, that was enough for now; racing flat out, dodging shoppers idling on the pavement, prams, bicycles, newspaper stands, a busker; glancing off parked cars and bollards, oblivious to the screeching traffic. Pickets in miner's helmets were milling around, gathering in small, snuffling groups on streets he barely recognised, finally slowing him to walking pace. City. Centre. So much was cordoned off, his elation gave way to irritation. He needed to keep going, somewhere, needed to get away from the gassy smells, the klaxons, the drums. There was a raggedy crowd of people milling about in the square, shouting, punching the air and waving placards. Undesirables. He would avoid cutting through. They were angry for sport. It was what they did best. Spoiling. He'd seen it before and it was getting worse; crude and undirected. Against everything. Brothers, shoulder to shoulder, swearing, spitting. One headline caught his eye: LATEST OUTAGE. He was sure it was meant to be 'outrage'. The thought broke the intensity in his brain, drew him back into a present world of slow working, electricity cuts, minor scuffles, empty shelves, snarling discontent. It all seemed so familiar, the unrest, the tension – it was a deeply unhappy world he was coming back to; that much registered. What he had previously lived was surely there before him, still to be lived out. He could have hoped for better.

Out of breath, he stood for a time, taking stock. He found himself staring through a department store window. The TV was showing riots on nine screens, bandaged limbs, shaky, high-voiced reporters, stretchers, walls of police behind plastic shields, bloodied foreheads. The noise was stereo. To him, all telly was in black and white, the horses talked to you, the kitchens were Rockwellian, the women wore crinoline and polka dots, ran after their men-folk. On these screens, in the window reflections, rattling around his ears, he began to realise he was watching exactly what was unfolding behind him on the other side of the square. He had a choice: the reality or the rendition. Perhaps he was feeling better after all, more in touch. Refusing to be swayed by the mystery. The desert man, The Old Crown man was looking for him. It had to be that way. He had the revelation. Now, he needed time to think; time to count the interruptions. He knew now the pull of the stranger in the pub, his own reluctance to let go of it. Stonie thrust his hands deep into his jacket pockets and tucked himself into a bus shelter as the pavement swelled; any bus would spirit him away. Anywhere.

Gemima had been observing Stonie for months. Perfect specimen, she had recorded. He talks then retreats. Nervous; looks out of window all the time, apparently at nothing much; usually the sky. Always on his own in the pub, on the bus, when shopping, at church. Right age. Interacts only occasionally with people. Definitely on the edge. Classic body language. The referral had come from immigration. San Diego was unreliable. Their medics wanted money for information, or did not like her questions and she had no clearance. She was still waiting for answers. An intriguing case, they wrote. Perhaps typical of the slippage. Said to be a UK citizen but no passport. Handed over by the US Border Agency. Traced quite possibly to the Midlands, but not a native of the region. A town dweller though there was no match with any missing persons file. Limited medical history available. Cited as temporary loss of memory and very little to build on. However, all the signs pointed to a gradual recovery, gradual self-realisation. He was making connections with local people. The one question mark, a tenuous link with the Annexe, Yuma, where he had first come to their attention. It was a question of waiting to see what he would do next, when he would make a move. Who did he know; was there anything to hand over?

In the days which followed, a pattern emerged. Stonie would be out and about by ten in the morning. With the Indian on his mind. His day would start with one round-city trip on the inner circle No.11. Top deck, one row back from the front seat, window, pavement side. He was not sure what this would achieve. There was something aimlessly reassuring about reconnecting. This was his way of doing it, looking out on worlds he didn't have to join. Tiny strips of decrepit garden history, rubbish-strewn housing estate lay-bys, flyovers arcing across sub-station scrapyards; ornate sandstone, freshly painted rust, terracotta Victoriana towering over shadowy canal tunnels. In his ears were all those working class snippets, the real opinions on the strikes, the economic casualties, characters at close quarters you could observe, scrutinise without having to open your mouth. He wanted to say, never mind your pathetic little struggles for survival, the cold-for-this-time-of-year bloody weather, the shopping list, have you seen this man, this Indian guy, he ended my life, he saved my life, I have to find him. I think I can tell you what he looks like.

The routine was recorded, sampled. Once, twice a week, varying the vantage points. Losing, picking up again. The pace, steady before lunchtime. Gradually becoming more erratic later in the day – until standing motionless, staring at the sky in the late afternoon opposite The Crown. The hair-twisting, nail-biting. The predictability. He would have to rediscover his appetite for work. Travel had not been kind to him.

The play of light, the colours, the taint of a city with its subtle divisions - it all came round again. Grey areas, university green, black areas. Brown. The asian streets, afro-caribbean corridors. These places, they were alive, colourful, inviting behind glass. Safe, from his double-decker vantage point. However, white and eye-to-eye, you needed a reason to be there. You needed a reason to drink in the aromas, move self-consciously to the strains of the music, pretend you ate the exotic. Stonie watched his reflection come and go in the window of the bus. He could have been at work, at his drawing board, being Mr. Nice Guy, fending off the freelancers, pretending to be an artist. He was blacklisted. No trade union sticker on his typesetting. Did he really want to be bullied again? No one at Brunnings had chased him and that was just fine.

Stonie wondered how long he could make it last, the money, the routine, the daily trawl, even the note from the GP. What else was there to do? Alight from the bus at the Bull Ring, coffee, a quick browse through the newspaper shelves, window shop the boutiques, argue his way through the market, find a toilet, decide on what to eat. The afternoon routine hardly varied. Finally, to the Old Crown. Enough money for one pint. He could feel the hollowness in the pit of his stomach every time he entered the pub. After all these months, there was still a numbness. He filled his day, walked slowly against the pace. Here in the city there was everyone to talk to and no one to know.

Perhaps it was Wednesday. It didn't seem to matter much. It was time to call someone. Gem, Kate, Zach? Fairweather friends were so uncomplicated; whatever excuse for a conversation, it would be nothing more than small talk. Of the up-to-date story, the Reuladair tale, there was so little to go on. Anyhow, he was proud that none of them knew the other, less sure that his phone had remained silent for days.

The first streetlights were popping, pink to yellow against the steel of the late afternoon sky. Almost two weeks and little to show for the missing months. This was cruel. It was the way the city treated him. Stonie leaned back against the café window, his bum uncomfortably edged against the low sill. The air was still. There was no wind and the traffic seemed muffled, not yet at the snarling end of the working day. He took stock of the square. The area seemed quieter, less threatening. One or two small groups of pickets, a cordoned off hole in the ground, a police car parked at an odd angle, the endless clearance sale signs. A wave of tiredness overtook him. It was the tiredness of the litany. Miners, IRA, football riots, election threats; union instructions, prescription drugs, fast food. The here-we-go-again search for holiness, for peace, for a slice of heaven on earth. All he had to show for it was the search. Everything was more uncertain than ever before. He rolled out his Mail from under his arm; last night's news. Why were they not down the pits where they belonged? Why were they not back driving the trains, polishing their fire engines? He closed his eyes, tightly, trying to recall a time when people claimed no rights to anything; everything was in its place.

Above the hissing and growling of the surrounding streets he could hear a voice, a distinct voice inside his head. Someone he knew he had to respond to. He turned around to face the window behind him. Through the steamed up glass and fine mesh curtain, barely perceptible between the peeling 'EGG & BACON BAPS' lettering, was the close up face of a stranger. Stonie stared, mouth wide open. Apparitions had been commonplace lately, a way of escape. 'Another haunting,' he breathed against the glass, frantically wiping at the dirt on the window with his palm, with his sleeve, spitting away the street grime over a bigger area in a wide, circular motion, his heart racing. It was real. Stonie rushed to the entrance of the café. He could barely push open the door, trembling, knocking his shin, stumbling between tables as he tried to find some composure. The man, standing on the far side, at a window seat, drew himself up to his full height, and opened his mouth to speak. Stonie stared at him wide-eyed. He had never seen the face before. But he knew.

'Please sit down,' the stranger said. Stonie, still trembling, continued to stare at him. Everything about the man was in sharp focus, every detail of his weathered face. The bone structure, the lines, the colour, the tone. He could taste the skin; somehow he knew the face, he knew the hair. 'My name is Wendy Soon,' he announced. Stonie opened his mouth but nothing happened. He moved forward slowly without taking his eyes off him, steadying himself against a chair. 'My name is Wendy Soon. I am Quechan.'

'Oh, yes,' Stonie managed. 'Yes, I see.'

'I will order a refreshment.' the Indian continued. 'You must drink.' Stonie was rigid, ashen faced. The interior of the café was spinning round. He held onto the edge of the table, breathing heavily, trying to concentrate on what he should say. Both men seemed to be waiting for the other to begin when sudden distraction broke the deadlock. They glanced out of the window at the same time as a klaxon blasted above the traffic noise. On the other side of the road, a large, vociferous group of protesters had formed. As the chanting intensified, a police line was locking in around them, swaying and tightening, yelling above the rasp of a loud hailer. It was becoming the soundtrack of the city. Wendy Soon turned his back on the window, sat down first and calmly sipped at his drink. 'I, that is, we searched for clues to the silent one. Many months. He has, he had a friend. Please, won't you sit down? I have found him, the silent one.'

Stonie hardly moved a muscle. The sentences were closed off. There was no fluency, they were tangents. He was in the Old Crown, that was the sensation; the voice, the same voice. He was sure he was missing whole chunks of what the Indian was saying. He could hear his own shallow breathing, had to concentrate hard in case he missed out on some vital moment. 'I know you but I don't know how I know you,' he said. 'It was the bus, today, yeh a few minutes ago. No, in my head it was you. The desert, a flash back, you're the guy, you must have been the one who - ' Stonie was searching the unsmiling face of the Indian. 'But what has the desert got to do with what you wrote on that mat? It was you in the Old Crown. You left a napkin, no, a beer mat. You had written on a beer mat. It freaked me out. Yeh, how come it's the same person? I've been looking for you ever since. Because of the name on the mat, right? What you said, the weird way it all happened. How do you know Jay, about Jay? What happened to her?' Stonie's voice was cracking. The Indian took his time.

'Mica?'

'Jay, she was called, well, is called Jay. Mica's none of your business. What's your connection? You need to tell me what you know. What do you know?'

'You are not who I was looking for,' the Indian said, ignoring Stone's question.

'Right, fine, but you are from my past and you seem to know something. This silent one…uhm, that was me…and, and I do know who you are.' Stonie was shaking, breathing hard, his gaunt face tightening into anger.

'I had first to find Canaletto. I have a description. You are not Canaletto. Things have to be done in order.'

'Who the hell is Canaletto?' Stonie asked. 'Oh yeh, yeh, Canaletto, whatever,' he said, shaking his head from side to side. He didn't want an answer. 'You're Indian. They told me two state uniform guys found me, some way outside Yuma. But it was you, wasn't it? It was you. I have it in my notes, these guys, the home, the patients or something.' Stonie slumped into a chair, pushing it backwards, almost crashing over as it scraped the floor. 'Yeh, okay, how would I know? That's what they told me. I must have been feeling it…that's what was making me react in the pub. But what were you doing writing about Mica on a beer mat. And how the hell, what on earth are you doing here?' He took a deep breath.

'I understand you have many questions' the Indian said, 'I will wait.'

'You have to tell me how you know about Jay, what you know about Jay.' He could feel the anger welling up, the confusion. He was loud, attracting attention, shifting self-consciously in his space, as if looking for a way out, a way not to hear any more, a way to hear everything. 'I do know who you are, don't I?' Stonie said, more calmly this time. 'And, and you know who I am. You found me, didn't you? And didn't you see me in the pub? You must have recognised me.' He had to go over it again. There were pieces missing. The games in the pub, the games we were playing, you were watching all the time, weren't you? Some elaborate joke? Who's in on all this, then?' He felt sick in his stomach. 'In fact, I had a premonition, just a little while ago. I was on the bus. It has all been coming back to me. They said it would. I have it in my notes. Said it might all happen at once. Maybe not at all.' The Indian broke his silence.

'I do not understand. Do you mind if I ask what has been coming back?'

'You, the past, my memory, never mind' Stonie answered. 'Not important for now.' He twisted around and gazed out through the window, across the square, this time over the rooftops and chimneys, up beyond the wafer thin city haze, towards the clouds. He was looking for dark blue. Even just for a split second. Something was drawing him skyward. He stared intently, as if searching for a sign, permission, reassurance.

'So you are Blu. That is the name you were given,' the Indian said. Stonie nodded slowly.

'I've spent weeks thinking of nothing else. Just knew I had to look, keep looking. Didn't really think I'd find anyone, if I'm honest. Couldn't have imagined there would be a double connection.' Stonie was moving from foot to foot, drawing short breaths and biting his lip. He was desperate yet did not seem able to go deep enough, to fully grasp the moment. 'We never met. Not properly. We never spoke. So tell me what happened to me. What you know. Tell me what you're doing here. And what you said, about Jay, why d'you write she's dead. Just...just start somewhere. Start, just get on with it.' As Stonie said this, he stretched out his arm and raised his hand as if in absolution, as if to halt the proceedings, calm thins down, give permission to start again.

'My friend, you are displaying stigmata. Your palms - ' the Indian said. 'I know about this from the Holy Bible story.'

'What?' Stonie replied. 'What? He turned his palms upward. 'Oh that. There is a perfectly reasonable explanation. I grabbed at some wire and - ' He wanted to say never mind, don't be so bloody clever, what would an Indian know. Tell you later. No, not at all. You wouldn't understand. He wanted to drift away. What if all this isn't happening, I'm going to waken up. I'll be on my own, back in my hospital bed. The guy has appeared out of nowhere. He's the freak, a throwback to another dream. It's the medicine. Side effects. He's the guilty conscience. He's an alien presence. Stonie was constantly losing his train of thought. He felt a growing sense of unease creeping over him, the beginnings of panic. He had to hold on to his sanity at all cost. But he hardly knew what that felt like; only the familiar dislocation of those days in Yuma, the Annexe it was called; the treatments, the endless questioning. This stranger seemed to have appeared out of his head.

'I am interested in what you have to tell me,' the Indian said. Stonie started again.

'All these months, I've been haunted by the things I don't know about myself. I would try to piece things together, lies, truth, what people decided to tell me. This morning, something tripped. I was on my way to nowhere in particular.' Stonie paused for a moment, unsure if he was being understood. He seemed unable to utter a sentence that made any sense. He was filling spaces.

'It was my mission to seek out Canaletto,' he heard the man say. 'My father said I would find the truth. He appeared to me. I knew I had to start with the mute. You are Blu.'

The Quechen was taking his time. Stonie wanted to interrupt him but fought back the questions. Every time the stranger spoke, he was robotic; the accent, an annoying form of broken English. His statements seemed to have been programmed into his brain along fixed lines. Stonie himself was in replay, back in that first Old Crown encounter, recalling the possibility the man was Spanish or South American or Mexican. Recalling the style, how the Indian would not reply to a question when it was asked. It was happening again. Stonie was finding it difficult to concentrate. Why didn't the man make himself known in the pub? He must have looked around at one point, seen me. What about Mica? Telling me he doesn't recognise the name. Doesn't he remember what he wrote? Did *he* write it? There had to be others involved.

'Listen, you need to tell me your story, my story, from the very beginning, right? Stonie said. 'I mean, did you play a part in getting me out of that Annexe place?' Wendy Soon took his time and Stonie knew there would be no direct answer.

'My father, in a dream he told me I should begin a journey.' the Indian was saying. 'Start from where you are, he said. Build on what you know. This was after finding Canaletto, the man from the desert. Many weeks passed before I was given the address for his child. I have travelled far to find her. She would make him speak again.'

Stonie shook his head. 'No. no, no you are mistaken. I am the guy you saved,' he said, 'but I am not Luca. I mean, Canaletto. Did I say Luca? Where did that come from? I don't know why I called him…how I know his, his - ' Stonie was stuttering, his lip trembling, his eyes filling up. He took a deep breath. 'I guess you saved my life. That is important enough, but what's it all got to do with this child of Canaletto bit?' he asked in frustration. 'That's what I don't get.' There was no answer. Perhaps it was best to let the Indian's story unfold.

'When I returned to the nursing home, they said he had been taken away, the man they called Blu. They did not say who took him or where he was taken. At the time, I had this information. I did not say I knew. It led me to this.' Wendy Soon thrust a crumpled piece of paper across the table. Stonie smoothed it out. The old address. Worthington Mews, George Road. Three roller-coaster years. The Mica years. The tale before.

'But how did you get this address?' Stonie asked.

'I will come to that. I did not trust his keepers,' the Indian went on. 'They had no names. They were friends with the military. They made fun of this man they called Blu. He could not speak for himself. It was a strange place. I heard it was called the Annexe. There is great evil there. There were many people who could not speak for themselves. This, I understand. My people too have no voice. It is my mission to give him back his life, to give him back his family. One day I had the courage to make a visit again. That is when I found out he had gone. I asked travellers who camp near the buildings. They said he had been taken to Yuma.'

Stonie sat in stunned silence. The Quechen was speaking in the present tense about Mica's father. That is what was happening. There were facts he did not know. The father must have been dead for six months, more. Probably much more. Mica's father; Jay's father. This was not the time to talk about details. The Indian would not know that Mica wanted the photograph or what was so special about it. As far as Stonie could recall, Luca Cambareri was still tucked inside 'The Little Prince'. He rehearsed an explanation. The last time I heard her voice, over the phone, it was then I knew for certain there was no reason for me to stay in one place. It was as if I was seeing the light, but the star had already died. I shivered at the sound of her voice. Anger, fear, emptiness, I don't know. I should have gone to see her. But I think I wanted to punish her for rejecting me; maybe punish myself for losing her. Momentarily, Stonie was not connecting with the stranger. He was organising a defence of sorts. Around them, café life continued unnoticed. At one point, he tried to attract the attention of a waitress, an automatic response to some peripheral movement, but no one seemed to be serving. Everything had turned itself around so quickly. He needed time to think, he needed a drink, but it looked as if the Indian had no intention of setting up drinks, of any semblance of civility. It was business. He needed to phone Zach, Kate, Gemima. Zach would be best.

'I came to England to find Jay,' he heard the Indian say. 'I came to tell her where to find her father. I wrote many letters. Each one told of our search. My friend, Sylviana, she discovered much. Then I knew what to do. She found the money somehow. It was not easy to leave home. I have been to Worthington Mews. The lady at Worthington Mews told me where I might find you, at this café. When I saw you, I knew in my heart you were not her father. You are more like a brother. But I was drawn here, the trail led me here,' he went on. 'The story is unfinished.' Stonie was tempted to grab him by the arms, shake him. It seemed impossible to look this man in the eye for any length of time, to interrupt the script.

'Look, I don't understand. How could I have been mistaken for an older guy? What kind of weird stuff is going on here? I mean creepy or what, the guy I'm mistaken for happens to be connected…well, let's just say I know about him.'

'You are not Mr. Cambareri. But you live at the same address as his child.' Child? Hardly a description Stonie recognised. He simply could not get to grips with the way this was going.

'I don't live there anymore. How did you get this information?' Stonie asked in exasperation.

'There was a military dog-tag beside the body; beside you, that is,' the Indian said, this time in serious enough flow to suggest he would not allow an interruption. 'I carried you to my pick-up. You were dying. I have seen the look many times. I had to get you to water and to medicine as soon as possible. These men and women promised to look after you. Months went by. I believe no one did anything to find out who you were. You could not help yourself. I visited you three times. On the third visit, they said you had gone away. It was dangerous for me to stay, or to ask any more questions. They suggested I did not return at another time. I saw soldiers.'

'Dangerous?' Stonie asked.

'You are not in the minority. You are not a nobody. We are chased away from these places. If we go near them we can be arrested. I could see that it was no ordinary rest home. You must understand, I was not welcome.' Stonie could feel reality slipping away. He had been hoping for more from the Indian, on the mix up.

'What was I doing with a dog-tag?'

'I do not know. But you are not Luca Cambareri. He is an American, a GI. You are not American, you are not a soldier.' Wendy Soon replied. He appeared calm and unruffled.

Stonie fidgeted in his seat. He did not wish to consider all the things he was not. 'I don't know who I am, what I am,' he answered. 'I don't know what I have been.'

There was a long pause. Stonie stared at this implacable figure, unable to absorb the full significance of being face to face with his saviour. Too many confusing things were happening at once. 'I could not remember anything for a time,' he said. 'I had a medical condition, a form of amnesia. Do you understand what that means? There are, there were things that made no sense.'

'I have told you everything,' the Indian cut in, defensively. 'It was a high sun; I was taking a short cut on a dirt road. I saw several vultures. I thought at first it was road-kill, then as I drew near, I realised that it was a human. You would not have seen the next moon.'

'That close?' Stonie asked. The full weight had never dawned on him, that something so life threatening had taken place. This was a new way of viewing things. Wendy Soon nodded slowly but made no reply. Stonie could see the Quechen was dignified, composed, other-worldly, that he was no part of the social ferment breaking out all around them. He was out of his place. Yet there was a message burned into those contours. Compassion? No. That was the wrong trophy. Duty? These were great lengths to go to for someone who owed him nothing. Truth? That was much more elusive. Stonie was on overload.

The café had emptied, leaving the two figures exposed, alone in the L shaped room, with its full-size Mocha prints peeling over them, the mock Charles Rennie Mackintosh lampshades dampening down the yellow light, creating spots on each table. At a distance, from the street, the scene had the ambience of a Hopper canvas. Dusk, two figures, sculpted into a single understanding, their histories mysteriously, momentarily intertwined. It was for the passer-by to choose. The waitress approached for the third time and began engaging in conversation, breaking into their unrehearsed dance of accommodation. This time an order was taken, but the interruption set Stonie even more on edge.

'I have no idea what I was doing there, in the desert. Well, yes I do. I had been travelling on my own, just travelling. I know they brought me back from Arizona to the coast. I have seen the reports. I was taken to San Diego.' Stonie could feel the desperation mounting. He was sure he had asked at least three times directly about Mica without once getting a clear answer, some explanation. All he wanted was an order to things.

'And then?' Wendy Soon asked. 'How long did it take you to come home?'

'Look...' Stonie lurched forward on impulse, as if to clutch at the Indian's collar, but changed his mind and held back. He could feel tears welling up inside him.

'You haven't told me anything about Jay,' he said. 'What's the connection?' There was no reply. The Indian was sharp enough to counter the move, leaning back hard against the wall, tilting his chair off its front legs. The table shuddered with the sudden jerk of his knees, spilling cold coffee over the Formica. Neither moved to mop it up; just eyed each other in anticipation. Neither commented on the spillage. The waitress pushed between them and leaned across the table, enough to block any further action.

'I tell you, I found this body, near to death, hardly a breath in him. He had nothing about him to tell me who he was. I did what I could.' Wendy Soon's voice remained steady as he calmly stood up. 'I must leave now.' Stonie jumped upright, at the same time jamming the table against the Indian's body.

‘You can’t, you mustn’t, can’t. Please, no not yet,’ Stonie pleaded, immediately realising the futility of his actions. Wendy Soon had raised his arms clear of the table, back against the wall and stiffened as the table edge jammed against his legs.

‘I’m sorry, I’m so sorry,’ Stonie said. ‘You’ve no idea what it has been like not knowing, not remembering,’ he continued, pulling the table free and turning to adjust his seat. The waitress, standing right behind him, grabbed Stonie by the shoulders and forced him back into his chair.

‘That’s quite enough of that,’ she said, ‘we’ll have no rough stuff around here.’

‘Right, oh yes, sorry,’ Stonie said, turning first one way then the other, trying to talk to both parties at the same time and finally facing the Indian. He shuddered and shook his head from side to side. ‘You have no idea what a shock this is, I mean, just a few minutes ago I could see this face in my head, this figure somehow, somebody I recognised but didn’t know why. The moment - it was in my head like some nagging, constant dream. Now I’m staring at the real thing.’ There was a pause, as the Quechen lowered himself back into his seat. He nodded slowly, his eyes fixed firmly on Stonie. ‘I was told that when my memory returned, it would come back quickly, it would all become clear. They were nearly right. I don’t have to ask who I am, what I’m doing here, but the reason for being on that journey, well - ’ Stonie broke off. The feeling was that the more he pressed, the more distance there was between the Indian and the truth. But he could not help himself. All he could sense was a muted fury. His whole being seemed to be floating above ground, with waves of numbness slowly shivering through his limbs. All the noises beyond the glass were muffled, sweet, comforting. They fitted well with the flickering glow above the roof horizon, the pricking star clusters gathering in the deeper velvet. They were part of the journey he continually craved. But the noises inside his space, within his boundaries, they were the opposite. The chink of spoon on cup, the grind of plate on plate, the high nasal conversation of the waitress on the telephone, the scratching of his fingernails on the underside of the chair. It was all the boom and hollow thunder of an imploding brain.

‘You can have a pot of tea on the house,’ the waitress said. ‘Just calm down.’ Both men took stock, Stonie breathing noisily, the

Indian quiet and assured. Finally Stonie felt ready for another question.

'Tell me, Mr. Soon. Mr. Wendy Soon,' he said in a measured voice, slowing almost to a whisper, "Tell me why you did not say anything, say that you knew me all those weeks ago, at the Old Crown. You must have seen me, knew who I was. Did you see me? Did you come there deliberately? It could not have been coincidence. You looked as if you were talking to someone you knew.' Wendy Soon looked straight at him but made no attempt to respond. He was a master of silences. Stonie knew someone else who had used silence to devastating effect. He had learned to wait. The Indian closed his eyes for a moment. Stonie went on. 'Don't you understand, I'm trying to piece things together here, get my life back. You have got to help me. Are you hearing me?' With that, Stonie flipped, launching himself fully across the table, grabbing both lapels, and hauling Wendy Soon with him as he slumped back into his chair. A plate of half-finished food was sent flying by the trailing body, both mugs of tea, a pen, cutlery, a notebook, it all sprayed onto the floor. For a second they were locked, motionless, nose to nose. 'You fucking little half-breed, say something. What you holding back? Who the hell is Canal…whatever? Jay, what happened to my Mica?'

The Indian remained calm, inexpressive, Stonie's coffee breath hot under his eyes, Stonie's dilated pupils registering way beyond him. In a quiet and dignified manner, the Indian straightened and began to prise Stonie's fingers free of his coat. He could see the terror, feel the helplessness. This was slow-release shock, alien, robotic, like the air tube severed to send his adversary waltzing out through space; that moment when the glow of recognition bounces in split-second shards of infinity across the visor as it twists beyond grasp, rolling wider and wider into blackness. He did not wish this on Stonie.

The waitress was on top of them in seconds, tray in hand. She knew how to use it as a weapon. This time, she was quick to sense there was no likelihood of further trouble. Without a word, she swept her mop-up cloth across the plastic table cover, tumbling what was left of the refreshments into her curled up apron, then bent to clear the floor. She would keep watch from the rear of the café, looking up every so often, checking. Both men sat looking at each other, frozen into denial. For each, this perhaps was closure; the opportunity for retreat into their separating worlds. In a far corner, new diners grunted and mumbled through their pastries about what the world was coming to; fighting outside in the street, fighting in here, I don't know. At the window table, ten minutes went by: ten minutes of silence, neither man seeming to know what to do next. When the waitress returned, she straightened the chairs around them, still without saying a word, set out fresh cutlery, place mats, the plastic flower, the cruet, and retired with uncharacteristic reverence.

'So they called me Blu?' Stonie said, to break the impasse. Wendy Soon nodded, but did not offer any more. He placed both hands on the table, stretched out, palms down on either side of the setting.

'I came here to unite a family,' he said. 'But there is none. There is no family.' He watched Stonie's ashen face tighten, the mouth half open and ready, the lips twitching, as if at any moment words would form. Wendy Soon felt strangely cold and detached. The caring had burnt itself out. Had he not dreamed of the sparkle in Jay's eyes, heard the shriek of joy as he announced he had found her father. The moment the mute spoke for the first time? Yes, he, Wendy Soon, had made it all possible. Yet there was no Jay. There was no Luca to awaken. He knew that now. The Italian GI could be anyone, any Cambareri picked at random from the Mount Kisco Tribune by a desperate rehab clerk in some grey office. God knows there had been enough phone calls from the reservation. The trail had gone cold, gone wrong. What had been a whim, a spur of the moment, a passion, it was all at an end; the promise to his own father. Wendy Soon had been hoping to carry his own story with him, find his voice, raise the profile of his people, return triumphant. All he had found was another kind of reservation. Unrest, protest, oppressed miners. A people who did not realise how much they had. All he found were shadows. The realisation was profound. The man in Old Crown. There was nothing to be gained by coming face to face with failure. The man in the desert, the man in his mind, the man in the rest home. This man in the café. There would be no redemption.

The face of the Quechen revealed no such turmoil. He would make his excuses and leave. He would fly home the next day. He would return to Sylviana. She had found the money. He would work to repay her. She knew something of the Indian heart, understood what had driven him. She was his unlikely confidante. For the honour, for the memory of all those who had ever risen from the pit, he had told himself. Back in Yuma; the dark history would again be drowned out in the clamour for survival. Just as in this darkening city here, closing in around him. The committees would be meeting, dividing the dirt, managing the trailer parks, stalling the DA, arguing over the revenue from the casino. While they squabbled, the chiefs would be doing deals, protecting their interests. It was the modern way. Yet it was no way to silence the cries of his ancestors. Stonie's tale, whatever it is, was nothing by comparison.

Outside, Wendy Soon could see the miners waving their arms, shouting, squaring up to each other. It was almost dark and starting to rain, the street lights and cars streaking their red and orange stains across the spatter. He could hear shouting, screaming, chanting. He knew of irony, wondered who considered being the true noble savage. Opposite, sat Stonie, the man who had invented himself, dreamed strange dreams of a past he had never been given. To Stonie, the thin blue wafts of cigarette smoke, the occasional shaft of low, yellow broken lamplight peppering the walls, the chattering radio chinking out the latest irrelevancies, it was all one vast, shimmering constellation. He was tumbling in slow motion, face to upside down face with some anodyne chaplain trying to reach his soul, the next moment being tugged, leg first towards that tin hut door flapping in the breeze. There were dogs yelping at his feet, beer-swilled piercing eyes drilling him out onto the frozen sand, fingers prodding at his ribs and genitals, the taste of spit spray, a million TV laughs hollowing out his ears, the queer chant of the high altar, above which, above which stood Mica, *his* Mica, beckoning.

There was no sense to anything either of them had heard or tried to imagine. Which of the worlds were they to choose? Around them, tables filled up and emptied. These were hungry people, distracted, animated, expectant; taking refuge from an increasingly hostile street; retreating into who knows what fantasy. Stonie felt he should draw them in as he tried to claw his way back to reality. They would know what the Indian had on Mica.

'Excuse me, can I take your order now, it has been half an hour since, I need the places. ' The waitress dropped her arms and notepad onto the table, pen at the ready as Stonie shook himself fully alert. As far as he was concerned, there was unfinished business. 'I see you've made up. Just as well.' The waitress flung her head back, rolled her eyes and waited. The Quechen made no movement at all, simply stared ahead, eyes unblinking, as if he had already left his body. He spoke slowly and quietly.

'May I have my bill? There is no need to take an order for my friend. He is leaving,' Wendy Soon announced abruptly.

'Yeh, well wait a minute,' Stonie exclaimed. 'You need to tell me about Jay Cambareri.'

As he spoke, the front window erupted, glass exploding everywhere as two locked figures burst onto the table, punching and kicking, splitting the table in two, sending Wendy Soon and Stonie sprawling. Stonie fell backwards, still on his chair, the wrestling couple toppling over onto him. Diners scattered, screaming and cursing as the two fighters rolled off the remains of the table and in amongst the chairs and tables, urged on by a yelling crowd who had quickly encircled the broken window and were encroaching on the café from the pavement. Within seconds, police batons began raining in as helmets and placards flew in all directions, customers jamming the doorway to escape. Outside, the square was teeming with police and pickets and commuters, barriers crashing down onto the road, mothers and children screaming to get clear in the melee. A double decker bus had ground to a halt, its upstairs passengers pressing against the windows like some make-shift pantomime balcony, clamouring for a better view. Stonie lay winded. He was stunned, barely able to move, bits of glass sprayed across him. He found himself trying to laugh at the sound of the metal tray crashing down on the heads of the fighters. He knew at once. The waitress, appearing from the refuge of the counter, was kicking and cursing, madly jumping onto the writhing duo. Stonie found a way of twisting sideways, enough to avoid a well-meaning foot in the groin as others joined in, grabbing at Stonie's sleeves to pull him free of the fighters, yanking frantically to get him to his feet. Finally, the men were hauled off Stonie's legs. He was bundled to one side as several policemen squeezed through the entrance and set about separating the still battling miners. Two officers, Stonie reckoned, setting about the fighters. They were having trouble dragging the enraged, cursing waitress out of the way. It was her café, after all, her livelihood, her domain.

The men were dragged free, their arms twisted between their shoulder blades, amidst the cheering and whooping of a no-rules wrestling ring. Stonie swayed against the counter, unable to make up his mind if it was blood or sweat. There was definitely a trickle. He drew his fingers over his forehead, across the hollow of his neck then back under his chin. No blood. He shook his head violently, stumbling into his helpers as he screwed his eyes tight shut, grit and tiny shards falling all around him. He tested his arms, twisting each elbow as he gripped it, methodically stamping out each leg at the same time. There was dirt in his eye, something tickling inside his ear, enough to make him shake the irritation to one side with a curse. The force rocked him sideways, but he was caught by the waitress, steadied and made to sit down as she began thrusting a chair behind his knees.

'You alright? Still in one piece, eh? Hell of a fight.' She sounded matter of fact, unconvincingly sympathetic. As he looked up, a glass of water was placed in his hand.

'Nothing broken, I don't think so anyway. Bloody hell, what was that? What a mess. Didn't get hurt yourself, did you? Yes, I'm okay, just shaken a bit,' he gasped. 'Thanks.' For a second or two there were flashes, but no pictures, just a warm, pleasing lightness, as if something, or someone was offering him a way out of the strife, an apology, an explanation. His helpers were forcing him to stay on the seat. He thought of resisting, in a sudden reflex at being contained, yet there was nothing left in his knees.

'Better stay sitting down,' the waitress said. 'Your coat's ripped. But it must have protected most of your body. Can't see no punctures. Let me see those hands.' Punctures? An odd concept, to be punctured, as if there was something to let out. Shakily, Stonie stretched out his hands, palms down. There were small cuts, one or two glints of glass around his knuckles. He'd had enough blood-letting of one sort or another. Without waiting for further examination, he ran his fingers up through his hair above his left ear and winced as a splinter caught his finger, burying itself under his nail. The pain made him jump. Now he could tell that he was aching. He stiffened. A voice asked if he was alright, not concussed, needed an ambulance, wanted to lie down, a cup of tea, a smoke, wanted to go home. He made no attempt to reply. When he saw the tweezers of a Swiss Army knife waving in front of his face, he held out his hand and isolated the finger. Stonie thought this was a good idea at last. He eyed the large, close-up face of the Samaritan without uttering a word, without putting a meaning to the sounds he was hearing. There was a virtual choir of words mouthing at him whichever way he turned, a familiar chorus, another opportunity to let go. Finally, in penitent fashion, he leaned forward with both arms across his knees, fingers slightly bent, and heaved a large slow sigh. He was in no position to argue.

What world was this he had come back to? There seemed to be no way forward and none back. All there was to remind him of anything were the scars; the interruptions. Had he been here before, just forgotten how to handle it? For a moment he thought he recognised the pain. Life was measured in moments like this. Perhaps he should simply let go. He closed and opened his eyes and waited for the wince. There would be no apology. Everyone always seemed to say sorry for everything. It was a way of spreading guilt, as if they've caused the problem and you're meant to forgive them or something. These were his own drops of blood, were they not? He did not deserve the attention. Leave it to spill. Leave it.

Stonie had forgotten what he was doing in the café. He pulled himself upright in his chair, mumbled a thanks and this time determinedly concentrated on what was going on around him. He looked out across the stooping figures at the space where the window table had been; where he had been sitting. Through the remaining spikes of plate glass, he could see people running across the square, a line of constables shielding themselves behind a clear plastic wall of linked arms, batons out, screaming orders. A mounted policeman crunched past, going backwards, rearing up. The streets were in chaos, with fire sirens, burglar alarms going off, ambulances wailing. Just behind the makeshift platform, bathed in the yellow street glow, in the centre of the grassy mound, he spotted two of the burliest miners, stripped to the waist, practically eating their loud hailers as they blasted orders in every direction. As he took this in, almost in slow motion, the figures disappeared under a ruck of blue.

Stonie, sitting rather limply and at an angle, turned his attention to whoever was still in the café. 'I was about to ask the Indian about me,' he whispered to his helper.

'Sorry?'

'I was talking to someone,' he said more distinctly, this time clearing his throat. All around him, chairs were being stacked, tables righted.

'I'm afraid I don't know what you are talking about, sir,' one of the waitresses said. 'Are you sure you haven't hurt your head? Let me see, can you focus?' The tweezer man leaned forward, waving the instrument in front of Stonie, as if to say I'm the one, is there anything else I can do for you. He put his well-meaning hand on Stonie's shoulder. This had the immediate effect of galvanising Stonie into action. He shivered and shook and straightened at the touch, pulled himself free and jumped to his feet in one seamless move.

'I'm okay now, I'm fine, really I am. Thanks for your help,' he said. There was no eye contact. His gaze was fixed on the far end of the room.

'You do seem to be a little disorientated,' came a voice from behind him.

'No, no, no I am not. Absolutely not. No, I - '

'No hurry, gentlemen. Just when you're ready. I'll carry on sweeping up over here.' The lady moved in front of Stonie and into the window alcove. 'I'll have to shut up shop though, have to lock the place, see. Just when you're ready. The police want me to close early, see? The joiner's here to board me up. And I thought the crowds would be good for business.' She continued to sweep the floor without looking at anyone in particular. 'Don't expect I'll get anybody to pay for this, even if I do manage to get my day in court. The insurance, see, they're bound to tell me this was another act of God. You know what insurance companies are like. Probably say I should have seen it coming, had bars on the windows, yeh? What with the bus shelter being so close.' The monologue was rapid. Stonie made no response.

There was no sign of the Quechen. All Stonie could remember were the staccato conversations, in between the screeching tyres and expletives, the groundswell, the mayhem. All he could recall, all he could think of were opening lines that petered out. Those first few heart-thumping moments across the table. The eyes of the one who had held him at the threshold. The voice. He could hear the voice in his head, the opening gambit. 'I am not a mystery to you, I am a mystery for you.' Did the Indian really say that? Perhaps, through the pall, Wendy Soon had been a figment. That had been Stonie's lot in recent times. He turned himself slowly in his space, surveying the scene, then made towards the gaping window. He was politely asked to use the door. No, you don't understand, he was saying to himself, no one understands. The talk was, get yourself checked out, can I give you a lift, hope you're not too shaken up. Stonie looked as if he would do what he was told, then decided to hold back. For some reason he did not feel that it was time to leave. He had always had a habit of hanging back, being one of the last to leave anywhere. It used to annoy him. This was different. Most people, it seemed to him, lived a half-life. To get the most out of the experience, he would have to get more out of this situation, though quite what that would look like, what it would amount to, he did not know. In his mind was the Old Crown. The stupid game. He should have left earlier; made his decision and stuck to it.

It was a peculiar kind of paralysis. He had no real affinity with the eatery, pity on it, no real affinity with the dazed and broken. Tomorrow, no doubt, the great and the good of the neighbourhood would read some proud piece analysing the dispersal. Easy headlines. The miners would get theirs. The pin stripes would mouth their anxieties, the flabby underbelly of the city would spread out in the morning through the A-Z once more with barely a nod in the direction of the boarded windows. For now. Shout, eat, stare, turn a blind eye. In the end, the suffering heart of the urban wasteland was creating its own blight. Conspicuous apathy, minority voices, the marginalised. The newspaper headlines and hoarding were full of it. The bullies on whatever side would have their day.

Stonie cared little for this. How many times would he have to be born again? Every dancing molecule in the fibre of his being was crying out to be found. He felt invisible. The reason he had quit the city in the first place. One of the reasons. Surely not again. He would have to ring Zach. He was often thinking of doing that. Zach always knew what to do next in life. He shook himself out of his reverie and forced his way through the stacked chairs, easing himself sideways between two jammed tables to squeeze his way into the corner seat where the Indian had been sitting. There seemed no point in going outside to search, no point at all.

'I'm closing up, dear,' came a shout from behind the counter. 'I did say. I thought you were about to leave? What are you standing over there for?' The voice was irate.

'Just give me a minute or two, if you would, 'Stonie said. 'I'll stay out of your way, I just need to…' He had no reason to stay, no reason to go. By now, he was the only customer left in the cafe. The officers had taken their notes, the last of the eaters had relived their encounters, built up the drama, dusted themselves off, gathered their belongings and filed out on cue. And the joiners had finished banging up the window, the sound of their hammers like the nailing of some old fashioned coffin. Stonie brushed some plaster from the chair, leaned over to blow on it and stood for a moment, stretching and arching his back. 'I just need to, to gather myself for a minute or two,' he said. He leaned against the tiles and stared out into the night. His head was resting on the rim of the screen-printed mirror behind him, his hands thrust deep into his pockets.

'So where to now, Mr. Blu?' It was the waitress. Stonie turned towards her, brushed some tiny beads of glass from the table with a menu card, blew on the dust and sat down, still muttering to himself. Mr Blu. Not much imagination there. The colour of my eyes. Deciding I was some kind of scientist, someone's father. I don't get what the alien said; the Indian. I'm back at square one. I definitely did not dream this. Not this time. He was here. So if someone comes up to me right now and says are you Mr. Blu, something like Sandy Blu, Sky Blu then I'll answer, I'll say, if that's what you want me to be. That's it. Whoever you want me to be.

He peered through the slats in the wood. The last of the cones and barriers were being piled up, only one or two rougher looking types squatting on the grass, arms on knees, still smoking and swearing and spitting. It's a hallmark, the swearing and spitting. And the cigarette, especially when it's tucked, burning side into the palm of the loosely curled fist, held between the thumb and the index finger. Labour, no doubt about it. Or lack of it. He watched a policeman jokingly coerce the men to move on, out of sight. 'You were listening?'

'Yeh, well you were loud. Excuse me, would you mind moving to that other chair, just that I haven't done over here yet,' the waitress interrupted. She was decked out in pan and brush and broom and assorted cloths. 'You alright, love? You do still look a bit dazed.'

'I'm fine.'

'Tell you what, I'll get you a cup of tea. Like one myself, I would; proper parched. Terrible, just awful, but I'll be open in the morning as usual, you mark my words. Take more than a bunch of left wing thugs to keep me at home. Sure you don't want to see a doctor?' Stonie nodded.

'Not very good for business, riots,'

'You can say that again,' the lady chuckled. Stonie was caught out; his mind picking over inconsequential details. It was a stupid expression. Why should anyone want to say it again if they have already been understood. He hated being so objective. He hated being so nit-pickingly obvious. There was definitely something wrong with him, in spite of being told he'd just about made a full recovery. Perhaps the something wrong with him was that he was normal. He breathed slowly, blowing out through full lips as if aiming at a candle, rather than exhaling quietly. He was trying to gauge his mood. He had to find a mood, a distraction. He knew that for now it would mask the muted anger, the outright frustration. Was it worth chasing around the city centre, searching? He would suffer for not knowing. Later, he would dream that he knew the truth about Mica. He could feel his palms stinging. With a flash of the barbed wire woven through his fingers, his whole body gave a sudden twitch, his leg kicking out, scuffing two or three times in reflex across the carpet, like some kind of electric shuffle. Rubbish shot out from under the table. Dog ends, screwed-up napkins, beads of glass, an old bus ticket, a penny.

'Missed all that,' the waitress was saying over his head, nodding in the direction of what was strewn across the floor. She was pouring out two mugs of tea at the next table. Stonie bent down under his seat to pick up the penny and something else caught his eye. A small green notebook.

'That yours?' she added, nodding at the book.

'Oh, yeh. Must have dropped it,' Stonie said.

'Never seen it in your life before, have you?' she said. Stuff you, Stonie muttered to himself. Everything's a battle, even the most inconsequential thing is a battle. What's it to her? What the fuck is wrong with the world. I'm never in the right place. Never get to make a decision that sticks. Just a bloody notebook.

'Shit.' Stonie had banged his head on the underside of the table as he unfolded himself, rattling the saucers close to the edge. It was the waitress who reacted quickest, catching a flying salt and pepper set.

'For God's sake, be careful now, will you, there's been enough mess.'

'Yeh, well actually it belongs to my friend. He left the book on the table.' The waitress gave him a look of disdain. She was tired, fed up with this unwanted pantomime.

'You mentioned more tea, thanks, good idea,' Stonie said.' 'Yes, my friend, the foreign looking gentleman. He's gone, disappeared. No sign of him,'

'Disappeared into thin air, has he?' The lady sat down side-on to the table, elbow and mug in a straight line along the edge. She looked quizzically at Stonie, straight into his eyes.

'But you came in alone, sat all alone just here,' she said.

'Of course I didn't, that's nonsense,' Stonie replied, raising his voice. 'I joined the guy at his table. You tried to serve us.' Not again, Stonie thought, this is not happening.

'Been a busy afternoon. Think you were on your own, my dear.' she said, her mug of tea at eye level. She sounded adversarial. Why would she lie? What did she know? Only a waitress. What's the point? Stonie decided to leave it; mounting any kind of protest seemed as futile as ever. Someone, somewhere was experimenting on him, with him. He had no idea where the line had been drawn. He sat back, trying to make up his mind where he was, what was going on, watching the lady in slow motion respond to a phone call from behind the counter. As the waitress gabbled on at the other end of the café, Stonie turned to peer out through the wooden slats, took a sip of his tepid tea and stared dispassionately at the narrow world outside. The slit in the wood made things dramatic, perhaps because of what he couldn't see. The emptying square had an epic scale to it. Like a David Lean film. Stonie had always wondered what it would have been like to have a walk-on part: one of a straggle of passengers spilling out from a mini-bus on the other side, an early drunk in the dim far corner of the bus shelter trying to vomit, his flat cheek hard against the glass, an idling taxi driver, his diesel engine coughing like a tractor as the last of the shop windows flicked to night mode. At a distance, between streets, an orange burglar alarm was hopefully flashing out the seconds, as if anyone ever took much notice of anything. Stonie tried, but he could not see the sky this time, no matter which way he turned. At one point, though, he was sure he could see a reflection of stars. Not enough. He sighed and turned inward. Everything to him seemed strategic. Each encounter was staged, each incident timed. All he had to do was make the connections.

Stonie's attention turned to the half-curled notebook in his hand. Thumbing through its pages, he was confronted by sheet after sheet of hand-written notes, diagrams and strange, timidly drawn sketches on plain, yellowing paper. Further towards the back were minute columns of figures. He checked through to the last page, bending it slightly against the spine, then flicked back to the opening page.

'Numbers. Just numbers and scribbles,' he mused. It was loud enough to draw the waitress into the observation as she made her way towards him. She stood beside the table, sipping her tea, saying nothing. Stonie wet his index finger on his tongue, flicked over the first page and began to take a closer look. There were several addresses above the first scribbled drawing. The last on the list was his previous address, Worthington mews, complete with phone number. But the name against it, that was Luca Cambareri. The realisation made him shiver. Made him angry. He instinctively lowered the book to his lap and looked up at the waitress.

'Don't ask me,' she said, noisily placing her saucer on the corner of the table. 'You sure you are alright? You look as if you've seen a ghost or something. Thought you'd been through enough today.' She moved closer. 'Here, what's that you've got there? Let me see,' she said, and snatched the book from Stonie's hand. 'You're obviously not going to leave till you've solved one mystery or another.' She sat with her back to the next table, her knees almost touching his knees.

'It's got nothing to do with you,' Stonie said half-heartedly. 'You wouldn't understand.'

'So then, what's so important about the imaginary foreigner?' she asked, handing the book back to Stonie after what seemed like a cursory inspection.

'What's it to you?' Stonie replied. He didn't mean to sound rude. In his head, he was trying to create this man, the father, this enigma. Recreate the story.

'You're right. Sorry. I'd better be getting on,' the waitress said, breaking the silence. 'None of my damn business. Got an eye for some of these things, though. I like the cryptic. Crosswords, riddles' that kind of thing. There's list in there. There's always a story in every list. Connections, see?' She stood up, glanced around the café and stared back at the figure of Stonie, hunched over his mug. 'Actually, since you're still here, you could help me shift the damaged tables and chairs out to the back yard. I knew there was a reason for letting you hang around.' With that, the waitress turned to walk towards the counter, then hesitated, as if to begin another wave of one-sided conversation.

Stonie was fully engrossed in the drawings. There were small arrangements of dots, some linked up to others. There were several scribbled drawings on each page. They had to mean something, connect with something. They had to have significance. With Stonie, everything had to mean something. It could not simply exist in its own space. It could not avoid his interference. What he saw were simple shapes. Animals, cars, a pair of scissors, an aeroplane. He stared, turning the book upside down, holding each page up to the light, close to his nose, squinting, scrutinising, flicking. The waitress could not resist the intrigue. She sat down again, opposite Stonie, confrontational, on edge.

'Lost your glasses dear? Can I help? I should know; gets difficult at a certain age. What you looking at, or what you looking for, I should say? Here, let me see.' She was leaning way beyond her personal boundaries, her nose practically on the other side of the paper by this time. Stonie made no attempt to pull back, his arms rigid against the edge of the table. But this time he tightened his grip on the book. 'You're a troubled fella and no mistake,' she began. 'I mean, should have left ages ago, scratched and beaten up like you are and acting weird since, peering through the boarded up window all the time, spilling stuff, emptying your pockets, squinting…telling me you were with some strange guy. And now this.' She tried to grip the top of the book with her left hand, almost spilling her drink. Stonie recoiled.

'Just curious; seems such weird little drawings.' Stonie drew the notebook close to his chest, waiting for the lady to try again, 'Stars, dear,' the waitress said, lowering her mug and looking him straight in the eye. 'Stars.'

'Well thanks for that but I'll make up my own mind,' Stonie countered. The outside world had faded by this time. It was finished. It had fallen silent, apart from the muffled shouts of police in the near deserted square. Apart from Stonie's racing heart. Yet again, he should have left, got out while he could. He had the feeling there would be a revelation. It was this familiar, uncomfortable hiatus, some kind of enforced waiting time between interruptions.

'Stars,' she repeated. 'I know my stars. All got numbers and names, see.' She forced the notebook down onto the flat of the table with Stonie's hand still attached, her finger pressed firmly onto the first page. This time, Stonie went with the flow, waitress page up. 'See?' she said, tapping at the paper. 'They've all got serial numbers, names of the discoverers here and there, that kind of thing.' She eased the book gently from Stonie's fingers, turned it around and took a much longer look than before, smoothing out the dog-eared corners, flicking through several of the pages. Stonie sat with his hand in the air, poised, as if to snatch it back.

'You'd better go on, Stonie said, 'since you seem to know what's in there.'

'Quite a lot of detail, really. Definitely star locations,' she announced in an authorative voice. Stonie looked on as she carefully placed the book back onto the table. The two of them were almost touching heads, concentrating, intense. 'Some well-known bits of one of the constellations, I'll wager,' she went on. 'There are definitely references. Tiny bits of writing, see? There's Procyan in Caris Minor and Sirius in Caris Major. Thought so.' Stonie eased back slightly, trying not to appear too surprised by the revelations. After a pause, he looked up over the book, straight at the lady, his mouth open, his eyes narrowing.

'Impressive.'

'Well, I must be getting on,' she said, pulling herself up to her full height and wiping her palms downward on either side of her apron. 'But see, love, there's Orion, or part of it, three together. And that one - ' she pointed with a fork, singling out a drawing with one of the prongs. 'Betelguese on Orion's right shoulder and, and eh, Ridge, no, Rigel, that's his foot. Surely you knew that - '

'But you're a waitress,' Stonie interrupted. The remark was out before he had time to check himself.

'Don't mean I've no brain.' The retort was fired off almost before Stonie's words had landed, the lady stabbing at the side of her head with the fork.

'Sorry, I didn't mean to offend'

'Well, there's things you know and things you don't let on you know,' she replied. Stonie looked on and said nothing. He simply could not gather his thoughts enough to keep up the apology. 'Right, as I was saying, I really must finish up here,' the waitress said, picking her way between the stacked chairs. 'When you're ready,' she shouted, as she disappeared into the kitchen. Stonie sat motionless, staring at the open booklet, trying to take in the revelation.

'Just coming,' he said, in a half-hearted way, at the same time drawing his thumb across the bent edges of the book till he held it at the last page. It was full of diagrams, each a dotted collection, some linked up, most of them annotated. The occasional pencil scribblings were faint, but legible. It had to be the work of the mysterious Wendy Soon. He repeated the name out loud.

'Pardon?' The waitress was in the doorway, twisting around to catch his eye as she balanced a tower of broken plates and saucers.

'No, it's nothing,' he replied. 'Just thinking.'

'Noisily,' she shouted. 'I could do with some help with these tables.' Stonie ignored her. He was scrutinising one of the pages intently. 'HD37328, or is that a 9?' he whispered to himself, as if it was now important to deliberate over every single digit, over every mark. The final few drawings, in black, spidery ink, filled a third of each page. Several of the star codes seemed to stand out; they were unlike the others. Most, however, were of uniform length and format. What now? The lady obviously knew a thing or two. For a moment, he thought of engaging her further, but resisted. He could hear her clattering on in the background, but was too engrossed to feel any guilt. Something else had caught his eye: as he bent the notebook back against its spine, between the last page and the inside cover there was a slit, hard against the stitching, split open, revealing a thin pocket – a second skin. There was something sticking out of it, a piece of paper or thin card. It tempted him. Instead, he dropped the book into his jacket pocket, smoothing down the flap, picked up the mug and glanced around to make sure he hadn't left anything behind. The cold tea tasted disgusting. As he turned, he was suddenly aware of just how much of him ached. The movement hurt. Twisting, raising his arm, leaning back; it all hurt. He clenched both fists and his fingers felt puffy.

Through the slats, the square was now in its mid-evening lull, the sky a yellowing, gassy canopy of neon punctuated by a flickering blue cast from the remaining police lamps. Buses were being allowed back through the cleared streets. He could see the last of the sweepers limbo dancing the police tape as they waited for their lifts. All those pot-bellied council workers had tattoos, he reckoned, arms, neck, some bare to the waist to reveal their innermost fears across their weathered torsos. Mother, girlfriend, dagger, naked breasts, God in clouds, angels with fangs. What did they know about God? He'd seen those kinds of guys crying like babies at funerals and football matches, yelling Christ as the macho ballet swept on into extra time. No reverence, no respect. Wonder if they ever looked up at the sky, waited for the clouds to clear, thought about the firmament. Now, there indeed was a concept. Stonie was often preoccupied by things like this, how people moved between the earthly and the divine, how they were wired for eternity. For as long as he could remember he had been looking for clues. In his drift, there were other worlds.

Stonie is in first person. It is the way he deals with the serious, the inevitable. Not for the first time, he is an angel. Only, in this, it is for real. He stretches his wings, careful of the space he inhabits. He is always careful of the space he inhabits. This is the dark alley, the fourth storey, poised on grey, guano-strewn sandstone, ready to swoop. It is time to take to the air. He drops off the crumbling window ledge and curves majestically within inches of the road, an arc of supreme geometry, which takes him high again into the urban therm. An angel with the eye of an eagle. His feathers rise at their tips, ripple and dance, tracing the gale. Here, high above the canal, he waits, skeletons of neon glinting in his pupils, the stench of the Black Country in his nostrils, the perfect wind holding him. He is still, yet still moving.

Where dogs bark and sirens wail, through the oppressive, pulsating white noise of an urban midnight, there is the sound of screaming. It is a woman in the far street, running from the hallway of an open door, its yellow light cutting the pavement in two. Three men are fighting and stumbling out of the house, down the tiny path onto the concrete slab of a road, almost within grabbing reach of the fleeing figure.

'Some family you've turned out to be, you're no father of mine, leave me alone'

'C'mere you bitch, you fuckin - '

'I'll never come back, you can rot in hell! You'll never see me again.'

'You ungrateful, pumped up, limey-loving bastard, you can keep your fancy degrees and good-for-nothing ideas and your poncey Edgbaston pub crowd. Fucking telling us how to run our lives. Don't you bloody ever – '

The words are muffled, trailing off as the woman flails her way out into the darkness. She slips and catches onto broken railings to steady herself, slowing enough for the first and biggest of the drunks to make a lunge at her arm. As the nicotined, broken fingernails dig into her wrist she is wrenched free and upwards on a warm draft, a few drifting feathers swirling down into the light. The men fall among themselves, cursing, ranting. There is no flap of wing, only Stonie's glide, as he draws her against his breast. His wings quiver, taut at the edge of the curve as he banks out over the rooftops. He feels the guilt of talons he thought he would never use, relief that his arms are gentle, comforting around his prey. There is no damage from the opposing forces. His heart pounds in perfect harmony with the fearful life he carries. After a few moments, he breaks the silence.

'I know the secret of flight' he whispers. The angel climbs effortlessly towards the first wisping cloud - no burst of speed, no buffeting - becoming one with the shimmering distance of a fading star. Katherine Sealey, wide-eyed, shivering, finally finds a voice. She is no longer limp, no longer passive, yet in her heart, she knows that to fight is futile.

'Where are you taking me?' The wind is singing in her ears, a strange, soothing music she has never heard before.

'No,' Stonie answers her, 'the question is, where are we going?'

'You going to sit there dreaming or whatever.' The voice was irate, the body language screaming 'had enough, clear off'. It was the hands on the hip. Stonie stood up to face the waitress across the table.

'Oh yeh, sorry. Overstayed my welcome. Was going to help, just that I ache all over. Took more of a pounding than I realised.'

'Course, dear, I should have thought, you're in no fit state. It did look a bit ugly. Mind you, it's not the first time the place has been roughed up.'

'Look thanks for everything,' Stonie butted in as he made towards the door. 'I do have a home to go to, in spite of what it looks like. You've been very kind.' He looked straight at her. "Stars, eh? Oh, can I pay you for - ' The words tailed off as she waved her arm in the air to usher him out. 'Oh, right, thanks, I'll, I'll let you know what I make of the puzzle.' Within seconds he was back in the street, his hand, his wrist, his whole arm buried deep in his pocket, clutching the book.

The next day, around breakfast time, there was another of those calls from America, this time, a male voice. Stonie thought he recognised the name. Federation of something something in the Arts. Would it be possible to go back over the information he had supplied as a reference for Zach Heimer. Mr. Heimer had applied to their agency for funds, was setting up shows in Europe, would he, Mr. Reuladair, mind up-dating them on Mr. Heimer's plans. He had cleared them to enquire. The deadline for the tranche was fast approaching. Lies. The same expressionless, neutral voice, the same patronising language. The last time there had been a transatlantic phone conversation, he was sure he was being tapped. Stonie slammed the receiver down. Nine-forty five a.m. They were calling in the middle of the night; nobody who was any good did that sort of stuff. He would maintain his silence, say nothing to Zach. He needed Zach's full attention. Stonie quickly blocked it from his mind. He cleared breakfast and decided on the same routine for the day, weaving through the crowds, window shopping, drifting in and out of his past, ready for The Encounter. This would be the day the Quechen would be sure to find him.

Between the pavement and the sky there was nothing of interest. He tracked his way through moments of sheer panic; that hollow knotted, sickly wave rippling through his whole body as he was sure he'd spotted the right Pony Tail, The Suit, his Saviour. The man would be leaning out of some tacky newsagent's doorway, his silver hair catching the belisha light, deep in thought, waiting. There would be the same weather-beaten lines and shadows across his angular face, his deep-set eyes firmly focussed on some other world. The Quechen would pull a fistful of sand out of his pocket, thrust it in Stonie's face and say, count this, count the grains. He would cup his hands to the air and capture a cloud for him, saying, listen, it has something to tell you. Listen, then let it go. He would sing with an angel voice and the desert music would heal, restore, bless. And the Indian would be ready this time to tell Stonie the whole story. Not just the facts, but an explanation, a resolution. Where he had been, where he was going. To Stonie, everything was about losing Mica. To the Indian, although Stonie did not know it, everything was about finding her. In those teeth-grinding moments on the pavement, a wave of helplessness would pour through Stonie as the crowds swarmed past him; a paralysis, a deep, deep cramp, a checked tear, before he would force one foot in front of the other towards yet another stranger. This day, he was calm. Slower for the pain, but calm. Perhaps he had had enough.

As the afternoon wore on, he grew tired of dreaming, tired of scanning every face, every posture. The working day was drawing to a close with the same, relentless certainty. The same sparrows arguing between the same buildings, dripping through the pavement branches for the day's crumbs. Queues formed at bus stops. They were all going home. Stonie was sure he was going home too. He had to call it something. Nothing was ever his for long. He found he was back in the square, staring across at the café yet again. There was already graffiti on the boarded up window. Above the shops, shutters were rattling closed, around him, cones were being collected, clouds of starlings were sweeping up over the crumbling eves. He began to pace himself between bus stops, checking every few minutes to make sure the unopened book was there, was still real, still his. Crowded into his seat on the upper deck, he would examine it without distraction, ponder its mysteries. There would be a right moment. Journeys at dusk were rich in philosophical possibilities, revelations, small decisions with huge implications.

Wk.1424
52° 29' N 1° 56.6' W

Stonie made the call while still half asleep, the curtain flapping gently just above his nose as he lay flat on the carpet beneath the window sill. He was watching the clouds, distracted, drifting, but he was in charge. The space was no longer his comfort zone, no longer the portal he would stare through for hours, plotting his escape. This time it was his vantage point. 'Red sky in the morning, shepherd's warning,' was going through his head. No stars tonight then. He was in resolute mood. Stonie was back.

'Look Zach, I have to see you while you're still on this side of the Atlantic. We have to talk. I need help.'

'Been thinking that for months.' The voice was confident, reassuring.

'Yeh, yeh, funny. Don't mess me around, this is serious,' Stonie followed up, the handset lying across his chest. 'I'll be ready in half an hour. Can we meet, then?'

'It's Sunday morning, for goodness sake. I don't have to rush anywhere. Ease up,' Zach replied. 'In any case, you said you'd give me a call two days ago. I've got things planned. I'm only over here for a couple of weeks then off to Italy.'

'My my, and you waited in all day Thursday?'

'Alright, okay, I get the point. So what's the problem?'

'I'll tell you later. Ten o'clock, Westbourne Road. Can you be there for ten? I need the rest of the day for the library. I'll fill you in when we meet.'

'Okay, well what do you mean Westbourne - '

'Ah, forgot, you've never been to the Botanical Gardens. Just get there; I'll pay,' Stonie interrupted. 'Got to go. See you soon.'

The morning mist was burning off, giving way to hazy blue skies by the time Stonie found his way into the glasshouse. It was hot, claustrophobic, with shards of sunlight criss-crossing the greenery.

‘So, what now?’ Zach was fiddling with his camera, talking through the lens at Stonie as he approached.

‘Stop pointing that thing at me, will you?’

‘Click, click,’’ Zach continued, cheekily, ignoring Stonie’s protestations.

‘What d’you mean, what now?’ Stonie fired back as he ducked out of line.

‘Well, you going to take up your job or what? I mean, now you know where you used to work and they’d like you back. That’s what we’re here to talk about, isn’t it?’

‘How the hell do you know that?’ Stonie replied. ‘No, it’s not what we’re here to talk about. You’re not really taking any shots are you? Put the camera away.’

‘Oh, just surmising, piecing things together from what you told me, Stonie, that’s all.’

‘You’re making this up as you go along,’ Stonie said, and stopped talking, distracted by the carp nibbling at his hand. He wiggled his fingers in the water. ‘You’ve no idea, have you? I mean, what I’ve been through. Or do you know more about me than I know about myself?’ There was a pause, long enough for Stonie to continue. ‘Actually, that’s how we find out who we are. I mean, from what other people think of us. Can’t help it. Trying to live up to their expectations, than kind of thing. It’s how we make decisions, ultimately.’ Zach looked directly at Stonie for the first time since they met, and spoke slowly.

‘What are you talking about?’ For a moment, he caught his breath. Did Stonie know after all that he’d rifled through his personal effects? Perhaps he had revealed something in conversation; the brain scan appointments, the pills, Yuma. Zach prepared himself ‘Not supposed to do that,’ he said, homing in with his camera on the gaping mouths of the carp flicking out of the water at Stonie’s fingers. He fired off several shots.

‘Yeh, well, as I said, you’ve no idea,’ Stonie repeated. ‘There’s more to it than you think.’

The two fell silent. They sat against the low wall of the pool, slowing up in the swelter of the tropical air, trying not to distance themselves too much from each other. Zach had lowered his camera onto his lap and was playing with the settings.

'Well, you can hold a pen now, paint, write, that sort of stuff,' he chipped in after a moment or two. 'That was a crazy crucifixion. God.' He pointed the camera at Stonie. 'They must be healing up well now, these hands of yours? How many holes was it?'

'Seven.' Stonie took his time as he shifted his position, embarrassed at the scrutiny. There was the faintest of rye smiles breaking across his face. 'Look, almost healed,' he said, offering his palms in a penitential gesture.

'Biblical,' Zach said, 'Yeh, very Biblical, I'll say that much. You must have been insanely angry not to notice the pain.' Stonie shook his head slowly from side to side and sighed, recalling the sacrificial canal side pose. It was so unnecessary. Pure theatrics. Costly.

'Yeh, well that's behind me now. Pretty intense at the time, though. Pretty stupid.'

'Kind of rounded off the Jay story, though,' Zach said. 'Put an end to it.' Stonie's response was measured.

'There won't ever be an end to it.'

Zach stood up and began pacing up and down on the wet slabs, stroking leaves, ducking behind the camera, pushing through overhanging foliage. He took no photographs. To Stonie, it was an irritation. 'Right, what am I doing here?' he asked as he moved away.

'That's just the point. There's no end to it. There's more stuff, much more,' Stonie said, raising his voice above conversation level. He stood up and wiped his hands on his jacket.

'Where the hell are you?' Zach reappeared and fired off a profile of Stonie. One, two. By the third shutter, Stonie's palm was across the lens. 'Cut it out, will you? I was going to call you on Thursday. Said I would. I definitely planned to catch up. Then things got a bit dramatic.' He pushed back the cuffs of his shirt and jacket. 'See, these bruises, well…'

'You been self-harming? I mean, the barbed wire was bad enough. It's a wonder you haven't thrown yourself into a canal or under a bus by now. Better not give you any ideas. No girl is worth it, Stonie. No job. No period of your life.' Zach had moved away again, ducking under fronds, parting leaves, till finally leaning over the low wall at the far end of the glasshouse to capture some exotic stamen in close up. He was feigning disinterest, in a conversation of his own making. The kind of slow, accentuated running commentary of the practiced photographer with his mind on technical minutia. But he was waiting. He had been summoned, after all.

'Nothing like that,' Stonie replied, in a slightly raised voice. 'I know I was in a state then, coming to the end of something. And I guess I should say thanks for being there. Spoiled the canal trip a bit. Sorry about that. But it's all coming together. Thursday in fact. That's what I want to tell you about. I was going to phone.' Zach was still hidden somewhere behind the foliage. Stonie, leaning with his shoulder against the rusting metal upright, drew his head back to stare up at the glass sky. The diffused light forced him to squint. It looked like a prayerful gesture, as if he was waiting for some divine guidance.

'Let's get out of here,' Zach said, reappearing suddenly through the giant ferns behind where Stonie was waiting. 'I need some air. This had better be good.' Zach took the lead towards the door and stepped out onto the veranda. The air was a relief, cool and clear, and the sun was breaking low through the trees beyond the tennis courts, strong beams cutting through the remaining strands of mist. Two peacocks were strutting gingerly between the deserted tearoom tables, looking for a confrontation. The two men walked past them, out onto the top path. To one side, there was a single diagonal track of dark green footprints across the dipping lawn, running all the way down to the bandstand: some lone trekker had scuffed his feet through the grass, breaking into the silky smooth carpet of dew. Zach let Stonie catch up with him. 'What's coming together?' he asked.

'My life. In a funny sort of way,' Stonie replied.

'Well, let me know how you did it.' The comment drew a quiet laugh from Stonie, but Zach's tone suggested he wasn't exactly joking. Stonie turned and fixed Zach with a direct listen-here look.

'Thursday was the craziest. I would have rung but I was too worn out. Friday, I was too confused. It just all became too much.'

'Get on with it. Do I need a notebook?' Zach quipped. In his head were the stolen facts of those missing months. Hopefully, they would stay there.

Stonie began with the Old Crown, taking an hour of slow-walking, meticulous detail to get anywhere near the truth. He would roll his eyes, stop to prise a thorn or two off a briar, dip low over a rose bush to sniff and cough his way out of a difficult moment, inventing reasons for back-tracking to some flower he's missed, playing phonetics with the Latin labels. Endless interruptions. All in bullet points. Never once did Zach say 'you've told me that.' It was not in his interest. All it would take was one additional fragment. He followed Stonie closely, occasionally mock shooting, setting him up in the viewfinder. Stonie would go over odd little details of his story, as if in some mid-evangelical flight around the altar, the occasional tear welling up in his eyes. Zach processed it all, sometimes feeding the silences, sometimes simply walking them out. It was no ordinary awakening. Stonie's face had changed. There was colour, a certain edge, narrower eyes. He appeared to be more in control, sinister for the first time. The episode seemed explosive enough in itself, at first risible, but it was becoming seriously weird by the café encounter. There was the distinct feeling he would probably never be told everything. All his energy was being used up trying to listen between the lines. He began to rehearse what he might say when Stonie finally ran out of steam. After all, they were on their third lap around the lawn, clockwise, idling past the patio doors yet again. He had been patient so far. No leading questions. During one of Stonie's more tortuous pauses, Zach stepped in.

'I caught the tail end of the riots on the radio,' he said. 'Three hurt or something, several arrests, one policeman in hospital, roads closed, a bit of local damage, that sort of thing. Bloody miners.' Stonie said nothing. He moved away from Zach to sit on the edge of the stone bench, to one side of the tropical glasshouse doors, arms by his side, ready to parry any questions. Zach hesitated, then sat down next to him and stared out across the lawn, rather than turning to address Stonie. 'And you were right in the thick of it, you and your Indian, well, Wendy Soon, if you like. Just think. Who would have thought. Dramatic stuff alright.'

Stonie made no reply. It looked as if he had finally given up trying to remember. 'This is pure speculation,' Zach began, 'but do I get the distinct impression that you still don't know who you are, don't really believe yourself?'

'No, no, no, nothing like that. I think the Indian believed I would be Jay's father, languishing in that goddam awful Yuma rest home, see? He obviously hadn't paid much attention. Well, I guess I looked pretty awful. Bad skin colour, bruised, kind of tanned but dirty. Jay, he was trying to find Jay, to tell her where her father was, trying to do something crazy, useful. It just feels now there's more to it than that, something creepy. Has to be that way. He had my address, well, ours at the time. How the hell did he get hold of that? Felt like he was talking in riddles at first, in his strange way of talking, his accent, you know? I just don't get it. There was this woman, an Italian waitress he befriended. This guy comes all this way to find my ex-girlfriend because he wants to reunite her with who he thinks is her father, who is actually me, because the only information he has leads him to believe I'm this military scientist guy. Have I told you that bit? Have I?' Zach shook his head wearily as Stonie looked over at him.

'You've told me everything several times and I've listened several times, Stonie.'

'Yeh, yeh, of course. As he'd never met any of us, he'd no idea what we looked like or the age thing, the Indian, I mean. Bet he thought Jay was a bit younger. Anyhow, that's why he showed up. His mission. Said he was on a mission. He must have found his way to the old flat and discovered we'd both left ages ago. That must be it. So he's hanging around wondering what went wrong and what to do next, totally preoccupied, totally lost and disillusioned. I suppose there would be some eternal shame for him not fulfilling his calling in life, coming from his culture. Hell, who paid for him to be here? What was it to him?' Stonie took a deep breath. Zach was tempted to offer something but decided against it. 'Hell, I don't know what I know and what I'm making up,' Stonie went on. He made eye contact with Zach, as if to say, you're turn, but Zach maintained his silence with a shrug and a tight, sympathetic smile.

'Scary moment on the bus, though, seeing his face in my head, Zach. What's the likelihood of that kind of revelation then finding the guy's right in my path moments later?' Stonie was rounding on Zach, forcing a reply.

'Very weird coincidence.'

'Coincidence? Don't believe in coincidence or luck. Stonie Reuladair is Wesleyan-evangelical. It's banned. Like gambling and art and ballet, and...and doubt.' Zach laughed, but he was not sure he understood. It was simply the right time to laugh. 'I'm trying to connect, trying to get a handle on how he could have got started, how he could ever think it was worthwhile to do something so, so altruistic, so sacrificial, so damned crazy.' Stonie went on. The two men finally set off again through the conservatory and out onto the terrace, walking slowly side by side.

'Well I'm not religious, not…but maybe you were destined to meet up again,' Zach said.

'No, don't think so. It was all set up. Has to be. But what was in it for him?' Stonie asked. 'I needed to know how he made the connection, how he managed to mistake me... then get off the reservation, find his way over here. Never got to that bit.'

"Are you sure you're not making this up, Stonie? Especially this meeting up in the café nonsense, getting landed on by drunks, the guy disappearing.' Stonie ignored the provocation.

'And I still haven't got to what happened to Jay after all those months. No one returned my calls when I did start to check it out.' Zach continued to nod at appropriate moments. 'Know what? One night I rang ten different numbers, people from our past. Plucked up the courage, broke all my rules about moving on. Every single telephone number was unavailable, continuous tone, or silence. Please call later, several times. Didn't feel strong enough to keep on trying. Anyhow I was running out of past. I just couldn't bring myself to, yeh, well, coincidence? I don't think so.' Stonie drew in a long breath and sighed noisily. 'I need a drink. A pub drink – take out,' he said.

'Now, that I understand,' Zach said, responding sharply to the idea with a pat on Stonie's shoulder. He moved ahead of Stonie towards the turnstile. 'Let's get out of here.' As he glanced back, he could see that Stonie was about to launch into another monologue. 'Save it,' he said. But Stonie continued.

'I knew, I just knew somehow the guy, I mean, when I glanced at that beer mat in the Old Crown, but I didn't link things up at the time. It must have awakened something. All those weeks of trying to find him and just when I do, or he finds me, for goodness sake I have a chance to piece it all together, I get flattened and he disappears. And you're starting to doubt me. That's bad form.'

'Playing devil's advocate, my friend,' Zach shouted back. He had quickened his pace, leaving Stonie trailing behind as he made his way out into the car park.

'So how the hell does that make sense, tell me that? How totally unfair?'

'You haven't been at work then?' Zach said, deliberately changing the subject as Stonie caught up with him.

'Couldn't face it,' Stonie replied. 'Just couldn't go back into the agency. I'm not an adman if I'm honest. Maybe I'll sign on. Don't know what I'll do. I did think about going back. I need the money. Or starting my own studio. I could start up on my own.'

'I didn't think you would go back.' Zach added.

'Really? What made you so sure? Take Vicarage Road, the Old Crown's just across from the lights. Or would you rather go down to The Midland?' Stonie had the waft of perfume in his nostrils. Gem. The smoothness of her cheek against his. Turning air kisses into the real, full on version. He could see the thin chain folding into her cleavage, hear her soft, reassuring voice, those clever, timed asides. It was fleeting. Studying soil sciences in the London, she had said. Okay. He must ask her if that's the truth. What's so interesting about dirt? One day.

The pace was slow, Zach matching Stonie step by step. 'One thing. How d'you know this Indian guy had your address in the first place. Why couldn't it have been random?'

'It's in the note book,' Stonie replied, stopping dead in his tracks and grabbing hold of Zach's elbow to hold him back. 'The book. Oh yes. I was going to get round to it. That's the reason I called you. Well, one of the reasons. Wait till we're inside.' Stonie chose a window seat, then changed his mind. He had to face the sky, had to watch. When Zach returned with the drinks, Stonie drew the notebook from his inside pocket. 'Look at this,' he said, laying it out in front of Zach. 'I did mean to tell you about it right away. Can't really make head nor tail, well, it seems to be in riddles or crossword stuff or in code or something. Or stars. That's what the waitress thinks anyway.'

'Waitress?'

'Oh, never mind,' Stonie said. 'Just take a look.' Zach picked the book up and flicked through the first few pages.

'Strange, very odd.'

'The lady in the café, she seemed to think it was all to do with the sky. She was a bit full of herself. I wasn't listening much, wasn't taking it in, I must admit,' Stonie continued.

'Definitely unusual notation. So whose is it, then?' Zach asked. 'Where did you get it?'

'Oh well, it was on the floor, amongst the broken crockery, under the table, the one I was sitting at when the pickets came through the window. I'm pretty certain it belongs to Wendy Soon,' Stonie said.

'You sticking with that name, then. That's what he called himself? No 'Snow Arrow' or 'Crouching Fox' or 'Chief Running Away' or...well, you know.'

'I didn't make it up. That's his name, Zach. I didn't make it up, for God's sake. You think this is all bullshit, don't you. Just made it up to get attention, eh? No point in telling you anything, really.' Stonie was getting tired of these strategic lighter touches, and his expression registered the fact. Zach, buying time, put his glass of beer to his mouth and made a gesture of contrition at the same time. It was enough to get the conversation flowing again.

'You were saying?

'I'm pretty sure I saw it sticking out of his coat now that I think about it,' Stonie said. He began running his finger down the columns, line by line, scanning each page in turn, searching for some recognisable starting point.

'All these little drawing things with numbers, what d'you make of it?'

'No idea. It's neat,' Zach answered. 'Deliberate. Must mean something to someone. A collection of sorts. But of what? Definitely not train spotting.' Stonie flattened out the pages across the threaded stitching.

'Perhaps he'll come looking for it,' he said.

'Or maybe he dropped it deliberately?' Zach spoke slowly, paused and watched for a response. The implication was not lost on Stonie. He took a long drink, leaned back in his chair and ran his fingers through his hair.

'I'm beginning to wonder,' he said, looking directly at Zach for the first time since they sat down together. He didn't like the idea. So much of what he had gone through, up until now at least, seemed to have been random. 'What you trying to tell me? It's some kind of game, some kind of test? Are you in on this? I mean, it's like I've been lied to by life itself. Don't need any more surprises.'

'Don't be ridiculous,' Zach said, his tone hardening. 'Who's the one who's been coming to the rescue, trying to get you back on track, that sort of thing?'

'Yeh, well that would be the best kind of cover,' Stonie replied. He was tiring. Everyone was fodder.

'It was just a thought, that's all,' Zach said. 'Do me a favour.'

The two sat in silence for a few minutes, Zach becoming more diffident, Stonie, more wary. Finally, Zach spoke. 'Well, I guess it does look more like a train-spotter's book, actually. Let me see it again.' Zach turned each page slowly, unfolding several dog-ears as he did so. 'Well, I'm good with crosswords, codes, riddles,' he said. I've got patience, but this looks as if it could try my patience to the limit.

'Let me see, what's that, Zach?' Stonie was trying to take the book out of Zach's hand as he bent the back of the book against its spine. A thin, folded sheet was jutting out from a slit in the cover. 'More of the same. More columns of numbers,' Zach said with a running commentary as he unfolded the paper and smoothed it out on the table.

'Watch!' Stonie warned, moving to grab a corner of the sheet. 'It's all wet, you'll ruin it.' He drew the side of his hand across the surface towards the edge of the table, sweeping a few dregs of beer onto the carpet as Zach lifted the paper up to the light.

'No harm done, see?' Zach said. 'Lighten up.'

'So, anything different, let me look.' Stonie could feel this was out of his control already. The knots were tightening in his stomach.

'In a minute, hang on!' Zach replied, twisting away from Stonie's advancing clutches. He knew he was doing it for effect. 'Just hang on.'

Stonie sat back for a moment. He was beginning to resent sharing the notebook, sharing his story, his life. It felt like a mistake. 'Did I hear you say 'cosmic' under your breath, Zach? Did I hear you actually use that word? We're supposed to have left the sixties behind. Dude.'

'Yeh, man, v cosmic, v Hippie, so Sixties. Look, you idiot, you yourself said it might be about the stars. What else is that but cosmic?' With both hands on the edges of the book, Zach shuffled his chair closer to Stonie and forced the spread in front of Stonie's face. 'Look, those diagrams, tracery, they're little sections of the heavens. They're maps,' he said, softening his stance. He laid the book down and pointed at one of the lists. 'And with the numbers, well, they're references, got to be. Hell, I reckon your waitress knew what she was talking about.'

'What's hell got to do with it?' Stonie countered.

'Oh yeh, heavens, yeh, well, okay, very droll,' Zach shrugged. He knew he had to back off. He was in danger of losing Stonie for the day. He closed the book and offered it up. Stonie looked at him with a slightly perturbed expression on his face, said thanks and dropped the book back into his inside jacket pocket with no further comment. He had had enough for the moment. In the silence which followed, both would have preferred to change the subject. One, completely talked out, the other, unsure what to do with the craziness, the pace, the new, tantalising twist. Within minutes the book was out on the table again

'Surely the Indian will miss it. He can't be finished with it,' Stonie began. Zach made a tight-lipped gesture before responding.

'Well, yes, maybe he can, maybe he is.' he replied, taking his time over every word. He had no idea which way to steer the conversation.

'He wouldn't have left it there for me to find, would he?' Stonie said, with the merest hint of a whimper. 'I mean surely not in those circumstances.'

'This is becoming seriously rhetorical, Stonie. How would either of us know? Let me see that separate piece of paper again.' The sheet folded out to something like twelve inches square, and every bit of it was taken up with fine columns of numbers on both sides. Most of the numbers were a combination of digits, letters and a few bracketed characters. Every so often as he scanned down the lists, Zach could see that certain references were much longer than the others in the pattern. There seemed to be an emerging sequence, a deliberation. 'Notice anything?' Zach asked after a pause. Stonie had gone quiet, drinking, sitting back, detached, looking around at the other tables full of hunched, chattering diners.

'I'm hungry,' he said. 'Sorry, what did you say?' Stonie turned back and made a conscious effort to follow Zach's finger as he traced down the sheet. 'Yeh, sorry. Getting hungry though.'

'See this,' Zach said, jabbing at the lists. 'Every reference is numbered, some in brackets, some without, but they are all in sequence, every last one of them, I'm sure of it. The short rows, with or without letters of the alphabet, they're numbered and it looks as if no two references are the same. They have to be sequential. Look.' Stonie was staring blankly at the paper, as close as he felt comfortable, vainly trying to follow Zach's explanation. 'See?' Zach continued, unconcerned at Stonie's stiff, hollow attention. 'Some of these entries are repeated on these little diagrams, here.' Zach had opened the notebook again, stretched the pages against the spine and flicked through to the first page. Then another, testing each with the opened sheet, making comparisons, matching up the information. He found a pencil and a scrap of paper and began making his own notes. Stonie's pained expression was lost on him. 'Are you taking any of this in?' he asked. 'Stonie, it's you're call here. Take an interest.' Stonie leaned back and put his glass to his mouth, but didn't take a drink. Instead, he lowered the glass slowly to the table and carefully, ceremoniously placed it on a beer mat, adjusting its position until it was perfectly centred on the square.

'I seem to have been surrounded by strange goings on ever since I came back. Like, there's been those calls from the states about, well, about…you. Very disconnected. I've told you about them, haven't I? And now this. I'll never fathom it out. I've had just about enough.' He rose from his seat and forced his way between the standing drinkers. 'I don't think I can keep up. I did tell you that people were calling me up about you, didn't I?' Zach waited for more but nothing was forthcoming. Stonie had stopped and was looking across at Zach, as if he was thinking of coming back to his seat, but he changed his mind and made for the door, hesitating for a moment with one hand on the door knob. He twisted round and faced Zach square on. 'The book,' he shouted across two or three people. 'Didn't expect to go into this much detail, not right now. I've had enough. You work it out.'

'What calls?' Zach yelled after him, but Stonie had turned his back. Zach watched Stonie push open the door then hesitate yet again. 'Shit. What calls?' Zach whispered after him.

The hazy sun was diffused through the partly stained glass window, seeds and leaves and road dust swirling up off the pavement. A fly poster was flapping up around a lamp post, more frayed with every passing car. Between the shoulders of the shifting drinkers, Zach watched Stonie lean forward over the empty wine bottles on the window ledge by the door, and begin to shade his eyes, with his hand in salute pose across his forehead, almost touching the glass pane with his nose. Zach had seen him staring out at the sky on a number of occasions. Perhaps Stonie believed this time he would see Jay window-shopping across the street, Luca staring out from a poster panel on the side of a slowly passing bus, the Quechen stoop out of a taxi and head straight through the door of the pub. Who knows what other actors were skulking around in the wings? This was a Stonie with complications. Zach sat back, closed his eyes and waited. He knew what calls.

'Is it really months since we were here together? You were in some kind of limbo, some kind of shock, I don't know. You'd handed in your notice or something and you looked as if you had completely lost it. Gem was talking in a more animated way than normal. 'I remember that much. I mean, you just sat there not wanting to be anywhere.' Stonie studied her, looking for anything other than her normal dispassionate expression.

'Particularly not in the UK,' he said. There was no way he was going to drop into full confessional mode again. He was beginning to wish he'd held back with everyone. But he couldn't tell her that. He watched closely as Gem talked on. The lips, the clean pores, the perfect sweep or her eye lashes. He was listening, but the unfolding mystery of Zach was still preying on his mind.

'You certainly didn't seem happy with your job, you - ' Gem stopped. She was the professional. Small talk was hard work, sincerity seemed even harder. Irritation was something to note, not to take on. She was curious to know how long it would take this guy to come back. Or to say anything meaningful. She continued with the reminiscing device. Up until then it had been a comfortable ploy.

'Oh, sorry; just had a thought,' Stonie said, with a vague nod of his head. 'Nothing for now. Later.' Gem continued, talking fast and thinking faster, wondering how to make the most of the opportunity. She crossed and re-crossed her legs several times, sweeping imaginary crumbs from her skirt, finally leaning forward to rest her elbows on the table edge, both hands cupped around her coffee cup, looking interested.

'And the thought? Are you not going to tell me? Never mind. Actually, you don't seem much different now, come to think of it. Is it me?' Gem went on. It was inane and uncharacteristic. 'Here, let's order some tea. You were sitting in a daze, actually, right here, in the same seat, funnily enough. Talking about getting away, doing something a bit radical and, eh, remember, didn't you tell me that dream you had about selling poetry but it was original copies and stuff like that and once the poems were given away you were angry that you couldn't buy them back. I never forgot the look on your face. Just weren't with it at all. I think it was to get money to travel and you were in America somewhere. But it wasn't real.'

'Right, well, anyway, dreams,' Stonie replied, shifting uneasily in his seat.

'I remember the picture you created. Anyhow, nothing wrong with dreams. And sometimes they come true', Gem said. Stonie started biting his nails

'Sometimes.' That was as much as he could say. He had to plan this. Gem was still someone to aim for. He composed himself, ran his fingers over the buttons on his shirt, discreetly checked his flies to make sure and sat forward. 'It really is good to see you, though,' he said, forcibly lightening up. 'Work going well?'

'Oh, just the same. So where have you been all this time?' Gem asked, weighing every word to avoid the possibility of a flippant response. She needed to know in detail. She began to realise that maybe she had missed him after all.

'So, what's been happening? Well, I could make it up, my own version, if you like. That would be fun. It's important to have plenty of gossip and nothing to talk about. But I'd say, if I'm honest, I'd say things have definitely changed. You've changed. Just being nosey.' Gem loosened the button on her jacket and relaxed back into her chair. 'You've been ill, or overseas, or just plain bored with us all,' she prompted. Stonie looked across at her. There it was, the fine little silver chain with its cross disappearing into her cleavage. He was still wondering what that would feel like when a look became a stare.

'You spent quite a bit of time thinking about this lately, then?' Gem asked. Stonie knew it was a leading question. For no reason, the interview feeling was creeping in on him again. No, well, okay, missed you, been busy. That's what he wanted to hear.

'Yes, well I'm back now. Had a few days out here and there, local stuff. Then reports to write; interesting project. It's for a study on Indians in a reservation.' He tried to make a connection but ran out of ideas. 'Behavioural issues, comparisons with certain kinds of people over here. I won't bore you with it.'

'Oh, you won't do that. Do go on. More coffee?'

'Good idea.'

'But I thought you were in advertising.' Gem said.

'Yeh, well I am, was. It's creative, related. I do all kinds of things, really. Copy writing, design, research. I'm good at it and this came up. Well, there's this guy. I got to know him a bit. Flies in and out of the place all the time. From the states. Zacharias P. Graffenheimer the Third. Now, there's a mouthful for you. But that is his actual name. He's an artist and kick-ass photographer. A bit of a conceptualist, I suppose. Mounts shows of his work, got a reputation in the states and seems to be establishing himself in Europe. He wanted someone to work for him at this end on a project. Can't say too much. It's all a bit subject to copyright, awkward deadlines, permissions, you know the kind of thing.'

'When is he around, then? You must introduce me to him one of these days,' Gem said, assuming a more formal pose as she replaced her cup on its saucer. There was a hint of embarrassment at the suggestion.

'Well, come to think of it, he did say, he mentioned some state-side photo shoot, some government commission. He's away at the moment,' Stonie said. Gem knew instinctively to move on.

'So then…what now? What have you got planned? I mean, the immediate future, after the report. Painter. Poet? Full time writer. Back to the agency?' With a grunt and shrug of his shoulders, Stonie took Wendy Soon's notebook out of his pocket and casually dropped it onto the coffee table.

'What do you make of this?'

Wk.1430

52º 29' N   1º 56.6' W

On the First Night of the Book, Stonie lay awake all night, his brain on overload, trying to work out just what it was about the Big Idea which had come back to haunt him. He felt he was back to his old self, flirting with escape, teasing out an exit strategy. That's when he knew enough healing had taken place. The less he thought of Mica, the easier life became. Wendy Soon was a figment. That was easier too. If he was chastened by his desert experience, his lost months, it hardly mattered. As far as he was concerned, everyone was in denial about something. For now, everything seemed to be back in its place. Almost everything. He still could not figure out the people he knew in his immediate circle. Gem, Kate, mostly Zach.

It was already time for a change, another gamble, something out of character. Ordinarily, he hated codes, loathed numbers, and had no patience with the cryptic. Calculation was a concept he would never get round to. There was too much order, too much pattern. Far too much logic. He preferred risk, turning the random into real. Yet this was different. He knew at once. Something had to be done with the book and these figures, if only to throw light on the soul of a stranger. Tomorrow he would continue to scour the city, praying for a second chance. Tonight, he was in commentary. So Reuladair takes a favourite star or two, several in fact. Plots the paths between them, all the permutations. It's a new angle. He transfers the grid to acetate and lays it across a map, any land mass of his choice. The stars touch the earth; he goes there, begins his journey. It is his way of securing a future. Only, it is not just any land mass of his choice. It is the Quechen's world. The next set of stars are a new time frame. He goes there, curious, engaged, each star a crossroads. The path before him is the one he leaves behind. He is caught between the warm desert mattress and the frosted concrete park bench. *He sleeps to wake, he falls to rise, he is baffled to fight better.*

The Second Night of the Book was more sobering. A deep, dark, clear night; so many more stars than he had seen before. They were light years away, and they all looked the same. Except, each was set in his own time, her own space. This was the way with the universe beyond his skin. A pulsating cocoon, whether asleep, or waking to filter out the ambient white noise beyond his four walls. The coordinates would be the starting point. Those at least, might make sense of the original *plan*. He would try to move between them. Yet again sleep eluded him.

The next morning, Stonie's breakfast conversation with himself took the form of an ultimatum. Wrap up the book and send it back to the reservation. It was bound to reach the Indian. Perhaps, then, letters would come, explanations. On the other hand, he could eventually turn up, this mysterious inquisitor. He would be spotted

at traffic lights, then swiped from his gaze as three double decker buses bumper-to-bumpered across his line of sight, leaving a shadow on the side of the road. He would be on the opposite platform as some slow-moving goods train rumbled through the station, captured fleetingly between coal hoppers. He would be way down there in the stalls just as the theatre lights were dimmed, with someone else rising from the same seat at the final curtain. And each time, there would be nothing but an after image, a vague certainty that he could have been stalked successfully if everyone had been more alert. It wasn't really the Quechen after all. It was a construction, an interruption. We were not meant to mean anything to each other; this was internal. The physician was healing himself.
On The Third Night of the Book, the phone rang. The voice was upbeat. 'Cracked it yet?'

'What d'you mean? The mystery of the notebook or the mystery of the disappearing Zach?' Stonie said.

'Yeh, sorry about that, just had to get back; stuff to sort out.' Zach replied.

'Biggest euphemism in the world, biggest excuse.'

'What is, my friend?' Zach asked.

'Stuff!' Stonie almost shouted down the line. 'Stuff, what stuff this time? Can't have been that important.' He was annoyed. His friends were strangers and this proved it. 'I mean, you just upped and away. I was depending on you.' He paused and lowered his voice. 'I needed you to be on hand. You know, your analytical brain. I needed an angle. Either you, or I try the waitress in the cafe, but that was just luck, most likely.' The line went silent for a moment.

'Ah well, well, I just thought I'd check you were okay. I haven't gone back to the States yet. Just had some urgent rolls of film to get processed…oh and invoices to sort out. And some clients in London...new business. Anyhow, have you solved the mystery?' Stonie sensed something. Insincerity, pressure, distance, more than the three and a half thousand miles. Zach had definitely crossed the Atlantic.

'So, you're not calling from the kiosk at the end of the street, are you?' He felt justified in being provocative. He hated being given the run-around.

'I wish,' Zach answered,

'Anyhow, what's with these calls I've been getting? People asking strange questions about you, Zach. Are you in any kind of trouble?'

'You've had calls?' Stonie sat on the arm of his chair, steadied himself.

'You know I have. Told you more than once. The guy was curious about you being in the UK, how long for. Wanted to know what you were planning for your show and I said you were just on holiday, visiting me. Then off to Italy to some photography conference. But how did they get my number? Did you give them this address? I kind of wondered if it was actually me they wanted information on.' There was no response. 'Zach, don't go dead on me, d'you hear? You there?' There seemed to be interference on the line. Stonie persisted, raising his voice, jamming the receiver even closer to his ear. He became aware of how tightly he was holding the receiver, grinding his teeth. 'Hello, Zach, you there?'

'Oh, yeh, sorry, something on the line; well, look, I had to leave an address with my agent, a phone number, in case I had to be contacted. Seemed like your number was best. I don't have an office yet in the UK. Seemed reasonable. Never know what hotel I will be going on to or who's place I will be crashing out at. Don't you remember I discussed it with you? I guess you weren't quite your old self.' Stonie was becoming irate. He slumped into his seat and leaned his head back till he was staring at the ceiling. 'Far as I'm concerned, they were snooping and it wasn't your normal work people, wasn't about you. It just made me feel odd, that's all.' There was a delay on the line. He could hear the 'what else' as he spoke. 'Said they had some information concerning a buyer, someone who had researched your work.' Stonie had slowed until his voice tailed off at the end of the sentence. 'But I think there is something else going on.'

'Oh, right, okay. It'll be some agent. Did you take a note of the guy's name, the company?' Zach went on, more concerned with what he needed to know than any slant Stonie was putting on things. He was talking without listening. Stonie was ready to cut him off and began to hold the receiver at arms length. He wasn't being taken seriously. There was no point in pursuing it. He knew something was not right, instinctively knew that the other parts of the Zach saga were beginning to sound hollow.

'Anyhow, if I'd cracked it, you'd be the first to know,' he shouted into the phone. He was rapidly changing his mind. The secrets of the book, if he ever found them, would be his. He would do this alone. 'One fraction of a second of inspiration and it will all fall into place. I swear it will. You know me, take my time. I just pretend I don't know what I'm doing. But if I have no option - ' He paused, thankful there was no eye contact.

'So, you okay? Sorry to have been a bit vague. You know how it is.' Zach paused and in spite of himself, Stonie felt obligated to fill the silence.

'Well, anyway, I'm in pretty good form if you want to know, getting on with the research. I've more or less given up on finding the Indian. He's history. It was wearing me out. I'm sure he's far gone by now. And that's disappointing.'

'Well, let me know how things work out. And best not to mess with my agent. Busy man. Doesn't seem to like jokes or small talk. They're a breed apart. Comes with the job. So I was sight-seeing, visiting you, right? Doing Italy, photo trip. Right? You did tell them that? Well he knows I'm working. Glad you're occupied, keeping the book thing going. It certainly is a bit of a teaser – and especially after all you've been through.' Again Stonie could hear a slight crackling on the line, clicks, interference.

'But I still don't understand, he didn't really get to any point. Said you hadn't left your last number, didn't have an itinery for you. Zach, what's you're problem, you sure you are not hitting problems, in some kind of trouble? It always comes across - ' Stonie was interrupted.

'Nothing, anyhow, have to go. I'll be back in two or three weeks. Take it easy. I'll send you an invite to the private view in Milan.' Zach's voice was normal. Stonie had been listening for nerves.

'As if I'm likely to make that kid of trip. Where would someone like me get the money? Yeh, well I have to get to the library. Closing soon. Thanks for the call. Ciao.'

Stonie replaced the receiver and surveyed the mess around him. The flat was littered with bits of paper, all shapes and sizes, complete spiral bound books ripped out and taped into a patchwork of ideas, scribbles, diagrams, calculations. A4 sheets, ruled, punched, screwed up and flattened back out for re-use. Every scrap with any space on it was marked and positioned. The paper trail into the kitchen was trampled on, torn and mended. More than once it had stuck to his feet, been sprayed with coffee and crumbs. The mirror was covered, hidden somewhere behind three days of worked-over drawings, pins and trails of thread. Piles of books had become weights to the drapes and folds of old wallpaper rolling off the mantelpiece and across the sofa. Every coffee cup had been pressed into service, holding down the curling corners of the galaxy.

The big stars were easy, Stonie could identify the planets. It was the sheer volume of small points, incidentals, those moments in history which had never mattered before, that no one had ever really noticed, those light years. Now, they seemed significant just for themselves and had to be fitted in, taken seriously. This was about interconnectedness. Everyone who had ever looked up into the heavens had been reached. This was about the fact that without each in its place, and at the right time, the story would be incomplete. Stonie raised himself from his doubled up position on the chair and picked his way towards the kitchen. One space, Stonie had kept free. Over by the window, he had left some carpet exposed. By three in the morning, he would be flat on his back, staring up at his familiar square of night and willing the clouds to break. He would recall the sky south of Jerome, one hundred and eighty degrees of sparkling Arizona. It could have been the sweeping Dutch canopy east of Zwolle or the jewelled Kenyan velvet of Marsabit. Could have been. Only now, he was wiser. Each signature, each sighting mapped out a different way of living, a different way of going somewhere. This time, Stonie was determined. This time, it would no longer be in his head. The nagging doubt was there. He had no one to leave behind.

'Fifth time in the same lounge, almost the same time of day; fifth time in three weeks,' Stonie said as he threw his jacket over the arm of the chair and slumped down into the soft leather. The lady was becoming a habit. The book was bringing people together and Gem was conveniently curious. Stonie needed no excuse. He was cultivating the mystery. She would joke about these numbers becoming his life's work, sense he was not to be trifled with. He would hide his irritation. But Stonie was tired. There was no breakthrough. Not with Gem, not with the book.

The hotel lounge mid-morning. It was a comfort zone. It brought hope 'You've been keeping count? I can hardly remember which day it is,' Gem said, her tone uncharacteristically relaxed.

'Very precise.'

'Well, not really. Look, back in a minute. Just realised I need to go to the toilet.' Stonie leapt up and briskly made for the corridor. He came back at a slower pace, already talking. 'Just can't get rid of this awful dank slab-grey sky, can we? It's depressing,' he was saying, immediately aware of how ridiculous the national preoccupation was.

'Who's this, then?' Gem enquired, holding up a small black and white photograph.

'Hey, what are you doing with that?' Stonie countered irately.

'I was just staring at the floor, needed picking up, that's all. Sorree.' Gem noted the discomfort. Stonie was by this time on the edge of his seat. 'You must have dropped it. Thought it was yours.'

'Okay thanks.' Stonie reached out for the photograph as Gem turned it over between her fingers. She was sorely tempted to tease things out.

'What's so special, who is he, then?' There was a pause.

'Probably a guy I never met, someone's father, somebody's lover, how the hell do I know; let me see,' Stonie replied, softening his tone. 'Let me see it; give it to me.'

'Tells me a lot. You've got a real knack for description. He looks like a Yank.' The comment took Stonie by surprise. There were things to remember, things to forget. It was hard to tell the difference.

'Let me see,' Stonie repeated, trying to stay calm under the mild provocation. 'Oh, right. Never seen it before. Probably fell out of one of these books I picked up, second hand job lot. I'm always book browsing, love second hand shops.' He fingered the photograph, holding it by thumb, index and middle finger, lightly by the edges, as if a fingerprint would mark the image. As he spoke, he kept the photograph at eye level.

'You know what old books are like. People use pictures and old photographs as bookmarks, so you find some strange stuff, odd bits, fascinating scribbles in the margins, newspaper cuttings, flowery dedications in fading brown copperplate, meticulous sometimes, they are. Found a lock of hair once. Looked like some kid's curl, now there's a memory for you. Course, you get mouldy petals and pressed earwigs and live book bugs, and pages that missed the guillotine. Can be quite a journey.' He took a deep breath and tried to sound reflective. 'No, no idea.' Stonie sat back, and placed the photo on the arm of the chair in a deliberate attempt to make it look as if it was unimportant. Luca Cambareri had been tucked away inside Antoine de Saint-Exupéry for months. Stonie had no recollection at all of thumbing through the book since his return, removing the picture; no idea why it came to be on the floor at his feet. 'Just a bookmark,' he said.

'Look, I have to ask you, you being here and in this state, well, what's going on? I've missed you. This is not the old Stonie. So, what have you been up to?' Stonie took a deep breath and shifted in his seat, leaning forward, his elbows propped on his knees, his hands cupped around his drink. The photo was caught in his knuckles like a cigarette as he slurped his coffee.

'It's no bloody business of yours, don't ask. Just don't ask,' he blurted out. The aggression caught both of them by surprise. Gem looked shocked and sat back abruptly in her seat trying to get the measure of what was going on. 'God, did I just say that? Where did that come from? Oh, so sorry; there was a rush of heat to my head, couldn't stop myself.'

'I'm right after all,' Gem said, 'you need help, Stonie, definitely need help.' She looked at him steadily. He was more of a stranger than she had thought. She had never heard him use the word. He was never that angry. Gem reached over, placed the mug squarely on the table, and stared intently at the hunched figure on the sofa. Stonie smile self-consciously.

'And stop looking so bloody concerned,' he said, fixing Gem with a stare. 'I mean, what do we know about each other in any case. No one has the right, I mean nobody lets anyone inside their world, really. Really. Just a bad moment. Caught out.' Gem drew back. This was exactly what she was looking for. The disjointed conversation, the other-worldliness of the exchanges, a mood swing. There was a definite change and it might be productive. It was time for creative pleasantries, time to push one or two buttons. She put her hand on Stonie's arm and tapped it gently.

'Look, I'll...I'll be on my way now. Better be getting along.'

'No no, no, sorry. It's okay. Really. Been through quite a lot lately. Didn't mean to, to lower the tone, to react like - ' There was no more sentence for Gem to finish off.

'Could do with another coffee, then. Back in a minute,' she said, heading over to the bar. From there, she could measure Stonie, try to second guess the next mood.

Stonie sat on, examining the back of the photograph. There was a faint set of numbers neatly inscribed in the top right hand corner, marks disappearing into the scratches and tiny cracks and the residue of countless fingerprints. He mouthed the configuration slowly, turning the surface towards the light as he read, 23230046. He wanted to say he recognised the number. He felt he ought to know. He felt connected but did not know why. At least, he knew the guy was Luca. That much. Perhaps he should share what he could remember, see what else he would be told about himself. That was usually the way of things. Your friends are a useless source of who you are, but your acquaintances, well, they are less careful. Here was the thin line between knowing the truth and dreaming it. But he held back. He turned the photograph over and looked at Luca staring straight to camera. Looked into his eyes. There seemed nothing to penetrate. What he missed, however, was the slightly disturbed surface, the minute ghosted impressions on the bromide, the equation, part of a formula.

Stonie felt he needed to lighten the mood, make up for his reaction if he was to make the most of the morning. Gem was looking uncomfortable, restless 'Well we can't go on meeting like this,' he joked.

'Or letting things get too heavy,' Gem replied. She looked knowingly at him, with a slight tip of the head to one side and did what she was best at, laughed to order. Stonie held back, consciously looking away from Gem. There it was again, the pause before responding. That slight, well-constructed silence. Stonie wished he knew her secret.

'You don't really like your job then?' she said, finally breaking the silence. 'I get that impression. But you're an artist, take photographs, do a lot of writing. Couldn't you make it as an artist on your own? You must know an artist or two who could help you out, maybe collaborate, put on a show.'

'Yeh' said Stonie, ' isn't that what everyone does?

'Well, just a thought. Must be difficult, of course. I've never come across any rich artists. I mean, how on earth can you afford to take me out like this? You're broke, aren't you?'

'Oh, I thought it was on you again,' Stonie joked. 'Anyhow, I'm getting money for my story,' he said, almost before he had thought about what he was saying.

'What story? What on earth are you talking about?' Gem asked. 'You know, I'm more convinced than ever you're just a dreamer, a romantic. What on earth are you on about now?'

Stonie waited his moment. He had begun to toy with the idea that he was more than the keeper of a mystery. He would weave the notebook quite seamlessly into his 'lost' five months. There was a book in it. The thought had only just occurred to him. In any case, Gem was still on his list. He knew he had to come up with something impressive soon. This felt like a good time for confession. For a few moments, he rolled with the small talk until the coffee had been served. Gem ceremoniously plunged the cafetière and poured the coffee in silence, before looking up.

'So, Mr. Dark Horse, why me? Why do I get the inside track?' It felt like the break through she had been waiting for. Stonie was looking for another kind of break through. 'I bet people have been trying to piece you together for months. I certainly have. Not that it's any of my business. But you know me, well, the absentee, that kind of thing, it makes a lady curious. She was trying not to patronise him, trying to put him at ease. There was a thin line.

She leaned forward; her pose was earnest, concentrated. 'Any progress then? I mean, on the notebook. That mystery you're trying to solve?'

'Oh, did I tell you about that? Stonie asked, looking surprised. He took a noisy sip of his hot, black coffee and sat back, wiping his mouth with his forefinger as he did so. There were times when he regarded every conversation as an interrogation. But this was Gem and he was weary of the quest. He needed to spice things up. Take the lead. He cast his eye around the lounge, as if establishing that there was no one in earshot. 'I'm working on it. I mean, he does exist, honestly.'

'Who?'

'Ah, well - '

In the next ten minutes, Stonie covered the highlights. No need to mention Mica. No need for an explanation, a motive, just the facts. Everyone has a reason to escape, the urge is in us all. That was his comfort. Stonie could hear himself dramatising the more intense encounters to himself. Facing the wrong end of a gun, the searing heat, cold, emptiness. Left for dead, the rest home with its smell of old age and wasted months, the endless medical examinations, those fleeting, lucid moments he had clung to until he could finally trust himself, the uncertain steps back to some form of reality. He wanted to say how he felt when he first walked back into his flat, the final shock of total recall. His form of recall. Instead, it was just the found book in the café which might have belonged to a strange foreigner who disappeared. Found after the disturbances, the riots. He managed the drama. Gem listened intently without interrupting. Finally, Stonie sank back into the armchair and drew breath. He had made it big, yet left out a great deal of detail.

'Goodness,' Gem said when the opportunity presented itself.

'That's it,' Stonie said. 'All I can tell you. That's me up to date, in a manner of speaking. I don't know whether I'll ever solve the mystery. It's absorbing and I guess it seems to be from another dimension. Then or now or the time before. Maybe I'm already the future. But my time off work, well I didn't really mind the space.' He paused for a moment, leaned forward in his chair and swept some tiny crumbs from the table edge. 'You'll understand why it has been difficult settling back into a job. I thought I could. I'm going to try a different route. I seem to be always travelling inside my head. Come to think of it, I suppose I could always do art.' Gem smiled approval, as composed as ever, and waited for a moment before responding. Her voice took on a playful tone.

'You've never shown me any of your work, you know. That would be a good excuse to meet up soon. I'd like that. Anyhow, about this guy. Maybe he is a real alien, the Indian-type guy,' she said. It was slight, the best she could do. The coffee was finished and it was almost time to go.

'That what do you think? What you really think? You big on mysteries?' Stonie asked.

'No, not particularly. It's worth writing up, though. I get the feeling there's plenty more you haven't told me, eh?' Gem chuckled and shook her head. She had stiffened, altered her pose and seemed more strategic. Stonie sensed it and made a mental note.

'So, that's it.'

'Great story. My lips are sealed. I'll buy the newspaper when it's serialised,' she said, standing up to take her leave. She was as in command as ever. Stonie envied that. She buttoned her jacket deftly with one hand, swept her bag onto her shoulder and moved round the table as Stonie rose from his chair. Time for air kisses.

'That's it. You have been entrusted with the task of finding the alien,' she joked. Stonie winced but managed a measured smile. He was not being taken absolutely seriously. Enough for Gem to notice. 'Sorry,' she said. 'But there's stuff going on. I need to get back to the office. Problems to solve, you know how it is.'

'Like what?' Stonie asked, defensively. It had not gone well.

'Another time,' she replied. 'Thanks for the company. It has been very interesting.' Stonie knew that with Gem, there was no point in pursuing the matter. The remark heightened his unease. And anyhow, he hated the word. Nothing was just interesting. It meant nothing, hid the truth. Had he said too much? At least Mica was still his private domain. 'Bet all these numbers are a secret code to call the guy back home. A special message,' she added with a melodramatic flourish. 'No, I'm serious. How do we know? And he chose you.' She looked at Stonie, fixed him straight on, a mischievous twinkle in her eye. 'I'll pay and no argument.'

For the next few weeks, Stonie kept everyone at a distance. Nothing new in that. He had done it most of his life. But he knew he had to work, finally persuading his old agency to take him back as a freelance artist. That suited. Every available moment away from work, there were still more permutations to consider, more tiny white dots on small black skies from large dusty books. There were lists. Lists of people to talk to, people to hide things from and no way to draw his own lines between them. Above him, the sky was no inspiration at all. Beside him, each dog-eared page in a library book was just another little sin. Inside him, the passion for closure was dying.

When the call came, he was half asleep, the curtain flapping gently just above his nose as he lay on his back beneath the window sill in his usual spot. The gap in the slash cord window was high enough for the occasional spit of light rain to catch his forehead. Stonie stretched out his foot and lazily knocked the receiver onto the carpet to bring it within reach. He looked at his watch. After eight and dusk falling quickly. The caller was someone he had spoken to only once before by telephone, yet she seemed to know every detail.

Yes, he was a former tenant, moved on some time ago, red hair, thinning, the fellow from the ad agency. Yes, occasionally at the Old Crown, thought so. How did you track me down? Oh, a regular. It was one of those calls where the preliminaries are leading nowhere, get on with it for goodness sake…get to the point. Did he want the envelope sent on to him or would he be anywhere near by to pick it up. For a certain Jay Cambareri, care of…well it has your name on it and it seems too much time has gone by to return it to the sender. Very old date. They said at the pub they knew where you'd gone. Stonie's mouth dried. Day twenty-four of the Book, page nine of the Drawing and now, the Envelope. He felt queasy. Three years of his life ransacked again in a single instant. Collect it? Would teatime tomorrow be convenient?

Picking up the envelope was easy. Opening it would be a different matter. It was that post-mark again. Stonie had never laid eyes on the lady, yet she had recognised him, said she'd been wondering where he'd gone, wasn't around these parts much any more, curious why Jay had vanished without a trace. Those were her words. Stonie thanked her profusely, his heart racing. The letter? Oh yes, it had been trapped behind the skirting board, corner sticking up deep in the back of the cupboard in the hallway, under the gas meter, you know the one. Sorry it's so crumpled. Stonie needed a drink. On his way back home, he changed his mind. Home was no good. He made for the Old Crown, found a quiet corner seat and sat for an eternity with the envelope in his pocket, one minute buried deep, the next, taken out and examined, held up to the light, stroked, smoothed out. It was still pressed deep inside his coat pocket, unopened, when he swayed into his flat hours later. A note for a dead woman. This was a moment drained of all reason. So much emotional baggage crammed into one freaky envelope. Whatever it contained, he would not be ready.

Hello Miss Cambareri, how are you today. This is Sylviana again. I told Wendy Soon I would let you know if I found anything new. I have not seen my Quechen friend for a few weeks but I always keep my promise. He used to sit here in the window with his little book of numbers. Remember I tell you he can only take numbers and letters down he read all the time but he no write words or stories very well. I don't think so. I write for him. Anyway, the diner is very busy. Did

I say we are on the edge of the reservation, overlook the railyard. That why we get the many customer. There have been two fights this week but I no allow beer.
Someone call me yesterday from the Veterans Association she say the number on the dog tag, it not the same as the number on the urn. They check it in a book but they wonder if I ask about the right person. Then they not sure who I talk about. My friend think the military maybe given out the wrong ashes. But the date they give me, that was '69 or '70 so maybe they forget already? I say why they no talk to Mrs Cambareri, your dear mama, they say your mama she never contact them. Sure they have other records but the authorities tell me nothing. I think this is my 19 letter but you have never reply but because I no get return to sender I keep writing. No one can tell if you exist, but the people in Mount Kisco still say this is your house owner. I live in Mount Kisco once. This better than city. Last time I see him, Wendy Soon is full of hope and I no wish to disappoint him. He has to find family for the man in the nursing home I ask time and again what it is to him and he tell me he do it for his father. Everyone respect their father. So I help. You know because he is Indian they not deal with him.
I think it is very wrong but make trouble if I talk about it here. I have to make living. He is a very nice person, most of them are. I invite again you come visit with us.
They install me a telephone soon. I write with the number and maybe you phone.
I no give up.

Signed Silviana

The handwriting was assured, obviously a fountain pen. The blue lined yellowing single sheet was punctured through to the other side, the dark brown ink feathering in places. The folds were sharp, ceremoniously sharp. This was the pride and deliberation of someone on a mission. Stonie folded the sheet of paper and tucked it back into its envelope. It was history. It explained nothing. He was still languishing in that God-forsaken Arizona hospice. He was still answering all those questions about who he thought he was. He was still pacing the world, unsaved, longing for the right interruption. Mica's father was dead. Mica's father was not dead. Mica was dead.

Mica was not dead. Stonie had an overwhelming desire to pick up the phone, hear her voice again, even in anger. He shuffled slowly out of the hallway and into the sitting room, without switching on the light, arching his back as he removed his coat, swaying, cursing the drink, cursing the whole fucking world. He hooked his finger through the tag, pulled the sleeves free, then held the coat out at arms length and slowly let it slide off his bending finger onto the floor. The alcohol was playing with his head. Did you know I once loved someone I called Mica but I don't know why? Why I called her Mica, why I loved her, hell doesn't matter now anyway. All too late and she's dead. That's what I have been told. History. I loved her because I needed to love her. Because it was time. Because the train ride was boring and there was no one else to chat up. Funny thing. I don't have a photograph. I mean, I can show you a photograph of her father. Weird, eh? The only photograph of her father I have ever seen. I shoved it into the back of a book about a planet and a flower and a little boy and travelling and trying to love too much. And, oh yes, about the stars. Screw the stars. I burnt her image, every last damned photo of her. Did you know that? Every last letter. Maybe I don't even know what she looks like. *I write you, maybe you phone, I no give up...* Sure, yeh yeh.

Stonie is standing in the centre of the room, rocking slightly from side to side, suddenly unsure of which way to move. The swaying is leading to a fall. Here he is, the plotter of all things inconsequential, crashing through endless bursts of stars, ripping the sky apart, quite possibly falling forever as he sees himself coming into view in that dark little section of exposed mirror, one tiny corner of his face, an ear, a tight lip, a stranger's eye staring emptily back at him; a tear. This is his next journey.

He swiped the sheets of paper off the cushion and slumped clumsily into the armchair. With his trailing arm over the side he found the phone, picked up the receiver and dialled. The number in his head was for a taxi. 'So how many letters arrived at the fucking flat from the time this one slipped away?'

'Pardon?' came the reply.

'I said, what was that bloody ashes thing all about then,' Stonie shouted. 'Eh, eh?' He was shaking, sniffing, trying to wipe away the snot on his shirt sleeve. 'Tell me that, then,' he said gruffly, trying to clear his throat.

'I'm sorry, you have a wrong number. Get some help.' Stonie held onto the receiver, listening to the intermittent, discontinued tone for a long time.

'She must have opened the first letter,' he said, speaking loudly into the receiver, 'then decided, then made up her mind she didn't really want a father any more. In any case he was fucking dead. Dead. You don't, you don't go chasing after a memory by letter. This was some crank, some sicko joke. It's all just a bloody sick joke, d'you hear, a great big fat transatlantic joke.' Stonie dropped the receiver and slumped deeper into the chair, slowing his breathing, both arms dangling limp at either side, his head back and off to one side. The tally was this. Two jobs he never cared for, a past he could hardly recall, one lost saviour, friends now beginning to steer clear of his shadow, a curious nether world teasing him from the pages of a battered little notebook. And, within him, this vague notion that at one point in his life he was sure there would be no more lapses in concentration.

A slight breeze had begun to rattle the edges of the myriad papers in the room, setting up a thin, soporific vibration in the air, over which Stonie could just about hear the strains of The Circle Game, yet again those lone pickings, that same plaintiff phrasing carried in the moist air across the roofs. How about that? The same bloody tune. I do not believe in coincidence. This he affirms to himself. The letter was on the floor by his feet. He positioned his foot on it and gently dragged it back and forth under his heel. The space was still his vantage point for hope and clear skies. He was back at the last, shocking voice in his ear, Mica's muted, unexpected coldness. 'The photograph of my father; I must have it.' But the Little Prince was still guarding it, unmoved since then. Yes, he could have sent her the photograph, let that be an end to it. Perhaps it too, like this mysterious notebook, was exercising some hold over him. The material world imbued with metaphysical power. Hard to tell. Yet for some reason, he had never got round to throwing Luca Cambareri away. He was connected. There had been neither passion nor pain when the final chapter in the father's story was told. One gloomy Christmas getting over him. Just one Christmas, that's all it took. So mother burns the last of her bridges, selfish cow. Auctions the house contents, whatever memories are left and within a month they're in England. That's how it happened. Dragged Mica, kicking and yelling, into my arms. I just never heard the screams. Mica. She never wanted England. Never wanted me.

As he stood up, Stonie kicked at the dangling receiver, sending it crashing against the wall. He seldom seemed to be fully in control of who he was at any point. It was a mess inside his head, a mess outside his head. He held himself steady by forcing the backs of his calves against the cushioned frame, his arms straight, outstretched fingers barely touching the arms of the chair. Stonie knew when the alcohol was doing the talking, arguing with him. Yet there seemed nothing to take charge of, nothing to control. After a moment or two, he dropped his hands onto the windowsill, leaned forward, stared out at the glistening roofs and breathed in the cool air. Perhaps this night, this darkness would be his other home.

The city seemed pleased with itself. And after all this time, he was regaining his place, surely, in spite of the anger. So, what was he doing night after night, indoors, pouring over some obscure little set of numbers. Obsessed. Stuck. He had to move on. He thrust his head further out of the window, as far as he could and twisted his whole body round until his face was almost pointing at the sky. The drizzle felt good. It was cool. After several minutes he eased himself in stages back into the room and began to pick his way awkwardly through the debris of stars to the kitchen, swaying as he went. Everything was spinning gently, just as it should. It was time to tidy the place, straighten things out. He followed this thought with a rasping vocal 'even if it takes all night, I can work off the drink. I can work off the fucking past, do you hear, Mr Reuladair?' Starting from the outer edges, he moved anti-clockwise around the room, making sure all the sheets, pages, threads were where he thought they ought to be. Everything pinned, everything taped, everything coded. Corner to corner.

Stonie smiled at the thought of falling upwards. If he could have negotiated his way sensibly in the semi-darkness through the plates of half-eaten toast and dried up coffee mugs, apple core and orange peel, the bus timetables, beer mats, pencils he'd stood on several times; if he could have found a resting place amongst the complicated charts, the little lengths of thread holding the constellations together, dark, brooding stacks of books, astronomical tables, his scratchy drawings, the maps, impenetrable colour systems, the numbers, references, things he'd forgotten the significance of, important pieces of sky…

At lunchtime, St Philip's Square filled up with criss-crossing snack-eaters and pub seekers. The business world taking a breather. Gem was making for her usual bench when she spotted Stonie idling through the park. In no time there were side by side and talking about their day, their week. Gem already had a rough idea where she might find him.

'Want one of these?' she asked. She handed him a chocolate finger. 'So, what's the whinge today then?' she asked. It was guaranteed he would take the bait.

'Is it that obvious?' Stonie said.

'The list is as long as my arm. You can't help it.' Gem was in playful mood.

'I'm a Protestant, for goodness sake. I protest. That's what I do. I reserve the right to invoke the heretical imperative, remember?'

'What on earth are you talking about?' Gem said, feigning annoyance. There was something about Stonie which drew her in. It was never a strain being with him. But he was a maxim freak. Proddy dogs hate catholic cats, better the devil you know, keep your friends close and your enemies closer. He seemed to live by them. At times she could not make up her mind if she enjoyed the tactic or if it was deliberate evasion.

'Well, you're always proselytising.'

'What?'

'Proslytising,' Stonie repeated. 'I'm never going to become a fully paid up member of The Church of Jesus Christ of Latter Day Saints, am I?' Stonie stretched out every word of the title. 'And neither are any of these, he added' waving his hands casually to embrace the passing traffic.

'Oh, so that's what I've been doing, have I? Now, it's my turn to protest.' The conversation was light-hearted. Gem knew how to court him.

'Sort of, yeh, you've been selling Mormonism or whatever it's called. Mormonites. I never know with these things. Don't trust the methods they use. Christadelphians, Scientology, Moonies, C of E.'

'Church of England? Gem laughed, pointing towards the Cathedral. 'Well, they'd be very happy. Don't be ridiculous. We're not in the same, the same -

'Well, just because the state blesses it doesn't make it okay, right? Not necessarily.'

'So that means you don't trust me?' Gem asked.

'I didn't say that, didn't mean that. You're winding me up.'

'Perhaps,' she said, with a knowing look. 'So, how long for lunch, then? When do you have to be back?'

Stonie glanced at his watch. 'Oh, about half an hour. They're flexible. Funny, bumping into you like this. I was sure, the other day, I saw you coming out of a shop. Sure it was you, but I had just got on a bus and it was pulling away. Too dangerous to jump, but I was tempted. I was on the platform. That's twice or three times. You're getting out and about.'

'Aw, you would have done that for me?' Gem said. 'Jump off a moving bus?' She knew Stonie hadn't been at work for days at a time. It was all plotted. She might have to change her pattern. The natural encounter had to be maintained.

'You don't half talk gibberish sometimes,' Gem said, shaking her head. 'I mean, for a start, take the Roman Catholics, right? You talk as if a Roman Catholic is the devil incarnate. You must have grown up a bigot and didn't even know it.'

'Well that's the way it was on the west coast of Scotland. Seriously. So, what is this, some kind of truth session, then? Some kind of confessional?'

'How long have you got?' she said playfully.

'I know,' Stonie said slowly, 'that's a good idea. Dangerous. Let's go for it. What are the rules? No rules? No rules.'

Stonie was good entertainment value. But she had a job to do. She looked directly at Stonie and made it obvious he should start.

'Well, you represent everything I'm searching for, can't get, yet despise,' he said, 'searching for, can't get, despise.'

'Goodness, okay...go on.'

'God, sex and money.'

Gem looked shocked, a steady-on expression, mouth open. She drew a deep breath.

'Well, not God, religion, really, Stonie added, before Gem had time to speak.' There was a pause. Buoyed by the lack of interruption, Stonie let go another volley. 'And while we're at it, God knows I've done my best with the body language routine. Innuendo. Eyes, hand gestures, proximity. Ever since we first met.'

'Proximity?' Gem turned to face him.

'Yeh, the distance between us, little touches,' Stonie said. Your perfume, whatever.' He knew he was getting out of his depth, but could do nothing to stop himself. 'And while we're at it, what about these gleaming stones dripping off your ears, the intimate silverware, the cut of the clothes? Who's bankrolling you? The lifestyle?'

'I beg your pardon. Hang on a minute, what in heaven's name gives you the right to - '

'Ah, ah, ah, wait a minute. No rules. You said so.' Stonie waved his finger from side to side and tilted his head in mock reproach. Gem shifted uneasily on the bench, creating more of a gap between them. Perhaps, Stonie thought, it was more adversarial than unease. Judging by the silence which followed, Stonie was convinced he'd blown it. Gem pulled her shopping bag closer in with her foot, tucked the flap across the opening, as if to mark some kind of closure, hide the contents; then she smoothed out the corner of her jacket. She made much of pinging several crumbs off the flap.

'Right. Right. Well sometimes you look so vacant you need to be sectioned. Not listening, to the point of rudeness. You bite your nails, or at least, scrape away at the cuticles'

'Given.' Stonie said.

'And, and the self-deprecation, laughter, mock humility which begs anyone within earshot to agree and say, how lively and endearing. Ad nauseam. '

'Guilty.'

'And it would never end up as an affair, I mean – Be ye not unequally yoked together with unbelievers - and that sort of thing. Anyway, you're too small.' Stonie laughed at the final insult; Gem was warming to the game. She gave a coy smile, even as she looked down at her knees rather than at him. 'You don't put a value on anything, look for advancement, fight your corner. You can't make money to save your life. You'll never make it in business, she said, looking up and straight at him. 'There, how's that?'

'Yup. Know that too,' Stonie countered. 'Notions of mammon never enter the equation, my dear. The artist is above that sort of value judgement, the business woman married to it.'
He winced. He had gone too far. This was getting serious, out of control.

'You know me too well. I like good stuff around me, and why not? But don't you think they aren't mutually exclusive? You can have it all, surely,' Gem said, without waiting for an answer. 'Actually, I don't care what people make of me, what they think.'

'That's a lie,' Stonie said. 'We all do. Nobody's that thick-skinned.'

'Yeh, well for what it's worth, I forgive you,' Gem said. 'Absolution, that kind of thing.' Both of them laughed, stood up at the same time and went in for the air kiss. 'Time to get back, Stonie. Got to earn my next outfit. See you sometime.' Stonie laughed uncomfortably. He wanted time and place, but said nothing. Gem was already several steps away when she slowed and turned to look at him. 'That was crazy...I think I enjoyed it. I'll let you know.'

'Pretty much TW3 stuff,' Stonie said. 'Two relative strangers making the most of what they don't know about each other. Great fun. Hate to think what damage has been done, though, and all while we're sober. Ought to know better.'

'Don't go all self-conscious on me now,' Gem shouted back at him. 'Can't take it back.'

Making the most of 'happy hour' was a mistake. By six-thirty, Stonie was drunk. For the first time in months he was properly angry at the effects of the alcohol. Angry with himself for believing he would ever find the Indian, angry at himself for wasting so much time deciphering the book. There were things he'd forgotten he was angry about. He sat quietly in his alcove, tracing wet lines on the varnished wood with his finger, scraping the spillage onto the carpet with the edge of a beer mat, squaring up several mats to form a line. The beer was actually beginning to taste good. That was the problem. The search had become a habit. Where else but the Old Crown. He tried to get as much air into his lungs as possible, a slow draft bringing with it the comforting mix of cigarette smoke, the occasional perfume, alcohol and tightly packed bodies. The idea was to steady his vision, aid concentration, be ready for the evening sky.

But he could hardly tell if it was dusk, if there were starlings; if the pavements were emptying. To him, the city was insensitive to such things. It was all noise and artificial lights and signs telling you how to live your life. Brutal, calculating, designed for the automaton. He had his eyes half closed and was trying to empty his head when he felt a tap on the shoulder.

'Twice in one day. Can't go on meeting like this.' It was Gem.

'Oh.'

'Can't stop, with someone. Just popped in for a booster before a party.' She moved around the table and leaned down to be face on with Stonie. 'You alright?' Stonie looked up, looked straight at Gem, taking a moment to focus and form his words.

'Remember you said that we might have one significant conversation with one person in our whole life? You said that.'

'Well, yes. I might have done.' Stonie took his time. He looked up and over Gem's shoulder at as much fading sky as he could find. It was too early for stars. His voice was barely audible.

'I think I might have killed someone.'

Wk. 1437
36º 7' N 115º 81' W

Everyone is laughing at his regional accent, his attempt to speak in French. There they are, those pathetic attempts at French lyrics, French poetry with the extra syllable. He himself knows what he means. How the Little Prince should dig up the flower, what to do with the stem to keep it moist, where to travel next, how to measure the distance between planets. Tears are rolling down the little boy's face, falling into the root ball. Stonie tries to tell him salt water is no good for the plant. Somehow, the Little Prince just can't get it.

And so Stonie's dream went on, drifting through those soporific blips at thirty-eight thousand feet, with the strongest urge now and then, as he opened his eyes to a slit, to walk out onto the carpet of white cloud, his sweaty forehead stuck to the inner skin of the window. He watched the thin wing cutting through the blue freezing ghost light with its orange tip flashing easy as a heartbeat. It was always going to be a crazy move. Night time and Monday and a bucket seat and a million light years from the chaos of his living space, this long silver tube pointing irredeemably towards a desert dawn.

'Times there's real turbulence these parts. I swear to God it's the Almighty shaking out every last silver dollar 'fore you go to hell,' Stonie's seat companion opined with a minty drawl. Stonie wiped a thin trail of saliva from the side of his mouth.

'Right', he replied.

'Ain't no escaping. What you sow you're gonna reap. Better get ready,' the man continued, straightening his glinting bolo and folding back his shirt sleeves. But no cabin lights flickered, no seatbelt signs ushered them into the upright position. Stonie noticed the blackjack cuff-links of a La Vegas junkie. He would have the row of seats and the San Diego run all to himself. He thanked the guy for his wise counsel, assuring his travelling companion that his mission was not the casinos, the wedding chapels and the crossing of the Styyx.

'Never gambled in my life,' he said. He cozied down, dropping the threadbare tartan blanket to his knees and spreading himself across the empty seats. Then the routine. Check for the letter, the passport. It was still there, Luca's photo, stuffed hurriedly in-between the Buffalo pages and Milan without ever taking a second look. As he drifted, he imagined Gemima peering through the letterbox, eyes narrowed against the gloom of the hallway. All those unanswered calls. The flat would not be empty, simply left without presence. She would be no wiser. In the front room, the constellations would still be there, not a star disturbed by his abdication.

In his nether world, he was struggling to recall Mica's face in detail. The deeper he searched, the less he recognised. What did she actually look like? He tipped his head back against the headrest and breathed in long and deep as the plane lurched and dipped and banked steeply onto its next highway. When he woke, rain was scattering light trails of tears onto the window, flashing, multi-coloured. Vegas apron.

Wk. 1440
32º 39' N   89º 57' W

The torrent of nickels and dimes endlessly rattling the empty coin box made tuning in to Silviana's tortured accent a tad more problematic than with transatlantic calls. He was having to shout. 'I'm at the bus station…running out of money. Just got off a Greyhound. Thought these calls were free for locals.' As the bleeps sounded, Stonie hammered in the last remaining coins sliding out of his sweaty palm and tried to catch what was being said. 'I need directions. Is it far to walk or should I find a - ' The line went dead. 'Never mind. I'll look for a cab.' His voice tailed off with the click as he slowly replaced the receiver with one hand, wiped his brow and flicked a drip from the end of his nose. A cab was unlikely but there would have to be someone ready to earn a buck. His shirt was clinging to his back, making him shiver. For the briefest of moments he was lying yet again in the sand, scraped and bleeding and winded and trying not to move. It seemed to be a backdrop, unsolicited, clear. He recognised the metallic texture, the electric taste on his lips. There was the same familiar wave of exhaustion and dizziness. He leaned on the glass door till it jerked open, pushed his bag through the gap with his feet and stumbled out onto the pavement, careful of the burning edges of the kiosk. There was metal beading hot enough to create a weal. Dropping his sunglasses back onto his eyes with a sharp flick of his head, he squinted at the street beyond the bus yard. It was empty. No one. Not a movement, only the distorting waves of watery heat lifting the far edges of the town. Stonie looked down at his feet. There was barely a shadow. With some difficulty he forced his sticky wrist down into his trouser pocket and dragged out the crumpled paper with the address of the Italian's diner. Silvania's place.

'I will take you there. I take you where he lives.' Sylviana sat down at the table next to Stonie and closed her eyes, as if in prayer. 'I show you first,' she said. Raking around in her apron pocket, she produced first a scrap of paper, then a pencil, well chewed at the end. She began to draw a map, all straight lines and tentative circles, crosses, arrows, pausing now and then without lifting the pen off the surface. 'He has a cabin. It no legal you see, but they no touch him. He live on the edge of the reservation, but on the wrong side, you understand?' She stabbed several times at a mark on the paper before writing something which Stonie could not quite make out. It might have been Soon. 'I no been out there,' she said. 'No seen him for a while. He never come here now.' In the silence which followed, Stonie strained to read what was written on the map, trying not to look up, not to look Sylviana in the eye. He could sense the sadness, found himself on edge trying to get to grips with the mystery, with the strange emptiness of what lay before him. There would be no small talk. It was too warm for that. He was uncomfortable for the first time, irritated, a familiar loneliness enveloping him. In the stultifying heat, it was dark shadows, the shimmering edges beyond the shaded window. There was no shape, no form to what he was doing, only the creeping fear of the unresolved.

'Okay, we go now.' Sylviana was by the shutters, leaning back through the door, the beginnings of a smile breaking on her lined face. Pretty, once, Stonie mused. There were still traces. Through the fine mesh of the bug door, a rusting, faded saloon was turning over; a course engine, knocking, spitting, sounding very unreliable. Stonie decided it was an old Ford, a Cortina, manual left-hand drive, on eighty or ninety thousand miles second time around. But there were no badges, no trim. The hinges rasped as he pulled open the door by grasping the lowered window, his fingers burning against the hot glass.

'How far, did you say?' he asked. Sylviana crunched the gear stick forward.

'I no say. Depends. Maybe one hour.'

'Right, thanks.' Stonie twisted to check for the third time that he had deposited his things on the rear seat. His jacket, his bottle of water, his leather satchel.

'I no been before,' Sylvania reminded him. My friend, Wendy Soon, I no get invitation. I never been that far.' Stonie wrestled with this. Madness. It had to be. Perhaps too late to question the wisdom, the romance, his perseverance. It would have been cheap to buy wheels in Yuma, or hire them; safer. This was free, but he was surrendering his independence. Was this to be a destination, a marker, or merely one more interruption? There was no air-conditioning, no sun-roof, the beaded seat sliding beneath his bum with a tickle, dust pumping in through the cracks in the sills, the radio crackling between Fire & Rain and tortured Navajo. Same love song, different language. He was not used to Ford, not used to being driven. Being driven had dangers, gave him no choice. That seemed to be his lot. But at least, the ride was to scale.

The wipers scratched at the dust as they pulled away, squeaking rhythmically with each ten yards of road as the couple settled into a complicated silence. The lady knew there was only fiction, rumour. The facts had long ago given way to Quechen story-telling, to myth. She was free to invent her own ending. This journey was as much for her as for the gaunt, fidgety Englishman.

Stonie stared emptily at the grey-green scrub, the far off dust devils, the occasional glint of fools gold sparking off the boulders, the tiny twisters of grass touching down along the track. By now, he had reconciled those wild, fearful landscapes, his loss, his incarceration, the flaming rocks and ice-cold sand. He had the marks. He could cope, would cope, if it lead to revelation, a settling.

'You no go back, eh? No go home again?' Sylviana suddenly prompted. It seemed more of an imperative than a question. Stonie saw no point in responding to the rising inflection. He shrugged. The lady knew. Either way, it seemed his future would lie in these endless, petty inconveniences, unannounced waves of hope. The hard roadstone had long since given way to the soft, sleep-inducing vibration of a dirt track. He rolled his head slowly back against his neck, drew deeply on the dry, warm air and closed his eyes.

From the sandstone overhang, Zach is spraying the remains of his breakfast cereal at the squabbling ducks, simultaneously wrestling in some mock embrace with Kate, who is trying to prevent him from falling into the water. Kate, of all people. Now he is threatening her with a dowsing as the low churn of the engine eases them into the shadow of Tunnel No. 5. All along the bridge parapet, men in white coats are waving at him, their hypodermic needles shining in the morning sun. Stonie knows he is ready for them this time, has the answers. Oh look - is that Gem, running down the muddy, sloping bank towards the narrow boat? She is screaming at him, frantic, her chain and silver cross twisted among her fingers. She wants me to have it. She wants me. Stonie laughs as he stands up and stretches out to grab the pendant - then stiffens in an instant as the stonework crunches against the side of his head.

Stonie opened his eyes enough to register that there was no pain from the encounter, but his heart was racing and he knew at least he was in touch with something. That was enough for now. He watched the boulders and dry brush racing past him, an out of focus and unremarkable landscape of accommodation, at one with the sound track of the tyres on the gritty road and the massaging movement of the car.

'Good morning, this is your captain speaking. Thank you for choosing Pan Am Flight zero zero zero. Our stewards will be coming round shortly with light refreshments and please do not hesitate to ask if you have any special dietary needs. Weather today? Well, average for this time of year. We will be flying at 34,000 feet, climbing in a short while to 36,000 feet to avoid the effects of the Gulf Stream. Wind speed is what it always is. Time to destination? Well we do not have a destination. This flight will simply keep on flying and flying, out into the blue yonder, the dark velvet sky, the myriad stars, light years of universe, super novas, black holes, you know the kind of thing.' The voice is light, jocular, purposeful. In seat 21A, Zach is leaning against the window, snoring loudly. On his lap there is a small, close-up black and white photograph of a man in military uniform. Zach wakens with a start, tears at the photograph three times and lets the pieces drop onto his lap. As he leans back and closes his eyes, the pieces re-form. He wakens up, tears at the photograph again, exactly three times, leans back and closes his eyes. As this continues, above Zach's head, the seat belt and no-smoking signs light up. 'This is your captain speaking. Ladies and gentlemen, would you please return to your seats and fasten your seatbelts. Nothing to worry about. We will be experiencing a little turbulence for the foreseeable future.'

Sylviana's own waking dream died in the instant her passenger shook himself upright. 'Oh, yeh, sorry, dozed off,' Stonie grunted, wiping a thin trail of saliva from the edge of his mouth. Sylviana barely moved her head, but took an odd, sucking intake of breath, leaned forward and switched off the rasping radio. 'Yeh, I was somewhere else.' Stonie said.

The township spread before them in an arc of shacks marked at its extremity by a leaning flagpole, its ragged, holed stars and stripes wrapped limply around the frayed halyard. At a rough count, twelve buildings, all single storey. Sylvania slowed to a crawl as they passed under the ranch-like white wood lintel, finally rolling to a halt in the middle of the open space. Stonie narrowed his eyes against the blazing light, tugged at the door handle and slid himself off his seat. Pulling himself upright, he arched his back, hands on the back of his waist, and stretched with a faintly musical yawn. Sylviana had not cut the engine. She was sitting with her hands on the steering wheel, looking straight forward. She seemed to be still driving inside her head. Stonie ducked back into the car. 'You okay?' he asked, barely concentrating as he leaned over to rescue his bags and jacket one at a time from the rear seat. He laid them neatly on the gravel beside the car and stood up, edging the car door shut with his heel as he surveyed the scene. That was the move, the unforced error. The Ford lurched forward a foot or two, catching Stonie by surprise. He swept round behind the vehicle and made towards the open driver's window. But the saloon began pulling away towards the divide between the first two shacks. Stonie stopped in his tracks, the car out of reach. She's parking up. No one parks up by accelerating, not in this kind of space. Perhaps circling. But the saloon seemed to be gathering speed, consumed by clouds of dust. Stonie watched, fully expecting Sylviana to reappear between the other buildings, then he wheeled around, with the vague notion that perhaps someone had caused the sudden move. There was nothing but empty space behind him. A few feet away, his crumpled satchel, bag, jacket and sunglasses lay abandoned in the heat. He turned to stare in the direction of the settling dust, the nape of his neck cold in the recall. This had happened before. Yet again, he was moving to the unmistakable fading rhythm of what was left behind. His shirt was clinging, his jeans rucked into his groin, his eyes gritty.

After a moment, he became aware of the blistering heat on his skin. He moved towards the first of the shacks, took the dry, splintered steps in one stride and began walking briskly along the stoop. The hollow clack of the boardwalk seemed loud and uninviting, as if every grain in the wood was objecting to the intrusion. There was shadow enough, but no relief. At each window, he cupped his hands against the cloudy window, pressed his nose to the glass and tried to blot out the glare. Inside, the sparse rooms gave no hint of character or individuality, no clue to gender. He took note. Dry hanging pelts, a brass paraffin mantle lamp, a stained gingham table cloth, empty Jack Daniels bottles, the ramped up candles with their spilled, cracked wax building stalactites on the metal hearth. In each of the windows he could see behind him, the ochre earth, smoked blue cloudless sky, the thin horizon. The tease of the horizon; it was out there, pressing in on him.

Stonie turned, leaned against the rail and took his time over every shack. What would Zach be looking for? Or Gem, or Kate. They seemed to have the hunger for detail, painstaking detail that he lacked. Well, they would never have allowed it to get this far, that's for sure. Theirs was a peculiar wisdom. He knew by the observations they made, questions they asked. A curious thought waved over him. Each of them asked different questions, but in the end, it amounted to much the same answer. Zach, forensic. Gem, business-like. Kate, philosophical. He liked to think he had given them just enough, second-guessed them. But Sylviana taking off without a word? Stonie felt this was a violent act. Just goes to show, faith has its limits. Loyalty can be found wanting. There it was again, the creeping loneliness, but it was too hot for tears. He held onto the silence, leaning with his fore-arms on the rail, statuesque, straining for the slightest disturbance, breathing more slowly, folding second by second into the perfect stillness.

It was likely to be mid-afternoon. Stonie was standing by the fifth shack. He was already exhausted, unsure if he was repeating himself in his search. This was hardly Sage-brush City. There were none of the B-movie cowboy cosmetics to comfort the eye, none of the Indian Myth, only the odd chipped enamel sign, split wooden doors, frayed jute awnings. Every living space seemed to have its own unique assortment of twisted tools and gas cans lurking in the lean-to shadows. To one side, the overgrown John Deere engine, to the rear, a flat-tired trailer chassis, at a distance, the tortured metal frame which may have once been living quarters on wheels. Stonie's thirst finally set him off again. There were no markers, there seemed to be nothing territorial, just a mesh of hard-dirt paths between buildings. He scuffed between two buildings to the marked-out edge of a homestead and tried a water pipe. The tap squeaked as it spun free, but nothing came out. Stonie rattled the stem till it spluttered and spat at him, but he could not bring himself to put his mouth to the opening. He quickly unhooked the tin mug from its wire bracket, blew out the dust and caught the trickle. It was tepid, tasted sweet, tasted of kale.

By now, he felt certain that the settlement was deserted. Someone would have seen him snooping, witnessed his arrival, been curious. There was always a feeling of being watched. He wiped his lips with the back of his hand and turned full circle, distrustful of the silence. This was not a peaceful experience. Most of the surrounding terrain was rock and brush, undulating, but with little cover. He would continue his search. There was nothing else for it. He was bound to hear Sylviana if she came back for him. Wherever the Quechens were, whatever they were doing - working, gambling, sleeping off their lunch - they would not return in the late afternoon heat. There was time.

Stonie inspected another shack, wondering how to size up the differences between each of them. He circled the dwelling with less enthusiasm, unsure of what to look for, peering through windows, trying to make sense of the interiors. This next dwelling seemed neater, cleaner lines, folded garments, moccasins arranged this time, tunics on hooks, all the paraphernalia of domesticity, but the contours, objects, the closed doors, the colours and shadows, they offered little clue to personality. Perhaps a squaw. There was nothing anywhere to suggest women or children. Nothing specific about what this person did for a living, nothing unusual. It was the romance Stonie had grown up with, the movie set, the Rockwellian detail. It was all déjà vu. He was becoming weary. Without his Italian guide, without intimate knowledge, he was lost. Sylviana would come back to help him, surely. He needed an explanation for being abandoned. Perhaps if he circled the shack seven times, trumpets would sound, the walls would collapse and all would be revealed in a moment of glory. Anything else was becoming hard work. For a fleeting moment, he was trudging his daily beat through the city, tramping aimlessly between stores, through underpasses, across parks, sitting in the open spaces, staring, waiting. Just waiting. The world reduced in his ears to the muffled white noise of despair.

He decided anti-clockwise would be a fresh way of looking at things. The reward was a slightly open window he had overlooked, in full sun, its shutters pinned back. He prised the frame open still further, cutting out the glaring landscape behind him and stretched on tiptoe. As his eyes adjusted to the dimness, he began to pick out details. It was a separate room, a bedroom. On the grainy slatted walls, some pouches, a hide jacket, a woven tunic all on one hook. He took note: two pairs of boots, beaded leather strapping, a ceramic cup on the floor, tipped onto its side, protruding from the shadow of the bunk, shirts of some sort draped over a chair, looking familiar. White man's shirts, thought Stonie. On a shelf over the bed, Stonie strained to make out a pocket watch, and something which might pass for a bolo. Hardly Indian, but an eclectic mix nevertheless. He relaxed back onto solid ground, let go his grip on the edge of the window and flexed his shoulders. Perhaps it was worth another look. Dragging over an old bucket with his feet, he tipped it upside down and pushed it against the stilts, careful not to let his toes touch the hot metal. This time he could lean in, blot out more light.

Deep in a recess, barely visible, was a shelf full of books. Books. Most of these reservation dwellers smoked, chewed, gambled, drank and argued their way to the next wage, if they could get one. They could read, but to own a book, to collect books, that marked you out. Stonie knew enough, had picked up enough. This had to be the one. He stepped down and studied the ground around him, suddenly animated, pleased with his deduction. Within seconds he was pumping at the rod of a cracked wing mirror on one of the car wrecks, both hands wrapped around his canvas jacket. It squealed and gave way in seconds. Back on the upturned bucket, awkward and trembling, he positioned the glass to feed sun into shadow. He could make out a King James Bible, of all things, what looked like folded maps, the faded spines of several hardbacks, something about Confederates, National Geographic Magazines, A History of Leech Mining. Stonie could no longer hold the pose. Anyhow, he had seen enough. He jumped down, threw the mirror into the nearby brush and stood for a moment, his heart thumping. So Sylviana was right. 'Who else would have a book on the English Countryside in a place like this? Stonie spoke out loud. The sound of his own voice dropping onto the silence startled him, made him aware of the urgency. Nothing was completed. He ran to the nearest water tap, cupped some water to his mouth and swallowed hard, gathered his belongings from the middle of the compound and sprinted over to the boardwalk. His mind was already rehearsing the next move. But the heat was taking its toll. He positioned the bags beside the door of the shack, singling out one of them for pummelling. This would be his pillow. Time to think. But, within five minutes, he was on his feet, the temptation too great. Checking again that nothing stirred, that there was no usable truck or pickup in site, he tried the door handle and the door eased open with no resistance.

Cautiously, Stonie walked into the middle of the room and took stock. There was an open notebook propped up on the shelf above the stove. He took a closer look, recognised the writing and so nearly picked it up. His heart was thumping; same style of writing, same size. But there was dust everywhere. There would be tell-tale marks. This was trespass. This was intrusion. Any minute now he would be found out, made to explain, all the effort immediately forfeited. He would go home empty-handed. Stonie felt paralysed. He was at the heart of his recent history, all those weeks pacing the city streets, certain of answers, feeling cheated. Surely he would hear a pick-up long before it pulled into the compound. There was time. He was breathing heavily. He had the right, ought to know, had to know. So far, all the weird incidents, connections, and now this, this moment; he had to stretch it out, get as far as he could. One more fact, that was all; something to pull everything together. He felt angry, adversarial, his eyes darting, his whole body tense. He was turning on the spot in a swirl of possibilities. Scratched shelf, mapping pin, shrivelled moths and crane flies, oil stained towel, candle droppings, chewed biro, conch shell, a cluster of tiny yellow feathers, note books. He had a right to know. This had to be The Centre.

He noticed a bureau to the left of the bedroom door. Bureau, cabinet, dressing table, it had drawers in it. Anyone can open and shut a drawer with no sign of disturbance. Just one look; possibly a gentle rummage through the contents. It felt like the right thing to do. He had no idea what he was looking for. Second drawer down, belts, buckles, fasteners, a sheath, its long knife intact, a dream catcher of all things, with 'Souvenir of Gila Bend' stitched onto its tag. Must have been meant as a gift. He eased the drawer closed and pulled on the knobs of the next drawer down. Empty. Stonie glanced across at the window and leaving the drawer open, moved over to the window sill for a wider view. As far as he could see, there was no movement, no sound but his own breathing and the creaking of the floorboards. He noticed he was standing on a rough, tufted mat with some kind of faded bear motif. It was snagging on the gravel caught in the tread of his sandal. Certain things just have to be straightened out at the time. One more check. He returned to the open drawer and pushed against it with his thigh. As it resisted, he bent closer to look at the lining. The face staring up at him, the capped, handsome face was Luca Cambareri. He knew the face well. It was tucked back in his book, Antoine de Saint-Exupéry's Little Prince, the traveller, the keeper of plants, the lone child in the desert.

'Like laughing stars, your joy brightens my planet' Jay had quoted at him. One of the first cards, he had received, now like someone else's celebration. Stonie gripped the side of the drawer, trying to take in what he was reading. The caption, the faded columns of the newspaper lining the drawer, the same photograph, the only photograph, the headline, lead story. He fumbled at the folded edges, trying to pick it up, but it would be unlikely to fold back to the original, not in the time. He squinted, scanning the small print, trying to absorb the faded story line as he eased the newspaper away from the base of the drawer towards the light. "Open-cast miner, father of Soon, Quechan Indian, State Penitentiary, part of a gang high on local alcohol, raped a white woman, wife of a visiting military scientist. By time of trial, woman found to be pregnant and has since gone into hiding." Stonie's hand was shaking so much he was in danger of tearing the paper, but he managed to smooth out a crease in the corner of the brittle newsprint. Date: 16 August 1952. The beginning of Mica. Had to be. Trembling, he tried to push the drawer shut, but it juddered, sending a cloud of dust, a clay pipe and what looked like a necklace of animal teeth crashing past his ear. He lunged out instinctively, snapping off the end of the pipe in his fingers as he caught it. It was time to leave. The clay pipe and teeth were picked up, arranged on top of the shelves at speed and the mat smoothed out with his heel. He was back on the stoop within a few seconds, the door eased to a click in the hope that nothing would alter the order, nothing disturb the tranquility.

Stonie leaned back beside the door, slid down the wall and crouched by his bags, resting his head against the palings, steadying his trembling body. He was in another dimension. He could feel the tension, picking over every word as Mica's very drunk and very angry mother cursed and swore and banned her from ever bringing up the subject again. Now it made sense. He tried to slow his breathing down, take charge of the whispering expletives. Wendy Soon had been trying to find his Jay, my Mica, his family, his half-sister. She was his step-sister. Jay had a half brother. In one move, Stonie stood bolt upright. He needed to get away, needed not to meet Wendy Soon. Not until he was ready. He sucked in the dry air, steeling himself for the heat of the unrelenting late afternoon sun bearing down, no more than a foot from the shadow of the cabin. He had to give himself space.

With so little money, it would be hard to coax one of the locals into giving him a ride to a telephone, to the rail yard. That is, if he could find a local. The place was eerily still; a ghost town, a place with a past and little future. He hadn't ever thought anything through. Now he was paying for it. Now there was nothing to follow. Trailing his bags and jacket, he walked to the end of the cabin, jumped down off the boardwalk and looked around. It was almost too hot to move. He eased himself onto the cooler wood, his legs half-dangling, feet scuffing the dirt. Something would come to him; a plan, a way forward. The connection between heaven and earth, this proof of what truly counted, perhaps that was for someone else. Whatever had drawn him to this, it was over. Whatever he knew about himself, it was enough.

'You wait long time for One Day.' The voice broke into Stonie's thoughts. 'You wait very long time.' Stonie looked up, startled at the sudden intrusion, and measured up the old Quechen who was shuffling towards him, a small, pony-tailed man, slightly bent, with a warm, weathered face, long grey hair in a middle parting held in place by a yellow headband. The eyes were narrow, leathery, knowing everything. 'They say he gone United Kingdom, Great Britain.' The old man paused. 'Me? I am from Great Yuma.' he added with a chuckle.'I never leave.'

'Right, oh, hello there.' Stonie, unnerved by the unexpected encounter, summoned up a degree of protocol. 'Excuse me? Did you say 'One Day?'

'That is so, my friend. He called One Day. That is who you seek.' The Indian rolled his shoulders in a good humoured display, spat a chew onto the dirt close to Stonie's sandals and drew himself as tall as he could. 'He no Wendy, he One Day,' he said slowly. The Indian fell silent, swaying backwards and forwards slightly from the waist, waiting. He had emphasised this last statement in a more determined voice.

'Yes, but how, I mean, where did you, well, what do you know about – ' Stonie began' The Indian nodded gently and gave an open-palm sign of peace. As far as Stonie was concerned, it was a sign for him to be silent for a moment.

'Counter of Stars, he father of One Day Soon, he say One Day, his unborn son will be great traveller, will bring much happiness beyond these sacred lands. That was many, many summers ago. He never see his son. They take Counter of Stars away long time. He bad omen when his squaw die. They say he lie with white woman. Bring much trouble.' Stonie wanted to go inside for the scrap of newspaper, but thought better of it. He sensed that it was better to wait for a natural ending. He stared at the Indian, nodded his head slowly and said nothing.

'One Day no dig for gold any more for white man. He worked for Diner woman,' the Indian continued. His voice had softened. He was using the past tense. Stonie sat down on the deck, still weak at the knees, trying desperately to process the story. This was becoming messy, unkind, unfair. With no warning, the Indian crouched down in front of him, squatted on the ground and crossed his legs. 'Ah,' he said, 'He foolish. But his son, he no foolish. He wait. One Day - ' Stonie slowly pushed himself away from the boardwalk and took a few steps beyond the squatting figure, fully expecting the Indian to continue. It was hard enough trying to understand the accent, the timing. But the Quechen had stopped talking altogether. Stonie circled him.

'You've been here all the time,' he said. The Indian tore off a piece of tobacco and began to roll it inside his cheeks.

'Yes,' he replied, bowing slowly. 'Yes.'

'You've been watching my every move, haven't you?'

'That is so,' the Indian answered. Stonie expected more, a reprimand, a description of his intrusion, a warning. But there was only a prolonged silence. Eventually, the Indian spoke. 'The lady from the diner, she wise. She no come here with One Day. I no see her. She no want to come here,' the Indian said, spitting onto the exact same spot on the gravel.

'But what about Wendy Soon, One Day Soon? Where is he?' Stonie asked. He could feel himself becoming irate. So the waitress had never visited the reservation before, why come all this way only to take off like that? She must have been scared of something.

'The woman called Sylviana, she too close. She say too much. She tired of Indian life. We do not mix well.'

The last assertion took Stonie by surprise, so measured, so assured, so English, every word pronounced. A wave of exhaustion swept over him. There were too many things to remember, to put in place.

'Look, I don't understand. Whatever has been going on between…I mean, something happened years ago and I just need to find somebody who knows the whole story,' he said. 'There was a trial – ' The Indian made a gesture Stonie didn't recognise, but he sensed it was unwise to continue.

'I feed you. Tonight you stay here,' the Quechen announced.

'Oh, right, yeh thanks,' Stonie stuttered. 'That is very kind, but Wen, One Day, what about your brother?' The Quechan rose from his seated position in one graceful movement, not a trace of his years, and turned to face his guest.

'You ask in reservation, no one know where he is.' There was a long pause. 'I know where he is,' the Indian answered obliquely, just as Stonie looked as if he was about to ask. 'They tell you he still to return from finding his, how you say, sister. He no find her. They say she dead.' At this, Stonie's heart leapt, with a reflex intake of breath. There was such finality in the word. No point in saying anything else, asking any more questions. He felt a shiver run through him. It was not what he came to hear. 'One Day very sick. He walk off the reservation,' the Indian went on, waving vaguely in the direction of the sloping land behind the shack. He paused and drew deeply. 'He is with his ancestors,' he added. I feel this.'

'But there must be more. You need to give me some kind of proof.' Stonie said. He tried to read the implacable face before him, looking for signs, tried to order his thoughts, but the provocation was ignored.

'Come.' The old man turned slowly and shuffled off towards the farthest shack, where the trodden path became unkept ground. Stonie let him go, staring after him, uncertain of his next move. It was late afternoon, the air as still as ever, the long tendrils of sunlight creeping into the yard from the distant horizon. He watched the Indian ease himself up onto the deck of his home and disappear into the lengthening shadow of the awning without once breaking stride, without once looking back.

Zach had woken with a headache. It was the jet-lag, it was the Rioja. It was the guilt. Yet instead of phone calls, here he was, nine-thirty in the morning, finally back at No. 10 Worthington Mews. Stonie, in whatever state, would be delighted to see him. There were dreams to unravel and more to replace them. There was more of the book. There were confessions. Zach was careful this time. No wrists stuck painfully in the gap, no attempt at finding a key. He lifted up the flap of the letterbox and peered through the bare bulb light. As far as he was concerned, it was a mess. Papers everywhere, pinned to every wall, as high as the cornices, spilling off the skirting boards. The trail of joiners didn't seem to make much sense. So this is Stonie's so-called research, he mused.

Zach had been kept at bay for weeks. Stonie must have been drunk half the time, taking the little green notebook far too seriously. He knocked much louder on the panels of the door with the palm of his hand, a flat, hollow smack that stung his fingers. Then another rattle of the letter box. He turned to face the street, self-conscious, suddenly feeling vulnerable. It felt as if this was how he'd spent most of his waking hours, peering through letterboxes, peering into other people's lives. It was the only way he saw his own life, was all he recognised of the people around him. Dramatic moments, highly edited versions. No longer. The thought did not sit well with his state of mind. He swore under his breath and placed the flat of his hand against the door, his shoulder against the back of his hand, vainly hoping the door might give. The varnish felt rough and sticky. It was another day, another opportunity to deal in mysteries. Not for him the teasing possibility of a clear sky and an open road.

'For God's sake, waken up, Stonie,' Zach hissed at the open slit. The element of surprise had gone. He might just be wasting his time. He backed off, jumped the two steps onto the pavement and went to the back seat of his car, returning with a small torch. Once again he lifted the flap, this time awkwardly peering in, shining the beam straight through to the lounge. The ring of light was picking up more of the same, more sheets of fuzzy, joined up dots, more lines, dense and crazy lines, open, blank spaces. They were all beginning to merge into one. He narrowed his eyes and concentrated, adjusting the length of the light till the image on the far wall became clear. It was the face of a girl.

Wk. 1440
51° 28.3' N 0° 27.3' W

It was one of those hard frost mornings, a ball of orange easing up over the mist-shrouded fields, coating the runways in glace pink. Zach watched as the baggage train pulled up alongside the cargo hold, nervously fingering his boarding pass and once again in rehearsal. One full day in the UK. All it took to convince him he'd got it wrong. Battjes needed hard facts, some resolution, yet he had nothing to offer. The written report was bullet-point stark, his explanation, pure conjecture. He had done what was asked of him. Perhaps Stonie was aware and had outwitted them all. Anyhow, he had questions of his own. What had they done with Cambareri? Was he dead yet? Was there no more to extract? He picked his way between chairs, through sprawling legs and carelessly dumped hand luggage to stand by the window, his back to the lounge, the shoulder strap of his camera cutting into his neck. The irritation fired off an urge to capture the rivulets of condensation on the massive pane. It was a soft, random, vaguely melancholic thing to do. Focus, click, ease away. Focus, click again. There was something reassuring in the movement. Flat of finger on the smooth shutter release. The management of pressure, the nano-second satisfaction of capture. Once more, he cranked the spool forward, an act of defiance, of connection. These were rare moments, when the questioning lens was enough conversation, his only true comfort. He was fascinated by the precise disturbance of light. In his head was the blemished film, the chemicals doing their work, the sharp edge of negative, the paper in the tray, waiting on the inevitable, timed revelation of a past moment of pleasure. A series of actions he could finally control.

Over the speakers, a calm voice invited him to board, bringing him back into the present. People were milling around, hands, caps, newspapers awkwardly shielding their eyes from the sudden angle of a low yellow morning sun, in a strange ballet of accommodation.

Everything seemed to be in slow motion. Everything needed to be captured. And in the turning, something happened. He became The Photographer. Pure and simple. He was, is the artist. This would be the first and last assignment. The Research Centre would have to do without him. He no longer had the stomach for the mask. He shuffled into the queue, a cool rippling reflex passing through the muscles in his back. Row 21A. He could watch the world go by. As he slumped into his window seat, the absurdity of the past few months waved over him. Easy money at an unimaginable cost. What had he been thinking of? And anyhow, who was watching the watcher? He didn't care anymore. The thought made his skin creep. It was time to get out. Battjes would have to believe the trail had gone cold.

Men in large ear mufflers and yellow tunics waved and shouted below him on the tarmac at the first judder of the aircraft as it was being pushed out from its berth. There were feathered Jack Frost patterns on the edges of his window, between the skeins of plastic. Zach reached into his coat pocket, took out his wallet, removed Luca Cambareri's photograph from one of the sleeves and began to tear it up with ritual deliberation, first one way, then the other. Three twists and he could tear it no more. He let the parts fall like confetti onto his lap and sat back with a sigh. The early rise was catching up with him. As the plane eased itself away from the runway, Zach stretched his legs as far as he could, nested into the wing of the headrest and watched the first criss-cross patterns of powder white fields drop below him, the pink sky reflecting in ox-bows and farm pools, drifting wisps of cloud closing in. He began to imagine the face he'd seen through the letterbox only a few hours ago. The girl was talking to him. He wanted to recognise her, wanted to know what she was saying, but nothing came.

Stonie Reuladair leaned back onto the stoop opposite the old man's cabin, at an awkward angle against the rail, hardly daring to move, reluctant to break into the silence. The air was cooler now, the heavens offering up the first hint of a star and the dull orange scratch of a jet trail on the far horizon. The Indian was nowhere to be seen. Two or three pick-ups had entered the compound unnoticed. Blue wisps of smoke were here and there twisting into the softening sky. There was food and conversation in the air.

Ceremoniously, he unfastened the strap on his satchel, the Bhavani satchel, pulled out a thin, battered canvas wallet and carefully removed his precious map. From beneath it, he slid out the sheet of acetate and held it up to the light. There were scratches all through the constellations, stars missing, scrapes, stress lines, unconquered worlds. Slowly, he unfolded the map, laid it on the wooden slats, stroking it several times as flat as possible. Then, methodically, he lowered the heavens onto unfamiliar territory.

FICTION FROM APS PUBLICATIONS
(www.andrewsparke.com)

Abuse Cocaine & Soft Furnishings (Andrew Sparke)
Copper Trance & Motorways (Andrew Sparke)
Initiation (Pete Sears)
The Horned God (Pete Sears)
Life Unfinished (Martin White)
Nothing Left To Hide (HR Beasley)
Mister Penny Whistle (Michel Henri)
The Death Of The Duchess of Grasmere (Michel Henri)
An Inspector Called (Ian Meacheam)
So You Want To Own An Art Gallery (Lee Benson)

CLASSIC REPRINTS
Jeremy (Hugh Walpole)